A TASTE FOR VENGEANCE

A Bruno,
Chief *of* Police
Novel

MARTIN WALKER

Quercus

First published in Great Britain in 2018 by Quercus

This paperback edition published in 2019 by

Quercus Editions Ltd
Carmelite House
50 Victoria Embankment
London EC4Y 0DZ

An Hachette UK company

A CIP catalogue record for this book is available from the British Library

PB ISBN 978 1 78648 615 8
OME ISBN 978 1 78747 602 8

10 9 8 7 6 5 4 3 2 1

Typeset by Jouve (UK), Milton Keynes

Printed and bound in Great Britain by Clays Ltd, Elcograf S.p.A.

'The Maigret of the Dordogne' Antony Beevor

'Sure to appeal to readers with a palate for mysteries with social nuance and understated charm' *Wall Street Journal*

'Enchanting country mysteries that embody the sublime physical beauty and intractable political problems of the Dordogne' *New York Times*

'One of the charms of the series is the detailed procession of French country cuisine that no investigation is ever allowed to impede; another is the character of Bruno himself – humane, sensible, honest and a very good cook ... A satisfyingly intriguing, wish-you-were-there read with lashings of gastroporn' *Guardian*

'[Courreges is] a truly winning character ... brave, bright and very human' *Independent on Sunday*

'The delights of [Walker's Dordogne] – from the chateaux along the rivers to the prehistoric cave paintings to the food on the tables – are very real ... Absorbing' *New York Times Book Review*

'Strikes a captivating balance between suspense and delight' *The Washingtonian*

'Martin Walker's delightful Bruno series makes you want to buy a ticket and immerse yourself in *la France Profonde*' *Irish Independent*

'Walker's relaxed style and good humour help to bring to life his engaging hero and delightful home' *Telegraph*

Martin Walker is a prize-winning journalist and historian who has worked for the *Guardian*, the *New York Times*, the *Washington Post* and *The New Yorker*. He is the author of *Cold War: A History* and *The President They Deserve: The Rise, Fall and Comebacks of Bill Clinton*. He is best known, though, for his Bruno, Chief of Police series of mysteries set in the Dordogne. Martin and his wife Julia Watson have two grown daughters. They spend most of their time in the Dordogne, where Martin rejoices in the titles of Grand Consul de la Vinée de Bergerac, and Chevalier de Foie Gras de la Confrérie du Pâté de Périgueux, roles he takes very seriously indeed.

Also by Martin Walker

Death in the Dordogne
(previously published as *Bruno, Chief of Police*)
The Dark Vineyard
Black Diamond
The Crowded Grave
The Devil's Cave
The Resistance Man
Death Undercover (previously published as *Children of War*)
The Dying Season
Fatal Pursuit
The Templars' Last Secret

To my fellow members of L'Académie des Lettres et des Arts du Périgord

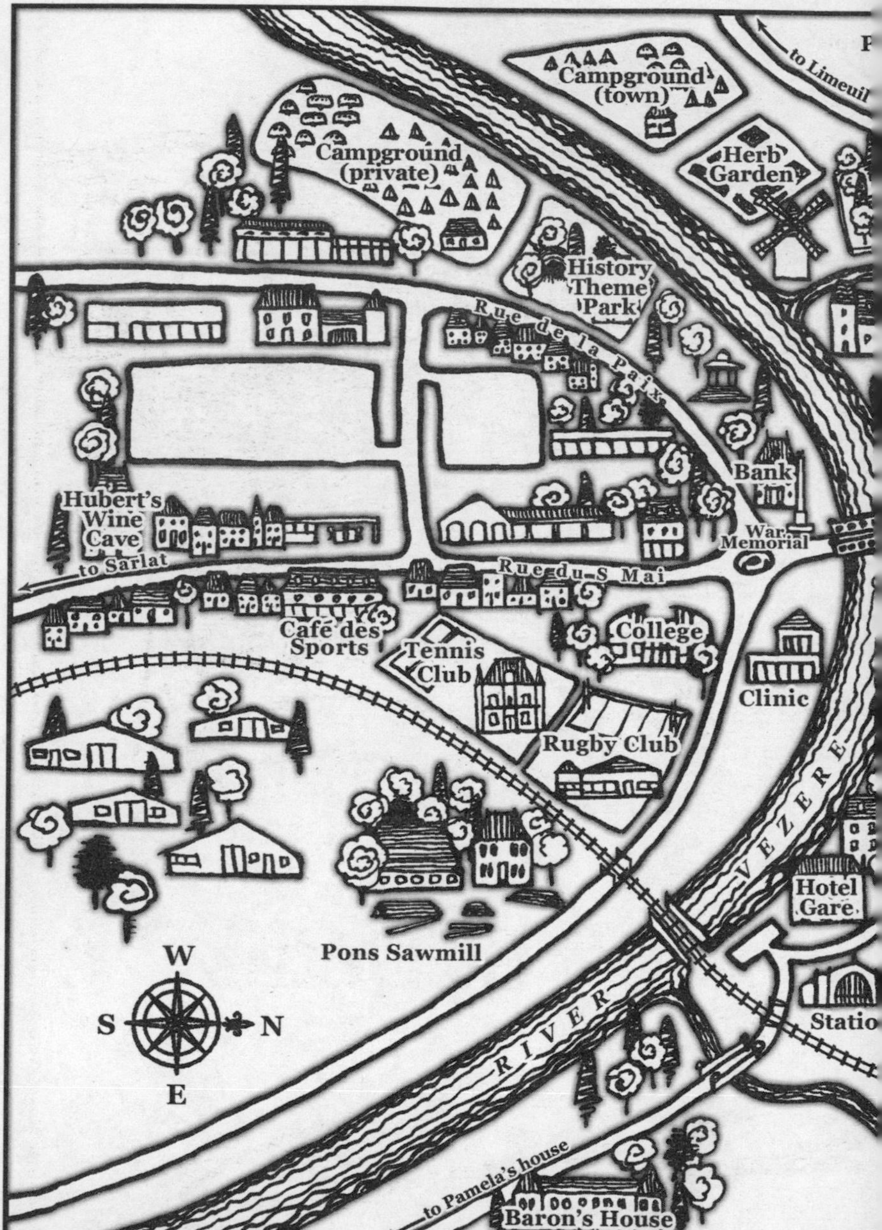

to Limeuil
Campground (town)
Campground (private)
Herb Garden
History Theme Park
Rue de la Paix
Bank
War Memorial
Hubert's Wine Cave
to Sarlat
Rue du 8 Mai
Café des Sports
Tennis Club
College
Clinic
Rugby Club
VEZERE
Hotel Gare
Pons Sawmill
W
S
N
E
RIVER
to Pamela's house
Baron's House

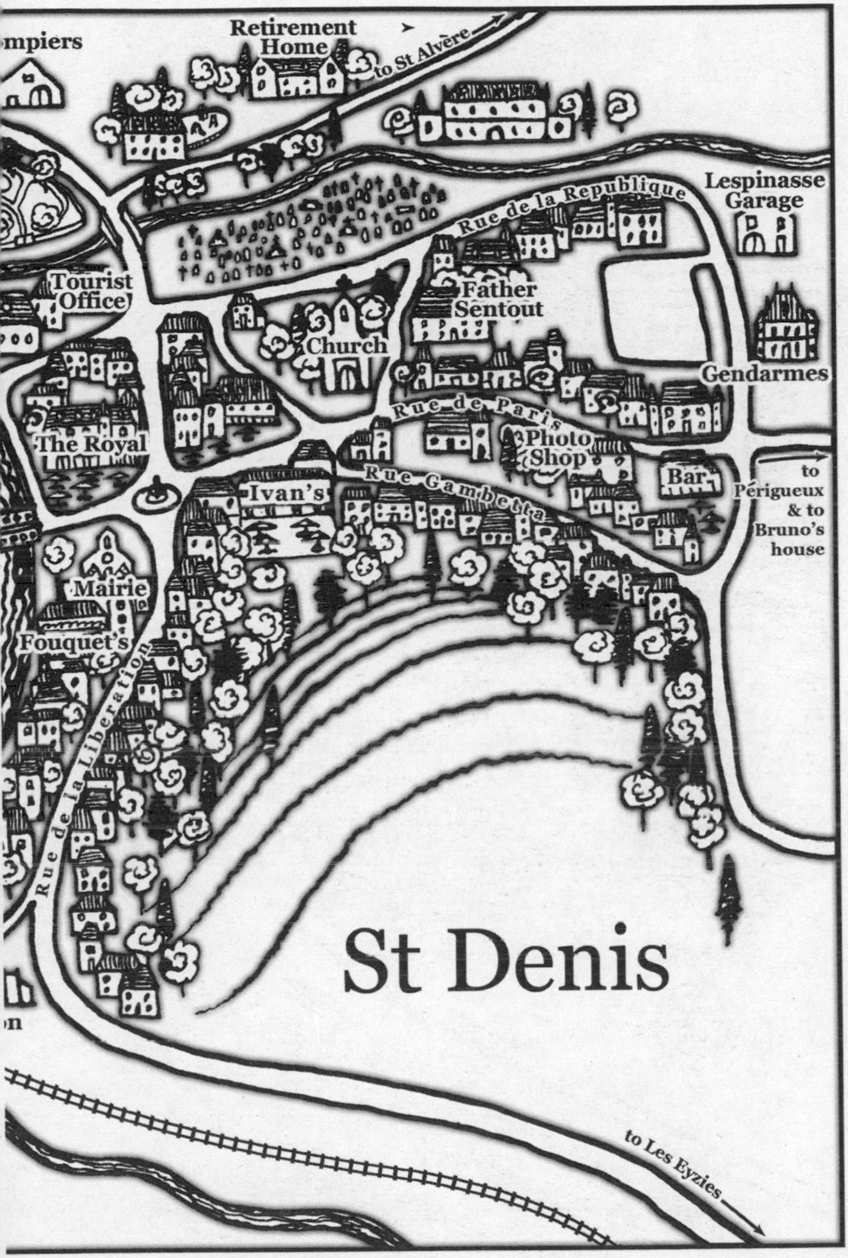
mpiers
Retirement Home
to St Alvère
Lespinasse Garage
Rue de la Republique
Tourist Office
Father Sentout
Church
Gendarmes
The Royal
Rue de Paris
Photo Shop
Ivan's
Rue Gambetta
Bar
to Périgueux & to Bruno's house
Mairie
Fouquet's
Rue de la Liberation
St Denis
on
to Les Eyzies

1

Bruno tried always to be reachable on his mobile phone, even when he wasn't on duty. And on this cool, damp Sunday afternoon in spring, with clouds and rain showers sweeping in from the Atlantic some sixty miles to the west, it was his day off. Bruno could think of few better ways to enjoy it than to accompany the local women's rugby team in the regional final.

They were all aged between sixteen and nineteen, and had been trained by Bruno over the past decade. Teaching wasn't part of his remit as town policeman of St Denis, but he relished his involvement with these young people and he was deeply proud of the team. Women's rugby was a relatively new sport in France and there were many, not least in the town's male teams, who thought the game was too rough for the fairer sex. But few could maintain that prejudice once they had seen the girls play. They tackled one another as hard as the men, but they ran and passed more, played a faster and more elegant game and kicked the ball ahead with as much skill and more finesse. They were seldom bogged down in the muddy, grinding mauls that often marked the play of the male teams. If Bruno had to sum up their style in a single word he'd have said they played with more grace.

That was not how it looked on the field this afternoon. The ball was slippery in the drizzle and most of the players were so smeared with mud that it was hard to tell one team from the other. The score was level, at twelve points each. The opponents came from the much bigger town of Mussidan and they had been champions of the Dordogne *département* the previous year. Few, except Bruno, gave the St Denis girls much chance.

Suddenly the mobile phone vibrated at Bruno's waist. He ignored it. With only ten minutes left to play, the St Denis team was just fifteen metres from the opponent's goal line and pressing hard. The ball had gone loose from a scrum and two players, one from each side, were wrestling for possession. As their teammates piled in behind, St Denis won possession and the ball went out towards their winger. Then Bruno groaned as the ball at the wing was passed forward for a foul. The referee blew his whistle and called for a formal scrum. Bruno took the opportunity to glance at the screen of his phone. It was Pamela, a former lover who had remained a close friend. He decided he'd better take the call.

'Bruno, dear, I need your help,' came the familiar voice. 'One of my cookery school clients who was coming from Bordeaux by train failed to turn up at the station as planned. And she's not answering her mobile phone. I tried to check with Bordeaux airport whether she'd been on the plane but they pleaded security and refused to tell me. I've got her photo. She sent one so that I could recognize her at the station. Can you help?'

On the pitch, the two squads, each of eight forwards, advanced upon each other like warriors from some far-distant age. The front rank of three had their arms around each other's shoulders and they were crouching, ready to duck their heads and slam into the interlocked shoulders of their opponents. Behind them the remaining forwards ducked down, locked into place and began to push. On each side were the flankers, and Bruno's eyes were on the nearer of the two, Paulette. About to turn nineteen, the daughter of the town florist, she was the finest natural athlete and ball player he'd ever trained, male or female. Bruno knew one of the scouts for the national team was somewhere in the stand. They always watched a regional final, looking for promising new players. Paulette was the first player he'd worked with who could reach the supreme level of playing for France.

'I'm tied up but I'll see what I can do later this afternoon,' he said quickly, his eyes fixed on the pitch. 'Send me a text message with the name and flight details and email me the photo.' After a brisk but affectionate farewell he closed his phone.

Pushing from the flank, Paulette added her strength to the St Denis forwards as the two squads slammed together, all of them shoving hard as the opponent's scrum half tossed the ball between the feet of the two front rows who vied for possession. Paulette's head was down to watch where the ball was going and as soon as she saw it being heeled back away from St Denis, she began to peel off from the scrum and anticipate the next move when the ball would emerge into open play.

It was a matter of delicate judgement. If she got ahead of the ball, Paulette would give away a penalty. If she hung too far back, the opposing scrum half would have time to pass the ball back to a teammate who could kick the ball safely up the field and out of play. The rule in rugby was that a passed ball flew faster than a human being could run. But in this instance, Bruno thought, the opposing fly half was standing a little too close. At the least, Paulette should be able to charge down a kick and, with enough speed, she could catch the fly half in possession.

Paulette timed it perfectly. As the scrum half began to pull the ball from the scrum and turned to pass it back, Paulette pounced. Her sprinter's acceleration matched the speed of the ball and she hit the opposing fly half just a second after the pass was received. Paulette wrenched the ball free, side-stepped and accelerated towards the line with only the full back to beat. She dropped the ball onto her foot, punted it neatly over the full back's head, caught the ball as it dropped and had time to run behind the posts to ensure an easy conversion. Five points for the try and two more from the conversion. Along with every other spectator except the Mussidan team's sullen trainer, Bruno leaped into the air with excitement and admiration for a dazzling piece of play.

'Well played, St Denis,' he called out, ignoring the beep of an incoming message on his phone as Paulette placed the ball for her conversion kick. He assumed it would be Pamela, sending the details she had promised about the missing woman. Paulette stepped back a few paces, focused carefully and then strode forward and kicked the ball easily between the posts.

'Now, don't let up,' Bruno shouted. 'Let's have another score.'

'*Mon Dieu*, that girl's a marvel,' said Lespinasse at Bruno's side, owner of the St Denis garage and this year's chairman of the rugby club. 'They never saw that coming. She'll play for France one day, you mark my words.'

Bruno nodded, distracted by the sight of Paulette bent double and retching and then dropping to one knee. The St Denis trainer ran onto the pitch, squeezed a damp sponge onto the back of her neck and gave her a bottle of water. Paulette took a swig, nodded and then jogged back to join her teammates.

As play resumed Mussidan tried a short kick, followed by a rush of all their forwards together. But the St Denis players held them, and when they slipped the ball to their scrum half and she tried to dart around the maul Paulette was there to bring her down just before the final whistle went. The girls of St Denis had won their first championship by a convincing score, nineteen points to twelve, and Bruno was dancing with joy on the touchline as the two teams filed past one another, exchanging handshakes in the traditional courtesy of the sport.

Cheering themselves and beaming with pride, their faces still flushed from the game, the whole team then lined up to hug and thank Bruno in a great crush of muddied womanhood. Bruno had tears in his eyes as he slapped them on the back and told them how splendidly they had played and how much they deserved to win the champions' cup.

Then the parents and families gathered round to praise and embrace their daughters. They were followed by the Mayor, who handed Bruno a flask of cognac and he took a celebratory swig. Philippe Delaron, the town photographer who worked for *Sud Ouest* newspaper, was trying to round up the girls for a team photo but they were all too excited to listen to his appeals until Bruno marshalled them into sufficient order for the photo. Somehow the Mayor placed himself with a politician's skill into the centre of the picture. Finally, with the winning trophy held high, the young women tugged Bruno into their ranks for a final photo. As they broke up he noted that Paulette was looking unusually pale.

'Are you okay?' he asked her, trying to look into her eyes for any sign of concussion. 'Did you get hurt in that tackle?'

'I'm fine,' she said briskly, avoiding his gaze. 'Just something I ate. Don't worry.' She turned and hugged him fiercely before greeting her parents, ignoring Philippe's appeal for one last photo and then joining the rest of the team heading for the showers.

Bruno scanned the small crowd of spectators as they began to leave the stadium, hoping to spot the scout for the national team. A solitary man still sat in the stand, tapping away at a tablet on his knee. A sports writer or the scout? Bruno wasn't sure but he knew better than to try and lobby the man on Paulette's behalf. If he hadn't been impressed by her skill and her sense for the game, the scout was in the wrong profession. Bruno knew that he would find out soon enough, when the French team announced the names of the thirty young women who would be invited to the summer camp to prepare for the next season. Now that women's rugby was starting to be televised, money was available to invest in the sport.

Bruno pulled out his phone and called an old police academy friend who worked in the security section at Bordeaux airport and passed on the details of the missing client at Pamela's cookery course. She had messaged him the name of Monika Felder, on the British Airways flight from Gatwick, adding a British mobile number and an address in Surrey along with the information that the cost of the week-long course had been paid in advance. Bruno was promised a call back after his friend had checked the airport computer.

Suddenly someone from the changing rooms was calling Bruno's name, asking if he could find a doctor. He trotted over to the beer tent, where Fabiola and her partner, Gilles, were eating grilled sausages on buns while waiting for the girls to dress and pile into the hired bus that would take them back to St Denis.

'There's a call for a doctor in the changing rooms,' he told Fabiola. 'Can you help?'

She nodded, her mouth still full of sausage, handed him the remaining half of her bun and headed to the changing rooms. Bruno followed, waiting outside while Fabiola went in.

Paulette's father, Bernard, came to join him and asked, 'What's this about wanting a doc? Who's it for?'

'No idea,' Bruno replied. 'We'll learn soon enough. Paulette played well.'

'We've been worried about her. She was sick just after breakfast this morning. Said it was just nerves before the big match.'

Bruno glanced quickly at him and patted Bernard on the shoulder, trying to conceal his own sudden alarm. Then Florence came to the door of the changing rooms. She taught science at the St Denis *collège* and acted as team manager. She was looking flustered and beckoned Bruno to join her.

'Paulette fainted in the showers,' she whispered, trying to ensure that Bernard couldn't overhear. 'She said she was just a bit dizzy and not to make a fuss. Fabiola is looking at her now.'

Florence went back inside and a few minutes later out came the players, some in jeans, others in short skirts and fashionable jackets, looking more as if they were coming from a disco than from a hard-fought match. At the tail came Florence and Fabiola, Paulette between them and looking fine, if a little pale.

'It was nothing,' she told her father, hugging him. 'Just the excitement.'

'She'll be fine,' said Fabiola, without smiling.

Bruno handed her the remains of the sausage and bun, now cold and not looking at all appetising. Fabiola tossed it into a nearby bin.

'I'd love one of those,' Paulette said. 'I'm famished.' She set off with her father to the food stand.

'Is she really okay?' Bruno asked when they had gone.

'Mother and babe both doing well,' Fabiola said grimly. 'She's nearly three months pregnant, hasn't seen a doctor yet and hasn't told her parents. She's in perfect health but I don't want her playing any more rugby this year.'

Bruno was about to say something about the trial for the national team but stopped himself in time and then closed his eyes and grimaced. There were now more important things in Paulette's life than rugby. He sighed, thinking of the hours of practice he had put into refining her skills.

'Did the other girls hear? Do they know about this?' he asked.

'I took her into the trainer's room for a quick examination so I don't think they overheard anything,' Fabiola replied. 'But her teammates aren't fools.'

'*Merde, merde, merde*,' said Florence.

She had put just as much effort into Paulette's future, maybe more. Paulette had been a poor pupil, kept back one year after failing her exams to get into a *lycée*, and it had taken the combined influence of Bruno and the Mayor to get the *lycée* to accept her. Bruno had called in some favours to secure a promise from a university with a special course for sports teachers that they would be happy to take her, if she passed the *bac*, the *baccalauréat* exam at the end of the two years at the *lycée*. Suddenly, what had seemed to be a very promising future for Paulette that matched her athletic gifts was now at risk.

'She must have known she was pregnant?' Bruno asked.

Fabiola gave him a pitying look. 'Don't be an idiot, Bruno. Of course she knew, she just didn't know what to do about it. I think she was hoping that with all the knocks from rugby it might just go away. But babies can be pretty resilient and Paulette is an extremely healthy young animal.'

Fabiola's jaw tightened. She and her partner had been trying to have a baby for some time, but without success. Bruno knew from Gilles that Fabiola was starting to fret about it, despite the advice that she always gave to her patients that nature would probably take its usual course and they should avoid worry and simply enjoy the process.

'Does the father know? The father of the baby, I mean, not her dad,' he asked.

'I have no idea. She just clammed up when I asked when her last period had been and refused to say another word. At least she promised to come into the clinic tomorrow so I can give her a full check and I'll try to ask her then. At a guess I'd say the baby is due in October – just when she was planning to go on to university. If she decides to go ahead and have the kid, that is.' She shook her head sadly. 'It's so damn unnecessary, these days.

They get the sex education, they know there's contraception available but they still make a mess of things.'

'That poor girl,' said Florence. 'What a prospect to face. Still, she can always take a year off and go to university later. When you see her tomorrow, tell her she should feel free to come and talk to me about it.'

She could always go to university, Bruno thought, but the chance of a place on the French under-20 team would not come again and he knew Paulette had set her heart on it. And a sports teacher who had played for her country would have a much easier career path than one without.

It should have been a joyous ride home to St Denis on the team bus with the championship cup aboard. But Paulette had handed the cup to Bruno without a word, before stomping up the aisle to sit alone on a rear seat where she leaned back and closed her eyes, as if asleep. Clearly she was determined neither to speak nor to take part in any celebrations and that put a damper on the journey.

At least it meant there were none of the usual singalongs to drown out the call to Bruno from the security desk at the airport. Monika Felder had not been on that day's flight, nor had she booked it. She had, however, flown in the previous day on the same British Airways flight. Her passport had been recorded by the Police aux Frontières before she passed through customs. And she was booked to take the return journey to London Gatwick in a week's time.

'Do you want the photo?' Bruno was asked. He knew that surveillance cameras had been installed at more and more airports and access points so he quickly agreed. He could check it against the image Pamela had promised to send. He thanked his old colleague, ended the call and found Pamela's email with the attachment. He clicked on it, expecting the drab near-anonymity of a passport-style photo. Instead, it could have been a studio portrait, carefully lit, of a strikingly lovely woman. She had blonde hair, artfully arranged to flatter her face and her large, dramatic eyes. Her cheekbones were high, her smile alluring while sufficiently restrained for the passport regulations, and her complexion seemed to glow with that soft perfection that so many Englishwomen enjoyed. It was a compensation, Bruno assumed, for living in that damp and foggy climate. She was standing slightly sideways while looking directly at the camera, a pose that showed off her long, elegant neck.

Bruno gave a low whistle of appreciation, thinking that anyone seeing a woman such as this would not easily forget her. That should make finding her much easier. His phone gave the double-beep sound of an incoming message. It came from his friend at the airport and even the grey image of the woman waiting at the passport desk could not conceal her beauty. She was evidently the woman in the photo Pamela had sent.

There could be any number of reasonable explanations for her failure to arrive as planned, Bruno thought. She may have missed the train, or decided to take a day off in Bordeaux, or been diverted by a sudden family emergency. Still, it was odd that she hadn't called Pamela to warn of her late arrival. He called the English phone number that Pamela had sent him and heard the bland tones of a recording saying the subscriber was not available. He left a message with his own number.

As soon as he put his phone away, his thoughts turned to

Paulette's pregnancy, wondering whether Paulette would be more forthcoming with him than she had been with Fabiola. And if not, he began to think how he might learn the identity of the father of Paulette's child and whether he should somehow let Paulette's parents learn of their daughter's condition. Legally, however, Paulette was no longer a minor, which meant she was entitled to her privacy.

Bruno sighed as he contemplated the cheap brass cup sitting on the coach seat beside him, far less impressive and much less costly than the cup for the young men's championship that had been bought a generation earlier. Still, Bruno would ensure that it took pride of place in the club's cabinet of trophies, despite the grumbles of the old guard who could still not bring themselves to take the women's game seriously. Perhaps the championship would change that but he doubted it. The old ways died hard in St Denis and Bruno himself had at first questioned whether the girls should continue to play after puberty. It was the insistence of the girls that had converted him and made him increasingly proud of the young women he had trained. This should have been a day of triumph but Paulette's situation had cast a shadow. Bruno's dream of watching her trotting out onto the pitch in the blue shirt of the nation at the Stade de France in Paris had turned hollow.

How would her family react? If she were to have the baby, the family would have some decisions to take. But the real choice would have to be up to Paulette. Bruno grunted to himself, thinking that more and more frequently he was faced with situations for which the police academy had left him wholly unprepared.

Perhaps he should consult his colleague Yveline, the impressive young woman who commanded the local Gendarmerie. An athlete who had been on the French Olympic squad for field hockey, Yveline had taken a friendly interest in Paulette's sporting prospects and she would have been at the match had she not been on duty. He'd visit the Gendarmerie before going home. He could tell her about Pamela's missing customer at the same time, and that thought reminded him that he should check with Pamela if she had any news.

As Pamela answered his call, he heard in the background women's voices and laughter. It was the time when her pupils would be preparing the classic Périgord dinner they would be eating that evening.

'What's on the menu?' he asked her.

'*Blanquette de veau*,' she replied. 'Since we have one empty place there's going to be lots left over if you'd like to come and join us.'

'I'd love to but I need to see the rugby team home and you'll be pleased to hear that they won the championship. Then I have to check in at the Gendarmerie so I'll call you after that to tell you if I can make it. Any news of your missing woman?'

'Not a word. But did she land?'

'Yes, but I've heard from the airport that she landed yesterday, not today. Could she have mistaken the date?'

'No, she emailed me two days ago to confirm her arrival at Le Buisson station today. The plane was scheduled to arrive at eleven this morning so I explained how to take the airport bus to the Bordeaux station and catch the train at two. She had lots of time, enough to get some lunch at the station and I was to meet her at four. But it's a daily flight. Maybe she just wanted a day sight-seeing in Bordeaux. Do you think something might have happened to her? A sudden illness, perhaps?'

'I'll check with the station,' he said.

As the homebound bus drew into St Denis's rugby club, Bruno closed his phone. He had learned that no woman had been taken ill at Bordeaux station, nor on the airport bus. The train had been on time. He climbed out to congratulate the team once more and waved them off in their various cars. He called Yveline but she was off duty that evening. Finally he phoned Pamela to learn that she and her cookery school pupils were about to sit down to dinner.

'The *blanquette de veau* looks perfect and I saved a place for you. We're drinking that rosé from Château Briand that you like,' she added.

'I'm on my way.'

2

Bruno rose early the next day to polish his boots and leather belt before his usual jog through the woods. His basset hound, Balzac, began by running at his heels but then as usual became distracted by some interesting scent and pottered off to fall increasingly behind. Bruno was confident that he'd turn up at the end of the run. And while Bruno knew he should be thinking of the special parade that was scheduled for later that morning, his mind turned again to Paulette's pregnancy. He'd have to wait for Fabiola to tell him the outcome of her meeting with the girl, although knowing Fabiola's care for the privacy of her patients, he did not expect to learn much. He would also have to call the ticket office in Le Buisson to see if there was any way they could check whether Pamela's missing guest had boarded a train or even bought a ticket.

The missing Monika had been the main topic of conversation at Pamela's dinner table the previous evening. Bruno had arrived late, just in time for the main course, and the introductions to the other clients had been hurried. There had been two middle-aged couples and three single women: two of them in their sixties and a fashionably dressed younger woman who was introduced as Kathleen. She was a journalist from one of the British Sunday newspapers, invited by Pamela to enjoy a free cookery course and write about the experience. She had prematurely grey hair, very well cut. Bruno guessed her to be in her mid-thirties, and was told she was a keen horsewoman who would be joining the morning rides to exercise the horses.

Bruno's English was now, thanks to Pamela, good enough to follow most of the conversation. But when Pamela explained that Bruno was the local policeman, he had to fend off a barrage of questions about Monika. Adult missing persons were not usually recorded until three days had passed, he explained, but since she was a foreigner who might not speak much French he'd be making an extra effort to locate her. He'd been grateful when Pamela had changed the subject to Bruno's other role as one of the several chefs on the course.

Bruno would be teaching them to make a pâté de foie gras and to show the customers how to get five separate meals from a single duck. The Baron would be showing how to make a stuffed neck of goose and then to use it in a classic cassoulet of the Périgord. Ivan from the bistro was giving up his day off – for a fee – to demonstrate his desserts, from crème brûlée to *tarte au noix*, pears poached in spiced red wine to *sabayon de fraises*, a dish of strawberries in a creamy custard, a favourite of Bruno's. Odette from Oudinot's farm was taking them to find various kinds of mushroom in her woods and then showing how best to cook them with veal. Stéphane was to demonstrate how he made his cheeses and yoghurts. Julien was giving them a tour of the town vineyard and winery and Hubert was giving them a wine-tasting session. Along with a tour of Bergerac vineyards and a couple of sightseeing trips to the Lascaux cave and some chateaux, they were in for a busy week, Bruno thought. Pamela and her English friend Miranda had planned it well.

Back at his cottage, Balzac was waiting patiently by the back door. Bruno showered and took special care with his shave before toasting the remains of yesterday's baguette and sharing it with his dog while listening to the local news on radio Périgord. The final item concerned him and this morning's parade which would mark Bruno's promotion in rank and the increase in his responsibilities. He took his dress uniform from the dry cleaner's bag, dressed and checked his appearance in the mirror before heading to his office in the Mairie. Usually his dog sat alongside him in the passenger seat, but Balzac sometimes laid his head on his master's thigh, so today the hound went in the back of the van to ensure that Bruno's impeccable uniform showed not a trace of canine hair.

As Bruno parked beside the Mairie, he noticed two other municipal police vans already there. From the window of Fauquet's café, two cops in uniform waved at him. One was an overweight and untidy man who looked too old for the job, and the other a young woman in a uniform that looked at once new and rather baggy on her slim build.

The man was Louis, the municipal policeman of Montignac, a small town further up the Vézère valley. It was wealthier than St Denis, thanks to the thousands of tourists who came each year to visit the fabled prehistoric art in the nearby Lascaux cave. Just eighteen months from retirement, Louis had twice to Bruno's knowledge been reprimanded for being drunk on duty. He made no secret of his resentment that Bruno had been given the promotion Louis felt was his due for long service.

The young woman was Juliette Robard, newly hired to replace the last policewoman of Les Eyzies, who had retired after being shot on duty. She had made a full recovery, but had decided to take a safer job at her Mairie. Juliette was a new graduate of the police academy. She was a local girl who had given up a secure job as a ticket inspector on the regional rail service to be nearer to her mother, who had been confined to a wheelchair after a car accident. Since her father was a long-standing member of the Les Eyzies town council, Juliette's appointment had been almost a formality. It had also been hurried through, to ensure that Juliette was securely in place before the reorganisation of the municipal police, which would have required the new commander – Bruno – to give his approval to her recruitment.

Bruno felt neither surprise nor resentment. That was how these matters were arranged in the region. He had known Juliette since, as a teenager, she had been one of the pupils in his tennis classes. He liked her and thought of her as a level-headed and shrewd young woman who would probably be a success in her new career. He appreciated Juliette's cheerful disposition and there was something both intelligent and kindly about her eyes that suggested she would make a fine colleague. Moreover, she spoke good English. Bruno thought this was becoming essential for any policeman in the Périgord, a region whose most important industry was now tourism. Louis spoke no language other than French. Luckily Bruno would be able to approve the appointment of Louis's replacement.

Bruno shook hands with Louis, kissed Juliette and gratefully accepted their offer of coffee. He was about to decline a croissant, but Balzac, who knew this café well, was giving him one of those appealing looks and Fauquet made the best croissants in the whole of the Périgord. And Fauquet had automatically brought one with Bruno's coffee. Leaning forward in his chair so no crumbs fell on his uniform, Bruno enjoyed this sublime example of the patissier's art and gave Balzac his usual portion.

'Are you on good terms with your former colleagues on the railways?' he asked Juliette.

'Yes, most of them,' she replied cautiously. 'What do you want to know?'

He told her of the missing Monika and asked whether it would be possible to find out if she had bought a ticket for any of the trains from Bordeaux to any of the local stations in the last two days.

'If she bought the ticket online from England, she'd have had to print it out and that would have been scanned by the inspector,' Juliette replied. 'If she used her credit card to buy the ticket at Bordeaux station, there would be a record, but you'd need her credit card number and it could take a while. And we'd need to open a formal missing persons' file to get around the data confidentiality regulations.'

'Are there any less formal ways to get an answer more quickly?' he asked.

'Of course,' she answered with a grin. 'Give me the full name and details and I'll check who was on the duty roster for the Sarlat route for the last two days.'

He gave Juliette the information and from his phone emailed her and Louis a copy of the photo Pamela had sent.

'Why all the fuss about some foreign woman missing her train?' Louis asked.

'The reason, Louis,' Bruno said, 'is that tourism is now the biggest industry in the *département* and that means we make a special effort to be sure everything goes smoothly for foreign visitors.'

Juliette gave him a playful punch on the arm and Louis grunted a reluctant assent, muttering something about not being quite up to speed with his new phone yet. Juliette, by contrast, was already speaking on hers, exchanging pleasantries with some former colleague and speaking in what sounded like technical terms known only to *cheminots*, as rail employees were universally known.

'Both of our Mayors are coming, along with Bossuet from the regional council,' said Louis, leaning forward and murmuring into Bruno's ear. 'I heard on the grapevine that Bossuet wanted to swear you in but your Mayor insisted on doing it himself.'

A recent study by the Ministry of Justice had decided that the local police forces needed more resources in computers, communications equipment and administrative support. Since Bruno had been one of the policemen surveyed in the study, his region had been picked for the pilot project to test the new system. Amélie, the young official who had made the survey, had strongly recommended that Bruno should lead the project. It meant that Bruno was being promoted to be chief of police of the entire valley, from Limeuil, where the River Vézère flowed into the Dordogne, all the way upstream to Montignac.

After today's swearing-in, he would be in command of Juliette and Louis, and a new administrative assistant, yet to be hired, who would occupy a disused storeroom beside Bruno's office, along with new computers and a secure communications system. For Bruno, it meant many more responsibilities, a modest pay rise, and the knowledge that he would spend much of his time driving back and forth to Les Eyzies and Montignac to coordinate his new team. He would have to learn how to get along with two new Mayors and their respective councils and the *Conseil Régional* of the elected politicians who ran the *département*. For Bruno, the most uncomfortable aspect of the change was that he would no longer be answerable solely to the Mayor of St Denis.

'The parade has been pushed back to eleven so we have some time to wait,' said Louis, with the sly look of a man with inside knowledge. 'A little bird told me you might want to brace yourself for a surprise. And I don't just mean a lunch, which is why it's all been delayed. Some brass hats are supposed to be coming so we'll be giving a lot of salutes.'

Bruno's heart sank. He had picked up a hint that the Mayor was arranging something special. He had expected the swearing-in to be a formality, held in the Mayor's office and all over and done with after a few minutes. If lots of saluting was to be involved, it seemed likely to be rather grander than that. And now he had two hours to kill. He should go up to his office to catch up on paperwork but it would not be a good idea to abandon his two colleagues.

'A friend of mine is pretty sure he checked your missing woman on the train from Bordeaux two days ago,' said Juliette.

'He'll be pulling into the station at Le Buisson on a change of shift and can give us half an hour.'

'Let's go,' said Bruno, rising. He caught himself and asked Louis if he'd like to come along. Louis gestured with his head towards some of his hunting friends at the bar and said he'd stay with them.

They took Bruno's van and pulled into the station forecourt about twenty minutes later. Juliette led the way around the back and through an anonymous door into a corridor lined with offices. At the far end was what Juliette called the relief room, where the train staff could rest on their breaks or between shifts. It had two sofas, a large dining table on which someone had set out a chess set, and a counter that contained a sink, a microwave oven and a coffee machine. Beneath the counter were a refrigerator, cupboards and a dishwasher. A small TV stood on a bookshelf half-filled with paperbacks, magazines and table games.

'This is Sylvain, chess champion of the *cheminots*,' said Juliette. A young man with a goatee beard turned from the coffee machine, embraced Juliette and held out a hand to Bruno.

'You must be Bruno. How do you like your coffee?' he asked.

'Black, no sugar, thanks.'

'So you're the guy who lured our Juliette off the rails?' said Sylvain, smiling before bending to take cups from a cupboard. 'The railways aren't the same without her.' He looked at Juliette. 'If it doesn't work out, I'm sure we'd all be delighted to have you back on the service. At least our uniforms fit, which is more than I can say for the copper's outfit they've given you.'

He suddenly noticed Balzac and kneeled down to caress the

dog. Then he reached into the cupboard, brought out a packet of biscuits and told his guests to help themselves.

'Is it okay if I give him one?' he asked Bruno, waving a biscuit. 'I had an uncle who had a basset, a lovely dog. What's his name?'

'Balzac,' said Bruno, enjoying once again the way his dog made friends wherever he went. It made his job much easier. 'And he'll be your friend for life after you give him that biscuit.'

Sylvain poured out three coffees and then pulled a small computer from his official shoulder bag that was hanging from a hook beside the bookshelves. Bruno recognized it as the digital system for checking rail tickets. Sylvain pressed two buttons, entered what seemed to be a password and then began scrolling through various screens.

'Monika Felder bought her ticket by computer from England, paid with an English credit card and printed it out herself. She paid full price so she could have used any train irrespective of peak or off-peak periods for the rest of this month.' Sylvain spoke clearly in a precise manner that would have made him an excellent witness in court, Bruno thought.

Sylvain looked up. 'We don't take reservations on this line, so she wasn't limited to any particular day. She took the daily 14:05 train from Bordeaux St Jean the day before yesterday and I checked her ticket before Bergerac. Because it was a print-out, I had to read it with my scanner which is why we have all these details. She was the kind of woman you notice, well-dressed, striking. She asked me about return trains next Sunday, saying she had a flight that afternoon. I recommended that she take the 9:05, getting into Bordeaux St Jean at 11.55, in time for the airport shuttle at noon.'

'Do you know at which station she got off?'

'I'm pretty sure it was Lalinde even though her ticket went all the way to Le Buisson. I have to be on the platform at each stop so I can be sure everybody's clear before I give the signal to the driver to start off again. So I remembered her, and the man she was with.'

'What man? Was he on the train with her?'

'Yes, they were chatting away in English when I checked her ticket. He didn't have one, said in good French that he hadn't had time to buy one at the station, so he paid in cash. But he had a *Grand Voyageur* card, which got him a small reduction.'

Bruno knew about this frequent traveller card. He'd have bought one himself but his police identity card got him even better reductions on the trains. 'So you have the number of this man's card.'

'More than that,' said Sylvain proudly. 'Thanks to the card, we've got his name and address on file. His name is Patrick James McBride and he lives at Sainte Colombe, wherever that is. But the postcode starts with 24 so it's in this *département*.'

'I know it,' said Juliette, opening her phone and accessing the local phone book. 'It's north of Lalinde, on the way to St Marcel. There's a landline listed for him.'

Bruno checked his watch as she began to dial. There wasn't enough time to get there and back before the parade was scheduled. Juliette shook her head to say there was no answer. She left a message, asking Monsieur McBride to call her back.

'How did these two people seem to you?' Bruno asked. 'You

said they were chatting away. Like old friends? Or strangers striking up an acquaintance?'

'I don't think they were married – they seemed too interested in each other for that. She was being flirtatious and he was being appreciative, you know, like people looking forward to jumping into bed together.'

'I never knew you were such a romantic, Sylvain,' said Juliette, rolling her eyes.

'You bring out the best in me,' he replied with a sly grin. Bruno got the impression this wasn't the first time he'd flirted with Juliette, and that she had no intention of responding.

'Thanks for your help,' said Bruno as they finished their coffee and headed back to St Denis. Louis was still in the café, installed at a small table at the rear, drinking a *petit blanc* with two hunters, arguing happily about the merits of various guns pictured in the issue of *Le Chasseur Français* that lay open before them.

Bruno told Juliette that he would just check his messages and install Balzac in his office and rejoin them in time for whatever sort of parade the Mayor had arranged. But as he approached the Mairie's main door, the Mayor's secretary, Claire, emerged carrying a dog leash and a large suit-carrier. Claire was a relentless flirt, especially around Bruno.

'*Bonjour*, Bruno, the Mayor wants Balzac to be there,' Claire said, waving the dog leash and batting her eyelashes. 'I'll take good care of him. And the Mayor says you have to wear this so take off your old jacket.'

She handed him the suit-carrier. Bruno unzipped it to find a new uniform jacket with the two broad white stripes of a *chef de service principal* on his epaulette. While Claire attached Balzac's leash Bruno ducked inside the Mairie's entrance to change. It was a kindly gesture, he thought, but they could simply have put the new epaulettes on the old jacket that he'd just had cleaned.

At that point, a van full of gendarmes came up the Rue de la République, followed by a familiar Citroën with its tell-tale double aerial of a police vehicle, plus another official-looking car. The van double-parked while the occupants descended. At that moment Bruno realized just what a serious ceremony the Mayor had planned. Yveline, commandant of the gendarmes of St Denis, marshalled her troops into two ranks, stood them to attention and saluted as the Prefect and the Procureur of the *département*, each in uniform, emerged from the official car.

Prunier, the Commissaire de Police for the whole department, was also in uniform. He and Jean-Jacques, the chief detective and known to all as J-J, climbed out of J-J's Citroën. Bruno counted each man as a friend. Years ago he had played rugby for the army against a police team which had included Prunier, an acquaintance that had led to an invitation to dine at Prunier's home and meet his wife and children. And Prunier had done a fine job in modernizing the force and raising its morale. Bruno had worked with him on a couple of sensitive cases and had come to trust his judgement and to admire the man's finesse in navigating the complex politics of the region. In the ten years that Bruno had worked with J-J, the chief detective had become a valued colleague and a regular dining companion. But Bruno suspected that his relationship with each man depended to a considerable extent upon his independence. As an employee of the Mayor of St Denis, Bruno was not in the usual police chain of command. Had he been their subordinate, neither Prunier nor J-J could have been nearly so cordial.

The two top policemen of the *département* came up to shake his hand just as the Mayor, wearing his tricolour sash of office, stepped out from the Mairie. He was followed by the Mayors of Les Eyzies and Montignac and then by the Mayors of all the other *communes* whose populations were too small to justify their own policeman: Limeuil and Audrix, St Cirq and Campagne, St Chamassy, Thonac and Thursac. When had this been planned? Bruno wondered. And how had they organized this sizeable assembly without his knowledge?

After hands had been shaken all around, two of Bruno's friends came out of the Mairie. The Baron was carrying the flag of *les anciens combattants*, the military veterans, and Xavier, the deputy Mayor, was carrying the red, white and blue flag of France.

'You take your place behind the gendarmes,' the Baron whispered to Bruno as he went past to the head of the parade. Then the school band appeared from behind the Mairie, playing 'Lorraine', the marching tune of the French army.

The two flag-bearers led them all across the bridge to the car park, where a gendarme lifted the metal barrier that had closed it to the public and saluted as they marched past him. They drew up before the town war memorial, a statue of a French soldier of the Great War standing on guard with bayonet fixed over a fallen comrade. The bronze eagle atop the obelisk that contained the names of the town's war dead had been newly polished. A crowd had gathered, mainly employees from the Mairie and their families. Some of the shopkeepers and local residents had joined them, along with Philippe Delaron, the photographer and local correspondent for *Sud Ouest* newspaper. Beside him stood a local radio reporter with microphone outstretched. The Mayor, the Prefect and the Procureur stepped onto a small dais that had been placed before the memorial and the band fell silent.

'Benoît Courrèges, chief of police of St Denis, come forward,' the Mayor commanded and Bruno stepped smartly forward and saluted.

'Do you solemnly swear to uphold the laws of the Republic as *chef de service principal* of the Police Municipale for the Vézère valley?' the Mayor demanded.

'I swear,' Bruno replied.

'Do you swear to observe the discipline and regulations of the Police Nationale as an *officier judiciaire* with the rank of lieutenant?' This time it was the Procureur who administered the oath as the chief judicial officer of the *département*; Bruno had not expected this.

'I swear,' he repeated, wondering just how many people could now claim some authority over him.

'Chef de Police Courrèges, step forward,' commanded the Prefect. And as Bruno advanced to stand to attention before him, the Prefect took from an aide the small silver medal with its red, white and blue ribbon and pinned it onto Bruno's chest.

'In the name of a grateful Republic and by decree of the Minister of the Interior, I hereby present you with the police

Médaille d'Honneur, for distinguished service,' the Prefect announced. He stepped back and he and Bruno exchanged salutes. The band began to play the 'Marseillaise' and the flags rose, which meant Bruno had to maintain his salute until the national anthem ended. Then the small crowd applauded and the parade was dismissed.

It was a strange moment, with a touch of sadness about it as Bruno realized that his professional life was about to change. No longer would he be responsible solely for St Denis, a town of just under two thousand souls, with another thousand scattered across the hills and valleys, the woodlands and plateaus of the vast *commune* that surrounded the town itself. He knew someone in every household, or at least every family in this *commune* that was larger than the city of Paris. Most of them were friends and there were few homes where he was not welcome, where he had not shared a meal or a drink, or danced at a wedding, held the baby at a baptism or helped carry the coffin at a funeral. He was as much a part of the flow of the town's life as the Mayor, the priest and the River Vézère itself.

Bruno could not even calculate how many people now lived in this new fiefdom of the whole valley that he had to police but there must be close to twenty thousand of them. He could never hope to develop among so many people the intimacy of his relationship with St Denis. And that personal knowledge, Bruno knew, had always been the key to his work as a country policeman. He would just have to try to train his colleagues in his methods, he concluded as the parade ended, the gendarmes were ordered to fall out and the dignitaries stepped down from the dais.

Bruno thanked them all, and then the various mayors came up and he shook each one's hands and kissed the Mayoress of Thonac on both cheeks. In the back of his mind he was thinking that Louis had been born and raised in Montignac and despite his grumpy moods, he was a well-known and familiar figure. Bruno could not expect to change him and did not intend to try. He would focus instead on picking and training Louis's successor. Juliette, however, seemed far more promising; quick-witted and engaging, she came with her own useful network of contacts among the *cheminots*.

He gave boilerplate replies to the two reporters, saying he was proud and honoured to be given the new job and what a privilege it was to serve the people of the Vézère valley. He was careful to call it *la vallée de l'homme*, the cradle of humankind, as the tourist board sought to label this region so rich in prehistoric sites and remains. Finally he escaped and strode quickly back across the bridge to the Mairie.

'You're improperly dressed, Lieutenant,' came a familiar voice and J-J loomed up beside him. 'Since you are now attached to the Police Nationale and our nation's President has seen fit to declare a state of emergency, you're going to have to wear a weapon at all times on duty. You will give up that old blunderbuss you use and start carrying the approved firearm, a lovely new SIG Sauer. I've got one ready for you at HQ and the armourer will give you a familiarization course on the range. You'll have to bring in your old PAMAS.'

'Why do we keep changing the personal weapons like this?'

'Because unlike the Americans we don't have hundreds of millions of civilians with firearms,' J-J said as they reached the Mairie. 'The only way we keep the European arms industry going is by buying new ones, different weapons for the police and the army, the gendarmes and the navy.'

Never one to forego an opportunity of politicking among the other mayors and the state officials, the Mayor had arranged a *vin d'honneur* to celebrate Bruno's promotion, followed by a lunch at the Mairie to cement relations with them all. Standing outside the Mairie, Bruno quickly rang his colleague at Lalinde, an ex-serviceman called Quatremer, and asked if he knew a foreigner called McBride at Sainte Colombe. No, came the reply but did Bruno want him to check on the man? Bruno said he'd be grateful and gave the address. He then climbed the old and well-worn stone stairs to the council chamber where the ancient wood table was laid for a formal lunch, the Mayor holding court for his guests while Claire circled with a tray of glasses holding champagne.

Bruno checked the menu card. They would be eating foie gras with a glass of sweet, golden Monbazillac wine, followed by fresh trout with toasted almonds, accompanied by a white wine from the town vineyard, then cheese and salad, *tarte au citron* and coffee. That meant four, maybe five speeches, Bruno calculated. The Mayor would offer a few words of welcome. After the foie gras Bruno would doubtless be expected to speak and Bossuet from the regional council would deliver his remarks after the fish, leaving the closing words to the Prefect, as senior representative of the French state.

'I had to check with the protocol department of the Ministry of Defence about your new medal and where you should wear the ribbon,' said the Prefect as they ate their foie gras. 'Apparently, your Croix de Guerre takes precedence, so that comes first on the breast with the Médaille d'Honneur alongside.'

'Thank you, *monsieur*,' said Bruno. 'I wouldn't have known.'

'It's quite a feather in our caps for this *département* to be chosen for the pilot scheme on police reform. I gather the justice minister was most insistent after the report from that charming young woman from Guadeloupe who did the survey. Apparently she's the minister's political *protégée*.'

'Amélie Duplessis,' said Bruno. 'A most impressive young woman, and did you know she's also a professional jazz singer? She'll be coming down this summer to perform at our summer concerts.'

So the lunch passed, political gossip, political speeches, Bruno's own brief remarks limited to his thanks to all present, his pleasure in his new colleagues and his good fortune in living in such a peerless part of France that his trips back and forth up the valley would make duty into a pleasure.

The Prefect had just sat down after his own speech and the coffee had been served when Bruno's phone vibrated. It was Quatremer from Lalinde, to say that Bruno should come right away and bring Jean-Jacques. McBride's home was now a crime scene.

3

Prunier agreed to drive back to Périgueux with the Prefect so J-J could use his own car. Bruno joined J-J to brief him on the way, Juliette following in Bruno's van. It would be her first serious crime scene, Bruno thought, and without her knowledge of the rail ticket system the murder could have gone unknown for some time.

McBride's home was charming, an old L-shaped stone farmhouse with a well-tended *potager* filled with the green tops of young carrots and radishes, beans, peas and a row of piled earth that promised asparagus. A mud-spattered Range Rover was parked beside a small tractor in the adjoining barn, which also contained a neat woodpile, the pump for the swimming pool and the oil-fuelled furnace for central heating. At the far end of the barn stood a workbench with a fine collection of tools that included a circular saw and a lathe.

In front of the house was a big courtyard with a large lime tree in the centre, surrounded by a neat herb garden that circled the trunk. Pots of young geraniums added splashes of colour and against one stretch of stone wall a small raised garden had been built, from which roses climbed up towards the windows of the upper floor. A crude wooden table surrounded by six chairs stood in the angle between the two wings of the farmhouse. Its main entrance seemed to be the open French windows where Quatremer was waiting for them.

'The door was open when I got here,' said Quatremer. 'I called out but there was no reply so I went in to look around, not touching anything. It all seemed normal and tidy until I looked in the bathroom. That's when I called your office, J-J, and then I called Bruno since he'd asked me to check on the owner.'

J-J nodded and told them all to put on evidence gloves and plastic bootees to cover their feet. Bruno always kept some in his car. J-J then led the way through a handsome sitting room at least six metres square. Several Persian rugs that looked expensive lay on the tiled floor. The remains of a wood fire in the *cheminée* had burned out, although Bruno noticed radiators to each side of the entrance doors and more under each window. A small hand axe was propped against the bricks of the *cheminée*, as though used to chop kindling.

Above the huge fireplace and on one wall hung hunting trophies; the skull of a mountain goat with formidably curved horns flanked by the antlers of several deer Bruno didn't recognize but thought might be African. Bookshelves lined one wall, filled more with DVDs and CDs than books. Two sofas faced one another on either side of the fireplace with a coffee table between them on which stood an ashtray and English newspapers and magazines.

Against one wall an antique wooden cabinet held a tray of bottles, a large TV set and a stereo. Above them were photographs of a man in safari jacket and dark glasses, holding a heavy bolt-action rifle, smiling proudly. In one he stood with his foot on the head of a dead rhinoceros, in another beside an elephant whose tusks had been bloodily removed. A third photo showed the same man, flanked by two Africans in khaki overalls, standing above a dead lion with a different, modern rifle in his hand.

Bruno shook his head in distaste. This was not hunting as he knew it, to put food on the table. It could even be illegal, although he vaguely recalled that some countries sold to rich hunters the right to hunt and kill elderly beasts. A fourth photo showed the same man bare-chested on a sunny beach, holding the same rifle. Clustered in a vaguely familiar background were Africans towing ashore an inflatable boat which had a very large outboard motor.

The wall with the photos was flanked by two doors. One opened into a big and well-equipped kitchen with room for a dining table that would seat six or even eight people; it looked home-made and sturdy, and Bruno recalled the circular saw in the barn. Perhaps McBride had made it himself. The other door led into a cloakroom that included a toilet, hand basin and a separate scullery with a washing machine and dryer. In one corner of the living room was a handsome old curving staircase that led upstairs. A door in the other corner was open and Bruno could see an unmade king-size bed, its sheets and duvet thrown back.

'Through here,' said Quatremer, walking past the bed and pointing to a doorway into the adjoining bathroom.

A woman's bra and panties lay on the floor beside the bed, a pair of shoes tumbled beside them and a blue silk dress had been tossed onto a chair. A small carry-on suitcase lay open beside the chair. At the foot of the bed were a man's shoes and socks, jeans and shirt. J-J paused to study the scene and pointed to the sheets.

'Don't touch that bed. We'll need to know if they had sex,' he said, and went into the bathroom.

The naked body of a woman with blonde hair lay sprawled in the shower cubicle, her head turned away so only a part of the side of her face could be seen. There was very little blood from the visible stab wound just underneath her left breast. Somebody, presumably her killer, had turned off the shower. Her body was cold and still stiff, the flesh livid where it lay against the floor. She had evidently been dead for some time.

'Is this the missing woman?' J-J asked.

Bruno bent over the body and used his pen to lift the blonde hair, then nodded. She was still beautiful, even in death. According to her passport details, she was in her late forties but her body seemed like that of a younger woman.

'That's Monika Felder,' he said, the sadness in his voice evident even to himself. 'It's the same face as the photo she sent to Pamela and the one from the Police aux Frontières camera at Bordeaux.'

There was no facial rictus, the snarl that Bruno recalled was one of the first signs of rigor mortis as the small muscles of the face contracted. That they had now relaxed again suggested she had been dead for more than twenty-four, maybe even thirty hours. He would have to look up his notes from the police academy to be sure.

'What do you make of the stab wound, Bruno?'

'Looks to me like a stiletto, a long and narrow blade,' Bruno said. 'That's why there's so little blood. Whoever used it knew what they were doing, where best to place it.'

'Where's the weapon? We need to find it.'

There was no sign of a knife in the bathroom, only male toiletries in the cupboard, the usual razor, comb and toothbrush in a glass beside the wash basin. Next to it was a woman's toilet bag, already open, and a transparent plastic bag containing liquids and gels, the kind that has to be taken out for security at airports.

'Sir, there's a woman's handbag and an open laptop in the kitchen,' said Juliette peeking around the door to the bathroom. Then she saw the body, put her hand to her mouth and exclaimed, 'Oh, dear Mother of God.'

'Is there no sign of this man, McBride?' J-J asked Quatremer.

'Not in the house, sir. I looked upstairs, two bedrooms, each with their own bathroom. They looked like guest rooms, beds not made, with bedding neatly piled on them. The car in the barn is registered to him. I haven't gone around the farmland behind the house. It's mainly vineyards and orchard, some woodland, about eight hectares in all, according to the *cadastre* at the Mairie.'

'So this McBride was what, a farmer, a winemaker?' J-J asked. 'There's no sign of a *chai*, no second barn for wine vats and bottling.'

'That's not uncommon round here,' said Quatremer. 'This is still in the area of the Bergerac *appellation* but there are hardly any named domains and not many winemakers. Mostly they grow grapes for the wine cooperative and some of them rent out their land to professional growers. But there's what looks like a very well-stocked wine cellar down some steps through the door in the kitchen. There's a barred door at the bottom of the stairs, still locked.'

'Right,' said J-J, pulling out his phone and looking at Quatremer, whose turf this was. 'While I'm calling the crime scene guys and the forensics team from Bergerac, perhaps you and Bruno could have a good look round the rest of the property.'

'He's a hunter,' said Bruno. 'He should have a gun cabinet. We'd better check for that.'

'It's in the scullery and it's not locked,' said Quatremer. 'I'll show you.'

The washing machine and dryer dominated one wall and on the other were hooks for outdoor and hunting clothes and a tall metal cabinet, its door closed. Bruno put on evidence gloves and opened it. Inside was a rack to hold four guns, only three places filled. He recognized a Lee Enfield 303, probably the best bolt-action infantry rifle ever made and still used in shooting competitions. Beside it was an old double-action shotgun, the metalwork beautifully scrolled. He looked closer and saw a small rose engraved behind the barrels.

'*Mon Dieu*,' he said to Quatremer. 'This one's a Purdey, English-made, twenty thousand euros at the very least.'

There was another shotgun, side-by-side barrels, with *l'Arquebusier* engraved on the stock, which Bruno recognized from his subscription to the monthly *Le Chasseur Français*. It was made in Bordeaux by Tony Gicquel, one of the finest gunsmiths in France, and cost about seven thousand euros. On a shelf below were some boxes of ammunition, the British 303 calibre and various shotgun shells, birdshot, buckshot and slugs. When Bruno pulled out the boxes to examine them a single loose cartridge rolled free, a big one. He brought it close to his eye to study it and saw BMG stamped into the rim. That made it a Browning half-inch calibre, or 12.7 millimetres, which these days meant a long-range sniper's rifle. But there was no gun to go with it.

The gun case was screwed into the wall at chest height, convenient for reaching into. Below was a chest of drawers with gun cleaning equipment, gun catalogues and hunting magazines. Leafing through them Bruno found a newspaper cutting from the Toronto *Globe*, about a Canadian sniper team which had used a McMillan TAC-50 rifle to kill two enemy combatants in Afghanistan's Shah-i-Kot valley at ranges of almost 2,400 metres. Bruno's eyes widened in surprise. In the army, he had been impressed by snipers who could hit their target at a thousand or even fifteen hundred metres. But 2,400 metres was almost unbelievable. He tried to imagine it, a distance at which a human being could barely be seen with the naked eye and that would probably take him ten minutes to run. The cutting was attached with a paperclip to a guarantee form from McMillan Firearms Manufacturing in Phoenix, Arizona.

'J-J, come look at this,' he called. 'He's got a bullet for a 12.7 millimetre sniper's rifle, a press cutting about a very special rifle that could fire it and this guarantee from the manufacturer. It would make a good elephant gun and we know from the photos that McBride hunted them. It might even be the gun in the hunting photos. So where is the gun now?'

'*Merde*, a killer at two thousand metres? That's just what we need. I'll check into it, see if it's registered. Meanwhile, go and look around to see if there's any trace of the owner.'

J-J turned to Juliette. 'And you, *mademoiselle*, please go door-to-door around all the neighbours and find out what you can about McBride and whether they heard or saw anything unusual over the past couple of days. Country folk tend to keep their eyes open so ask if they saw any visitors or strangers or unfamiliar cars.'

Bruno and Quatremer removed their bootees and walked around the side of the house, passing a small swimming pool that was still covered with its winter *bâche*, and a rear terrace flanked by four upright posts that held a well-pruned trellis of young vines, just coming into bud. It would be a pleasantly shaded spot in summer.

'Do you want to check the pool first while I look over the land?' Bruno asked. Quatremer nodded, went to the side of the pool and bent to untie the fastenings that held down the cover.

Were it not for the circumstances, Bruno would have enjoyed the walk up and down the rows of vines and then through an orchard of apple and pear trees. By the time he reached the woodland, Quatremer had joined him, saying the pool had been empty except for the usual log floating on the surface to prevent it freezing over.

The vineyard was on a gentle uphill slope which grew steeper as the woods began. Mature walnut and chestnut trees were interspersed with hemlocks, sycamores and some young oaks but Bruno saw no sign of the darkened earth that might have signalled the presence of truffles. They followed tracks of heavy vehicles to an area where the wood had been clear cut, low stumps remaining, and at one side neat piles of branches and thinner logs. A metal horse that would hold the branches for cutting stood beside a trailer which was already half-filled with trimmed logs that looked as if they would fit the big *cheminée* at the house.

At the far side of the cleared woodland Bruno saw what looked like a path. He headed towards it, leaving Quatremer to scour the other side of the log pile. He tramped through the tree stumps, careful where he placed his feet among the thick and tangled layers of twigs and small branches, wishing Balzac were with him. The undergrowth looked perfect for the wily *bécasse* that Bruno liked to hunt, thinking them the best eating of the game birds.

There was a well-trodden footpath in the opening between the chestnut trees and he followed it through a belt of mature woodland. It opened into another clearing where he was pleased to find rows of beehives. Bruno had often wondered whether that was a hobby he might one day take up. Something caught his eye, a quick flash of metal. At the far side of the clearing, below a great chestnut just starting to bud, lay a fallen stepladder. He moved closer, marvelling at the size of it, at least four metres high, one of the specialist ladders used by pickers in orchards seeking the highest fruit. But what would the pickers want from a chestnut tree?

It was only then that Bruno looked up. A single moccasin dangled from a foot just a few inches above his own head. The other foot was bare. He was suddenly aware of a stink of shit and the buzzing of flies. An almost naked man was dangling above him.

The man was hanging from a high and sturdy branch, an item of clothing drooping from one shoulder. Bruno moved closer, careful not to tread in the mess beneath the man's feet where his bowels had voided. The body was stone cold but he called out to Quatremer anyway and used his phone to dial 15 for the SAMU emergency medical service. He then erected the stepladder and clambered up to see how the man was attached. He'd never used such a tall stepladder; it felt perilously far from the ground. By accident, he brushed against the body and the garment, a blue flannel dressing gown, slipped from the hanging man's arm.

Bruno felt his gorge rise as he saw that the fingers appeared to have been put through a mincer, the ends bloodied and some of the nails gone. He must have clawed at the rope, trying to loosen it as he died. Bruno climbed higher, sickened by the number of beetles and other insects crawling around the body, clustering around the ears and nose. Something, he presumed birds, had already been at the man's eyes. The rope around his neck had bitten so deeply into the skin that Bruno could only see the knot of the noose emerging from torn and swollen flesh beneath the man's ear. Could this be the man in the hunting photos? Bruno had no idea.

'*Putain*,' said Quatremer, panting from his run to join Bruno and looking up at the horror of the red and swollen face, the lolling tongue, the smears down one leg from the emptied bowels. 'His own mother wouldn't recognize him.'

'Call J-J and get him up here,' Bruno said. 'No point us trying to cut him down. The poor sod's been dead for hours.'

'He didn't go quickly, did he?' said Quatremer. 'Won't be easy to identify.'

He began to dial and Bruno climbed down. He heard Quatremer asking for Commissaire Jalipeau and realized he was calling police HQ in Périgueux and so probably didn't have J-J's cellphone number. Bruno used his own phone and J-J answered at once.

'We've found another body, a male, looks like he hanged himself,' Bruno said. 'Come up through the vineyard and orchard to the clear-cut woodland and you'll see an opening on the left with a pathway. We're in the clearing just after the beehives. I called the *urgences* but there's not much point. He's cold as the grave.'

'Stay there,' J-J said. 'I'll come on up as soon as the *urgences* arrive. The handbag we found in the kitchen belonged to Monika Felder. Her passport's in the bag along with a purse. It still has pounds and euros and credit cards inside so it doesn't look like a robbery. The scene of crime team is just pulling up outside and forensics aren't far behind. And we found what looks like a suicide note in the printer. Send that Lalinde copper back down here. Presumably he can find someone local who can tell us if the dead man is McBride, maybe the local bank manager or someone from the wine co-op.'

'Right.' Bruno ended the call, told Quatremer what J-J wanted and watched him set off. Bruno was still wearing the evidence gloves so he reached inside the two side pockets of the crumpled dressing gown. He found a couple of paper tissues, a pack of Dunhill cigarettes and a Bic lighter. He looked around the straggling grass beneath the trees, seeing the indentations made by the legs of the stepladder and the second moccasin but not much more. Perhaps forensics could make something of the scene.

The man had been in good shape, not much fat on him and he was well muscled. Beyond the ravaged and bloodied fingers, his hands looked roughened, not with manual work but like Bruno's own hands, showing signs of gardening and chopping wood. There was a small, puckered scar high up on the chest beneath the shoulder and Bruno knew at once what it was. He had a similar scar on his own hip that had been made by a high-velocity bullet from a Serbian sniper in the hills above Sarajevo. On the side of the dead man's left leg, swollen with the blood that had been drawn down by gravity, were a series of small indentations and old scars of the kind made by shrapnel from a grenade or a mine.

Bruno assumed at once that the man had been a soldier like him, a combat veteran. He wondered where he had got the wounds. Presuming the body would prove to be McBride, who had spoken English on the train; he had probably been in the British forces. Bruno knew they had most recently seen combat in Afghanistan and Iraq, possibly in Bosnia or Kosovo.

He took out his phone again and called his friend Jack Crimson, a retired British diplomat and former intelligence officer who lived nearby. His daughter, Miranda, had moved to the Périgord with her two children after a messy divorce and was now Pamela's partner in the riding school and the new cookery classes. Jack knew most of the British people in the area and was likely to know of any old soldiers. He also spent a lot of his time visiting the local vineyards.

'Hi, Jack, Bruno here.'

'Ah, congratulations, my dear fellow, both on your promotion and on the medal. I was in the crowd at your parade with Miranda and the children. I must say you French people do these events very well.'

'Thanks, Jack, but this is business. I'm at a small farmhouse and vineyard just north of Lalinde, owned by one of your countrymen called McBride. He's probably an ex-soldier. Do you know him?'

'It doesn't ring a bell. There are thousands of Brits around here and I don't know them all. What's up? Is this chap McBride in trouble?'

'He's dead, if it's him. Looks like he hanged himself and there's a dead British woman in his bathroom, the one who never turned up for the cookery class. She was stabbed, a single strike to the heart. You'll keep this to yourself, Jack, and for God's sake don't tell Pamela or Miranda. Let me handle that. Could you ask around a few of your friends in Lalinde? They might know a fellow Brit.'

'I'll do that but why do you say he's an ex-soldier?'

'There's a long-healed bullet scar on his chest and an exit wound scar on his back, both small so I'd say a high-velocity bullet, probably military. And there are smaller scars on one leg, as if he was clipped by a grenade, maybe a mortar.'

'I could try calling our military records office. Do you have a full name and date of birth, any other details?'

'Patrick James McBride,' Bruno replied, quickly opening his notebook. 'That's all I have. Bullet scar in right shoulder, looks to be in his forties, maybe early fifties.'

'Leave it with me and I'll keep it under my hat.'

'You'll do what?' Bruno asked, wondering what Crimson meant by '*sous mon chapeau*'.

'Ah, under my hat. It's an English saying. It means I'll keep it secret. What about the woman? Do you have her name?'

'Yes, Monika Felder, British passport so I can call you back with her date of birth. She looked to be in her forties.'

'Felder? That does ring a bell, but nothing to do with the Périgord. When you get the date of birth, check the back page of her passport. She may have filled in the section about next of kin.'

As he closed the phone, Bruno heard the sound of a siren, which would probably be the *urgences*. A few minutes later, he heard the ambulance coming closer and went back to the clearing to show them the way. He saw it lumbering up the track by the log pile to stop where the tree stumps blocked the way. Two medics got out of the back and J-J climbed down from the passenger seat. He trudged after the medics and across the undergrowth to Bruno.

'Have you got her passport?' Bruno asked.

J-J pulled an evidence bag from his pocket, checked that Bruno was wearing gloves and handed it across. Bruno looked for the date of birth, 27 October 1970, and inside the back cover saw that the next of kin had been listed as Michael George Felder, with a British telephone number and an address in a place called East Grinstead. He noted down the details and then scanned the rest of the passport. It was full of entry and exit stamps: the United States, Canada, South Africa, Dubai, Australia, Chile, Turkey and

Hong Kong. There were four trips to the US in the last four months, each landing at Houston.

'*Mon Dieu*, she certainly got around,' he said, returning the passport to J-J, but not before noting the date of issue, four years earlier. 'That's a lot of trips. She's almost commuting to Houston.'

'No reply from the husband's phone number,' said J-J. 'I've got onto British police liaison and I called the Consul in Bordeaux. And now, where's this body?'

The two medics were standing beneath the body, smoking. 'I don't know why you called us in,' said one of them. 'The poor bugger's been dead for over a day. There's nothing we can do.'

As the medics went back to their van, Bruno pointed to the scars and explained why he thought the man had been a soldier. 'What are you making of it?' he asked J-J. 'Some kind of *crime passionel*, a murder-suicide? He wanted to make a new life with her but she wouldn't leave her husband?'

'It looks that way, but you know how I hate to leap to conclusions,' J-J replied. 'And maybe it's meant to look that way. We can't find the murder weapon so I suppose we'll have to bring some metal detectors to search all this woodland. We couldn't find his passport until it turned up in the ashes of the fire. Yves from the forensics team did some sort of magic on the cover with a special lamp and he says it's Irish, but he couldn't get any of the inside details. We've informed their embassy in Paris.'

'Irish?' Bruno exclaimed. 'But they're neutrals, not even NATO members. Where would he have got combat scars like that?'

J-J shrugged. 'I don't know. Maybe he was in the IRA, maybe he served with some other army, or maybe he's a mercenary. We'll find out. But to me the most important thing is the open laptop.'

'You mean it was open to work on? What's odd about that?' Bruno asked. 'Is this the laptop he wrote the suicide note on?'

'The suicide note was in the printer tray, the only sheet that was printed. All the control buttons and the keyboard had been wiped clean of any prints. The laptop was not just open – the back had been taken off and the hard disc removed. We found the bits in the ashes of the fire along with the passport. It had been smashed with that hand axe by the fire before it was burned.'

Bruno's eyes widened in surprise. 'Really? Can the technicians get anything from it?'

'I don't know yet but I doubt it. And I don't know what it means. Maybe he was just obsessed about his privacy or maybe there was something more significant to hide. I think I'd like to know a lot more about this McBride and his girlfriend before we can take this much further. One thing I know from looking at his wine cellar is that he was a wealthy man; it's full of bottles you and I could never afford. He has cases of Château Pétrus and Pape Clément, Lafite and Latour and Margaux. There must be a hundred thousand euros' worth of wine down there.

'One more thing, and it's important,' J-J went on as they walked back to the house. 'Absolutely no talking to anyone in the press, not even that friend of yours on *Sud Ouest*, and above all not to any British reporters who might turn up. I've dealt with them before and they're a nightmare, a real wild bunch.

They'll steal family photos, pretend to be doctors or cops, even tap phones in the hunt for an exclusive. And along the way they'll probably try to make us look bad. So if any of them gets onto you, refer them to the official police spokesman. All queries to go to Périgueux or the international liaison desk at Scotland Yard.'

4

Bruno collected Balzac from the Mairie and walked him across the bridge to the clinic to ask Fabiola about the result of her examination of Paulette.

'All I can say is that I saw her, confirmed my diagnosis and the expected date of delivery and we discussed the situation,' Fabiola said briskly. She had her coat on and her hand reaching into her bag for her car keys, ready to go, but she softened at the sight of Balzac.

'Paulette asked about her options and I explained them. You know perfectly well what those options include and she said she'd think about it.' Fabiola looked up from where she was petting Bruno's dog. 'She also asked me not to discuss this with anybody else. And that includes you, Bruno. This is not in any way a police matter.'

'Does that include her parents?'

'Of course. She may be living at home with them but she's over eighteen, an adult who is fit to make her own decisions. And you know them both, very devout Catholics, in church every Sunday. Given their religious convictions, there's not much doubt what their view will be.'

Bruno nodded, trying to think this through rationally and

discount his own ambitions for Paulette's future in rugby. Of course, Fabiola was right. It would be up to Paulette whether or not to go ahead with the pregnancy. He knew Fabiola; she believed that every woman, and only the woman, had the right to make that decision.

In principle, Bruno agreed but he wished he could share Fabiola's certainty. He wasn't sure just what was right. Abortion meant the death of a potential human being. Bruno had tried to avoid the issue by telling himself that he was sworn to uphold the law, and the laws of France were on Fabiola's side. An adult woman had the right to total control over her own body. And in this case, the thought came that Paulette having the baby would be a sad waste of a brilliant sporting talent. He caught himself. The coming of a new life could never, ever be dismissed as anything remotely like a waste.

'I'm afraid I'm being selfish,' he said with a sigh. 'I'm sorry. I was so caught up in the hope that one day someone I'd trained might play for France. For someone like me, it's akin to the Nobel Prize for medicine for you. It's a dream. But I guess it's my dream, not necessarily Paulette's.'

Fabiola gave him a rueful smile as she gave Balzac a last pat and stood up. 'Dear Bruno, you do love your sport, but this is about her, not about you. And I knew you'd eventually come round and see it from her point of view. She may not be quite as sports-mad as you. Maybe her sporting career is taking second place to her love affair.'

'If that's so, why is she so secretive about the father of her child?'

'Good question, and I wish I had an answer. But I don't, and nor will anybody else until Paulette chooses to tell us. She's quite a private person and maybe her own dream is different. Maybe what she really wants is to have a home, a man she loves, and to cook and have babies and raise children. There are a lot of women like that around here, particularly if they were raised like Paulette in a traditional family that goes to church, where Mother cooks lunch for them all every day and defers to her man. We aren't all like that high-powered friend of yours, Martine, with her business degree and her own company in London. And we want to please a man we love, to pretend an interest in things he likes. Look at me, keeping up with all the boring detail of politics because that's what Gilles likes to talk about even though he never tries to follow my interests. You won't catch him reading the *New England Journal of Medicine*.'

Fabiola sighed, ran her hand through her hair and looked at him, a challenge in her eyes. Bruno stared at her, knowing he'd just been allowed to see a side of Fabiola that he'd never suspected. He found himself nodding, not just in agreement but in appreciation of Fabiola's character and her honesty.

'Thank you,' he said, smiling at her with affection. 'I'll need to think about all that.'

'All right, lecture over,' she said. A brief, almost perfunctory smile flickered across her features. 'And in the meantime, we have the horses to exercise since Pamela is tied up with that cooking school of hers.' Her last phrase was spoken curtly.

'It's your horse and mine that we're going to ride,' Bruno replied, surprised by Fabiola's obvious irritation. 'It will be no trouble to take the others on a long rein. And Pamela has exercised our horses often enough when we've been caught up in our work so it seems reasonable to me.'

'Fair enough, that makes us even,' said Fabiola, with a shrug. 'I've put you in your place over Paulette and now you've put me in mine over the horses. How agreeable to know we can both be in the right.'

They set off in their separate cars for the stables. On the way Bruno thought about Fabiola's resentment at how the cookery courses were taking up so much of Pamela's life. The only irritation that Bruno felt was the interruption of their Monday evening ritual, when the same group of friends would gather each week to cook and eat together. But the cookery clients were now Pamela's priority.

The cookery school had been Miranda's idea. The riding school had originally been a farm and the barns and outbuildings had long since been converted into *gîtes* which were rented out each summer to tourists. Even with the rental income, money was tight. So Miranda came up with the idea of the residential cookery school, which would operate in spring and autumn and thus lengthen the letting season beyond the usual months of June to September. They had started the school the previous autumn and after a friendly write-up in a British magazine they were now fully booked until the end of May. Their *gîtes* were booked throughout the summer for holiday rentals rather than the cookery school, so their Monday evenings would resume, until the cooking classes started again in autumn.

Bruno missed the Monday evenings, just like Fabiola. And he knew that Fabiola's partner, Gilles, missed them too. And so did the Baron and Miranda's dad, Jack Crimson, and also Florence, the science teacher at the local college. Her two young twins kept asking when would they have bath times and suppers with Miranda's kids again. For Bruno, the pleasure of the Monday evenings together was more than just the company and the way they all shared the cooking. It was the sense of family that moved him, more profoundly than he would ever admit. It was the blend of generations: Jack and the Baron as the elders; Florence and Miranda as the mothers; Fabiola and Gilles as the young couple. He didn't want to think where that left him and Pamela, now that they had become friends rather than lovers. As he tugged his thoughts away from that uncomfortable area, he had a sudden flash of inspiration.

Why didn't he start holding the Monday evenings himself at his own place? There were spare bedrooms upstairs where the children could sleep and a big bath for the four of them to share. And there was Balzac, whom they all adored, and Bruno's chickens and geese, whom the children found endlessly fascinating.

'I've had an idea,' he told Fabiola as they saddled up their horses. He explained his plan for Monday evenings, and she replied that similar thoughts had crossed her mind. She offered to raise it with Gilles and Florence and leave Bruno to suggest it to Jack and the Baron.

'Jack never declines any prospect of spending time with his grandchildren,' Fabiola said, her voice eager. 'I'm sure he'll want to join in. And it solves Miranda's babysitting problem.'

Bruno was attaching leading reins to the other horses when one of the women from the cookery class came into the yard, dressed in riding clothes and carrying a riding cap. He recognized Kathleen the journalist from her prematurely grey, almost white hair. It contrasted strangely with her jet-black eyebrows. Strikingly thin with a brittle manner and heavy eye make-up, she had eaten little at the dinner of *blanquette de veau* the previous evening, drunk a lot of wine and had darted outside between courses for a cigarette. She had also shown great interest in the missing Monika Felder, knowing the name because Pamela had circulated the names and home towns of the current clients among them as a way to help break the ice.

Bruno had exchanged only a few words with Kathleen over dinner. But he had been impressed when he heard her explain to a neighbour who had asked about the origin of the word *blanquette* for the dish they were eating. Kathleen had said that it came from the word *blanc*, for white, since neither the veal nor the butter in which it was initially fried were ever allowed to go brown. Bruno hadn't known that.

'I think it was your horse I rode yesterday evening, the big one, Hector,' she said to Bruno in good French, shaking hands with him and Fabiola. 'He's a fine animal, a pleasure to ride. But this evening, Pamela said I should ride Primrose.'

She bent down to greet Balzac, then went straight to Primrose, murmuring something in a low voice, holding out her hand, a carrot cupped in her palm. Primrose sniffed and nuzzled at the hand, then bared her lips and seemed to suck the carrot into her mouth. Kathleen detached the leading rein, took Primrose into the stable, saddled her with speed and competence and led her out to join Bruno and Fabiola.

'Which way did you ride yesterday?' Bruno asked.

Kathleen pointed. 'Straight up to the ridge for a long canter and then down through some woods to a trail that led to a big quarry.'

'Would you like to try another route?' Bruno asked. 'The only problem is I'm not sure about galloping with all these horses on the long rein.'

'You're right, but I'll be happy with just an easy canter,' Kathleen replied. 'Primrose probably knows what she's doing but she's a new horse to me.'

They went along the flank of the ridge, skirting the edge of the woodland, and then up the shallow rise of the firebreak to the plateau and the open fields that led to St Chamassy. As they paused to admire the view an unfamiliar cellphone trilled with an incoming call. Kathleen pulled a slim phone from an inside pocket, turning away to answer and signalling that the others should ride on. She didn't rejoin them for some minutes and remained silent until they were back at the stables.

'That was my news desk in London,' she said to Bruno as they unsaddled. 'They say their crime reporter has picked up a rumour about the murder of an Englishwoman here in the Dordogne. They want to know if I could get some details from the French police. Do you know anything about this?'

'I'm very local police, just for this immediate area,' said Bruno, J-J's instruction about the British press fresh in his mind. His answer was not quite a falsehood. Lalinde, where Monika's body had been found, was not even on Bruno's enlarged turf of the Vézère valley. 'Murder is a matter for the Police Nationale in Périgueux. There's a Bureau de Presse there for media enquiries. I can give you their phone number.'

She took the number, dialled and was put on hold for a while. Bruno and Fabiola rubbed down the horses, refilled their water troughs and sluiced off in the sink. Kathleen was still talking in French when Bruno was ready to go.

'*Un instant,*' Kathleen called out as he headed for the door. 'Could you possibly help? They say that since I'm not an accredited member of the French press they can't talk to me. They want me to get the Paris correspondent to call. Perhaps you could talk to them?'

Several thoughts raced through Bruno's mind at the same time. The first was J-J's lecture. The second was that this journalist might not be able to make or break Pamela's cooking course, but an unhappy Kathleen would not be likely to write a good review about it. The third was that J-J was being over-cautious. There would have to be an announcement of suspicious death in the daily incident report that went out to the local media each evening, usually at about this time.

He pulled out his own phone, called J-J and asked if the incident report had been published yet. It was just about to go out over the wire, J-J said, and it was as blandly worded as he could make it: two deaths, possibly unnatural, of an unknown male and female, at a farmhouse near Lalinde. Police were at the scene, investigating the causes of death and trying to establish the identities of the victims.

Bruno thanked him, ended the call, and passed on the information to Kathleen.

'Is that all?' she asked. 'You can't confirm that the woman is English? Could it be this Monika Felder who was supposed to join us?'

Bruno held up a hand.

'I regret, *madame*, that I can only tell you what the official incident report says, which has not yet been released. If you call your news desk now, you'll be ahead of the competition. But there's no more I can do for you, sorry. And you should know that in France we never release a name until the next of kin has been informed and an identity confirmed.'

By the time he reached his vehicle, his phone was ringing.

'Why did you want to know about the incident report?' asked J-J, his voice heavy with suspicion.

'I'm at the riding school and by coincidence there's an English journalist here, doing a report on the new cookery school,' Bruno replied. 'Her paper called her from London after hearing some rumour from the British police about a dead Englishwoman. So I gave her what you drafted for the incident report, which any minute now will be out on the radio news.'

'Dammit, Bruno, you know what I said . . .'

'That's all she has and all she's getting from me,' Bruno interrupted, keeping his voice reasonable. 'I'm not going to piss off some writer doing a report that could hurt Pamela's livelihood, not for the sake of an incident report that's already being made public. You'd do the same, J-J. You've eaten Pamela's food often enough.'

'Look, Bruno, you're not just a village copper any more. You have command responsibilities . . . Oh, bugger it. It's always the same with you and women. Just make sure you stay well out of her way from now on.' J-J rang off.

As Bruno started his car, the radio came on automatically, tuned to France Bleu Périgord. The deaths were the lead item of the news report, phrased exactly as J-J had confided. But when Bruno heard the newscaster call them 'the mystery deaths of Lalinde', he wondered whether J-J had made a mistake. The very vagueness of the report stirred curiosity. An unknown man and woman in a country farmhouse, in a rural district where people tended to know quite a lot about each other's business? How long would it take for one of the neighbours being canvassed by Juliette to take a look up the lane and see the police presence at McBride's place?

His phone rang. He sighed and pulled in to the side of the road to check the screen. It was Philippe Delaron from *Sud Ouest*. He ignored the call and drove on. Within moments it rang again, this time with an English number. He assumed it would be Kathleen and he ignored that call, too. Shortly after that came the beeps of two text messages coming in.

What Bruno had not told J-J was that the following morning he would be at the St Denis weekly market, and Miranda was bringing her entire class along to have coffee and croissants and then buy the various foodstuffs they would be cooking that evening. He was supposed to give them a quick tour, introduce them all to the stallholders and explain how to pick out a good duck liver. Later in the afternoon, he'd promised Pamela to give her guests a demonstration of how to make pâté de foie gras, and also how to cook duck and discuss the wines that would best accompany each dish.

It worried him a little, the way Pamela and Miranda were running their cookery classes on the cheap, using friends like him, Jack and the Baron to cut costs. There were only two real chefs. The first was Ivan from the local bistro, who stayed open for lunch all year round but closed on weekday evenings out of season. So Ivan was free to earn some extra cash by giving two afternoon lessons. The highlight of the week was Raoul, a retired chef from a Michelin-starred restaurant, who was teaching another session. On the penultimate evening of the course, Pamela was taking all her guests to the Vieux Logis, Raoul's old restaurant in Trémolat, where he would give them a tour of the kitchens before they ate. On the final evening, the pupils were in charge of the meal, from shopping in the market in the morning to picking the wines and preparing the food, all within the budget Pamela had set.

Still, they would probably be eating better this evening than he would, Bruno thought, as he turned into the driveway that led to his cottage. He parked, let Balzac out to make his customary patrol of the grounds, then refilled the water bowls in his hen coop and brought in some fresh wood for his stove. Evenings could be cool and he lit a fire, looking forward to a quiet couple of hours with Jean-Marie Constant's new biography of Henri IV. He was Bruno's favourite French king, the one who had given his name to a classic dish, *poulet Henri Quatre*, after he had announced his desire that every French household should have a chicken in the pot each Sunday.

The large pot atop Bruno's woodstove provided his solitary meals, shared only with Balzac. One week, it would be a quartered chicken, to which he added some of his prepared *bouillon*, garlic, spices and various vegetables, topping it up with wine and fresh vegetables as needed. On Sundays, he would give what remained to Balzac then start all over again with knuckle of pork or a kilo of stewing beef, chopped into bite-size portions.

His friend the Baron, who had unexpectedly dropped by one Friday evening, had become a fan of the way the stew had thickened by the end of the week and now the Friday suppers had become a ritual, with Jack Crimson making a third. He brought the wine, the Baron brought bread, cheese and a *tarte au citron* from the patisserie counter at Fauquet's café. Bruno contributed his stew, salad from his garden and the inevitable glass of *pastis* to begin.

Two or three times a week, Bruno dined alone and had come to enjoy it, his book propped open on the table before him, a glass of Bergerac wine at his side and Balzac at his feet. This week's stovetop ragout was based on a large pork hock stewed with onions, carrots, leeks and lentils and a quarter bottle of cooking wine left over from a dinner party.

As the heat built up in the stove and the two-days-old stew began to simmer once more, Bruno checked the messages on his phone. There were two from Philippe Delaron, requesting information, another from Kathleen and one from J-J, asking him to be at police HQ in Périgueux at seven the next morning. That was odd; case conferences usually began at eight. There was one more, signed simply with the letter I, noting that there had been another murder in the Périgord.

It was Isabelle's way of staying in touch, letting him know that she was thinking of him even while holding down her high-powered job as liaison between the French and other European counterterrorism agencies.

'Wish you were here to help us solve it,' he texted back, and then went to his cabinet and took out a bottle of the Balvenie malt whisky she had given him on her last visit. He poured out two fingers and added half that amount of water, just as Jack Crimson had taught him. Bruno sat in his armchair, watching the fire through the stove door, aware of the aroma of the stew as it warmed, and thought of the evenings he and Isabelle had spent entwined before this very fire. And then, inevitably, he thought of the time she had told him, after the event, that she had decided to abort their child. She hadn't told him she was pregnant. It was the first time he had ever himself confronted the question of abortion, when it was already too late to do anything but mourn.

It was his memory of that grief – as much if not more than his hopes of Paulette wearing the blue shirt of a French rugby team – that had troubled him so profoundly since Fabiola told him that Paulette was pregnant. He sipped at his Scotch, wondering if Paulette would share the news and perhaps the decision with her lover, or whether she would take all the burden onto herself as Isabelle had done.

Ever sensitive to his master's mood, Balzac nuzzled his leg and stared up with his mournful basset eyes. Or perhaps he was just hungry for his supper, like Bruno. He finished his Scotch, caressed his dog, rose to stir the stewpot and then went out to the garden to look at the stars while Balzac shuffled his way discreetly into the bushes. Perhaps that was what Balzac had wanted all along. Moments of introspection, however gloomy, would always be interrupted by calls of nature.

He went back indoors, ready to eat, and saw another text from Isabelle's number. It contained two words: 'Googled Felder?'

'I will, thanks,' he replied and brought his laptop into the living room, pushing aside his book on Henri IV and sitting down at his dining table. He put the name Michael George Felder into the search window and a Wikipedia entry appeared in English.

Felder had been born in 1940, son of a British army officer, went to the officer training school at Sandhurst at the age of eighteen, joined the British army and retired in 1992 with the rank of Brigadier as Director of the Intelligence Corps. He had then founded a private firm, Special Security Services, which provided bodyguards, as well as anti-burglary and cyber-security systems to private clients. The company enjoyed a modest but growing success until the occupation of Iraq after the 2003 war, when it expanded dramatically, providing ex-military security staff to the US and British occupation forces. As CEO, Felder had become a very wealthy man.

He had been married twice, once in 1970 to an Englishwoman by whom he had two children. They had divorced in 1988 and he had the following year married Monika Eschinger, a West German citizen, then aged twenty. That was remarkably young to be a stepmother, particularly when she was barely older than Felder's two teenage children. That could not have been an easy relationship, Bruno thought. And Felder was now in his seventies, so it was hardly surprising that his much younger and beautiful wife should have found a younger lover. Could that act of adultery have led to her death?

Bruno then Googled the name of Felder's company, and found a website which listed offices in London, New York, Washington, Dubai, Baghdad, Kabul, Sydney and Johannesburg. The focus now seemed to be more on cyber-security than on bodyguards, and more on corporate clients than governments.

Bruno kept looking, finding a reference to Felder in a book in English about BRIXMIS, a small group of some thirty British soldiers allowed to be based in the old East Germany throughout the Cold War under the original four-power agreements on the occupation of Germany after 1945. Bruno knew a little of this since the French, like the US, were allowed a similar mission and the Soviet Union had their own such mission in West Germany. They were, in effect, legal spies, free to roam most of the territory where they were based, to observe military manoeuvres and spot new types of military equipment.

Felder had made his reputation by establishing the calibre of an unknown new cannon mounted on Soviet armoured military vehicles by pushing an apple into the muzzle and later measuring the size of the hole as thirty millimetres.

Bruno smiled at that, took his bubbling pot from atop the stove, and resumed his place in the biography of the good King Henri IV, who had at least temporarily stopped the French religious wars. Although a Protestant, Henri had negotiated an entry into the Catholic stronghold of Paris by agreeing to go directly to Notre Dame to attend a Catholic religious service, with the words, 'Paris is worth a mass.' A wise man, thought Bruno. It was sad that few of his successors on the French throne had shared his common sense.

As he ended his meal, he pushed the book away, unable to concentrate. His thoughts kept returning to Isabelle, just as she kept returning to him, however briefly. The last time he'd seen her, she had come down from Paris for the opening of the new cave beneath the chateau of Commarque, invited herself to lunch and stayed for the night before taking the morning train back to Paris. She remained irresistible to him, despite knowing there was no future for them, at least, not the future he wanted of a life together and children. The fierce fire of her ambition meant she could never settle down.

He shook his head to end that train of thought before taking his dirty plate to the kitchen to wash up. Then he let Balzac out for his usual patrol of the grounds and Bruno's own nightly look at the sky. With no other house in sight, when he turned out the light in his hallway the stars shone so clearly and in such profusion that he felt awed and a sense of calm came over him. The constellations were all so wonderfully predictable, exactly where he knew they would be. He followed the lines of the *Grande Ourse*, which the English called the Plough, to identify Polaris, the north star. Then he looked for the twins of Gemini and the three stars of Orion's belt with *Grand Chien*, Canis Major, beside them. Someday, Bruno told himself, he'd visit the southern hemisphere to see their different sky.

With that thought, he turned in and fell asleep as soon as his head touched his pillow.

5

At seven the next morning, J-J was waiting for Bruno in the corridor outside Prunier's office at police headquarters. A uniformed officer stood beside him, a sharpshooter's clasp on his lapel. This was the armourer, whom Bruno knew slightly from his annual firearms check.

'Case conference at eight, but you have to do this first,' J-J said, leading the way down into the basement. 'Seen the paper yet?' He handed over a copy of the latest *Sud Ouest*. The front page headline read **Murder in Lalinde** and carried a photo of police vehicles outside McBride's house.

'Just our luck,' J-J said. 'One of the houses on that road up to McBride's place belongs to a guy who does the local sports reports for *Sud Ouest*. That new policewoman of yours canvassed him along with all the other neighbours. He took photos of the house and called his newsdesk.'

Once in the deep basement, a level below the cells, they came to an armoured door, locked with two sets of keys. The armourer let them into the small firing range, just thirty metres long. Bruno turned in his old weapon, was given a receipt in return and was then handed a new handgun with two holsters, one made of webbing as a waist belt with a small pouch for the cleaning kit, and the other of leather for when he wore the gun under his armpit.

'It's a lot lighter than my last weapon,' said Bruno. 'What does this short barrel do to the accuracy?'

'It's a SIG Sauer Pro 2022 and light because it's mostly made of polymer. I assure you it's accurate to fifty metres,' said the armourer, stripping the weapon down, checking the breech and then squinting down the barrel before reassembling it. 'Note the slide stop pin, it goes all the way through the gun and you have to remove it to strip the weapon. It's metal because it takes the recoil and distributes it through the less resilient polymer frame.

'It's two hundred grams lighter, more accurate, less liable to jam and above all it doesn't become a danger to the user after six thousand rounds,' he went on. 'That's why we got rid of the PAMAS you've been using. The PAMAS was based on the Beretta but our French version used inferior steel so it started blowing up in people's hands. The SIG is a better gun. Same calibre, NATO-standard 9 millimetre, and it has a flat magazine base plate that shortens the grip by seven millimetres and makes it easier to draw even though you still have fifteen rounds in the magazine. You have no manual safety but you don't need one because there's an automatic lock on the firing pin.'

'Any problems I should expect?' Bruno asked.

'Your first shots may be a little off because the trigger is a bit slack by comparison with the PAMAS but you'll get used to that.'

The armourer had set up each of the three firing lanes, one with the paper target hanging from its wires at ten metres, the second at twenty and the third at the far end of the range. He handed Bruno the gun and told him to strip it down. Bruno complied, fumbling a little at the unfamiliar decocking lever and the slide stop pin, and then placed the reassembled weapon back on the table, the empty magazine to one side.

'Load your mag.' The armourer pushed across a box of 9mm Parabellum rounds.

Bruno loaded the rounds one by one, checking each time that the spring was smooth.

'Load your weapon.'

He slid the magazine home, gave the heel a gentle tap and it clicked into place. Making sure the muzzle pointed downrange, Bruno laid it back on the table and put on the pair of ear protectors the armourer handed to him.

'When you're ready, the full mag at ten metres.'

Bruno's first two rounds were outside the small circle, clipping the right edge of the cardboard square. The armourer was right about the trigger pull. He adjusted, fired a single round and saw it had hit the black circle. He then fired the rest of the magazine in double-taps, the way he'd been taught in the army, a short pause between each one. After the first few shots, Bruno began to change his position with a swift turn or a step to the side. That was how the army trained on handguns – it was not often in a gunfight that one could afford to keep firing from the same spot. The armourer hauled back the shredded target, most of the black circle now disintegrated.

'You pulled a little to your right at first,' he said. 'I already tested this gun and centred the sights so it was probably just the trigger slack. Now try the twenty-metre range. You don't need to clean the barrel yet. Just reload.' He handed Bruno a full magazine. Bruno ejected one round to test the spring and then replaced it. The armourer nodded in approval.

His first shot was a single and in the black circle. He then emptied the mag with seven double taps, moving his position between each burst. Once again the target was shredded. The armourer adjusted the next target and signalled Bruno to shoot again. At thirty metres he had three holes on the white edges of the target but most of the black circle had gone.

'She's a beauty,' Bruno said, ejecting the magazine and opening the cleaning kit.

He stripped the gun and sighted down the barrel. It still looked clean but he pulled an oiled rag through and then followed it with the phosphor-bronze brush. He used the tiny nylon brush and a little solvent to clean the carbon from the feed plate and the mouth of the magazine. He used the rag to clean the spring guide and spring and the long grooves, lightly lubricated them and reassembled the gun.

'Sign here,' said the armourer, handing over a form which acknowledged the receipt of the weapon, two holsters, a spare magazine, a cleaning kit and a box of 144 rounds. 'You are good to load and go. Remember to remove and unload the magazine when not on duty and all live rounds are to be kept locked away. You can expect at least one surprise visit to your home in the course of the next three months to ascertain that the weapon and rounds are being kept safely. Failure to abide by these regulations will result in disciplinary action.'

Conscious of the weight of the gun on his belt and with the box of rounds and the other holster straining the handles of the thin plastic bag the armourer had found, Bruno followed J-J back upstairs to the conference room where Commissaire Prunier had taken the head of the table.

J-J sat to his right and Yves from the forensic unit to his left. Bruno had expected to be at the distant foot of the table, below various detective inspectors, but J-J pointed to the vacant seat beside him. Bruno took his seat, noting that only he and Prunier were in uniform. There were pots of coffee, cups and glasses with fruit juice and bottles of mineral water on the table, and the coffee smelled a great deal better than the usual brew he had been served here in the past. Prunier was evidently launching some long-overdue improvements, Bruno thought with approval. He poured himself a cup and sipped.

'This case is obviously our priority,' Prunier began. 'Two foreign nationals are dead so the British and Irish police are both counting on us to resolve this. We can't have any mistakes. I know this looks like a murder-suicide involving two lovers but I don't want us making any assumptions. Let's double-check everything. The Procureur will be appointing a magistrate at some point today or at the latest tomorrow so let's see how far we can get while this is still entirely in police hands.'

Prunier gestured to J-J to start the briefing. Despite finding the passports, French law still needed formal identification of the two bodies, J-J began. British and Irish police had run the fingerprints of the two dead people through their criminal records and found no match. They were still waiting for a response from the Interpol fingerprint records. The only new item was that the murder weapon had been found by a metal detector in the undergrowth near McBride's body, an unusual knife that J-J said should be recognizable from its length and the handle that looked as if it had been made from a series of wooden rings. It lay before J-J in a clear plastic evidence bag and he picked it up to show it around, its slim blade almost twenty centimetres long.

Bruno raised a hand. 'I recognize it. That's a British commando knife, called a Fairbairn–Sykes after the two men who designed it during World War Two. The blade was long so it could kill through a heavy military greatcoat. They're still widely used by Special Forces throughout NATO. Along with the scar from a bullet wound, that adds to the suggestion that McBride had a military background.'

J-J made a note on the pad in front of him and continued. 'We're still waiting to hear from the Irish police about McBride. The British police sent a patrol car to the Felder address but there was no reply. Neighbours said Monsieur Felder had not been home for some time and Madame Monika Felder, the murdered woman, travelled a lot. Apparently the Felders valued their privacy and the neighbours barely knew them. The British police entered the house, found a family address book and were trying to contact Felder's two adult children.

'We did better with door-to-door inquiries,' J-J went on and explained that they had learned McBride sold his wine to the cooperative through a tenant who tended his vines. He had a little more than four hectares of vines, usually producing around thirty thousand litres a year. McBride and the tenant shared the money and usually got around ten thousand euros each. The tenant, a neighbour, had reported that McBride spoke decent French and described him as 'correct rather than friendly', a man who kept himself to himself and who travelled for weeks at a time.

McBride had lived alone and had few visitors but sometimes went to local rugby matches when he was at home. Being a European citizen, he had the right to live and work in France and didn't need a *carnet de séjour*. He paid French taxes, declaring an income of thirty-eight thousand euros last year from his grapes and private investments. He'd bought his farmhouse with its land shortly after the financial crisis when prices slumped. There was no mortgage on the property. He had a local doctor whom he saw once a year and who said he was in excellent health and gave a date of birth of 17 March 1965.

'When the doctor asked about the scar of a bullet wound, McBride said he'd been in the Irish army and had been wounded when serving with United Nations peacekeepers in the Lebanon,' J-J said. 'He had nearly two hundred euros in cash in his wallet and debit cards for three bank accounts, one in Dublin, another with HSBC in London and one here with Crédit Agricole, where he had a current and a savings account with just over twenty thousand euros. We hope to have details of the other accounts later today. He had a French driving licence, clean except for three points for speeding.

'We're still waiting for the pathologist's report after the autopsies, but it looks pretty clear that Madame Felder was killed by a knife thrust to the heart while in the shower, probably by this commando knife. We're awaiting confirmation from blood tests. McBride died by hanging, apparently by his own hand. There's no immediate evidence of anyone else being involved.'

The two dead people seem to have shared a dinner at

McBride's home on the evening after they were seen on the train that afternoon. The dishes had all been left in the dishwasher but there were remains of bread, salad, cheese rinds and steaks in the black refuse bag under the sink.

'We'll see if the pathologist confirms that,' J-J went on. 'There was an almost empty bottle of vintage champagne in the bedroom and an empty bottle of Château Haut-Brion, 2005, on the kitchen counter. That costs around seven hundred euros a bottle.'

J-J looked up. 'Like the wine in his cellar, that's a whole lot better than the stuff he grew himself. Beside the Haut-Brion was a half-empty bottle of a malt Scotch whisky called Camas an Staca from Jura, thirty years old, and when we looked it up it costs about six hundred euros a bottle. It had apparently been opened after the meal. The little metallic cover over the cork was found on top of the food remains in the refuse bin. I wish I could afford to drink like that.

'We don't know what happened after the meal, although we now know they had sex at some point. We found a pharmacist's bottle of Viagra in a drawer in the bedside table. We also found one glass with some whisky still in it, so either the two of them were drinking from it or McBride drank a lot of it alone. The autopsy should tell us how drunk he was. His tastes in wine and whisky were very expensive by comparison with his apparent income.'

'Anything else?' Prunier looked around the table.

With a grateful glance at Bruno, J-J read out the single paragraph that Bruno had handed him in J-J's office just before the meeting began.

'Chief of Police Courrèges did some internet research. According to his Wikipedia entry, Monsieur Felder – the husband of the dead woman – was the director of British military intelligence until 1992 when he left to start a very successful private security company. He's rich and he's thirty years older than his wife, the late Monika, who was a German citizen when she married him shortly after Felder divorced his first wife. He had two children by his first marriage, who presumably stand to inherit their father's very considerable wealth, now that Monika is dead.'

J-J looked up again. 'We've asked the British and Irish authorities to help us contact next of kin. There's no reply from Felder's home number so we've asked the British police to check with his company. They have offices all over the world, but not in Paris.'

'Did you go through the police liaison office with Scotland Yard or the Consulate in Bordeaux?' Prunier asked.

'Both, but what little information we have came through the liaison office. Somebody from the Irish Embassy in Paris is supposed to be calling me back later this morning. And we've already had some calls from the British press. So far, we've said nothing that wasn't in last night's incident report, which is how I'd like to keep it.'

'Let's speed this up,' said Prunier. 'Get an English-speaking officer to call this company of Felder's this morning and say we want him or somebody who knew his wife well to get here as soon as possible to make a formal identification of the body. Is she here or in Bergerac?'

'Bergerac, it was closer. McBride's body was also taken to the morgue there.'

'Get onto the banks and the tax office again,' Prunier said. 'I want to know exactly where his money came from, whether there were any significant transfers or changes in his bank accounts. What about the computer hard drive he tried to destroy?'

'Nothing useful left of it, sir,' said Yves. 'But he was a subscriber to Orange so we're trying to get something from them about his internet history. We can't find the SIM cards from his and Monika's cellphones, and forensics are sifting the ashes to see if they were also put into the fire. We have her number so we've asked the British police to see what their telecoms people can find. Destroying the hard drive is very unusual. If it weren't for the apparent suicide, I'd say this looked like a professional hit. So we'll be looking closely to see if we can confirm whether McBride really hanged himself or whether he might have had help. Given the amount of alcohol he seems to have drunk, I'm surprised that he could have climbed up that stepladder on his own.'

'Thank you, *messieurs*,' Prunier said. 'Despite the media interest, I don't think we need to add anything to the statement we issued last night. I'll suggest that any further press statement should come from whichever magistrate the Procureur will assign to this case. And I don't want any off-the-record chats with any friends in the media.'

As the meeting broke up, Prunier signalled to Bruno to follow him into his office overlooking the roundabout on Rue

Gambetta. He stood behind the big desk and scratched his head as if trying to work out what to say.

'We have to thank you, Bruno. J-J says you started this inquiry, looking for this woman who failed to turn up on time for a cooking course,' he said. 'I'm sorry it had to happen just as you took on this new job, but unless you particularly want to stay involved, I think it's in your own best interest to get back and start making a success of the Vézère valley. It's a big job and these first days taking charge of your new team are important.'

Bruno nodded, torn between knowing Prunier was right and his own interest in the case, triggered by that moment of sudden kinship he had felt when he realized that McBride, too, had been a combat soldier. And he was grateful that Prunier had not appealed to their friendship to help ease Bruno out of the inquiry and back to his real job.

'You're showing me the door just as you start serving decent coffee,' Bruno said, smiling.

Prunier laughed. 'You aren't missing much at this stage. This case is now a matter of waiting for the pathologist and the forensics report. After that we have to wait for the Procureur to decide upon a magistrate to lead the inquiry. So if you want to come back to join it once you've got your new team settled in, we'll keep a seat warm for you. And the coffee.'

6

Bruno left the police HQ building and headed for Place Bugeaud where he had parked. As he waited for the lights to change on the pedestrian crossing he saw a sudden scene in the car park, a young woman standing at an open passenger door of a car and shouting angrily at a man sitting in the driver's seat. Bruno could only see her back as she climbed into the car, a handkerchief to her face and her shoulders rocking as if weeping.

The lights changed and people standing beside him began to cross the road. He followed suit, taking his eyes off the couple in the car. It was only when they drove past him out of the car park that Bruno saw the young woman was Paulette, looking different with her hair down. She normally wore it in a tight bun when training or playing rugby. He craned his neck to spot the vehicle's registration number. His eye was distracted by a Green party sticker but he caught the first two letters, C and V, and then the digits 9 and perhaps 7. It had been a red Renault Clio, not very new. He scribbled down as much of the number as he had seen before the car was blocked by other vehicles and then lost in traffic.

It was no surprise that Paulette was in the city, Bruno thought. Like most students from St Denis, she was at the *lycée* five days a week, staying in the attached dormitory Monday to Thursday nights and returning home at weekends. But who had her companion been and was he the father? Certainly it looked more like a fraught argument than just a lovers' tiff.

Bruno knew the mind remembered things it had even briefly seen and he tried to use the tricks he'd learned at the police academy to trigger visual memory by singling out specific images, gestures and items of clothing. The man had been sitting in the car, at the wheel but leaning across to the passenger door. He'd had one arm on the wheel and the other had been outstretched and beckoning, as if trying to coax Paulette to enter. He'd been wearing a leather jacket with a cotton scarf looped fashionably around his neck. He'd been slim, clean-shaven, wearing glasses, but the features wouldn't come together. Bruno suspected he'd recognize him if he saw him again. He could have been a fellow student, and it was the kind of car a student might drive, or possibly a very young teacher with little money.

He climbed into his van and prepared to head back to St Denis. The nine o'clock news was on the radio, followed by local news and announcements. The second item was a report that the British press had named Monika Felder as the woman found dead in Lalinde at McBride's home. Prunier and J-J would not be happy, but the London newspaper had cited British police sources so there was not much they could do.

The last item was a reference to a charity drive at the *lycée* Bertran de Born which triggered the memory that this was the school Paulette attended. Bruno drove to it and weaved his way slowly around the car park, looking for a red Renault Clio without success. He drove on to the student dormitory, where the car park was so small he could see that there was no red vehicle inside. Quickly, he drove to the two other *lycées* in the city but again drew a blank.

He shrugged. Time to get back to St Denis. He could always ask for a search of the registration lists but officially he would need an operational reason for that. In the past, he had asked J-J or the gendarmes to do so as a favour but he wanted to keep Paulette's problem to himself while he could. Once her parents knew of her pregnancy, they would probably call in the priest and the whole affair would become even more complicated. Perhaps he should try to arrange to see Paulette in the course of this week while she was in Périgueux and get an idea of what she wanted. But he'd better take Florence along since she knew the girl as well or even better than Bruno did and it might be easier for Paulette to talk to a woman.

Fifty minutes later and still in uniform, Bruno was standing in front of Jean-François's stall in the St Denis market, explaining to Pamela's clients why he usually bought his ducks and geese from his friends at the Lac Noir farm. Knowing the limits of Bruno's makeshift English, Pamela had insisted on rehearsing what he would say. He pulled an evidence glove onto his right hand, and pressed his thumb into the plump, golden flesh of a raw duck liver.

'See the indentation and now I lift my thumb and the flesh comes back,' he said. 'That shows the foie is fresh and good. And it is not too big so the duck has not been stuffed too much.'

Pamela had already explained to them that ducks and geese

stuffed themselves to store in their livers the energy required for their long migration flights. As a result, their livers quite naturally swelled to three times their usual size and more. The kind of factory force-feeding still used in some Eastern European countries to swell the livers up to eight and nine times normal size was banned in the Périgord where the birds roamed free.

'The important thing about the duck is that we eat all of it except the feathers,' Bruno went on. 'And we can use those for cushions and for wonderful feather beds. This duck can give us five different meals.' He held up separately a liver, a *magret* or breast, the legs and then the *aiguillettes*, the two long, thin strips of the sweetest meat that ran down each side of the duck's belly. Finally he held up a *carcasse* from which all the other items he'd mentioned had been removed.

'And this we use to make a soup, or a *bouillon*, a stock. Nothing is wasted, and this afternoon, I will show you how to make each one. *Au revoir, messieurs, dames. Et bon appetit.*'

He turned and moved briskly away towards his office in the Mairie, keen to avoid Kathleen. At the Lac Noir stall, she had been eyeing him with that relentless, predatory look reporters develop when chasing a story. He knew it only too well from Philippe Delaron.

Bruno had been told that Pamela's clients were buying their own lunch of pâté, cheese, bread and the first of the new strawberries, and he was not expected to rejoin them at the riding school until around four in the afternoon. He'd already arranged for Louis and Juliette to meet him for a picnic lunch in the grounds of the chateau of Puymartin, which was equidistant from him in St Denis and Louis in Montignac. Bruno preferred the casual atmosphere of a picnic meeting rather than something more formal in an office.

He started going swiftly through the paperwork, more and more of which was coming to his computer screen rather than by post. But the pile of mail on his desk was still daunting, with a large folio-sized parcel balanced on top. He opened it to find two classic expressions of the French bureaucratic art: a work book for each of his new subordinates, Juliette at Les Eyzies and Louis in Montignac.

For each week of the year there was a white sheet, and beneath it was a blue, a green and a pink sheet, each with its own sheaf of carbon paper. One copy was for the Préfecture, the second for Bruno's files in his own Mairie and the other two for the regional council and for the Mairies of Juliette and Louis respectively. The first set of columns was headed by the day of the week, with blanks to be filled in for hours worked, the second for nature of activity, the third for fines issued and so on. There were other columns for training courses completed, work in support of the Police Nationale, liaison with the gendarmes, time spent giving road safety and other classes at schools. Bruno ignored the other columns, gave a shrug of despair at his nation's love of administrative complexity, and put both books on the windowsill. He would leave such ridiculous paperwork to the office aide who was being assigned to him. He put his head round the door to ask the Mayor's secretary if she could check with the Préfecture when his aide was supposed to arrive.

'They haven't had the *concours* yet,' she replied. The rules said that all jobs in the public service had to be filled by qualified personnel, either equipped with a suitable diploma or certificate of expertise or selected after sitting a *concours*, a competitive exam. Those who passed the exam had then to undergo a training course in order to obtain the requisite certificate.

'So when should this aide arrive?' he asked.

'The *concours* results will come next month, then they have the two-month training course and then it will be July and the holidays so if the budget has been approved in Bordeaux as the capital of our new region, Nouvelle-Aquitaine, and then authorized by Paris, you might get someone in September,' she replied. 'Until then, you'll have to do the paperwork yourself, as you really should have done on your own working hours since those new forms came in.'

'So who's been completing my forms until now? I don't think I've ever seen one before.'

'The Mayor said it was all nonsense and not to bother. But he's the Mayor and can get away with it. You can't.'

'Thank you, Claire,' he said and headed downstairs to the sanity of the market to buy the picnic lunch for his colleagues. Once outside, and with a sinking feeling, he saw Philippe Delaron sitting at a table outside Fauquet's café talking to Kathleen who was scribbling in a notebook. When reporters joined forces, they could be even more of a menace, and this new alliance would probably inspire more complaints from J-J. Luckily, they seemed too absorbed to notice him.

His shopping completed, Bruno set off to pick up Balzac and the picnic basket from his home, and then drove out past Les Eyzies to Puymartin. He had a fondness for the chateau that had been built in the thirteenth century and then restored in neo-Gothic style six hundred years later by an eccentric Marquis whose family still owned the place. Bruno thought of it as the basset hound of chateaux; improbable to look at but impossible not to like.

Juliette was already in the car park, leaning against her van in her shirtsleeves with her eyes closed, enjoying the sun on her face. Louis arrived as Balzac was energetically renewing his acquaintance with her. Bruno collected his picnic basket and led them through a path in the woods to a sunny spot where they could enjoy the view of the chateau. With a smile of quiet pride Juliette brought out a quiche she had prepared at home. Louis contributed one of his wife's walnut tarts and some home-made peach chutney. He also brought a folding chair, pleading that if he sat on the ground he might never get up again. Bruno set out the plates of ham, pâté and cheese he had bought in the market, opened the bottle of Bergerac rosé from Château Briand and began to slice the *pain*, giving the heel of the loaf to Balzac.

'This is a good idea, much better than meeting in some cramped office and trying to find a place to park,' said Juliette.

'Good quiche, Juliette,' said Louis. 'You've got the pastry just right.' He clinked his glass against hers and then against Bruno's.

'This is how business meetings ought to be,' said Bruno, grinning. 'Any problems I should know about or can we concentrate on lunch?'

'There is an unsolved murder, well, unpunished anyway,' said Louis. '*La Dame Blanche*, right here in this chateau. You know this place is haunted by the White Lady? Her husband came back from the wars and found her in the arms of a handsome young neighbour. He killed the youth and sealed her up in the north tower for fifteen years until she died. Her ghost comes out at midnight, looking for her lost lover. Lots of people have seen her, including my wife's sister.'

Bruno smiled at the old tale and Juliette rolled her eyes and said, 'This is a new job for me. Is this how we're going to meet from now on?'

'It's new to me, too. We're going to have to invent a way of working that helps us to support one another,' said Bruno. 'I thought we should stay in touch daily. Maybe if I start by sending you an email in the evening saying what I plan to be doing the next day and each of you send me an email at the end of the day saying what you've done. I don't want to hear about every road safety class for the children or traffic duties, but I do want to hear about anything important or unusual. On a quiet day, just say routine patrols. We should share lists of each of the main events like town saints' days, fairs and so on, in case we need to support one another, like Louis came to support me when we had that emergency at Lascaux.'

'So as far as Montignac is concerned, I'm still in charge?' Louis asked.

'Certainly,' Bruno replied. 'You know the town better than I ever will. And Juliette's in charge of Les Eyzies. I'm on call if you think you need my help and I may call on you from time to time. But I think we should meet at least once a week, preferably like this, but I suppose we had better be seen to be in regular contact so at least once a month we should have a meeting in one another's office, by rotation.'

'That makes sense,' said Juliette. 'If we start meeting in restaurants and have even a glass of wine, people will start to talk.'

'A lot of my work is done in restaurants and bars,' said Louis. 'That's where you learn what's going on. I make a point of knowing all the waiters and barmen, and I never forget a face.'

'I learn quite a lot chatting to the mothers outside the primary school at lunchtime,' said Juliette.

'You're both right,' said Bruno. 'But a little bit of social life together might be good. How about you come to dinner at my place one evening? Louis, bring your wife; and Juliette, would you like to bring a guest? I thought I might invite that young magistrate, Annette, in Sarlat, who deals with juvenile matters, and maybe Commandante Yveline from our local gendarmes, and J-J, the chief detective. We need to stay on good terms with them.'

Louis turned to Juliette, his expression suddenly grumpy. 'That's how he got the promotion, hobnobbing with the top brass.'

'It sounds like a good idea to me,' said Juliette, crisply. 'But since I'm new in this job maybe I should come alone at first.'

'Up to you,' said Bruno, ignoring Louis's remark.

'I'll think about it,' she said. 'And that reminds me, what do you make of your mystery man now?'

Bruno was enjoying a piece of her excellent quiche. He looked at her sharply.

'How do you mean? I was at police HQ this morning and nothing much new had come through. What have you heard?'

'That guy Yves from forensics we met yesterday rang me when I was on the way here, asking if I'd like to meet him for a drink some evening or maybe a meal. We were chatting and I think he was trying to show off a bit with what he knew about the case. The Irishman who hanged himself, McBride, apparently he's not a real Irishman. They had just heard from Dublin that the passport is a fake and he was never in the Irish army, nor the UN peacekeepers.'

'Well, it's not our business now, if it ever was,' said Louis. 'Lalinde isn't in our area and it's up to the Police Nationale.'

'That's not all,' Juliette added. 'There's news about Monika's husband. They found him through his company. He's in a special hospital in Texas somewhere, trying a last-ditch treatment for terminal cancer and he's too ill to talk.'

7

Bruno tracked down Jack Crimson to the bar of the St Denis tennis club, where he was helping Florence to make some sense of the club's chaotic accounts kept by the various volunteers the previous year.

'It's hopeless,' said Florence, throwing down her pencil and giving Bruno a despairing look. 'We issued ninety-two membership cards last year but only fifty-two seem to have paid their subscription, not including me, nor you, Bruno. And I know we paid because I have a receipt and so did you because we were playing mixed doubles together against Fabiola and Gilles. I remember they paid their dues at the same time and they're not listed. Worse still, we don't seem to have received any money for court fees for non-members. Using volunteers to keep the accounts is costing us more than we'd have to pay to employ someone full-time.'

'The bar accounts are even worse,' said Crimson cheerfully. 'We seem to have been paid for just over one barrel of beer but we bought three. Can I get you a beer, Bruno? If we start to charge two euros for a beer instead of one it seems like the easiest way to repair the damage and it's still cheaper than any of the bars in town.'

'I'll have a coffee but let me buy you one.' He turned to Florence. 'How are the children?'

'Getting lost in the bushes while hunting tennis balls,' she replied. 'Do you have any idea how many cans of balls we get through each season? And if we don't send our annual subscription to the national federation before the end of the month we won't get our usual allocation of tickets to the French Open.'

'Maths was never my strong point,' said Bruno, sniffing at the coffee pot before deeming the contents fresh enough to be worth drinking. 'Do you want me to go and look for them? The kids, I mean.'

Florence's head rose from the accounts as she picked up something in Bruno's tone. She looked at the two men, sighed and put down her pencil. She rose, murmured something about finding the children and left the club.

'I wanted to follow up with you, Jack, about Monika Felder,' Bruno said once they were alone. 'You said her name rang a bell.'

'Not her so much, but I knew a Mike Felder, military intelligence, married a gorgeous German girl called Monika,' Crimson said, pouring himself a beer from the tap on the bar and putting a two-euro coin into the cash box. 'Sorry, I should have got back to you on it but the imminent bankruptcy of the tennis club took priority. Still, I made a couple of phone calls about Felder. It seems he's at death's door in some American cancer hospital and his wife has taken an apartment to be near him so she can't be your dead woman.'

'It is her, I'm afraid,' Bruno said. 'Monika Felder has been in and out of Houston a lot lately but she died in Lalinde two days ago while supposedly on the way to your daughter's cookery classes. And this McBride chap I told you about had an Irish passport that turns out to be a forgery, but from the scars on his body he certainly saw combat.'

'Why do you think I can help?' Crimson replied, his face the very picture of innocence.

'Felder ran British military intelligence, which means he must have spent time in Northern Ireland,' Bruno said. 'So it's interesting that his wife seems to have been murdered by a former soldier with a fake Irish identity who then hanged himself. Criminal records have nothing on the fingerprints but I was thinking that if McBride had been in the British military . . .'

'That our defence ministry would have his fingerprints on file. Yes, I understand,' said Crimson. 'Why not just ask the British police liaison to do that?'

'We asked them in the usual way to search all available databases. Their report came back saying Monika Felder and McBride were both clean according to criminal records, which may be true but isn't quite what we requested. So if the British are being a little coy I wonder if that's because we seem to have both a military intelligence and an Irish connection. I can understand that Northern Ireland remains a sensitive issue for you British. But since the dead woman was your daughter's customer, and before your retirement you ran the Joint Intelligence Committee, I was hoping you might be able to help.'

Crimson stared at Bruno for a long moment before taking a deep gulp of his beer.

'Very well,' he said. 'You said maths was not your strong

point. You may be adding two and two and getting five but email me a scan of their prints and I'll see what I can do.'

As Bruno opened the door, Florence was approaching with her two children, their little arms filled with tennis balls, some of which fell as they scampered towards him. Florence asked drily, 'May we come in now?'

'Of course you may,' he said, bending down to scoop up the children as more tennis balls tumbled and Daniel and Dora shrieked with delight while complaining that Bruno was losing all their balls again. They spent a couple of happy minutes searching for them and then found a bucket to contain them all, counting them in one by one.

'That's eighteen,' he said as the nineteenth ball went in.

'No, Bruno, nineteen,' they cried out together.

'Nineteen balls at five cents a ball is ninety-five cents but I have no change so here's a euro and now we have to give it to your mother for the club as a lost ball fee. Will you give it to her while I go looking for dangerous criminals who might be on the lookout for more of our tennis balls?'

'Will you shoot them?' Dora asked, and Bruno was suddenly conscious of the SIG Sauer that was on his belt, and that under Police Nationale regulations he would now be required to carry it every day.

'No, we'll just make them look for more lost balls,' he said, and then quietly asked their mother when would be a good time to talk about Paulette.

'I'll call you,' Florence replied, gathering up her children.

Bruno kissed each of them goodbye, thinking he'd forgotten

to ask Jack about holding the Monday evenings at his own place. And now he had to worry about whether or not he'd get the tickets he expected for the French Open tennis tournament at the Roland Garros stadium if St Denis could not pay its dues to the federation. He'd already arranged to take two days' leave and make a long weekend of it and he had a date: Isabelle had already arranged to be in Paris that weekend. Still, he mused, Paris in early summer with Isabelle on his arm. And he'd always rather play tennis than watch it.

'How did you know to google Felder?' he texted Isabelle, and headed back to the Mairie to see if he could access the *département*'s vehicle registration records over the internet. It turned out that he could, if he could provide his logon and password as an *officier judiciaire*, which as a result of his promotion he now was. Typical of the police, he thought; they had been assiduous in giving him his new weapon, but he had not yet been given the appropriate access codes. He called Marie-Pierre, Prunier's secretary, who said she had a sealed envelope for him which probably contained them, along with details of his new pay scale, pension rights and system for reclaiming expenses. But she could only give it to him in person, after he had signed for the package. He could pick it up tomorrow, she went on, since Prunier had added Bruno's name to the list of those on the murder inquiry team which meant being at police HQ each morning at eight.

'But he told me just this morning that I should concentrate on my new job,' Bruno objected.

'Yes, he took you off the list this morning but just now told me to put you back on again and your name is on his list to call. I think he wants to explain.' She paused. 'He had one of those calls from Paris, you know, on the special line.'

'Ah,' said Bruno, as if all were now clear. But it wasn't. Calls on a special line from Paris meant either Isabelle or the Brigadier, a senior official in the interior ministry with wide-ranging responsibilities for intelligence and security. Why would he be interested in a squalid murder and suicide in the Périgord? Bruno thanked Marie-Pierre, said he'd see her in the morning and rang off, thinking he must remember to take her some chocolates. Marie-Pierre was likely to become an important figure in his new life. But his old life still had its obligations. He checked his watch, realized that he was due to tell the cookery clients about foie gras, and set off for home to wash and change, collect Balzac and arrive on time at Pamela's riding school.

Between them, Pamela and Miranda had done a clever design job to convert the old barn into a cookery school. The place already had water and electricity, and they had installed a large central island with two sinks, two ovens – each with six gas burners – and vast amounts of work surface. They had done it cheaply, buying the ovens and sinks second-hand through Le Bon Coin. Pamela's stable-lad, Félix, and his father had put down a concrete floor and then laid terracotta tiles on top. Bruno and the Baron had installed the cookers and the lighting and Claude, a retired plumber and keen member of the local hunting club, had taken care of the plumbing and bathrooms in return for free riding lessons for his twin granddaughters.

Bruno was now standing behind the island, the cookery

class lined up before it. At Pamela's insistence he was wearing a white chef's jacket. In front of him on the work surface was a duck carcass, two breasts, two legs and wings, a fat liver and a kilo of *aiguillettes*.

'We start with the *bouillon*,' he said, and smashed a kitchen chopper down to flatten the skeleton. He covered the bones with cold water and added a chopped carrot, a celery stalk and two peeled cloves of garlic which he crushed with the side of the chopper. He tossed in a coffee spoon of salt and half a dozen crushed black peppercorns and turned on the heat beneath the pan.

'We bring this gently to simmer and leave it for a couple of hours, strain it, and then reduce by about two-thirds at a fast boil. Then I always add a *hachis*. Do you know what that is? I chop very finely two garlic cloves, a bunch of parsley and two slices of dry, cured bacon. I throw that into the stock, add a glass of cheap wine and let it cook together, barely simmering, for another hour and it will reduce even further. I strain it once more, let it cool, and then pour the liquid into a tray for ice cubes and put it into the freezer so I always have stock when I need it. In the old days, the farmers would bury the softened bones deep in their *potager*, the vegetable garden. But my dog likes to dig for bones so I don't do that.'

Bruno looked down at Balzac who had been sitting looking up at his master but now rose to wag his tail as if aware he was being discussed.

'Now we make the foie gras. You see we have two. Here on the left is the one we bought in the market today and this second one in the white terrine dish is a liver we prepared earlier, from which we already removed the veins. What I will now do to the fresh liver is what we did earlier to the one in the terrine dish.'

He showed them how to remove the veins from the liver and then poured a tablespoon of cognac into a second, empty terrine dish. He added a generous pinch of salt, some black pepper and a smaller pinch of *quatre-épices*, which he knew from Pamela was called 'all-spice' by the British. Then he added half of the liver, sprinkled another pinch of salt, more pepper and the spice before putting the remaining half of the liver on top. Then again he sprinkled another pinch of salt, some pepper and another tablespoon of cognac.

'We leave this one in the fridge overnight,' he said, covering the dish with foil and reaching for the one already prepared.

'You can experiment with the alcohol. We have tried it with good Scotch whisky, which is excellent, or champagne, which was a bit disappointing. Armagnac works very well and so does Monbazillac, our local dessert wine, and since we tend to drink a glass of chilled Monbazillac with our foie gras, it makes a happy addition.

'We call this method of making foie gras, which is the most common way these days, *mi-cuit*, which means half-cooked,' he went on, covering the foie with some greaseproof paper which he moistened with tap water before putting the top on the terrine dish. 'The oven is now at a hundred degrees centigrade – earlier I placed in there a large dish half-filled with boiling water, into which I now put the terrine dish. This is an indirect way of cooking which we call a bain-marie. I now turn the heat down very low, to ninety degrees, and leave it for twenty minutes. We remove it from the oven, let it cool and pour out any excess fat.'

While the bain-marie simmered, Bruno took one of the *magrets* of duck, laid it fat side down and, using the flat of the knife, began gently to remove the thin, white membranes, explaining that if they were left on the breast, it would curl up in the cooking. Then he turned it fat side up, scored a criss-cross pattern deep into the fat with a sharp knife, showing that his knife had gone through the fat and sliced about a centimetre into the flesh. He seasoned it on both sides with sea salt and black pepper and invited one of the two middle-aged men to do the same with the other *magret*.

'The secret of cooking *magret* is to use a searing hot and dry pan to release much of the fat,' he went on. 'Then turn it over and reduce the heat so you have slow cooking on the flesh, but the fat from the breast seeps down into the flesh as it cooks. You can also do this in the oven but I like the control that I get from watching it cook. Now the twenty minutes have passed and I must take the foie from the bain-marie.'

He did so, then took a sheet of cardboard, trimming it with scissors to the exact size of the terrine dish. He removed the lid and put the cardboard sheet on top of the greaseproof paper that covered the foie gras. Then he pressed down before pouring out the excess fat. He put two tins of tomatoes on top to maintain the pressure and returned it to the fridge.

'You see that I saved the excess fat,' he said. 'After I leave the foie overnight in the fridge, I will melt this extra fat and pour it over the foie to seal it. We can then keep it in the fridge for a week. Always remember to use a hot knife when you slice it before serving.'

While the *magret* cooked, Bruno got the two older women, who had claimed to speak 'only restaurant French', to slice some fingerling potatoes and bring them to the boil. Then he asked one of the two wives of the middle-aged men to peel and slice four cloves of garlic, while the other squeezed the juice from two oranges, peeled another and carefully separated the orange segments. Miranda had drummed into him the need for the pupils to participate and Pamela had rehearsed his English script until he sounded reasonably fluent.

'You want the potatoes parboiled, not fully cooked, so I let them simmer for about five minutes, then take them out to dry them on kitchen paper,' he said, inviting Kathleen to do so.

'Now pour off the excess fat from the duck into a separate frying pan,' he told her. 'Add the potatoes and the garlic and let them cook over a low heat.'

She handled the tasks with a kind of careful competence that suggested she might have had more professional training in cooking than Bruno. All the pupils seemed to know their way around a kitchen and Bruno found himself wondering, not for the first time, why the reputation of British food was so bad in France.

'Now watch how I prepare the sauce,' he announced.

He put the two *magrets* onto a warm plate and poured the squeezed orange juice into the pan that had held the *magrets* to deglaze it, then added two tablespoons of sugar, the orange segments and a glass of Cointreau and left it on a medium heat to reduce. He carefully turned the potatoes, and then put the *aiguillettes* of duck onto his chopping board and showed his rapt audience how to remove the tendons with the flat of his knife.

'When I buy my *aiguillettes* from Jean-François in the market or from a good butcher, he does this for me. But if you buy them from a supermarket you have to learn to do this for yourself.'

He then asked each of the pupils in turn to tackle two *aiguillettes*, which most of them managed well. Kathleen had clearly done this before. Bruno seasoned the meat and put the pieces into separate frying pans to cook with some of the duck fat, and then asked each of the men to deglaze the pans with a splash of white wine. Bruno removed the *aiguillettes*, added two spoonfuls of honey and another two of old-fashioned mustard containing seeds, and invited the two husbands to mix them into a sauce. The orange sauce had reduced sufficiently so he put the two *magrets* back into the pan, and began to serve the potatoes, then the *aiguillettes* with the honey-mustard sauce, and finally the *magrets* which he sliced before adding the orange sauce.

'Now taste these dishes and *bon appetit*,' he said, handing out forks and pouring them each a glass of Pierre Desmartis's Cuvée Quercus, a Bergerac dry white wine with the body to enhance the duck and to offset the sweetness of the orange sauce.

They perched on stools around the counter to eat and Bruno tore up a large *pain*, twice the size of a baguette, so they could wipe up the juices. He took from the fridge a chilled bottle of Monbazillac to go with the foie gras he had prepared and also opened a bottle of Château Lestevenie. This was an elegant red made from Cabernet Franc and Merlot grapes by an English couple whose wines Bruno rated among the finest in the Bergerac. Bruno knew that Pamela's customers around the table would be visiting the vineyard.

As the wine flowed and the customers dipped into the foie gras and the *aiguillettes*, the slices of *magret* and the potatoes, Bruno was quickly on first-name terms with them all. The two older women, who lived in a town near London, had been teachers at the same school before retiring the previous year. One was Vera and the other Alice, and they said they had been attracted by the idea of a cookery course at a riding school even though neither of them rode. But they had enjoyed walking through the stables and looking at the horses and were hoping to watch some of the children whom Pamela was teaching to ride.

Was this their first cooking course? he asked.

No, they had been on a weekend course at an English country house, but each had felt it wasn't long enough, and since their husbands liked going off on golfing holidays together they had decided to treat themselves to this one after reading about it in a magazine. They were pleasant women, making compliments about Bruno's limited English and evidently enjoying the food and the wine.

He assigned them their tasks, making the supper they would eat once it was ready. The two men were to make a foie gras, Alice and Vera to prepare the *aiguillettes*, and the two younger wives to cook the *magrets*. He invited Kathleen, who confessed that she had been on several cooking courses, to try her hand at *tourain*, the traditional soup of the Périgord. Pamela had asked him not to add chunks of stale country bread to the soup, claiming the British usually preferred to have their bread separately. Instead, he quickly chopped some bread into cubes and fried them in duck fat to make croutons.

Pamela came in briefly to share a glass of wine and a bowl of soup. After a moment she tapped her spoon against the side of her wine glass and said that they should know that the egg in the *tourain* and all the eggs they would be eating this week came from Bruno's hens. Bruno raised a hand.

'What about *chabrol*? It is a custom our guests should know about.'

He poured a little red wine, about a third of a glass, into the last of his soup and swirled it around before raising the bowl to his lips and drinking it down.

'*Qu'ei lou chabrol que ravicolo, qu'ei lou pu grand doux medicis*,' he intoned, explaining it was the local patois of the region, still spoken by some of the older people. 'It is the *chabrol* that brings you strength, and that is the best medicine.'

'Do you speak it?' Alice asked, pouring some of the wine into her own bowl to follow his example. Several of the other guests did the same. He noticed that Kathleen gave the *chabrol* a token sip, grimaced and then returned her plate to the table.

'A little, and I understand it quite well,' he answered. 'It would be sad to see such an old language die.'

'It sounds like Italian,' said one of the husbands at the other end of the table.

'The locals say it is rather like the Catalan they speak just over the Pyrenees in Spain,' said Pamela, clearing the plates.

'If you're a policeman does that make you a gendarme?'

asked the prettier of the two wives at the end of the table. Her dark hair was piled into a loose bun and she wore no make-up and a man's blue denim shirt.

'No, *madame*. The gendarmes are with the Ministry of Defence. The police are under the authority of the Ministry of the Interior. I am a simple country policeman and my boss is the Mayor.'

As Bruno said it, aware of Kathleen's sardonic glance, he wished it were still true. He turned to her. 'Was the *chabrol* not to your taste, *madame*?'

'It seems like a waste of good wine,' she replied, rising from the table. 'I'm full, thanks. I probably had more than my fair share of those lovely *aiguillettes*. Unusual to have soup at the end of my meal but very filling.'

At the door, she turned to Bruno. 'Would you have a minute for me? My newspaper has been onto me again.'

Bruno nodded politely to the rest of the table, gave a shrug to Pamela and joined Kathleen in the garden. She was already lighting a cigarette.

'You understand there's nothing I can tell you,' he began. 'This is not my case.'

'Look, please don't treat me as hostile,' she began. 'I'm not a news reporter. I just happened to be on the spot and I'm not the kind of person who would threaten to write something bad about this cooking course to make you cooperate. Anyway, this is no longer my story. The paper's Paris correspondent has come down by fast train to take over. I've just sent a short sidebar story on the cookery school and the food of the Dordogne region to accompany the full-page spread about Monika being stabbed to death. It seems her husband is some kind of tycoon, quite well known in England. Obviously I'd be grateful of you could tell me something more about this man McBride who hanged himself but I imagine our official crime reporter will get that from Scotland Yard.'

'I have not treated you as hostile,' he said politely, recalling J-J's warning about the British press but keeping the scepticism from his voice. And he wondered how she had learned that Monika had been stabbed and McBride hanged. At least she did not know that McBride's identity was faked. 'I did my best to help you yesterday.'

'Yes, thank you. But do you have any idea what Madame Felder was doing at McBride's house? Were they having an affair?'

'How should I know?' Bruno replied. 'As I said, this is not my case.'

'From what I hear, it sounds like a love nest,' Kathleen said. 'Wasn't she naked when she was found, dead in the shower?'

Bruno shook his head, raised his eyebrows and shrugged, trying to appear a picture of innocence and ignorance as he wondered who might have told her that.

'I'm told you were there at the house in Lalinde where Monika was found,' Kathleen went on. 'A man from *Sud Ouest* caught you on camera along with your colleague from Lalinde.'

'I can't help you,' Bruno said, feeling it was a pathetic response even as he spoke.

'So you keep saying. I'm glad to say that French journalists have been much more helpful. And the *urgences* people were even more outspoken than the police. One of them recognized you when they were called to McBride's body and said you were the one who found him hanging in the woods.'

There was nothing Bruno could say so he retreated into official jargon. 'You must realize that the police have different responsibilities.'

'And so do the media,' she retorted, stubbing out her cigarette before looking up and smiling at him as if convinced she had got the better of the exchange. 'I enjoyed watching you cook. Will you be giving any more lessons this week?'

'No, I've done my session but I think all of us, cooks and clients, get together for a glass of wine at the end of the course.'

'Until then, but one word of advice. Duck *à l'orange* is a very dated dish for the British. It was popular for our parents' generation but now it's seen as old-fashioned. You might want to try something different, like a sour cherry sauce or a reduction of blackcurrants. But the *aiguillettes* were great.'

'Thank you, I'll remember that. But I still like *canard à l'orange*.'

'Me too, it's a classic. But food is more and more about fashion these days. Since you're doing this professionally, you'll need to remember that, don't you think?'

As she went back into the barn, Bruno checked his messages. Isabelle had sent a reply to his query about her suggestion that he should run an internet search on Felder.

'Friend of the Brigadier. They were on EU security advisory group together,' she had sent.

Prunier had left a message asking him to call back and giving his mobile number. Bruno called and found him just reaching his home.

'We'll need you back on the murder team,' Prunier said. 'On the strong recommendation of our friend the Brigadier. It seems he knew the Felders, even had dinner at their place outside London. And he said you should be sure to talk to Jack Crimson, who also knows Felder quite well.'

'I already have,' Bruno replied. 'He's looking into it.'

'Very good, see you tomorrow morning, as usual.'

8

Prunier, wearing civilian clothes, took his place at the head of the table again the next morning at the stroke of eight o'clock. Bruno was the only one present in uniform. The coffee was fresh and Bruno had remembered to give some of Fauquet's home-made chocolates to Prunier's secretary, a cheerful woman with photographs of her grandchildren on her desk. Prunier signalled to J-J to go ahead and the big chief of detectives loosened his collar button and tie and ran through the familiar list. McBride was not the dead man's real name but his partner in wine had identified the body as the man he'd known as McBride. Monsieur Felder was in a Houston hospital, too ill to speak, and the British police as well as Felder's company were trying to contact his two children by his first marriage.

'They are our obvious suspects, maybe too obvious, since after the death of Monika Felder they stand to inherit,' said J-J. 'Once we are in touch, we need to look over them very carefully, double-check all alibis.

'And now we have the rather surprising results of the autopsy. For Monika, cause of death is straightforward. She was killed by a single knife thrust to the heart. Evidence of consensual sex not long before death, and although precise amounts of alcohol are hard to measure post-mortem, she was drunk when she died, certainly unfit to drive. Her last meal had been a steak in pepper sauce that was cooked in McBride's kitchen. The surprise is that both she and McBride had ingested an unusual drug called GHB, for Gamma-hydroxybutyric acid.

'It's a date-rape drug, but it used to be quite popular in dance clubs, known as Liquid-E for ecstasy, or as Juice,' J-J went on. 'It is used clinically to treat narcolepsy and alcoholism, but it is also known to increase libido and athletic performance. In larger quantities it can cause loss of consciousness and in conjunction with a lot of alcohol it can be dangerous, in extreme cases even lethal.'

J-J looked up with that cheerful half-grin that Bruno knew well; it meant he was about to tell a joke.

'You might say a little bit turns you on, but too much can turn you off – for ever.' J-J looked around as if expecting applause. None came, and the few discreet grins did not last beyond Prunier's stony expression.

'Any pills found?' Prunier asked. 'And do we know how much they took?'

'No pills or containers found and no traces on any glasses or plates. The lab is still trying to estimate how much they took but they say it's often found in powdered form. It tends to have a strong salty flavour, so used as a date-rape drug it is usually added to a cocktail or to spicy food to disguise the taste. Maybe that's why they had steak au poivre. The lab is certain, however, that McBride was still alive when he died of asphyxiation while hanging. He – or someone – had made a noose but it was in the wrong place to break his neck.'

J-J looked down the table at one of the detectives. 'You used to be on the drugs beat, Louis. Do we have much of this GHB round here?'

'Yes, boss, but it's not common. That Dutch mob who were dealing around the campsites a couple of years ago, they were selling Liquid-E. And it came up in a couple of date rape cases last year in powdered form, both involving that disco in Bergerac that later closed down.'

'Check with the drugs squad, see if they can tell us anything more, and then go and talk to some of the known dealers,' said Prunier. 'Were any other narcotics found in the Lalinde house?'

J-J shook his head, then pointed to another detective and said, 'Bank statements.'

'We have the French bank account, which mainly pays local bills from the money he gets from his grapes,' came the reply. 'The payments for utilities, insurance and property taxes are all automatic. We're waiting for the British to send us details of the HSBC accounts but the Irish police have come through and show his debit card to be linked to an Irish company account in the name of McBride Creative Associates at the Allied Irish bank. The nature of the business is listed as consulting, with varying payments from companies based in Panama, the Bahamas and the Cayman Islands that totalled over a hundred and eighty thousand euros last year after being converted from dollars. Each payment was referenced to a different invoice number. The company address was at the office of his Irish accountancy firm. Irish company taxes were paid but those are known tax havens and these accounts were not reported to the French tax authorities. His debit card was used mainly for travel. In the past year he flew business class to the US twice, to Moscow, Istanbul, Hong Kong and Singapore once each. He usually stayed in Intercontinental hotels. The British say they are being slow because he has more than one account at HSBC but they promise to be in touch in the course of today.'

J-J turned to another detective. 'His vehicle?'

'Leased from the Jaguar–Land Rover dealer here in Périgueux, paid by his Irish company account. He gets a new Range Rover every three years and the dealer does the servicing. This one is halfway through the second year and he'd done forty-four thousand kilometres, quite a lot of driving. The tyres fit the tracks we found in the lane leading to his house and on the dirt track up to his woodland, but they'd also fit any other Range Rover. He had a sticker in his windscreen that allowed him to drive on Swiss motorways. We're still working on the GPS to track his recent searches. He had maps for the Dordogne and CDs of jazz and audio books in English of Charles Dickens novels. He has an almost clean French driving licence and paid two fines this year for minor speeding infringements.'

'Do we know what kind of consulting services he offered?' Prunier asked. 'Or anything about the companies who hired him?'

'We've asked Interpol to forward our inquiries to the relevant bank authorities but those offshore places are not known for being helpful.' J-J shrugged. 'We can ask the fraud experts in Paris but they're understaffed and it will take some time. We have some of McBride's phone records from Orange. They are mostly routine local calls and some were to and from the number of Madame Felder. It certainly wasn't a phone he used for business. If he had another, we haven't found it.'

'If he used Orange for his telephone he must have used them for his internet connection,' said Prunier.

'Most people would since it's cheaper buying the package,' J-J replied. 'We're trying to find which Internet he did use but we've drawn a blank on Bouygues, SFR and Free, all the usual ones. We'll try all the others. And he had a satellite dish, with the TV set tuned to the BBC, so he could have used a satellite phone and then he could have internet access through almost any international company he chose. We've asked Interpol to inquire with the various satellite operators but since we didn't find a satellite phone and we don't have a number we'll have to wait until we can get into all his bank accounts and see which company he was paying.'

Yves then intervened. 'It's possible that one or other of the companies who were paying him also paid for his satellite subscription so his bank accounts might not tell us anything. We already know that this is a man who took his privacy very seriously indeed. It's as if he knew exactly how law enforcement would go about tracking his moves and making sure we couldn't.'

Prunier nodded and then sighed. 'Are the Irish inquiring into this fake passport of his?'

'The passport itself isn't fake,' J-J said. 'It was a genuine Irish document, renewed seven years ago, not long before the Irish computerized their register of births and deaths. It was when they checked that for us that they realised his identity had been faked when the passport was first issued nearly thirty years ago. There was no such person with that date and place of birth that McBride listed. And his original application form has disappeared from the Irish records. It was in the days before computers, everything on paper.'

'Very convenient,' said Prunier, looking at Bruno with one eyebrow raised. Bruno shrugged in return.

'So what are our next lines of inquiry?' Prunier went on.

'The British bank, timelines of McBride's travels, tracking down the Felder children,' J-J replied. 'And we've asked the Irish police if they can find McBride's Irish lawyer, the one who drew up his company statutes, to see if he left a will.'

'Anything else?' Prunier asked, looking around the room.

'Monika Felder was a German citizen when she married Felder,' Bruno said. 'Is she a dual national? Can we find out if she still had a German passport and if so, where it might be? And can we take a look at the exact times and dates of her visits to Houston and what kind of visa she had? I don't know how long US tourist visas last, or maybe there's a special visa for relatives of people in hospital. But it would be useful to track her movements – on both passports – and see if they correlate with any of McBride's travels. Maybe we can check her travels through her credit card history.'

'It's worth a try,' said Prunier, rising to end the meeting. 'Bruno, my office, please.'

Once in his room, Prunier called in his secretary, who carried a large, sealed envelope with Bruno's name on it and a computer bag holding his new laptop.

'All the paperwork is in here and your access codes for our computer system,' said Marie-Pierre. 'It's a double encryption system for security, do you know how that works?'

Bruno shook his head. 'No.'

'Just sign here to show you've received all this and then go with Marie-Pierre. She'll show you how it works. And let me know as soon as you hear anything from Crimson,' Prunier said, turning away to lift his phone.

Marie-Pierre explained that when using his new laptop on official business, he would have to join the VPN, or Virtual Private Network, of the Police Nationale. She gave him a log-in ID, his full name plus 24 for his *département*, plus eight digits for his date of birth. Then she gave him a USB stick.

'Once you've logged on, you'll be asked to enter your password.' She made him open the laptop, log on and complete the various steps required.

'I've given you a temporary one but you'll have to create your own password, known only to you. It must contain at least twelve characters, at least one in capital letters, one numeral and one grammar sign like an exclamation mark or an ampersand. Once you enter that, you will be asked for the second security code. At that point, put this USB stick into your laptop and it will automatically generate a random code. You don't have to know what it is and once you've done it from your laptop, the laptop will supply it automatically from then on. But if you want to log on to the police VPN from another computer, you will need your code and the USB stick. Try not to do that.'

She gave him an envelope, asked him to write down the twelve-character password he intended to use, put it in the envelope, seal it, sign the seal and then hand it to her, where it would join the others in Prunier's safe.

'Now you can check on specific case files where you're

listed as a crime team member,' she said. 'We no longer have the old murder book, where you write down the progress of the inquiry each day. Instead, it goes into the case file on the computer. You can read it all, add information, post queries and suggestions, look up transcripts of interviews, scene of crime photos, autopsy reports and so on. You can also use it as an ordinary laptop and do searches or send private emails in the usual way without having to join our VPN. But the laptop remains our property so don't use it for anything you wouldn't want your mother to see.' Marie-Pierre surprised him by flashing a cheeky grin and a cheerful wink. 'Of course, grandmothers like me have seen it all so use your private computer for all that, like I do. And now off you go, Bruno, and thank you for the chocolates.'

He stopped in the waiting room, logged onto the VPN network and began searching the vehicle registration database for the owner of the red Renault in which he had seen Paulette the previous day. It was searchable so he put in the letters and numbers he had scribbled into his notebook. It gave him thirty-seven options, only five of which belonged to a Renault Clio. Three were for new registrations and it had been an older car. Of the final two, one was registered to a Madame Véronique Leverrier in Nontron, on the northern edge of the Périgord. The other was for a Gérard Jean-Luc Bollinet at an address in Périgueux, with a date of birth that made him twenty-six years old, and his profession was listed as teacher.

Bruno then went into the website of *département* employees and learned that he taught drama and French literature at the *lycée* that Paulette attended. He went into the *lycée*'s website and found that Bollinet had directed a student play the previous term, Alfred Jarry's *Ubu Roi*, in which Paulette had played the role of Ubu's wife.

Bollinet's address was across the river in the southern suburb of the city, on Bruno's route back to St Denis, in a small street of tiny houses just off the Route de Pommier. He drove slowly past, seeing a narrow door, a single window to one side. It was on a slope and he turned and headed back to drive past the rear of the house and saw a washing line festooned with baby clothes drying in the feeble sunlight that came spasmodically through the clouds.

Merde, thought Bruno. So Bollinet was a father already. He wondered if Paulette knew. The road seemed to be a dead end so he turned and went back the way he had come. As he drove past the front of Bollinet's house, a woman with a pushchair that contained a crying toddler was closing the front door behind her. She turned to push it down the street and Bruno saw that she was heavily pregnant. The toddler tossed a soft toy into the gutter and howled more loudly. The young woman looked hopelessly at the discarded toy, as if wondering how in her condition she could bend down and pick it up.

Bruno stopped his car, climbed out, saluted and said, '*Bonjour, madame*, with your permission.'

He bent down and picked up what he saw was a teddy bear and handed it to the child, who promptly threw it out again. Bruno went back to his car, took a piece of string from his sports bag and then returned to tie it firmly around the bear's neck. Then he tied it to the strut on the side of the pushchair and watched the toddler throw it, and then pull it back and throw it again. By this time the toddler had become fascinated with the new game and had stopped crying.

'*Merci, monsieur,*' the young woman said. 'At this age he can be quite a handful.'

She looked to be in her mid-twenties, with good features and a generous mouth but her hair was lank. She wore no make-up, had dark circles under her eyes and straightened up with her hands pressing into the small of her back.

'When is the baby due?' Bruno asked, smiling.

'About six weeks,' she said, with a smile that swept away the tiredness and made her look much younger. 'I'm hoping for a girl this time.'

'May your wish be granted, *madame*,' he said, saluted once more and returned to his car to drive off, feeling a new surge of anger at Bollinet for risking his own wife and family as well as threatening to disrupt Paulette's young life. But what could he do about it? He would have to have another talk with Fabiola and at some point see if Paulette wanted to discuss it with him, and if she knew of Bollinet's family. But it was not a subject he could broach; it would have to be up to her.

He was back on the main road that led through a succession of roundabouts to Niversac and the turnoff to Les Eyzies when his mobile vibrated. He pulled off the road onto the forecourt of a mason's yard and saw the caller was Jack Crimson.

'We need to have a chat,' said Crimson. 'Do you want to drop by my house, have some soup and salad and cheese for lunch?'

'With pleasure, shall I get some bread or wine?'

'No shortage of either. Shall I see you about noon? It has to be early because something important has come up.'

Bruno agreed and drove on to St Denis. Once in his office he checked his emails and saw one from Louis in Montignac saying 'Routine patrols'. The one from Juliette used the same phrase but added 'planning and review meeting with colleagues'. He had just acknowledged them when the Mayor came in, closed the door and sat down.

'What's this I hear about Paulette being pregnant?' he began, keeping his voice low.

Merde, thought Bruno again. It would soon be all over town at this rate. 'What have you heard, exactly?'

'Overheard, in fact. Roberte and Claire were chatting in whispers around the coffee pot when I was about to leave my office and I couldn't help but overhear. They were speculating who the father might be.'

Claire's colleague in the Mairie, Roberte, looked after the social security files. As soon as Bruno asked himself how they might have known, the map in his head of the various gossip networks in the town threw up the answer. Roberte's sister-in-law was one of the receptionists at the town's medical clinic. She had been in the job long enough to know what it meant when a doctor like Fabiola took certain medical products from the storeroom before returning to Paulette waiting in her office.

'It's true. She's about ten or eleven weeks gone, Fabiola thinks. Officially, I know nothing about it and I don't think Paulette's parents know. But I believe the father to be a drama teacher called Bollinet at her *lycée* in Périgueux. He's in his late twenties, married with a toddler and his wife is seven months pregnant.'

'How the devil do you know that? Paulette must have told you.'

Bruno shook his head and recounted the scene between Paulette and her lover in the car park, his check of the car's licence plates and his drive-by of Bollinet's home. He did not mention the incident with the teddy bear.

'That's a relief,' the Mayor said. 'From what I overheard, Roberte seems to suspect Philippe Delaron to be the father since he's always covering Paulette's rugby games.'

'I think Paulette has better taste than that,' said Bruno.

'Yes, I agree,' said the Mayor with a grin. 'Except that Claire was suggesting it might be significant that the unmarried male Paulette spent most time with was you, as her rugby coach.'

Bruno rolled his eyes and said, 'Thank heavens nobody takes Claire's gossip seriously.'

'Don't underestimate Claire. Most people like gossip and some of them in this town are prepared to believe absolutely anything,' the Mayor said. 'But what do we do now? If you're right about Bollinet, this is very serious. He's a teacher and I know it won't be the first time it's happened but officially to have an affair with a pupil is a sacking offence. Don't we have a duty to inform the education authorities?'

'Sacking is too good for the bastard, if you ask me,' said Bruno. 'But unless and until Paulette confirms that he's the father we have no proof. And we don't want to do anything that would make things worse for her, least of all when the list of the thirty young women selected for the French national team should come out at the end of this week. They'll be invited to join the adult team in training at Val d'Isère and Paulette will have to decide whether to have the baby or not.'

'Val d'Isère is in the Alps. How can they train there?'

'There are flat bits,' Bruno replied, thinking that by now he knew his Mayor well enough to know he wasn't really interested in Val d'Isère but had simply asked the question to buy some time while he thought about Paulette's dilemma. 'The women do team-building exercises there just like the men; mountain biking and rock-climbing and hiking up the Grande Motte glacier.'

'How interesting,' the Mayor said and then gave Bruno a sharp glance. 'Paulette's parents are regular churchgoers, loyal Catholics, which means they believe that abortion is a mortal sin.'

'The question is whether Paulette believes that. She's over eighteen. It's her decision, whatever her parents might want.'

'Have you talked to her about this?'

Bruno shook his head. 'I thought I was the only one who knew, apart from Fabiola. Oh, and Florence, she also knows. But now that Roberte and Claire are chatting it won't be long before some kind citizen passes the word to Paulette's parents and matters will then become even more complicated.'

'So what do we do?'

'I think I have to tell Fabiola and Florence about Bollinet's family,' Bruno said. 'I have no idea whether Paulette knows he's married and about to have another baby by his wife. The problem is that when I tell Fabiola, she'll assume I'm bringing pressure to bear to get Paulette to have an abortion so she can play for France and she'll be furious with me.'

'I see.' The Mayor nodded sagely. 'But knowing you, Bruno, I imagine you will do so anyway.'

'I thought I might consult Florence when school comes out today and see what she says.'

'Just what I was going to recommend. We can't let this young girl's future be derailed because of some adulterous drama teacher. He sounds like a real piece of *merde*.'

Bruno nodded in agreement, and at the back of his mind he wondered how he might report this particular aspect of the work of a country policeman to his colleagues. 'Routine patrols' would have to cover it.

9

Bruno always enjoyed his visits to Jack Crimson's house, and not just because of the genial hospitality, the customary glass of single malt whisky and the excellent wines Crimson liked to offer his friends. The house itself was charming, the kind estate agents would call a small chateau. It was built of well-weathered golden stone with a noble, pillared porch and symmetrical windows, approached through an avenue of rose bushes that had been allowed to grow and spread. The view from the rear terrace, which Bruno knew well, fell away to a gentle valley and then rose again to a sloping plateau dotted with grazing cows and then ridge upon wooded ridge into the far distance.

This visit, however, was more duty than pleasure. Bruno was no innocent. He had obeyed orders as a soldier, served the interests of France in secret wars in Chad and Libya, and seen comrades die knowing that their extinction would be listed as 'a training accident'. But Jack Crimson and the Brigadier were of a different kind, men who had lived and made their careers in that murky terrain of national interest and ruthless intrigue. They were two lifelong captains of the dark forces of the secret world of intelligence and Bruno expected he was now, on this gentle and sunny afternoon with his dog sniffing playfully at the rose bushes, to be given a brief glimpse into its shadows.

He had his own suspicions. McBride had been a combat soldier, probably an Englishman, living quietly in a foreign land under an assumed name, and enjoying a romantic liaison with the wife of a former director of British military intelligence. Iraq and Afghanistan were possible battlefields for such a man, and Northern Ireland perhaps more likely, given that false Irish passport. Crimson had probably worked with and doubtless would have known Brigadier Felder and he may well have come across the dead man once known as McBride.

Bruno had even worked out why he was to be the conduit for whatever information Crimson was now ready to impart. For Crimson to speak directly to his old friend the Brigadier would be too formal, a meeting too difficult to be subsequently denied. Crimson would like to be able to say, in all honesty, that he had spoken to no intelligence official, nor to any representative of the French state. Bruno was a friend, a fellow member of the tennis club, so to meet him was but passing the time of day with an old acquaintance over a welcoming drink. An encounter with Bruno was, in that favourite word of intelligence agencies, deniable.

'Good to see you, Bruno, and you, Balzac,' said the former chairman of Her Majesty's Joint Intelligence Committee, opening the door while Bruno was still halfway down the path. Crimson must have been watching for Bruno's arrival. 'Come through onto the terrace and enjoy this fine day over a glass of Scotch while Balzac makes his usual patrol of the garden.'

Crimson picked up a loaded tray from the kitchen, with

plates, bread, cheese, pâté and cherry tomatoes and asked Bruno to bring a smaller tray with glasses, a carafe of wine and a bottle of Scotch. On the terrace, Bruno was surprised to see that the table had been moved so that the view over the countryside was blocked by various bushes. Why would his friend do that, Bruno wondered, when he took such pleasure in the view?

A glass of Bowmore in his hand, softened with a splash of the Malvern water that Crimson favoured, Bruno asked why Jack wanted to see him so urgently.

'Glad you could make it so soon because I have to leave,' Crimson began. 'I'm on the afternoon train to Paris, Metro to the Gare du Nord and then the Eurostar to London. I'll sleep at my club tonight and then head north to spend a few days at a very pleasant country house belonging to an old friend and colleague. We haven't that much time so it will be a makeshift lunch.'

'This is very sudden,' said Bruno, although he had noticed a small suitcase standing ready and apparently packed in Crimson's hallway. 'You're supposed to be giving Miranda's clients a guided tour of the Bergerac vineyards later this week and you've been looking forward to that.'

Crimson shrugged and began to slice the bread. 'I don't have much choice. The powers that be in London think I'll be safer out of this country. Even if I doubted their advice, and I'm not sure that I do, I'd rather not take the risk, nor see any unpleasantness happening to Miranda and the children.'

'Your friends in England think you are not safe here in the Périgord?' Bruno asked, surprised.

'They think it's better to be safe than sorry when they suspect an IRA killer squad is operating around here,' Crimson said, almost casually.

'An IRA killer squad, here?' said Bruno, sitting up in alarm. He suddenly understood why the table on the terrace had been moved behind a screen of bushes. 'You are worried about a sniper?'

'It's only a routine precaution. And I just spent half an hour trying to find my old mirror on a stick to check the underside of my car, something I used to have to do every day when the IRA was planting car bombs. It's rather depressing, going back to all that. Here, have some of this excellent pâté that Miranda made me. And help yourself to more Scotch, or try the wine. It's a rather good Montravel from Daniel Hecquet at Château Puy-Servain.

'My old colleagues in London are assuming that McBride was murdered by some IRA hard-liners in a revenge killing,' Crimson went on, pouring out two glasses of wine. 'So they are now worried about some other British potential targets in the region. That means a couple of retired ambassadors, and me.'

'Do you think they're right?'

'It's very possible, people like me have been IRA targets before,' Crimson replied, sniffing at his glass of wine. 'And given these two latest deaths, it's one of the few explanations that makes sense to my old colleagues in London. I'm sure it won't take you long to work out why they have reached that conclusion.'

Crimson was avoiding Bruno's gaze, focusing on his food and then looking out over the garden to watch Balzac sniff his way around the flower beds.

'I suppose that means McBride was a British intelligence man who was using his false Irish identity to work undercover against the IRA,' Bruno said slowly, almost as if thinking aloud. 'And it would also mean that he had been doing so in such an effective or perhaps brutal way that the IRA still want to kill him, nearly twenty years after you reached a political settlement in Northern Ireland. Either this is personal revenge upon him or this man we know as McBride is a symbol of something for them.'

'That sums it up, Bruno,' Crimson replied and turned his gaze back to Bruno. 'You're right on both counts, personal revenge and symbolism. Have you ever heard of Operation Flavius?'

Bruno shook his head, his mouth full of bread and cheese.

'It was in Gibraltar in March, 1988,' Crimson began. 'Three members of a Provisional IRA active service unit, Sean Savage, Danny McCann and Mairead Farrell, had planned a bomb attack on the changing of the guard outside the Governor's house. As British soldiers, the troops on guard were seen by the IRA as a legitimate target. Thanks to good intelligence, we knew they were coming. The three of them were shot dead in circumstances which remain disputed.'

Crimson leaned forward, put his hand on Bruno's arm and looked at him intently.

'There's no doubt what they planned. Farrell had the keys in her handbag to a rental car that contained over sixty kilos of Semtex explosive, enough to make a very big bang indeed. Detonators and timers were also found in the car. The explosives were stuffed with two hundred bullets. That was vicious, Bruno. It would have been carnage, not just an explosion that would have blown off the front of the Governor's building and demolished half the town but bullets flying everywhere. What's more, Savage was an explosives expert and a known killer who had shot dead two police officers in an ambush in the Belfast docks. McCann and Farrell had already been in prison for explosives offences. Mairead Farrell served eight years for planting a bomb at the Conway hotel, hoping to kill British soldiers who sometimes drank there.

'These were hardened terrorists, probably the top team of the Provisional IRA.' Crimson's grip on Bruno's arm tightened. 'There is no doubt what they planned, but at the time they were killed they were unarmed and some eyewitnesses said on camera to British TV reporters that they were shot in cold blood as they lay on the ground.

'The official inquest in Gibraltar found that the SAS members who had laid the ambush and killed them had acted lawfully,' Crimson went on after a long sip at his drink. 'A subsequent judgement by the European Court of Human Rights said there had been no plot to kill the three Provos out of hand, but the operation had been so poorly planned and full of flaws it was likely to end badly.'

'The Provos, were they the people who tried to kill Prime Minister Thatcher with a bomb in her hotel room?' Bruno asked. He took a final portion of Cantal cheese and sipped at the dry white wine.

'Indeed they were. They were the hard-line wing of the IRA who broke away when we started to cooperate seriously with the Irish government in Dublin and began secret peace talks with the official IRA. The Provos said the official IRA were traitors and they tried to stop all the talks by killing Thatcher's successor, John Major, with a mortar bomb attack on Downing Street in 1991. That time they failed, thank God. It was war, Bruno, a very vicious and bloody little war with no holds barred.'

'I understand,' said Bruno. 'I think after the terrorist attacks we have seen in France in recent years, any French citizen would understand.'

'The reason why we think they may have been hunting this man known as McBride is that for the Provos, the Gibraltar operation was never really over. They did their best to make propaganda out of it but the fact was that their operation had failed. They had lost some of their best militants and they wanted revenge. Two years after the event, the Governor of Gibraltar they had targeted, a retired senior Royal Air Force officer called Sir Peter Terry, was shot, along with his wife, in front of their daughter at their home in Staffordshire. For the Provos, anything to do with Operation Flavius was personal and that's why my old colleagues want me back in a safe place in Britain while this inquiry unfolds.'

'And this man McBride was one of those SAS men in Gibraltar?'

'Not exactly, although he was in Gibraltar at the time and worked closely with the SAS. He was a career soldier in military intelligence, and he was in a special unit known as Fourteen. It stands for Fourteenth Intelligence Company. They specialized in reconnaissance, concealed observation posts and taking endless photographs of known IRA members. He was one of the planners of Operation Flavius but his name never emerged and he never gave evidence to any inquiry. But he'd been undercover in Northern Ireland long enough to know two of the bombers by sight.'

'And he had the false passport?'

'It wasn't false!' Crimson exclaimed with a barking laugh and a wide smile, as though proud of what he was saying. 'That was the beauty of it.'

He went on to explain that McBride had possessed a genuine Irish passport, printed and issued by the Irish government, thanks to a corrupt employee working in the Irish passport office. McBride's passport was renewed several times because the back-up documents were equally good. British Intelligence had even devised what looked like a real Irish birth certificate to justify it.

But the Provos had some very good counter-intelligence people and a lot of sympathizers in Dublin. They mounted a counter-operation of their own. Assuming that the British had someone in the passport office, they gambled that a clerk who'd take pay from the British to steal blank passports might want to earn some more money and do the same for a foreigner who needed a new identity. They found the clerk, bribed him to issue a passport to an Indian for a thousand pounds and then passed the information to the Irish authorities. The clerk went to prison, where other friends of the IRA went to work on him. He gave them a number of names but they all seemed – thanks to the birth certificates – to be real Irishmen.

'We got wind of their work and got the endangered men out of Ireland,' Crimson went on. 'But lately, the remnants of the Provos recruited an ex-priest who realized that although we might be able to forge the birth certificates we could never fake the baptismal certificates in the churches. They checked the Catholic church records and found nothing. After worrying where he'd gone wrong, the ex-priest realized they ought to be looking at the Protestant churches. And that's when our scheme began to unravel. Still, it had been good while it lasted.'

'And you never got back the fake passport from McBride?'

'You were in the military, Bruno, so you know how these things work. It was listed as lost in action and no questions were asked. And by that time we were working so closely with the Dublin government that we were told to stop the false passport game. We let sleeping dogs lie.'

'So who was McBride?'

'This is where it gets complicated,' said Crimson, pouring himself another glass of wine. Bruno declined. He wanted to remember all this.

'His real name was Rentoul, Richard Rentoul, and he retired as a captain after the first Gulf War in 1991 and went into the private security business with his old commander, Felder, and they began to make money. Rentoul became a specialist in working kidnap cases, setting up personal security systems, burglar alarms, bodyguards, training drivers in evasion techniques and so on. He was also a very good shot, passed out top of his class at sniper school. I believe he also made arrangements to pay ransoms which on a couple of occasions led to the arrest of the kidnappers. But after the Iraq War, Felder's company had so many contracts with the British and American occupation forces that they were in urgent need of trained men. Felder brought Rentoul into Iraq to help run the business and recruit more ex-army types. They were desperate for trained manpower, offering them two and three thousand dollars a week. It was like an El Dorado for those old soldiers. We and the Americans even had problems with serving soldiers resigning to take up the jobs.'

'How long was Rentoul in Iraq?'

'Not that long, just over a year, and then in 2004 he was killed in an ambush outside Baghdad while escorting an American convoy that was carrying cash. A lot of cash, nearly twenty million dollars. The ambushers got away with the money.'

'So if Rentoul is dead, who is using the McBride passport now?' Bruno asked. 'And how did he get hold of it?'

'That's the question, but I don't have to tell you that someone who knew both Rentoul and Felder's wife would very probably either have served with them in the British army, whether in Germany or Northern Ireland, or worked for Felder's company.'

'An investigation into all of them would have been done by the British police, who are not being very helpful,' Bruno said.

Crimson shrugged. 'I'm retired. There are limits to my influence but I will do what I can. And I'm confident that the British authorities will do anything they can to help round up this Provo murder squad – if that's who it was that killed Monika Felder and the man known as McBride.'

'Do you have any reason to think there might have been another motive for the killings?'

'No,' Crimson replied. 'And since Felder had been running an intelligence unit at a time when an ambush in County

Tyrone saw three IRA men shot dead, it is entirely possible that Monika Felder was the target.'

Bruno nodded thoughtfully. The inquiry had not yet really focused on motives for the murder of Madame Felder. Perhaps it should. He made a mental note.

'Was any official inquiry made into the ambush that killed Rentoul?' Bruno then asked.

'Not by us. Felder was a private company, nothing to do with us. And there were a lot of ambushes in Iraq in those days. I think the Americans did an investigation but I imagine they were more concerned with the money than with a handful of dead mercenaries.'

'Did they get any of the money back?'

'Not to my knowledge. You'd have to ask the Americans. Maybe they'd let you take a look at their report into the ambush.' Crimson shrugged again.

Bruno nodded, trying to think of what else Crimson might be able to tell him before disappearing off to Britain.

'Did Rentoul have a wife or next of kin?' he asked, suddenly struck by the thought that there might be a trail to Rentoul. 'In the French army, we have to name someone to receive any personal effects or pension rights.'

'So do we. Rentoul named his mother, a widow, and she died ten years ago. His pension rights died with her. That's all I know, except for one bit of bad news about those fingerprints you sent me. I asked an old friend in army records to see if we had any records of the prints, with particular reference to Fourteen, Rentoul's old unit. All damaged in an accidental fire, said the report. Believe that if you will, or conclude as I do that they were deliberately destroyed to stop any old IRA men getting hold of them. Filing clerks tend to be poorly paid and easily corrupted.'

Crimson looked at his watch, evidently worrying about catching his train. 'Is there anything else you can tell me that might be useful when I'm debriefed back in London?' he asked.

'Both Rentoul and Madame Felder had taken a drug called GHB,' Bruno said. 'It can be dangerous when taken with alcohol and they'd been drinking a fair amount. But your police will get that in our interim report, along with what we have so far about his finances, his car and so on. But he was a secretive man. I think we're still not sure how he got onto the internet.'

'Interesting.' Crimson finished his drink, looked at his watch again and rose. 'No time for coffee, I'm afraid. I need to get to the station for my train and since I don't know how long I'll be gone I'd rather not leave my car there. I have to ask you for a lift. I'm going to Le Buisson, then changing onto the fast train at Libourne.'

'Of course, I'll be glad to,' said Bruno. 'On the way I can tell you about this idea I've had about resuming our Monday dinners, even though Pamela and Miranda are tied up with the cooking school. And that reminds me, who's going to babysit Miranda's children while you're away?'

'Not my problem,' said Crimson, picking up the glasses and bottle of Scotch and stewarding Bruno inside before locking the French windows. He left the drinks and bottle on a side table before putting on a jacket and scarf. He picked up the small suitcase he'd already packed and handed it to Bruno before collecting a laptop bag and then tapping his pockets to be sure he had his phone.

'What about the washing-up?' Bruno asked, pointing to the empty plates and glasses on the table.

'The cleaner can take care of them.'

'Can I reach you on your usual mobile number, the French one?'

'I'd rather you didn't since it's too easily tracked. I'll mainly be using an English SIM card that I'll buy when I get to London. But yes, if it's really urgent. I'll arrange to have my French number checked once a day. And in case of any real emergency, Miranda knows how to get in touch with people who can reach me.

'By the way,' Crimson added. 'Just one final nugget. I presume what I have said will somehow find its way back to our mutual friend, the Brigadier. Don't forget to tell him that the Semtex we found in that car in Gibraltar was supplied by none other than the unlamented Colonel Gaddafi of Libya. He may have gone and Libya may be in chaos, but in my experience people involved in this kind of business tend to remain in touch with old contacts.'

Once they were in the car, Crimson spoke again. 'You probably won't need to remind the Brigadier since as a young officer he was involved in the operation, but you might mention the *Eksund*.'

'What's that?' Bruno asked.

'It's the name of a ship the French stopped at sea in 1987. It was carrying a thousand AK-47 assault rifles, fifty Soviet-made Strela ground-to-air missiles, anti-tank rockets and two tons of

Semtex, a gift from Libya to the IRA. Along with four others, an IRA man called Gabriel Cleary was found on board and spent five years in a French prison. Since he spoke good English, it was our friend the Brigadier who arrested and interrogated Cleary and gave evidence at the trial. I know that because I was the one who contacted the Brigadier when Cleary was arrested again in 1996 by the Irish police, who were acting on information my team had collected, when they raided an underground bomb factory in the Irish Republic.'

10

Once he'd dropped Crimson at the station in Le Buisson, Bruno parked at the entrance to the Pont de Vicq campsite and made some hurried notes of what he had been told. Then he called the Brigadier on the special phone he'd been given during a previous operation. It was shielded and encrypted in ways he didn't understand and a small green light glowed when he was in contact with anyone on the Brigadier's own network. A duty officer answered and Bruno asked to speak to the Brigadier on a matter concerning Jack Crimson.

'He's been called home. I just dropped him off at the station,' Bruno said when the Brigadier came on the line. He went on to explain the concern about the IRA and the Libyan connection. 'He told me to remind you of the *Eksund*,' he added.

The Brigadier ignored this, asking simply, 'What train is he on?'

'He's just left Le Buisson, so he'll catch the TGV at Libourne and arrive at Montparnasse at about six this evening. Then he plans to get the Metro to Gare du Nord for the Eurostar to London.'

'Very good, I'll meet him off the train at Montparnasse. Thanks, Bruno, and congratulations on the promotion.'

He ended the call and Bruno then rang J-J to repeat once more what he'd heard from Crimson.

'*Putain*, the IRA, that's all we need,' J-J replied. 'Still, there is some good news. The Procureur has appointed Bernard Ardouin as magistrate in this case. You worked with him before and he's a good man. We could have done a lot worse.'

That was a relief, thought Bruno. Under French law a magistrate placed in charge of the case had very wide powers, including the right to decide on criminal charges, to interview witnesses and to direct the police inquiries. Some of them saw the job as a stepping stone to a political career and others took a messianic approach to their work, pursuing their own political or ecological agendas, or mistrusting the police with whom they were supposed to work. That was sad but understandable, Bruno thought; people given unaccustomed powers were often like that. But Ardouin was a level-headed type who knew the law, liked his work and performed it well.

'The bad news is that the forensics guys are still arguing among themselves whether the guy hanged himself or someone did it for him,' J-J went on. 'There are no signs of his being tied up so I don't see how anyone else can have been involved in the hanging. And he botched the suicide anyway. He put the knot behind his ear rather than in front of it, which is the best way to be sure the drop breaks the neck.'

Amazing, the things you learn in this job, thought Bruno. But J-J was still talking.

'And they're involved in some technical argument about the reliability of blood tests for alcohol that long after death. Did you know that a dead body produces alcohol? It seems that even after death internal fungi and microbes and yeasts can make a corpse technically drunk even if he was teetotal.'

Bruno dimly recalled reading something about that in the forensics textbook he had to study at the police academy, but the details were long forgotten.

'I suppose that date-rape drug he took complicates matters,' Bruno said. 'I forget the name.'

'They found some in Monika's suitcase. The idiots missed it on the first search. It looks as though she brought it with her.'

'Could that have made him pass out?' Bruno asked. 'That could be a way for someone to hang him without tying him up.'

'Listen, Bruno. We've been round and round on this. Even if he had passed out, they'd have to carry him through the vineyard and into the woods, across all the brush and undergrowth and in the dark. You'd need two, maybe three people for that and probably more than one ladder.'

'I see your point.' As he spoke, Bruno was trying to remember how the rope had been fixed to the tree. He closed his eyes to summon the image from his memory. It had been slung over the branch and then tied to the trunk. So in theory, a strong man could have hauled the weight of McBride – he should start thinking of him as Rentoul – from the ground and then secured the rope to the trunk. But J-J was right; Bruno couldn't see a single man getting the body through the vines and woodland at night.

'Do we have a definite time of death?'

'No, a window, from around ten in the evening of the day Monika arrived until two or three the next morning. The poor bastard was hanging there for at least thirty-six hours. By the way, do you have a contact number for Crimson in England if we need to talk to him?'

'Yes, if it's really urgent. He said he was going to a safe place and he wouldn't want to risk being tracked by his mobile.'

'Okay, I'll see you tomorrow morning, as usual. We'll convene at police HQ but Ardouin may want us to go over the Procureur's office since it's now his baby.' J-J ended the call.

Bruno sat in his van, thinking, and then on impulse got out, walked through the gates of the campsite and down to the long stretch of grass on the riverbank that was known locally as the beach. Bruno had swum there often in summer. The river here was the Dordogne, on its way to be joined by the Vézère at Limeuil, the charming hillside village that was a pleasant stroll away and just a kilometre or so by river. He had swum it once, with Isabelle half-paddling and half-drifting alongside in a canoe with his old dog, Gigi, standing in the prow. He smiled at the memory as he walked along the beach to the bridge. There was a path beneath the first arch that led to the riverside café, not yet open for the tourist season, but the river was running high after the rains and he turned back to admire the view upstream.

He was still thinking about those arms on the ship, *Eksund*. Anti-aircraft missiles, anti-tank rockets and two tons of Semtex explosives. Bruno had been a combat engineer and had taken courses in demolition and he knew that with two tons of Semtex he could destroy half the bridges in Paris. This wasn't the small-time, almost amateurish terrorism that had become grimly familiar in France. This was sophisticated heavy weaponry that to Bruno was more associated with a real army than a terrorist gang. He felt out of his depth.

Could there really be an IRA murder squad here in this placid region? He found it hard to believe. There had been peace in Northern Ireland for nearly twenty years. People looking for revenge for the events three decades ago in Gibraltar must be getting on in years, or their sons and daughters had taken up the task. It didn't ring true to him, but then terrorists had their own rules. One of those, he thought as he strolled, was that killing had to be a political statement, a demonstration of the terrorists' ability to strike when and where they chose. So why would an IRA murder squad seek to make Rentoul's death look like a suicide, even leaving a suicide note, when they could have made publicity out of his killing? Perhaps they did that just to buy themselves time to get away, and their claim for Rentoul's execution would be announced later. He'd have to see what the others thought at tomorrow's meeting, and meanwhile, he had time to get to the *collège* in St Denis.

Whenever his other duties allowed, Bruno liked to be at the infants' school at noon when it closed, to stop the traffic and allow the mothers and children to cross the road safely. He always enjoyed the few minutes chatting to them as he and they waited for the storm of rushing feet and excited childish voices once they were let out. Most of the young mothers he had known from his earliest tennis classes and he went hunting with many of the fathers and husbands. He'd eaten and drunk in most of their homes and danced at more than a few birthdays. It was useful to him to hear the gossip but these moments at the school gates were also a pleasure in keeping up with old friends. And it was a way to remind himself that these mothers and children were in his charge, that their peace and security were his responsibility.

It was the same now in the afternoon when the *collège* day ended and the students came out. Aged between twelve and sixteen, they were mostly old and self-conscious enough to walk rather than race out like the younger children at the primary school. Only a few were being met by mothers in their cars, and the teenage youths looked slightly shamefaced as they climbed into the passenger seats. Almost half of the *collège* students boarded the school buses that took the rural kids to their scattered hamlets or villages that were too small for their own *collège*. They were noisy as they jostled their way aboard, greeting friends and sporting teammates.

Only a small number had paired off into couples, walking closely together or hand in hand. Some of them were teased by their classmates, perhaps from envy, perhaps because the rules of courtship were still unclear. They were mostly of an age that meant the boys all vied loudly to fill the back of the bus while the girls clustered, heads bowed together as they exchanged confidences. Half the marriages in the region had probably begun in these school buses, Bruno thought. But he wondered whether that would continue now that more and more of the youngsters had earphones playing their music and some of them were intent on the screens of their mobile phones, watching some video or texting.

He knew almost all of them by name from his tennis and rugby classes. He had watched them grow and form their friendships and launch their little feuds and establish the pecking order that would probably endure for years to come. Bruno knew that his presence at the school gates was one of the rituals that marked their day. It also, he hoped, served to remind them that the police were not some alien group but familiar figures, neighbours, part of the town's life.

He held up the traffic for the school buses to depart and then headed for the small row of maisonettes, subsidized lodgings for the teachers. This almost free housing was a way to entice staff to come to rural France at a time when most newly qualified young teachers wanted jobs in the big cities. He climbed the steps to the upper floor and rang the bell for Florence's apartment. She answered the door in her apron, a wooden spoon in one hand, the other rising automatically to smooth her hair when she saw Bruno grinning at her.

'Sorry I'm such a mess, I'm just baking something for the children while they have their snack,' she said, leaning her head forward for Bruno's *bise*. 'Come in, such a nice surprise, have some coffee or perhaps tea.'

Florence began to ask what brought him to her door when her children erupted into the hallway from the kitchen, clutching at Bruno's legs until he bent down and kissed each of them as they demanded he lift them both up.

'*Bonjour*, Dora, *bonjour*, Daniel, you're getting too big and strong for me,' he said, putting an arm around each child and then rising to his full height while sticky fingers clutched at his neck. 'Oh, you're so heavy now. Soon you'll have to carry me.'

He took them back into the kitchen, deposited each of them in the high chairs they still used, and accepted a cup of mint tea from Florence, the bite of an apple from Dora and a narrow sliver of sausage roll from Daniel. Little known in France, this

English delicacy had become a favourite after they had first eaten it at Miranda's house.

'You can have this bit, Bruno, because *Maman* is making some more,' said Daniel.

'Such lucky children to have such a clever *maman*,' he said, pronouncing both apple and roll to be delicious.

Once the snack was finished and the children had spread out on the floor with their colouring books, Bruno and Florence sat at opposite sides of the small table and he said, 'It's about Paulette. Word is getting around town, I think from someone at the clinic, and I'm pretty sure I know who the father is, her drama teacher at her *lycée*. Nearly ten years older than Paulette. His name is Bollinet but that's not all. He's married with a baby and another child on the way.'

'Oh no, that poor child,' said Florence. 'How do you know this? Have you talked to her?'

'No, I happened to see them having a row in his car when I was in Périgueux. He directed a play she was in last term.'

'I'm not going to ask how you tracked him down but for once I'm grateful for your snooping. What do you think we should do?'

'I'm not sure. I think Paulette deserves to know about Bollinet's wife being pregnant, but it's possible that she already does. That could be what the row was about. I wanted your advice, whether I should tell her, or you, or the two of us together. The sooner the better, I think, and it may be easier to talk to her in Périgueux in the week than once she gets home to her parents' place this weekend while the gossip spreads.'

'Who exactly knows about this in town?'

'The Mayor overheard two women talking in hushed tones about it in the Mairie, both of them employees.'

'Have you told Fabiola?'

'Not yet, I wanted to see you first.'

'Why? She's the doctor.'

'You're much closer to Paulette than she is and you're a single mother. You can tell her what it means.'

Florence rolled her eyes and looked down fondly at her children. 'It's not bad when you get used to it. I love being their mother.'

'It helps when you have a decent job and almost free accommodation,' said Bruno. 'That won't be the case for Paulette. And I remember how tough things were for you when we first met in Sainte Alvère before you got this job, having to put up with part-time work that was way below your talents and with a lecherous bastard for a boss. You weren't happy then.'

'It doesn't have to be like that for her. She has her parents here.' Florence paused, looking off through the window at the church spire. It seemed to trigger a thought. 'But I can imagine how the atmosphere would be in that home, the silent recriminations, church every Sunday, doing penance.'

She sat up and looked him in the eye. 'All right, I'll do it, but we'll both go. I'll talk to her. You should hover out of earshot but be ready to step in when I call for you or she asks for you to join us. When do you want to do this?'

'As soon as we can. How are you fixed for time?'

'I'm not, but we'll make time. I'll have to find a babysitter. I can't ask Miranda, with the cooking school. But Jack will be looking after her children so two more won't hurt him.'

'Jack had to leave town, called back to England. Gilles can do it, or the Baron.'

'That's all right, I'll get one of my schoolgirls,' she said, smiling. 'I have rather more faith in them. I'd better call Paulette, see if we can drive up there this evening.' She picked up the phone, scrolled through her contacts, pressed a couple of buttons and waited while Bruno listened intently.

'Paulette? It's Florence in St Denis. Could you possibly make some time to see me this evening?'

Bruno wished he could hear the other end of the call but had to wait, controlling his impatience, until Florence spoke again.

'I'll tell you when I see you but it's important.'

Another pause. Bruno bit his lip.

'Yes, we can be there at seven. Shall we meet at that wine bar on the Avenue Woodrow Wilson that we went to before? Yes? Fine, see you then.' She ended the call and put her phone back on the shelf, high above prying infant hands.

'How did she sound?' Bruno asked.

'Just like herself, a bit tense. We'll have to leave at six fifteen, it won't be rush hour but it will still be busy at that time. And we can't take your police van, nor should you wear uniform. Can you get your Land Rover?'

'No problem, I'll be here at six.' He rose to go. 'Thank you, Florence.'

'Just remember, this has to be for Paulette to decide. Not you, not me, not the Pope in Rome. She's the one who matters here.'

Bruno had time to walk his dog and tend his geese and chickens before having a quick shower and changing into jeans, a clean shirt and his blazer. He reached for the phone to call Pamela to say he would not be able to exercise the horses that evening but it rang just before he touched it.

'*Mon Dieu*,' he said on hearing her voice. 'That's a coincidence. I was just picking up the phone to call you, to say I have to be in Périgueux so can't come riding this evening.'

'That's fine, no problem. Kathleen has been hoping to ride your Hector, but look, Bruno, this is an emergency. Jack Crimson has left for London, something urgent came up. That leaves me right in the lurch without a guide for tomorrow's vineyard tour. Could you possibly help?'

'I'm not qualified and I don't know all those English terms. What about Hubert from the *cave*? He speaks good English and is a real expert.'

'He's at some wine fair in Düsseldorf.'

'There's Julien at the town vineyard.'

'Not enough English. And I already tried Monique at the wine bar in town but she's got a dentist's appointment. Anyway, the arrangements are all made for the visits and you know all the *vignerons*. You even get to have lunch with the clients at the Tour des Vents at Monbazillac. But if you're too busy for lunch you can pick them up at the restaurant but you'd better be there by two o'clock. I'm taking them around Bergerac and the Monbazillac chateau in the morning, and we'll taste some Monbazillac there as our *apéritif*. You have tastings arranged at Château Lestevenie, at Château de la Jaubertie and then ending with your own dear Château de Tiregand. It's all set up. You just have to give me three or four hours to help me out.'

'I'll make it work somehow,' he said, knowing he could

not turn her down. 'But you know, if a police emergency comes up . . .'

'Yes, but now you're in charge of the whole valley you have other policemen working for you and you can ask them to do it. I'm very grateful, dear Bruno. Let me know in the morning if you can join us for lunch and if I know my Bruno you're not going to turn down the chance to eat at a place with a Michelin star. I'll have the minibus with me and we can swap vehicles at the restaurant. You can take them all in the minibus and I'll bring back your Land Rover.'

He agreed and then listened to the news headlines at six on his radio before driving to collect Florence. They were still referring to the dead man as McBride and Monika as the wife of a wealthy English businessman. Inevitably they were reporting it as a *crime passionnel*, a tragic end to an illicit romance and the kind of story the French love. Bruno had already had a call from Gilles, who had been asked to file a report for his old employer, *Paris Match*. If only Gilles knew what his friend Crimson had just recounted to Bruno, he'd have a dramatic tale and a real exclusive.

Florence was looking lovely when he knocked on her door, in a blue dress that somehow lifted the colour in her grey eyes, simple pearl earrings and a belt of dark blue leather that was studded with silver coins, matching a simple silver necklace. Usually he saw her in the bland suits or white lab coat she wore for teaching or wearing an apron over a pair of jeans. Dressed up, she looked a different woman.

'You look terrific,' he said, before Dora and Daniel descended on him for a goodnight kiss. Muriel from one of his tennis classes was grinning at him from the door to the children's bedroom. He and Florence extricated themselves and headed down to his Land Rover.

'What are you going to say?' he asked as he drove past Lespinasse's garage on the road to Périgueux.

'It will depend a bit on the mood she's in, but at some point I'll have to tell her that we know who the father is and we also know his own family circumstances. If she goes ahead and has the baby despite that, then I'll say we will continue to support her as best we can. That's probably the point at which I'll ask you to join us, and you'd better have a cheerful story to tell her. We have to leave her persuaded that this isn't the end of the world, she can still go to university and pick up her sporting career. And we'll help her all the way.'

'Right,' said Bruno. 'I can do that.'

They arrived at the wine bar a few minutes early. The tables outside were full, mainly of people smoking and Florence said she'd prefer to be inside anyway, where they might find a table quiet enough for privacy. She asked for a glass of chilled Monbazillac and sat alone by the door. Bruno got her drink and a glass of Bergerac Sec for himself and then found a spot that was partly hidden by the bar counter.

About five minutes later, Paulette arrived, looking pretty in jeans, leather boots and a heavy fisherman's sweater. Her hair had been loosened from its usual bun, her eyes were made up and her lipstick boldly crimson. She embraced Florence before she sat down and ordered a mineral water. From what Bruno could see they exchanged small talk until her drink arrived and then Florence leaned forward, put her hand on Paulette's arm and spoke urgently.

Paulette responded curtly. Florence spoke again. Paulette pulled her arm from Florence's grip and tossed her hair angrily, as if about to stand up and storm out. Florence kept on talking and then someone took a position at the bar that blocked Bruno's view. He tried to crane his neck to see but it was hopeless. And there were no other tables or places where he could station himself without coming into Paulette's line of sight. He stood, most of his view still blocked by the man at the bar, but he could see part of Florence's head. She wasn't talking, which meant Paulette must be replying and had not walked out.

Instead, she had come to find him, walking around the bar and catching his eye. She must have known he was there. Her face was set, determined, but not angry. She forced a thin smile.

'Thank you for your concern, Bruno, and thank you for everything. Florence knows what I'm thinking so I'll let her tell you.' She leaned forward, pecked him on the cheek and left.

Bruno took her place at Florence's table, and looked at Florence who was staring into the distance, as if not yet aware of his presence. He remained silent, twirling his almost empty glass in his fingers.

Finally, Florence spoke, her voice dull. 'I don't know for the life of me if we've done the right thing. She knew Bollinet was married with a child. She didn't know his wife was pregnant but she said she was not greatly surprised. But that was nothing to do with her and why did we think he was the father?'

'What did you say to that?' Bruno asked.

'She didn't give me time to interrupt. She just said whoever the father was, it was no business of ours and anyway, the affair was over. She's already thinking about having an abortion and has an appointment with a gynaecologist at the hospital here next week. I suggested I would go with her but she said she had a school friend who would be there.'

A silence fell between them, all the heavier because of the chatter and laughter of the people around them.

'Can I get you another drink?'

Florence shook her head. 'No, thanks.'

'Perhaps you'd let me take you to dinner here in Périgueux,' he asked, hesitantly, more to break the silence than because he was hungry.

'Thank you, Bruno, and any other time I'd be delighted to go out to dinner with you but not this evening. It's all so depressing. I just want to go home to my children and think about this.'

Florence barely spoke on the forty-minute drive back to St Denis even though, in the absence of a radio in his elderly Land Rover, Bruno tried various topics of conversation. The progress of the *collège* garden and the computer club, both of which she had launched, failed to stimulate her. It was only when Bruno asked whether Paulette had said anything more about the father of her baby that she responded.

'I wonder if it was really him. You might have misinterpreted that scene you saw in the car park.'

'Who else?' he replied. 'She doesn't seem that close to anyone in St Denis.'

'It could be someone else in Périgueux. We don't know much

about her life there and she doesn't seem at all ready to tell us. And why should she?'

Florence pecked him on the cheek when he drew up in front of her apartment and darted inside. Bruno was hungry now and not particularly keen on his own company so he drove to the Bar des Amateurs where he'd be sure to meet some friends from the rugby club. He turned into the old parade ground opposite the Gendarmerie, now used as overflow for the market and for parking. Only a handful of other cars were there but he saw the glow of a cigarette in one of them. A strange place for a courting couple, he thought as he entered the bar.

Half a dozen men turned to greet him from watching football on the big TV screen where Paris St Germain was beating the Girondins of Bordeaux. Gilbert, a big, hook-nosed man whose jumping skills helped the St Denis rugby team win line-outs, was behind the bar and he poured Bruno a beer without being asked.

'Is it this week when we should hear about the national team?' Gilbert enquired. 'It will be great if Paulette gets selected.'

'The list should be announced Saturday, so fingers crossed,' said Bruno, relieved that the gossip about Paulette's pregnancy had not reached this far. 'Can you do me a pizza? Just cheese and tomato, maybe some ham if you have it.'

He watched the game, cheering with the others when the Girondins equalized, groaning when Paris scored again, and then Gilbert's wife came out from the kitchen with a tray full of pizzas and salad. Three of the men sat down to eat with him, keeping an eye on the match and sharing a carafe of the house red wine from the local vineyard. Bordeaux lost by a single goal and they were watching the post-match interviews when the bar was illuminated by someone's headlights coming into the parking lot. Then Bruno heard the slam of car doors and a shout.

He turned to look and saw silhouettes moving against the flare of the headlights and what looked like a scuffle with blows being struck – even over the noise of the TV he could hear grunts of pain. Were they mad, to fight in front of the Gendarmerie? He rose and went out, trying to shield his eyes against the glare to see what was happening. It looked like two men beating up a third. Bruno called to Gilbert for support and ran forward into the fight, shouting 'Police. Stop this.'

One man with blood on his face was being held by another while a second man was punching the first in the stomach. He had time for three hard blows before Bruno was on him, grabbing the arm of the man swinging the punches, twisting it hard behind his back and kicking his feet from under him.

'Police,' he shouted again, and then half-fell as the man being punched was hurled bodily into him. By then Gilbert and some others from the rugby team were there. Gilbert kicked the second man between his legs, he sank down and the fight was over.

Bruno was kneeling on the back of the man he had felled, searched in his trousers pocket for a wallet and pulled it out, finding an identity card.

'Gilbert, could you inform the gendarmes we have some customers for them, please?' he said, and asked Lespinasse to take his place holding down the man on the ground. Still chewing some pizza, Lespinasse mumbled agreement. The man kicked in the balls was going nowhere and Bruno turned to see how badly they had beaten the man they'd been attacking. He was on his hands and knees, groaning and being sick. He raised his head and Bruno recognized Philippe Delaron. Sergeant Jules arrived from the Gendarmerie with some handcuffs, applied them to the wrists of the two attackers and they were hauled away.

Philippe had a nose bleed and had taken a few punches to the stomach. Raoul, a volunteer fireman who was the rugby team's medical attendant, took him into the bar, looked him over and said he'd seen worse damage on the rugby field. The blood down his shirt made it look worse than it was. When he could talk without panting, Philippe said it was a fight about a woman called Mathilde and he did not want to file a formal complaint against the two men.

In the Gendarmerie, Bruno established that the two attackers were cousins, sawmill workers from La Douze, just up the valley, and they had been lying in wait for Philippe 'to teach that bastard reporter a lesson'. Fabrice, the one whose wallet Bruno had taken, was engaged to a young woman from Journiac. Philippe, who had a reputation in such matters, had managed to seduce her. And in the course of a row earlier that day between Fabrice and Mathilde, she had suggested that her fiancé wasn't half the man that Philippe was. Masculine pride being what it was, Fabrice had collected his cousin and over a few drinks they had decided to come and take their revenge on the Casanova of St Denis.

'I reckon young Philippe had that coming. You know his

reputation with the girls,' Sergeant Jules said to Bruno when the two cousins had been put in separate cells to cool off. 'But we can't hold those two unless Philippe files a formal complaint, or you do.'

'Get your breathalyser kit and leave the talking to me,' said Bruno, and led the way down to Fabrice's cell, collecting the cousin on the way.

'You've been drinking while in charge of a vehicle,' he began. 'And your cousin threw Philippe at me while I was making an arrest and had identified myself as a police officer. That's assault. Since I can smell the booze on your breath, we'll start with a breath test.'

'If I lose my driving licence, I'll lose my job,' said Fabrice, nursing his twisted arm. 'And that bastard Philippe Delaron needs a good smacking. My Mathilde's not the only one he's been after, with his press pass and his fancy camera, offering to take studio portraits of all the girls in the valley.'

'I'll give you a choice,' said Bruno. 'We can do the breath test and I file a charge of assaulting a policeman and we take a statement from Philippe and the law takes its course. Or you two stay in the cells overnight and in the morning we'll release you without any charges. I'll tell Philippe he got off lightly and then we'll all forget this happened and I can get back to the pizza I was enjoying when you two fools interrupted me. What do you say?'

'We'll stay here tonight,' said Fabrice and his cousin nodded in agreement.

11

When he awoke the next morning Bruno found a text message on his phone from J-J. This morning's meeting was cancelled while the magistrate reviewed all the case files. It would probably be held in the evening instead. That meant Bruno could exercise his horse, something he'd been missing. He took a brisk jog through the woods with Balzac, fed his chickens and with his uniform in the back of his van, he drove to the Gendarmerie to find Fabrice and his cousin had already gone. He went on to Pamela's riding school. It was still early, only a little after seven, but the light was on in the barn where he found Pamela and Miranda brewing coffee and setting tables for breakfast. There was a smell of baking and through the glass door of the oven Bruno could see a tray of bread rolls. He kissed them both, accepted a coffee and a glass of apple juice and told them the bread smelled wonderful. He asked them if anyone else would be riding that morning.

'Just me and Félix and maybe Kathleen if she's up in time. She went out for dinner and the light was on in her *gîte* until late. I think she had a visitor,' Pamela said with a grin. 'Not a car I recognized, I think it might have been a rental.'

'She said something about her paper's Paris correspondent being sent down to write about the murder,' Bruno said.

'Hector will be pleased to see you. He was a bit frisky with Kathleen yesterday. You'll find Félix in the stables, saddling up. You might take him his coffee. He takes it with milk, two sugars.'

Bruno walked carefully across the yard behind Balzac, balancing two cups and trying not to spill anything, when he saw Kathleen coming down from her *gîte*. She was dressed for riding. She waved a greeting and he told her she'd find fresh coffee in the barn.

A few minutes later, when Hector began to canter as the slope flattened and the plateau opened out before him, Bruno knew he'd been missing this. The sun was hidden behind a long bank of cloud, but it was strong enough to give a magical gilding to the tips and edges of the cloud. The sky was a pale blue that promised a fine day to come. The air smelled fresh and new and some of the trees in the woods down the slope had gone beyond budding to produce delicate leaves.

'You two go on ahead,' Pamela called. 'We'll see you at the quarry.'

She and Félix each had a string of horses on a long rein, and she kept them to a gentle trot. Kathleen leaned forward in the saddle, tapped the Andalusian horse with her heels and urged her mount into a swift canter that soon became a gallop. Hector needed no signal from Bruno to follow suit and the ride became thrilling, their speed creating its own wind in Bruno's face. That sudden, intense moment of communion between horse and rider came upon him and Bruno could feel each of the mighty muscles beneath him gathering, stretching and then contracting.

Hector hated to see another horse's heels ahead of him. He caught up with Kathleen as they reached the firebreak through the trees, barely wide enough for two horses to gallop side by side, but the nimble Andalusian was still a nose ahead. Not wanting to take a risk with one of Pamela's customers on an unfamiliar horse, Bruno pulled firmly on the reins and Hector reluctantly but obediently slowed, snorting to let Bruno know his displeasure. Bruno patted his horse's neck by way of apology, trying to convey his confidence that of course Hector could have won the race. He loosened the reins a little and Hector eased into that smooth not-quite-gallop that he could keep up for hours. By the time they reached the end of the firebreak they were close behind the Andalusian, tiring now, but then Hector slowed of his own accord, knowing this route and the location of the bridle path down through the trees. Kathleen had gone beyond it and Bruno called her back.

'This way,' he shouted, waiting to be sure she had heard and then waiting a little more until she turned her horse and came trotting towards him. She gave him a cheeky grin, as if to emphasize what she surely felt to be her victory. Bruno smiled indulgently. He would not spoil her moment by saying he'd held back Hector in case she had trouble handling her own steed when Hector came thundering alongside.

He led the way down to the hunter's trail that skirted the woods and ended at the quarry. Hector set off at a fast pace until he rounded the bend and saw the other horses ahead,

Pamela and Félix having taken the short route. Bruno reined in to let Kathleen catch up.

'What a lovely horse this is, as fast as the wind,' Kathleen said, coming alongside and slowing her horse. She was breathing hard and her face was glowing. 'That was a glorious ride.'

'It certainly was,' he agreed. 'You must have been riding for some time.'

'Since I was a little girl. I had my first pony at the age of six. There was a time when I thought I might go in for competitions but I broke a collarbone and then came exams that I had to pass to go to university.' She shrugged. 'No regrets, that's how life goes.'

'Do you still ride in England?'

'Not in London. It costs an arm and a leg and I travel so much for my job. But my parents live in the country where my childhood sweetheart runs a stable so I keep my horse there and in return I let him use it for his riding school. It's not an ideal solution. Novice riders can ruin a horse's mouth and upset its temperament but it's the best I can do.' As they caught up with Pamela and Félix she asked, 'Why haven't you come riding in the mornings before?'

'I usually do, but we've had meetings at police HQ in Périgueux,' he answered before he could stop himself. *Merde*, he thought. She'll know I'm part of the team on this murder case.

'On Monika Felder's murder?'

'Boring administrative stuff, learning new computer systems and doing my annual firearms check on the range.' It wasn't entirely a lie.

'So you're no longer involved in the case?'

'I'm riding today, am I not? And what about you? Didn't you say your paper's Paris correspondent was coming down to take over?'

'Yes, but he's thinking of going back to Paris already,' she said, rather too casually, and Bruno recalled J-J's warning about the media.

'I spoke to him last night,' she went on. 'Our crime expert back in London says he's heard that the heat is going off the case. It looks as though Monika was killed by this mystery man claiming to be McBride who then hanged himself. Is that what you hear?'

'So it seems,' said Bruno, relieved to hear the press had not yet picked up on the possible IRA connection.

'That's what Philippe Delaron from *Sud Ouest* told us. He's been very helpful so Gordon – that's our man in Paris – took us both to dinner at the Vieux Logis in Trémolat last night. Philippe seems to know you quite well.'

'St Denis is a small town.'

'And Philippe says you know pretty much everything that happens in this region.' She nudged her horse so they were riding very close, almost knee to knee, and lowered her voice. 'So I'd really be very grateful for any guidance you can give me on this story. Life isn't easy for a freelance journalist in these days of the internet and this could be a big chance for me.'

Her meaning was obvious enough, Bruno thought, but it was depressing to be seen as a man who could be so easily tempted by the suggestion of sexual favours. She seemed generous about spreading them – he recalled Pamela saying that

Kathleen had been entertaining a late-night visitor the previous evening.

He said nothing but edged his horse away and looked back, saying he wanted to be sure that Balzac was still with them. When Balzac finally caught up, Bruno took refuge in talking about his dog until they reached the rear entrance to the riding school. He swung down, led Hector into the stables, removed his saddle and began to rub him down.

'You'd better hurry up and get some breakfast,' Pamela told Kathleen as she came in with her own saddle. 'We're off to the truffle expert soon and you'll see Bruno again later today. He'll be guiding you all round the vineyards.'

'Oh good. Will Balzac come too?' Kathleen said, squatting on the ground and petting the basset hound.

Balzac, who had a particular fondness for women, rolled onto his back, inviting her to scratch his tummy. He then closed his eyes and looked ecstatically happy when she complied, all the while telling him what a fine and handsome dog he was. She looked and sounded as though she meant it, but Bruno's suspicions of her motives remained as he strolled up to Pamela's house to shower, shave and change into his uniform before heading for the Mairie.

Juliette's message from Les Eyzies was longer than the usual 'routine patrols'. She had added 'possible smuggling inquiry'. He phoned her and learned that the local tobacconist was complaining of a sudden drop in cigarette sales, which meant that somebody had obtained a cheaper supply.

'Let me come over to Les Eyzies and buy you a coffee,' he said. As he drove there along the River Vézère, he pondered how best to explain to a keen but inexperienced policewoman that the law was one thing but enforcement was quite another. They took an outside table at the Hostellerie du Passeur that did all sorts of fancy mochas and lattes but they ordered the traditional small espresso and Bruno began Juliette's education in the realities of village policing life.

'This always happens between December and March,' he explained. 'It tends to peak in the school holidays when coach-loads of ski clubs and school trips drive to the Pyrenees. Most of them go to Spain because the hotels and restaurants are cheaper and so are the cigarettes. And the smart ones visit Andorra which is virtually tax free, fifteen euros for a carton of cigarettes compared to seventy here in France. Everybody comes back with at least a couple of cartons, plus food mixers, wide-screen TVs, laptops. You can bring back up to five hundred euros of manufactured goods. That means a big family can pretty much pay for the ski trip. And the return trip is free because you can fill up a car or van with diesel or petrol for about ten euros in Andorra.'

'What do we do about it?'

'Does your Mayor smoke?'

'I don't know. My dad does, though.'

'And he's on the council. My Mayor smokes a pipe. I'm pretty sure he'd be unhappy if I went around persecuting his fellow smokers. It's the kind of thing that can lose a lot of votes. What's more, most of those tax-free cigarettes are legal because they only come in as duty-free allowances during the peak skiing season. And as far as French voters are concerned a little fiddle like this is one of the minor pleasures of life. It means they've got the better of the state.'

'You sound as though you approve.' Juliette was looking confused.

'I don't mean to do that. Let me put it this way: it's not our job. It's up to the *douanes* to enforce our customs laws. That's why they're stationed at the border. If they wanted, they could stop every vehicle returning to France from Andorra and they would probably find a few cartons of cigarettes more than the regulations allow. The people they want are professional smugglers who ship stuff out by the truckload.'

'So we ignore it?' Her tone was doubtful.

'Oh no, that would never do. The public has to know that we know what they're up to,' Bruno replied, smiling. 'Say you're in a café and you see someone's packet of cigarettes on the bar or on the table. Pick it up and look for the little printed mark that says *Vente en France*. That shows French taxes were paid. If you don't see that, you can say, "A good trip abroad, was it? Lots of duty-free?" Word will go round that you're no fool, but neither are you looking to give people a hard time.'

'They don't teach us that at the police academy.'

'Well, in my experience they do, they just don't teach it in the classroom. It's what you hear over a drink in the bar from the old veterans, or at the booze-up after your graduation parade. You know Louise, your predecessor. Take her out for a pizza one evening and ask her advice because there'll be aspects of being a female cop which I can't help you with.'

'Thanks for the tip. But what do I tell the tobacconist? I promised her that I'd look into it.'

'You have. You consulted your senior officer. You tell her that inquiries at a much higher level have established this pattern of people coming back from ski trips. It's the same in summer when they come back from abroad. They bring in enough cheap fags to keep going for a couple of weeks and then they're back in the usual *tabac*. So you tell her it's the duty-free allowances and you shrug and commiserate a bit. If it were me, I'd express some surprise that she hadn't noted this seasonal pattern already. Every other tobacconist in France knows it well.'

'You think she's trying it on with me?'

'Probably. People try to test us a bit, see if we're a soft touch, what they can get away with. It's normal, the way people are. Pretty soon the novelty will wear off and they'll get used to you and remember that you grew up here.'

'Okay. Now is there anything you can tell me about the murder case? People keep asking me about it.'

'I can imagine. You were at school with Philippe Delaron, weren't you? I bet he's been at you.'

Juliette blushed. 'Yes, well, we went out together for a bit when we were at the *collège*. I know where he heard about the dead man being McBride. He got it from Sylvain. They were at the *lycée* together in Sarlat.'

'You're going to be good at this,' Bruno said. 'You're already putting the patterns together, working out who knows whom, and why.'

'Beware of flatterers,' she said, smiling in response.

'Don't blame yourself. You'll be dealing with Philippe for years to come. Cops and reporters, we're often covering the same case. We have to stay in contact. Anyway, another guy from *Sud Ouest* just happened to be one of the neighbours you visited that afternoon to ask if they had seen anything suspicious. It was a coincidence. These things happen.'

'So he killed her and then hanged himself?'

'That's the most obvious explanation but J-J is still working on it. I understand the pathology is not conclusive, but this stuff is all way above my head. Anything else I can help you with?'

'Do you get anonymous letters?'

'Yes, we all do. They've been a feature of French life for more than two hundred years, ever since the Revolution when people started denouncing their neighbours, often in the hope of grabbing their land. I get two or three a week, glance through to see if I recognize the handwriting or typeface. We have to file them and if we get a visit from the Inspector General, he'll want to see them and ask what action you took. Most of the ones I get are pathetic, dark suspicions about other people's sex lives. You can ignore those. Some of the others have a bit of fire beneath the smoke, usually the ones about people working on the side without paying taxes. This is where you have to use your common sense. If you are told about the same person two or three times, go and have a friendly chat with them and say how embarrassing it would be to call in the *fisc* police. If they're working for foreigners, explain to the foreigners about the *chèque service* system. The employer pays a surcharge which covers the social security payment but also insures the employer against any injury the worker gets on the job. It could save them a fortune. The Mairie will have pamphlets about it.'

'Any more advice?'

'Make a courtesy call to every house in your *commune* at

least once a year and leave each of them your card with your mobile phone number. Make a note of birthdays and weddings and baptisms. Make yourself into a friendly fixture of everyone's life and find some way to have regular involvement with all the kids, just as you got to know me through tennis.'

Bruno drove home to pick up his Land Rover and a civilian shirt and jacket. He put his uniform on a hanger and hung it on the hook in the back of his vehicle. He texted Claire at the Mairie that he was taking the afternoon off because he'd be spending the evening at police HQ in Périgueux. Then he called Prunier's secretary to ask what time the meeting would be.

'We still don't know, but certainly after six. That's when the Paris plane gets in and there are a couple of people coming down to talk about the case. One has an English name, Hodge. That's all I know. I'll text you as soon as a time is confirmed.'

Bruno took the road through Le Buisson and Lalinde to get to the roundabout by Bergerac airport and then drove through the vineyards, a landscape he always enjoyed. He found the neat rows of vines calming, making the world seem an orderly and well-tended place. Being a winemaker was another of alternative fantasy lives he occasionally dreamed up for himself, along with being an archaeologist and the manager of a top-rank rugby club. When he'd been a boy, he'd wanted to be a fighter pilot. Perhaps when he grew older the fantasies would change again but he suspected the lure of the vines would always be at the back of his mind. Which was why he liked to help out his friends by picking grapes at harvest time, sharing in that glorious sense of abundance when basket after basket of grapes was tumbled into the giant vats.

The landscape was changing as he approached the slope that rose to the low ridge looking down onto the town of Bergerac. Fewer of the vineyards presented the traditional disciplined appearance of soldiers on parade in straight lines with gleaming white chalk and gravel between the rows. More and more of them showed grass between the vines, some of it trimmed but increasingly left to grow for the insects and wildlife to flourish as more vineyards became organic. As a boy, he'd been accustomed to seeing the workers wearing masks as they treated the vines with chemicals that had now been withdrawn as too dangerous. That was the fashion then, when so-called scientific farming was all the rage. Now the fashion was changing. After Alsace, the Bergerac vineyards were the most organic in France and in Bruno's view the wine was all the better for it.

As his vehicle began to climb, Bruno could see the pointed turrets of the Château de Monbazillac. It was a Renaissance jewel, built just after King Francis I came back from his Italian wars in the early sixteenth century, bringing with him Leonardo da Vinci and the new style and learning that had enchanted the French. Now a museum, it was at the heart of the Monbazillac *appellation* and symbolized the venerable heritage of the region's wines.

He saw Pamela's minivan already parked in the forecourt of La Tour des Vents restaurant and hastened inside to join her and her clients. He'd been looking forward to this lunch since he had a deep respect for Marie Rougier, the self-taught chef. She had taken over her mother's small vineyard and modest restaurant serving *crèpes* and slowly but surely transformed it into one of the handful of restaurants in the region with a Michelin rosette. Bruno had eaten there only once, invited by J-J in return for his help on a difficult case, and they had feasted on her signature dish, *ris de veau à l'ancienne.* He recalled it also as the first time he'd tasted a lovely Bergerac red wine from the nearby vineyard of Clos d'Yvigne.

Today they offered what was known in France as a light lunch, a *formule pause déjeuner.* Today that meant a first course of fresh asparagus in a rich *brouillade* of fresh eggs and butter, and a main course of a duet of capon, the thigh as a *confit* and the breast served roasted with spiced aubergine. The dessert was another signature dish, a presentation of chocolate mousse, bananas flambé and home-made caramel and rum ice cream. Not bad for thirty-five euros, Bruno thought as he scanned the menu and considered how many people would be working in the kitchen of a Michelin-starred restaurant. It was a place that had traditionally kept its prices down by growing its own food.

A chorus of greetings welcomed him as Bruno took the place that had been left for him, one of the younger wives to one side and the schoolteacher, Alice, on the other. The younger woman, whose name he recalled just in time was Nicole, asked him in stilted French how he would define a *brouillade.*

'A scrambled egg cooked in the very best butter by angels, with a little cream added, and taken from the heat while not quite set and placed on a very warm plate so when it arrives before you it is perfect,' he replied. 'It is not easy to get the timing right. I almost never succeed.'

'Tell us about the vineyards we're going to visit,' said Alice.

'We are seeing two that are run by English people,' he told

them carefully in English. 'Château Lestevenie is run by a man whose wife has a seat in your House of Lords. He makes very good wine from the Cabernet Franc grape. Most Bergerac wine comes from Merlot and Cabernet Sauvignon grapes. His name is hard for a French person to pronounce, it sounds like Omfray.'

'Humphrey?' suggested Nicole.

'Exactly, thank you,' said Bruno. 'Then we go to Château de la Jaubertie, which used to be a hunting lodge for my favourite King of France, Henri IV. It was bought nearly fifty years ago by the Ryman family, great innovators, using new techniques developed in California and Australia. They pick the grapes for white wine at night when it is cooler, and keep them chilled. And they use green harvesting, taking out some grapes in early summer so the others ripen better. They were among the first to reintroduce the old grape, Malbec, in some of their red wines. Their cuvée Mirabelle, hand-picked from specially chosen grapes, is magnificent, full of fruit and very smooth. Then we go to Château de Tiregand, one of my favourites, an elegant and classic wine of the Pécharmant, a small and special region. The name means hill of charm.'

'We chose these wines because if you like them, you can get them in England,' Pamela said from the end of the table, tapping her glass with a spoon to gain their attention. 'Before you leave, I'll give each of you a brochure which tells you where to find these wines and other essentials like duck fat and walnut oil.'

'And if we have time, we might also visit a friend of mine, Pierre Desmartis. He speaks a little English,' said Bruno. 'His wine won the gold medal year after year at the big exposition in Paris.'

The *brouillade* arrived and, as always in a fine restaurant, Bruno wondered what kitchen magic allowed them to produce nine plates, each with perfect *brouillade*, at precisely the same time.

'*Bon appetit*,' he declared, and took a tiny sip of the white wine, noting that Pamela had ordered a Jaubertie. He would allow himself a half glass of white and another half glass of red. That was all since he would be driving. He'd be careful to taste and spit at the *dégustations*.

'How was your visit to Château de Monbazillac?' he asked Nicole, who replied that she greatly admired the building but liked the wine even more.

'I loved it when you served their wine with the foie gras but I had no idea it would make such a good aperitif,' she said.

As their plates were removed, Bruno again wondered at the precision of the restaurant's organization. He knew from friends in the restaurant trade that there was a rule of thumb that a good *maître d'hotel* used to plan the time the diners were allowed between courses. A relatively large group such as theirs, who tended to take longer over each course, or a table with young children who were easily bored, were usually given a fairly short pause at lunch, between five and seven minutes. A romantic couple, staring into each other's eyes, would be allowed ten to fifteen minutes. The timings were different at dinner, when it was assumed guests liked to linger over their food and there were usually more courses.

Bruno used the interval to sketch briefly the history of the wine of Bergerac from Roman times, the destruction of the vineyards in the Arab invasion of the eighth century, the role of the monks in re-founding the vineyards and developing the sweet wine of Monbazillac. In Bruno's experience, the English loved to hear of the importance of their country in developing and expanding the French wine trade. From 1152, when Eleanor, Duchess of Aquitaine, married England's King Henry II, until 1453 when they were finally driven from their last bastions in the south-west corner of France, the English had transformed the French wine trade and become its best customers. The whole of what was now known as the Bordeaux wine region was in English hands, along with much of the Bergerac.

Even before the Hundred Years War, when prices rose due to the heavy taxes the French kings imposed on the sweet wines made by the monks of Bergerac, the English offered the monks tax-free status if they moved to their side of the Dordogne river. It proved to be an excellent location for the wines that became known as Monbazillac. In the Médoc, in St Emilion and in the Bergerac the English established a system of self-government and quality control for the wine trade. The Consulat de la Vinée de Bergerac was founded by the English nearly eight centuries ago and existed to this day, Bruno explained.

Dutch tourists, by contrast, enjoyed hearing of their importance for the wine trade in the seventeenth and eighteenth centuries. The Bergerac was a Protestant region so many of the region's winemakers fled to Holland and England to escape the religious intolerance of Louis XIV and established themselves as wine importers. The ones in Holland invented the concept of the brand. They urged the winemakers in Bergerac to begin stamping their barrels with the Consulat's symbol of a griffon's claw and later, when they began pasting labels onto their bottles, inscribed them with special insignia like the pine tree of Château Tirecul la Gravière. To this day, the best of the Monbazillac vineyards are still entitled to call themselves *Marque Hollandaise*.

'I know that you English think of your King John as a bad monarch, although he gave you Magna Carta,' Bruno went on. 'But did you know that he invented the wine of St Emilion? He granted land to peasants there on condition that they cut down the woodland and grew grapes.'

Bruno was aware that he was, as the English phrase put it, singing for his supper. Pamela expected him to entertain her customers as well as guide them, and he took his obligations to her seriously. He also enjoyed talking about the wines of his region and sharing his fondness for them. But he felt more than recompensed by this very fine meal as the capon was put before him, the breast perfectly roasted and the *confit* making the thigh as juicy as it was tender. He saw with approval that the waiters were offering red wine from Tiregand to go with the fowl and took a sip of the half glass he permitted himself.

Pamela's clients were arranging themselves in the minibus when Bruno's phone signalled an incoming message. It was from Marie-Pierre, Prunier's secretary, to say that Prunier was to host a working dinner in his conference room at police HQ with Ardouin, the magistrate, J-J and some officials from Paris. Bruno should arrive in time to begin at eight.

'Will do,' he texted back. 'Who is providing the food?'

'Police canteen,' came the laconic reply. Bruno settled himself behind the wheel of the minibus to visit the first vineyard on his list. Ah well, he thought. At least I've had a memorable lunch. He noted that Kathleen had managed the seating so that she was alongside him in the passenger seat.

12

It could have been worse, Bruno thought, surveying the dishes of various salads, cheeses and plates of cold chicken. Even the police canteen couldn't mess them up. But the baguettes had that uniform look that suggested they had come from a supermarket. Bowls of grated carrot, coleslaw and fruit salad betrayed a similar origin, as did the apple pie. Mineral water, apple juice and coffee were the only beverages.

'Welcome, Bruno,' said Prunier, rising to shake hands from his place at the head of the table. Ardouin the magistrate sat on one side of him, J-J on the other, and a stranger beside him.

'One of the people we're waiting for is an American, the FBI man at their embassy,' Prunier said. 'He has diplomatic status as a legal attaché and I assume he's here to tell us something interesting.'

The plane from Paris had arrived late, Prunier continued, but the officials would come as soon as they had checked into the Ibis hotel behind the cathedral. He introduced the stranger, a shaven-headed and burly man of Bruno's age, as a liaison officer sent from London by Scotland Yard.

'Chief Inspector Moore, Denis Moore,' the newcomer said, standing to shake Bruno's hand. He was wearing a dark suit, blue shirt and a tie of blue and white stripes with narrow yellow edging and some kind of crest. His handshake was firm without being crushing and the look from his blue eyes was direct.

'I met him on the rugby field when he was playing for the Metropolitan Police,' said Prunier with a grin. 'Like me, Denis gets his exercise as a referee these days. He's with their Special Branch, the English political police.'

'I wouldn't put it like that,' the Englishman said equably in serviceable French. He turned his gaze back to Bruno. 'The Commissioner tells me you used to play for the army.'

'Not regularly,' Bruno said. 'I only made the numbers up when one of the first-team players was injured. I'm Benoît Courrèges, chief of police for the Vézère valley, but everyone calls me Bruno.'

'Quite a coincidence, all you rugby players together,' said Ardouin, rising to shake Bruno's hand. 'At least Bruno and I share a fondness for tennis.'

It was interesting, Bruno thought, how men in a meeting always began by seeking some common ground, preferably around a neutral theme like sports rather than something potentially divisive like politics. Women, he had noticed, usually began by an exchange of mutual compliments on their dress, or with talk of their children. He could never decide whether this was something intrinsic to male and female natures or whether it was simply a social convention. But he knew that he always seemed to be attracted to women who broke this pattern and who fitted comfortably into male company, like Isabelle or Pamela. Florence, he suddenly thought, was one of the few who operated easily in either context. Perhaps it was something teachers had to learn.

'I want to clear up some loose ends before our friends from Paris arrive,' Ardouin continued. 'I presume we're all familiar with the interim reports from forensics and from the pathologist. It's unfortunate that they can't be more precise whether the hanging was murder or suicide. We might have to ask for a second opinion from Bordeaux or even Paris.

'Next, are we paying sufficient attention to this date-rape drug they were using? I know it was found in Madame Felder's suitcase but are we sure she brought it in or might it have been bought here or even planted? And I see no report in the file on the inquiries among local drug dealers.'

'The report will be ready tomorrow morning, but it's inconclusive, I believe,' said J-J. 'Forensics found no firm evidence of anyone else in the house so we don't think it was planted. They did find some traces in the remnants of pepper sauce on the steak. It seems that was how it was ingested.'

'And the origin of the rope?' Ardouin went on.

'Available in any hardware store. And the dead man's garage was also a workshop. There was similar rope there and in the trailer at the log pile. Some of it was used to tie bundles of branches together, presumably for kindling.'

'What would have been the minimum number of people needed if the dead man were rendered unconscious and then hanged?'

'I would think three, and they'd have to be strong,' said J-J. 'And they'd have to know the area well, perhaps by keeping the place under observation for a day or so. We're looking at all recent arrivals at hotels and letting agencies but that's a long shot. With airports at Bordeaux, Bergerac and Limoges, Ryanair alone is bringing in over a thousand people a day from the UK and Ireland. And they may have come via Belgium or Holland, travelled to Paris by train and then rented a car.'

There was a knock on the door and a uniformed officer showed in one very tall man, who must be the American, thought Bruno before his heart gave a skip at the sight of Isabelle, dwarfed by her companion. Her hair was a little longer than when he'd last seen her but her look of fierce and questioning energy was unchanged. Her presence came as a complete surprise. In view of the international aspects of the case, Bruno had been expecting the Brigadier. But it made sense to include Isabelle; she had been seconded from Eurojust to coordinate counterterrorism efforts among European member states. The bulk of her work concerned Islamic militants but the IRA would also involve her.

'*Bonsoir, messieurs*,' she began, with that smile Bruno knew so well. 'Apologies that we're late. May I present Monsieur Jason Hodge of the FBI, who is currently a legal attaché at the American Embassy.'

She then introduced each of the Périgueux team and the Scotland Yard man by name. Since she had worked with them before, Isabelle greeted Prunier, J-J and Bruno with a *bise* on each cheek. Ardouin and Moore each got a handshake.

'General Lannes sends his compliments but in view of my liaison role with international colleagues and my familiarity with the region, he asked me to take his place,' Isabelle said, effortlessly taking control of the meeting. 'Thank you for arranging this dinner, Monsieur le Commissaire, and might I suggest we begin with some new data from our American friend?'

'Fine,' Prunier replied. 'Help yourself to drinks or coffee, everyone. Let's hear what our American friends have to tell us and then perhaps Inspector Moore might brief us after Monsieur Hodge and then we should eat. This will probably be a long evening but let me say you are both very welcome.'

Isabelle took a seat at the head of the table, facing Prunier. Hodge sat beside her, brought a laptop from his case and a transparent folder filled with papers.

'You'll each be getting this digitally but I also have a print-out of the report made by the FBI into the ambush on Thunder Run alley on November 30, 2004,' Hodge began, speaking slow but excellent French. His deep, slow drawl reminded Bruno of Western movie heroes he'd enjoyed. 'I should explain,' Hodge went on, 'that "Thunder Run" was our name for that route, named for the surprise attack into the centre of Baghdad by armoured vehicles of our Third Infantry Division on April 7, 2003. That was the attack that toppled Saddam Hussein and ended the war.'

Maybe it had ended one war, Bruno thought, but it had launched another. Hodge's remark suggested to Bruno that he had been in the US military and had probably served in the Iraq war. Hodge began, apparently translating into French as he went.

'A convoy carrying eighteen million dollars in US currency was being taken from the secure zone at the airport to the treasury of the Iraqi interim government under Prime Minister

Allawi,' Hodge read. 'Because of pressing demands elsewhere on coalition military forces, the convoy was being escorted by an experienced team of twenty civilian paramilitary contractors. They were all British ex-military and equipped with armoured cars and Humvee jeeps with mounted heavy machine guns and their personal weapons, under the command of former British Army Captain Rentoul.

'The convoy was ambushed first by the detonation of explosives hidden at the roadside and then by rocket-propelled grenades. The escort vehicles at the front and rear of the convoy were badly damaged with serious casualties. Four of them were injured and three killed, including Captain Rentoul. The convoy was pinned down by heavy fire and the armoured truck with the money disappeared. The money was never recovered.

'A subsequent inquiry by US military police with FBI support looked at the possibility, despite their casualties, of this being a carefully arranged theft by some of the contractors, possibly with Iraqi help. This was judged unlikely because Captain Rentoul was a marked man. He had provoked a riot just a few days before this when he killed four Iraqi civilians in a car which he believed was a suicide vehicle. The civilians turned out to be a father with his three children in the back seat. The Iraqi government wanted Rentoul's head and he was about to be shipped out when the Iraqis made an urgent request for cash to pay police wages. Rentoul's team was available, and he volunteered to escort the convoy at no more than three hours' notice, hardly long enough to plan and set up a fake ambush and robbery. His body was badly burned but he was identified by his boss, former British General Felder, from the ID tags around his neck, his watch, and later from dental records supplied by the British authorities.'

Hodge looked up from his reading.

'We never closed the case,' he said. 'But there was little to go on and the ambush was clearly no fake.'

In bundles of $100 bills, Hodge explained, eighteen million dollars weighs almost two hundred kilos. He invited them to imagine sixteen stacks of bills, each a metre high. Naturally, the Americans had the serial numbers and subsequently found some of the bills on the bodies of Muqtadar al-Sadr's Shia militia fighters, some others circulating in Dubai and the largest amount that was recovered, thirty thousand dollars, was found in the home of an Iraqi government official who was in the pay of Iranian intelligence. More of the bills began to circulate through Hezbollah circles in Lebanon, which again were funded by Iran. The US investigators therefore assumed this had been an organized robbery by Shi'ite militants who had very close Iranian connections, and were probably acting under Iranian orders.

'So we stopped thinking Captain Rentoul could have been culpable,' Hodge went on. 'Frankly, we dropped the ball. Other crises came up and we moved on, and just wrote off the money.

'Then last night I was informed of the new questions about Captain Rentoul's fate by Commissioner Perrault here,' he went on, glancing at Isabelle. 'We can no longer conclude that he died in Iraq and obviously we now have to question the identification of the body made by General Felder. So we dug out the tape the military police made of that interview.'

Hodge clicked some of the keys on his laptop and the room

heard an American voice identifying the date, time and nature of the interview. This was followed by a cultivated English voice saying: 'I'm afraid neither I nor anyone else could make a positive ID of this corpse. It has been badly burned, charred and reduced to about half life size. The watch on the left wrist appears to be similar to the one I have seen worn by Captain Rentoul and his initials are engraved on its back. The ID tags are his. Maybe dental records would give you certainty but all I can say is that I think it's Rentoul and I'm terribly saddened by his death. He was a close friend and colleague.'

Hodge ended the digital recording and looked around the room.

'So we checked on General Felder. Thanks to information provided by the French authorities, we confirmed that he is currently in intensive care at the Anderson Cancer Center of the University of Texas in Houston. It's one of the best in the world. He has been there for the past four months and his family have rented an apartment to be near him, and where he can stay between treatments. He has terminal cancer of the oesophagus and his doctors have suggested that after the next and last round of treatment his family should consider removing him to a hospice to ease his passing. When I say his family, I should add that the apartment is rented by his two adult children and their mother, General Felder's first wife, who still uses his name. His current wife, Monika Felder, was in Houston frequently but always chose to stay in a hotel. Relations between her and the two children do not appear to be good, according to medical personnel at the hospital. She never visited her husband when the others were there, and vice versa. Usually whenever she was in Houston, at least one, and sometimes both the children would take off for a break or simply to go about their business. Their mother, Felder's first wife, was also often in the apartment with them or visiting her former husband.'

'*Mon Dieu*,' Isabelle interrupted, with a harsh laugh. 'That is either very sophisticated, very French, or there is something strange about those relationships. How do they arrange their visiting hours? Or are they keeping an eye on one another as the rich old man dies?'

'Good point,' said Prunier. 'We should look into that. But Monsieur 'Odge, please continue.'

'Here's something I find interesting,' Hodge said, in his measured way. 'If she had not been killed, it seems Monika Felder was planning to return to Houston. She was booked back into the Zaza hotel in Houston from next Tuesday, and she had a first-class return ticket from London to Houston with a confirmed booking for next Tuesday.' He shrugged and gave a lopsided half-grin, half-grimace.

'Thanks to the new information on Rentoul's finances using his identity as McBride, we have now asked the US Treasury to launch an inquiry through TFTP, the Terrorist Finance Tracking Programme, investigating those Panamanian companies and those payments Rentoul's Irish bank account has been receiving from the Caymans and similar havens. That's what we have so far. Are there any questions?'

'I have a comment,' said the English policeman, Moore, holding up a hand. 'Julian, General Felder's son, went to the Royal Military Academy, Sandhurst, and spent eight years in the

Parachute Regiment, during which time he tried but failed to secure admission to the SAS. He had various odd jobs and then worked for his father's company until four years ago when he left to become a partner in a London property agency. His sister, Portia, is a patent lawyer in private practice, also in London. She is still in Houston and her brother was taking a break at the Vail ski resort in Colorado. We emailed him and left a message with his hotel in Vail asking him to come to France to identify the body of his stepmother, Monika. If he agrees, there's a flight to Paris that could get him here to Périgueux sometime late tomorrow. But I haven't heard if he's agreed to do that. If not, we'll get someone from Felder's company to identify her body. So far we have zero information about any family she may have back in Germany but I gather our German colleagues are making inquiries.'

Moore paused and looked at Prunier. 'Shall I go on with the main part of my briefing? Or can we eat first? I haven't eaten since a sandwich on the plane this morning and I'm starving.'

'Let's get some food.' Prunier rose and led Isabelle to take the head of the line, Hodge after her. Everybody except Bruno chose the chicken. Bruno thought nostalgically about the lunch he had enjoyed and helped himself to some green salad, and cheese.

'Not many rugby players are vegetarian,' said Moore, sitting down beside him. Bruno forced a smile. He'd been hoping that Isabelle would join him but J-J, Isabelle's old boss when she'd been a humble detective in Périgueux, seemed to have monopolized her.

'Nor am I, usually,' said Bruno. 'But I had a good lunch. Tell me, this Special Branch you work for, what is it you do?'

'Special Branch no longer exists,' Moore said. 'A few years ago we merged with the anti-terrorist squad to become Counter Terrorism Command which includes intelligence. We're part of the police, which means that where the intelligence agencies don't have the power to arrest and recommend prosecutions, we do so on their behalf. Special Branch was originally founded back in the 1880s to confront Irish terrorism and that's still part of our work. I'll be briefing you about that.'

'How come you speak such good French?'

'I did Social Studies and French at university. I always liked the language and our school arranged exchange visits every year. I spent time in Paris, Lyon, Nantes and Grenoble. I met my wife on the ski slopes near Grenoble. She's originally from Perpignan. She and Isabelle have become good friends. Whenever her duties bring her to London, Isabelle comes to have dinner at our place.'

Bruno put down his fork and looked at Moore with renewed interest. This was a part of Isabelle's life of which he had no knowledge, this high-powered, international life she'd forged for herself since leaving the Périgord. And it made him think again of the dour and unimaginative school he'd attended in Bergerac, where no such international exchange visits were ever thought of.

'I wish we'd had that kind of programme at my school,' he said. 'Have you always been in this anti-terrorism unit?'

'No, I'm one of the last survivors of the old Special Branch. I even spent some time on the IRA beat, which I believe is why

I've been brought over for this, although I suppose Isabelle may have had something to do with it.'

'I thought you had peace in Northern Ireland.'

'So did I, and so we did, after a fashion, with a power-sharing government, but some of the old diehards don't give up and many of them try to raise their kids the same old way, with the same old songs and legends of the holy war against British imperialism and Protestant invaders.' Moore smiled as he said this.

Bruno went to get apple pie for himself and Moore. The tall figure of Hodge loomed up beside him.

'Were you in the military in Iraq?' Bruno asked.

'Yes, attached to the Third Infantry Division but I wasn't part of the Thunder Runs and I wasn't even fighting,' the American replied. 'I was in the Judge Advocate Corps, a military lawyer. Uncle Sam paid for me to go to law school so I did nine years in the service before joining the FBI.'

'Where did you learn your excellent French?'

'From my mom, she's French. She met my dad when he was at NATO HQ in Rocquencourt near Versailles. She brought us all up speaking French at home in Kentucky. After he left the service, my dad became a county sheriff.' He grinned. 'A bit like your job, from what Isabelle tells me.'

After apple pie and coffee, Prunier tapped his water glass with a spoon and invited Moore to give his briefing.

'As you probably all know, we have over the past twenty years seen a dramatic improvement in the security and political situation in Northern Ireland,' Moore began. 'Most members of the original IRA support the new power-sharing government in which former IRA leaders now sit alongside former Protestant militants. But the threat has not gone away. The province saw over fifty bomb attacks last year, the work of a new organization formed in 2012 and calling itself the New IRA.'

Moore went on to explain that this was an alliance of hardline anti-ceasefire republicans. It included a Londonderry-based vigilante organization and former members of the Provisional IRA's East Tyrone Brigade. These latter were the most ruthless and best-trained militants of the Republican movement and the ones responsible for the bombs that exploded in British cities, including the City of London, in the 1990s. In its first-ever communiqué, the New IRA said it had created a 'unified structure, under a single leadership' and warned of further violence against its 'age-old enemy Britain'.

Moore paused and looked around the table before continuing.

'It's clear that the threat remains and we have identified a number of former IRA militants living in France who may be prepared to offer assistance to old comrades. There are two former Provos, each of whom served time as convicted prisoners in Long Kesh and was later freed in the amnesty, who now live in the Dordogne. There are another three in the neighbouring *départements* of Corrèze and Lot-et-Garonne. All of them, we believe, bought properties and now live on the proceeds of the drug-running and protection rackets that IRA members traditionally operated to fund their operations, along with a number of bank robberies.'

Moore pushed a slim sheaf of papers across the table to Prunier. 'Here are their names, current addresses, arrest records, fingerprints and photos. If the killing of Monika Felder and

Captain Rentoul was an IRA operation, which is by no means certain, then we think those most likely to be involved are Damien O'Rourke, who runs a small construction business from his house just outside Montignac, and Sean Kelly, who runs a modest landscape gardening company based at Eymet. Neither operation appears to do much business or bring in much money. Both men have Irish passports, although, coming from Northern Ireland, Kelly is officially a British citizen. They each have wives who were also active in the Republican movement. We say these men are likely because we believe each of them had met Rentoul when he was working undercover in the late 1980s and may have recognized him recently around here.

'But I'm not yet convinced they or the New IRA were involved,' Moore concluded, with a challenging glance at each person round the table. 'My question is this – if this was an IRA execution, why aren't they boasting about it?'

'It could be to protect these two men, O'Rourke and Kelly,' said Isabelle. 'We think they were together in the vicinity of Rentoul's house. When Inspector Moore emailed details of the two men last night, I set up some initial inquiries. O'Rourke's van was caught speeding by an automatic camera at Couze, on the way to Lalinde, two weeks ago. And on the same Thursday, a market day in Lalinde, Kelly was also in the town, which as we know is near McBride's home. His vehicle got a parking ticket. I think we should pick them both up for questioning and DNA tests.'

'I agree,' said Ardouin. 'Commissaire Prunier, I leave the details up to you and your men, but I would like to interview each of these men. Of course, as yet we have no grounds for arrest.'

'Make it a tax enquiry, I can fix it with a friend in the *fisc*,' said J-J, referring to the specialist financial police. 'They're both small businessmen, they all have trouble with the *fisc*. We'll take a look at their tax records and bank accounts.'

'Both of them also had convictions for drug offences before they were sent to Long Kesh,' Moore added.

'Better still,' said J-J, 'we can make it a drugs raid. I'll see if our narcotics boys in Bergerac have ever heard of them.'

Bruno was already calling Louis in Montignac and was not surprised, from the background noise, to find him in a bar. Did Louis know an Irishman in the neighbourhood with a construction business named O'Rourke and had he received any anonymous letters about him?

'Damien, yes I know him,' Louis replied. 'Likes a drink. We had one or two complaints early on about his work, nothing serious, electricity installation not up to the norm but he fixed that. And I've had letters claiming he likes to pay cash for part-time work, but you know how it is with taxes, Bruno. If he didn't do that he wouldn't be able to hire anybody. Why do you want to know?'

'Keep it to yourself, Louis, but I hear the *fisc* might be onto him about those taxes.'

'*Merde*, the poor bastard. Thanks for letting me know, Bruno. And I just did routine patrols again today.'

Suddenly Isabelle was at Bruno's side as he ended the call. 'Who was that you were talking to?'

'My colleague in Montignac, asking what he knew about O'Rourke. It's all right, I just mentioned the *fisc* might be interested in him.'

'Are you mad?' Isabelle glared at him. 'Drunken Louis in Montignac was notorious even when I was based here. I wouldn't trust him a millimetre. And did your Louis know him?'

'They sometimes drink together.'

'*Merde*, Bruno, you try my patience.' She almost spat the words and turned to Prunier. 'Can we get some roadblocks set up around Montignac? Gendarmes, police, whatever. O'Rourke might be getting a tip-off. And we'd better get some police to Kelly in Bergerac. We'll have to hit them tonight . . .'

Prunier glanced quickly at Ardouin, and Bruno could see him weighing the options. One didn't get to be head of police of the entire *département* without considering the politics as well as the law. And on this occasion Prunier had the added pressure of the presence of British and American counterterrorism officers. He gave a quick, decisive nod, as if to reassure himself before he spoke.

'J-J, you get the police raid organized for Kelly's place in Bergerac and I'll get onto the gendarmes for Sarlat. Bruno, get me those two addresses and we'll talk about this later.'

Isabelle, always aware of the delicate protocol between police and magistrate, smiled sweetly at Ardouin. 'Since time may be of the essence, may we assume that you approve, *monsieur*?'

Ardouin looked at Bruno. 'Can't you just call your colleague in Montignac, Bruno, and tell him to say nothing to anyone about this?'

'I already told him that but perhaps I should stress it.' Bruno called again but got a busy signal. He kept trying while Prunier and J-J went ahead with the arrangements for the raids. As the others in the room carefully avoided his eyes, Bruno was left feeling like a bumbling amateur making a fool of himself among professionals.

13

Prunier led the way, the blue light flashing as he raced along the autoroute from Périgueux with Moore beside him and another police car in tow, leaving Bruno lagging behind in his van. He caught up with them at the first roadblock at Auriac-du-Périgord, just north of the town of Montignac. It was manned by gendarmes from Sarlat.

'All quiet, sir.' The *capitaine* in charge saluted as he reported to Prunier. 'Our colleagues from Montignac have the house and building yard surrounded but they are staying out of sight. They report no lights on, no sound of a TV and a builder's truck is parked in the yard. And gendarmes from Terrasson have roadblocks on the other access roads to the autoroute.'

'His wife drives a blue Peugeot 204,' said Prunier. 'Any sign of it?'

'First I've heard of it, sir. There's a garage but it's closed. It could be in there.'

'When did you get these roadblocks established?'

'About ten minutes ago, just thirty minutes after we got your call.'

'Good work, *Capitaine*, and thank you. I'll be sure to let your commander know of your efficiency. Please ensure that all the other roadblocks have the details of the blue Peugeot.' He read out the licence number, then led the way through the town to the road that ran alongside the River Vézère towards Les Eyzies. O'Rourke's house and builder's yard were part of a group of new buildings between the road and the river, close to the big new supermarket complex. They parked by the supermarket and waited for one of the gendarmes on watch to come and guide them.

'I'd better knock and see if they're home, sir,' said Bruno. 'In municipal police uniform, I don't look too threatening.' He loosened his gun belt and handed it to Prunier. 'Here, now I don't even look armed.'

'Don't be an idiot, Bruno,' Prunier said, removing the gun from the holster and handing it back. 'Take it, just in case. What will you say if he's there?'

'That we've been sent a warrant by the *fisc* and he has to come with us to Montignac to answer some questions.' Bruno put the gun into his trouser pocket, glad of its small size. He could never have done that with his old weapon.

'That's pretty thin.'

'Better than announcing a drugs raid. That would make anyone nervous.'

'Go ahead, take your van and keep the lights on so he can see the Police Municipale sign. Take care.'

Bruno drove slowly to the house and parked with his lights on, just short of the barred metal gate that closed the entrance. Beyond the gate was a builder's yard, filled with stacks of bricks, heaped sand, gravel and scaffolding, all dominated by what looked like an old wooden barn of the kind traditionally used to dry tobacco. Its entrance was now closed by sliding metal door, at least three metres tall and padlocked with a heavy chain. A flatbed truck with ladders leaning against its sides was parked beside the barn. Bruno could see it all clearly since his approach had triggered a motion detector that turned on a floodlight. Beyond the brick wall that sealed off one side of the yard he saw a small wooden gate and pathway that led to the house. It was a single-storey structure that could have come from a kit, with a shallow tiled roof, French windows to the right of the front door, and two conventional windows to the left. It did not seem an impressive advertisement for the skills of the builder who lived there. Bruno could see a garage behind the house.

As he opened the gate and walked slowly towards the house, wondering whether a hardened Irish terrorist was waiting for him with a gun, Bruno told himself that he deserved to be taking this risk because he'd been such an idiot. I should never have called Louis like that, he thought. I was showing off in front of all that top brass. Above all, of course, I was showing off for Isabelle, demonstrating the wide networks and local knowledge of a simple village copper. I should have realized that Louis would probably be half-drunk by this time of an evening, and could never keep his mouth shut. *Merde, merde,* and now I'm on the property of a known terrorist and ex-con with little to lose and no love for any kind of police. Feeling self-conscious, he slid his hand into his pocket and took a hesitant grip on his gun.

There was no reply when he rang the bell repeatedly, nor when he went to the back of the house to knock at what seemed like a kitchen door. He went to the garage, triggering another motion detector, but he was able to see through a side window that it was empty.

Prunier joined him at the front of the house and shone a torch on two impressive locks. The back door was equally secure. The double sliding French windows, however, looked as if they had only the usual internal lock. Prunier shone his torch down on the slide track and they saw the glint of a steel bar, holding the doors firmly closed.

'Did we not hear the sound of someone crying for help?' Prunier asked.

'Certainly, sir.'

Prunier took out his own gun and crossed to the two small windows, smashed the lower pane and reached in to undo the catch. He brushed away the loose glass, turned to Bruno and said, 'After you, Bruno.'

Bruno clambered in, catching the scent of female perfume. He found the light switch by the door. He was in a bedroom with an unmade bed, pyjamas and other clothes scattered around. The wardrobe doors were open, revealing gaps, as though clothes had been hastily removed.

'Police,' he called but there was no reply, only the vague echo of an empty house. He looked in the kitchen, saw the remains of a meal on the table and a pot of what looked like stew on the stove, still slightly warm. He went back to find the living room, turning on lights as he went, bent down to lift the locking bar and opened the French windows.

'Empty, but they were just here,' he said as Prunier entered, followed by Moore. He showed them the warm pot in the kitchen. Moore found a room that seemed to be used as an office, with a desk, a computer and several filing cabinets, the drawers open and some files sticking out. Then Prunier's phone rang.

'What? . . . I see . . . Well, that's good news, better than we found in Montignac. Our bird has flown. I want a very thorough search of the house and car, particularly any papers, computer, phones or SIM cards. Thanks, J-J.'

'They got the other one, Kelly, as he was pulling out of his driveway, suitcases and briefcases in the back of his wife's car,' Prunier said. 'Two minutes later we'd have lost him. He was armed with a handgun but he and his wife came quietly and are now demanding a lawyer. We can hold him on the firearms charge and forensics are working on the car. His wife had a map of southern France on her lap, open to show the route to Spain.

'I have to organize roadblocks and contact the Police aux Frontières,' Prunier went on. 'Inspector Moore will search what papers have been left here and we'll get another forensics team to come over. And you, Bruno, had better find out just how it was they were tipped off. I suggest you start with your colleague, Louis.'

'Yes, sir. I'm sorry for this.' Bruno felt his face turning brick-red with shame as he left. The story would be all around the entire police force of the *département* by morning and he'd never live it down. It would give ammunition to all those who argued that the Police Municipale were a bunch of amateurs who should be pensioned off and the work left to real policemen.

He was driving to Louis's place on the other side of town when he stopped at a pedestrian crossing for a bunch of men who were walking none too steadily. Behind them were the lights of a bar, with its name above the lace-curtained window, Le Relais du Chasseur. A hunter's bar was the kind of place where Louis would drink. On an impulse, Bruno parked, entered the bar and found the owner sweeping up. Another employee was stacking chairs onto plain wooden tables.

'*Bonsoir à tous*, and sorry to disturb you just as you're closing,' he said, putting out his hand to be shaken by a tired-looking man in his fifties with a shaven head and goatee beard. 'Was my colleague Louis in here tonight? I think it was here that I phoned him.'

'Yes, Louis is in most evenings but he left half an hour ago. You'll find him at home but knowing him he'll probably be snoring his head off by now.'

'What about that Irish friend of his, Damien? Was he in tonight?'

'Yes, a nice guy. Damien Aroque, something like that. He's in the same hunting club as Louis. His French isn't up to much but he has a lovely voice, sings like an angel and always ready to stand his round. They were all at the same table at the back, their usual place. I remember Louis got up to answer a phone call and came back and made some joke. Soon after that Damien left.'

'Thanks, I'll catch Louis at home and hope I don't have to wake him up.'

'Good luck.' The landlord shrugged and gave a half-smile. 'You're Louis's new boss, aren't you, Bruno from St Denis? I saw something in the paper this week and I don't think Louis is very happy about that.'

'Understandable,' said Bruno. 'I might feel the same way if I were in his shoes. Is Louis a friend of yours?'

'He's a good . . .' The man paused and then went on, 'He's a regular customer and his being a cop means I don't get much trouble, which suits me fine.'

'So he doesn't try to drink for free?'

The landlord shrugged. 'Let's just say I don't get much profit from him, but he'll buy his round once in a while.'

Bruno nodded and sighed. 'So long as he's not abusing his position.' He put out his hand again. 'Call me Bruno and thanks for the chat.'

'I'm Laurent,' said the landlord. 'Fancy a quick one for the road?'

'No thanks,' said Bruno. 'I'm on duty, and anyway I have to wake up Louis and I wouldn't want my breath smelling like his.'

The landlord grinned. 'Good night, take care.'

Louis lived on an estate built in the 1950s in a semi-detached house with a big rear garden but no garage. His police van was parked on the street. The only light Bruno could see was a dim glow through the frosted glass above the front door. Bruno went round the back, where Louis kept his vegetable garden and his hunting dogs. These were new puppies in training since his old dogs had been killed in sniffing out an attempted terrorist attack at the Lascaux cave. He had been handsomely compensated for their loss but Bruno could imagine the grief Louis must have felt.

The kitchen light was on and Louis was sitting at the table, a glass of what looked like cognac before him, smoking his pipe and nodding off in front of a TV that stood on a counter beside the fridge. Bruno tapped on the window. And Louis sat up with a start, rubbed his eyes, saw Bruno at the back door and his face fell.

'What time do you call this?' he began, blustering and holding the door half-closed.

'Time for you to tell me exactly what you said to your Irish friend tonight in the Relais du Chasseur,' Bruno said, pushing Louis back into the kitchen and into his chair. Bruno then perched on the table beside him.

'What do you mean?'

'That little joke you told in the bar just after I called you.'

Louis's eyes dropped. 'I don't remember. Here, have a drink. A nice bit of Armagnac from my cousin in Condom.'

'I'm on duty, Louis. This not a social call and you are in real trouble. What did you tell your Irish friend tonight?'

'Just that he ought to take care because I'd just heard the *fisc* were after him. It was just a joke. A lot of people have problems with the *fisc*.'

'The *fisc* are in law enforcement, just like you're supposed to be. And your Irish friend turns out to be a convicted terrorist who has now flown the coop with his wife just a few minutes before we raided his house. The damn cooking pot in his kitchen was still warm. And it was you who tipped him off, you damn fool.'

'Don't you talk to me like that, you young sod, still wet behind the ears.' Louis was angry now, gripping the arms of his chair. A big vein was throbbing on his forehead. 'All high and mighty and the darling of the newspapers with your shiny new medal. I should have had that job, you smug bastard.'

'Watch your tongue, Louis, I'm your boss.'

Was this drunken fool actually thinking of taking a swing at him? Louis was bigger and weighed a lot more than Bruno, but he was nearly twenty years older, out of condition, and he'd never been trained to fight. Bruno suspected it was the Armagnac speaking, but he stood up from the table. He edged his right foot back a little so he could slam Louis's face down onto his rising knee if the old fool tried to come at him out of his chair. But Louis must have seen something in Bruno's eye and he sat back.

'Screw you, Bruno, and screw your fancy women and your stupid little dog. It was you who got my dogs killed, the best hunting dogs in the valley. And I don't care if Damien got away, he's worth ten of you any day. And what's this crap about him being a terrorist? You're making it up.'

'He served time for it. And it wasn't just him who got away, it was also his friend in Bergerac. Luckily we managed to get him at a roadblock. He was armed and fleeing. We're still checking the phones but we reckon that when you tipped off Damien, he tipped off Kelly and they both made a run for it. Do you realize how much trouble you're in?'

'Not my fault, it's yours,' said Louis, with something like cunning in his eyes. He had let go of the arms of his chair and reached for his glass of Armagnac. 'It was you who told me about Damien and the *fisc*, Bruno. And you didn't tell me it was a state secret.'

'I told you to keep it to yourself, and my phone has an auto-record function. You'll hear it for yourself when this comes up in your disciplinary hearing, you stupid old drunk. Commissaire Prunier was on this raid tonight, along with British and American officers from counterterrorism, and you blew the operation. This is on your head, Louis, and I think there's a good chance that you might lose your job, and probably your pension with it.'

With that speedy switching of emotions that Bruno had seen so often with drunks, Louis seemed to shrink back into himself. The eyes that had been blazing with anger and indignation a moment earlier were now mournful and self-pitying.

'They couldn't do that, not after thirty years of service,' he said, trying to sound confident, but there was a whine in his voice and tears welling in his eyes. Bruno wasn't sure whether he felt saddened or sickened.

'Read the regulations, Louis, and what it says about dismissal with cause. Revealing police operational details to a member of the public is a serious offence, let alone to a convicted terrorist. And you've got half the cops in the *département* hunting an armed and dangerous man. Prunier will have every right to throw the book at you and I don't think your drinking chums in the Mairie will lift a finger to help.'

The tears were now trickling down Louis's fat cheeks and his hands were twisting together in his lap. Bruno felt a stab of compassion and then the kitchen door opened.

'What's all this damn shouting about? You'll wake all the neighbours, you and your drunken . . .'

Louis's wife, in a vast and floppy nightgown and bare feet,

her face gleaming with cream and her hair in curlers, suddenly caught sight of Bruno standing there sternly in uniform. Her hand came up to her mouth, belatedly trying to hide the fact that she had removed her dentures.

'*Putain*, Louis, what the devil have you gone and done now?'

Bruno felt a wave of pity wash over him for her, and just a little of it for Louis, as well. It wasn't entirely Louis's fault, he reminded himself. He'd been showing off that evening and he knew about the man's loose tongue.

'*Bonsoir, monsieur*,' Louis's wife said. 'I'm sorry, I didn't realize it was you. Can I make you some coffee?'

'No, thank you, *madame*. I'm just going. I think you'd better get Louis to bed. He'll need to be in good shape in the morning. Good night.'

Bruno let himself out the way he had come in and went back to his van, thinking that both he and Louis would almost certainly be hauled in front of Prunier tomorrow morning. He checked his phone automatically. There was a terse message from Prunier, requesting that Bruno deliver a written report on the affair to be on Prunier's desk by noon the next day.

'I expect you to come in person,' Prunier had added.

It was not just Prunier's official response that alarmed him as he drove back to St Denis but Bruno's own sense of shame. He had behaved like a foolish young recruit, trying too hard to make an impression before his superiors. And at a much deeper level, Bruno had been shaken by the outrage and anger that Isabelle had displayed. There had been something close to contempt in her reaction and that was the most wounding of all.

14

The next morning Bruno was woken up by the *cocorico* of his cockerel, Blanco, greeting the break of day. And a beautiful day it looked to be when he stepped outside in his old army tracksuit and running shoes. There was not a cloud in the sky and the air was so fresh he could almost taste it, and so clear that each leaf on the trees and each wrinkle in their bark seemed distinct. His gloomy mood of the night before had gone and as he and Balzac jogged through the woods Bruno felt a new resolve. With it came a determination to establish just what his new role entailed and under whose orders he now came.

There had been no further messages from Prunier nor from J-J about his attending that morning's staff meeting in Périgueux. Bruno decided to remain in St Denis and at the stroke of eight he was waiting outside the door of the Mayor's office.

'*Bonjour*, Bruno. What can I do for you?' the Mayor asked at the sight of him. 'You look as if you have something on your mind. Come in and have a coffee.'

'It's this new job, sir,' Bruno began, once Claire had brought in two coffees from the Mayor's private stock. 'I'm rather confused. Do I still work for you and for St Denis or what?'

The Mayor sat back, considering. 'It's complicated but yes,

you are still chief of police of St Denis and your traditional salary is paid by the town budget. But you are also chief of police for the whole valley, so you work for the community of *communes*, the standing committee of all the Mayors who are supposed to pay for your extra salary and your higher pension rights. But for the next year that's supposed to be paid by a special grant from the Ministry of Justice, since this is their pilot project, and they'll also pay for your administrative assistant once one is hired. We haven't seen their money yet so right now you are still wholly employed by St Denis.'

'But what about that oath that I swore, administered by the Procureur, to uphold the discipline and regulations of the Police Nationale as an *officier judiciaire*?'

'I was interested by that so I looked it up,' the Mayor said. 'Article fourteen of the Penal Code says such an officer is charged with determining infractions of the law, establishing proofs and seeking out the authors of such crimes. It gives you powers of arrest and detention and of requisition, according to the rules and regulations of the Police Nationale and subject to the authority of the Procureur.'

'So I don't come under the authority of the Police Nationale?'

'Not as such, since you're not formally in their chain of command. But as a courtesy and as a matter of efficiency, you'll naturally cooperate with them to the best of your ability. Your duties here take precedence, though.'

The Mayor smiled. 'Tell me, has our friend Commissaire Prunier been seeking to bring you under his command?'

Bruno nodded.

'I thought as much. You may have heard, Bruno, of *La Guerre des Polices*, a famous film in the seventies, about two competing police forces seeking the same criminal and getting in each other's way. It was probably before your time, but it pretty much sums up the relationship between the gendarmes and the Police Nationale. They are rivals, competitors, sometimes almost enemies. And that's not necessarily a bad thing. The system was designed that way, quite deliberately. Ever since the Revolution, the Republic has always been wary of one single, all-powerful police force. Better to have two competing sets of police so the elected politicians can count on the support of at least one. We may lose some efficiency, but we gain constitutional security.'

'You mean the way so many countries have separate intelligence services, one for domestic affairs and the other for international work, like the CIA and FBI.'

'Exactly,' the Mayor said. 'Or MI5 and MI6 in Britain and Mossad and Shin Bet in Israel. It's the same principle. Ambitious officers like Commissaire Prunier always seek to widen their authority but he's not your boss, Bruno. I am. Or rather, the people of St Denis, as represented by the Mayor and council, pay your wages and define your work. Should you have any trouble with Prunier, tell him that and let me know about it. Now, explain to me what brought this on.'

Bruno described the events of the previous evening and the context of the IRA connection, the presence of Moore, Hodge and Isabelle and Prunier's demand for a written report. In conclusion, he confessed that he had doubtless been guilty of showing off.

'But wasn't Prunier showing off too before this august bunch of officers? How often does a *commissaire* race off in the night to lead a raid on a suspect's house?' the Mayor asked. 'Your call to Louis in Montignac triggered the flight of these two Irishmen. That in itself suggests guilt. I'd say you cunningly smoked them out. No, Bruno, I don't think you should worry about that. Nor about Prunier's request for a report. You may tell him that you have reported to your own chain of command, which means me. If Prunier wants anything further, he's free to contact me. But take note that whenever several bureaucracies are involved in a project, they'll inevitably try to pick someone to take the blame if things go wrong. Make sure it isn't you.

'Now that's out of the way, let's talk about road traffic,' the Mayor went on, rising from his desk to look at the large map of the *commune* on the wall. 'The transport ministry has authorized the funds for two speed-trap cameras to be installed on our roads. Where do you recommend we put them?'

Twenty minutes later, having sent his brief but polite email to Prunier, Bruno was reaching for the paperwork in his in tray when his desk phone rang. Assuming it would be Prunier, he sighed as he reached for it.

'You're the luckiest amateur cop I ever knew,' J-J announced. 'A gendarme roadblock at Montauban picked up your Irishman from Montignac. And my forensic guys found cocaine traces in the car of the one we got in Bergerac. The narcotics squad sent their dog team in to sniff through his market garden and just found a stash of two kilos under his compost heap.'

'Which wouldn't have happened if I hadn't called Louis and he hadn't tipped off the one in Montignac to make them run,' Bruno said, feeling emboldened.

'I wouldn't try that on Prunier if I were you. I hear he's told you to deliver a report on it all this morning. When are you coming in? If you want, I can give you a hand with the phrasing. After all, it was me who put that idea into your head about using the *fisc*.'

'Thanks, J-J, and I appreciate that but I'm not coming in and I'm not filing a report,' said Bruno. 'I reported to my own chain of command, the Mayor, and that's all. I don't work for Prunier.'

'*Putain*, Bruno, are you out of your mind?' The shock in J-J's voice was evident down the line. Bruno could imagine the look on his face. 'You can't flout his authority like that, he'll go ballistic.'

'I have no choice. I'm under orders from the Mayor, who also chairs the committee of *communes* for whom I work. The Mayor wants to make the point that I don't work for the Police Nationale.'

'If it comes to a turf war between Prunier and your Mayor, you're going to be in the middle. And in that tussle, my money's on Prunier.'

'You could be right and don't think I'm feeling comfortable about being in the middle of this situation. But I doubt whether it will come to that,' Bruno said, thinking that J-J was probably the man best placed to defuse the situation. He could talk to Prunier and warn him against picking a fight with a professional politician. So he'd better make sure J-J knew how serious this could become.

'My Mayor is one of the most powerful in the Périgord,' Bruno went on. 'He's also deputy chairman of the Conseil

Régional. He's worked in the Elysée Palace, in the European Commission in Brussels and he was a Senator. He has friends and allies all over the *département*, not to mention Paris. And legally speaking, the Mayor is right. If he wants to make this an issue of Prunier doing a power grab and trying to take away the prerogative of an elected mayor, all the other mayors will back him. Prunier will be on very weak ground.'

There was a long pause on the other end of the line before J-J spoke. 'All right. I'll have a word with him, but you'd better have some kind of olive branch ready.'

'What do you suggest?'

'We're all tied up with the Irishmen but Hodge, the American, wants to take a look at McBride's place in Lalinde and Moore wants the same. Could you do that, help us out?'

'I'd be glad to but doesn't Moore want to sit in on the interrogations? He's the one who knows the Irishmen.'

'That's the point. They know him and he reckons his presence would be counterproductive. He's already suggested some lines of questioning but he wants to stay below the radar. Listen, I'll get a car to drive them down to St Denis and you can take them on to Lalinde then give them lunch at Ivan's and send us the bill. And I'll make sure Prunier knows you're doing your best to be helpful.'

Within the hour, Bruno was in the front seat of an unmarked police car. He twisted around to face Moore and Hodge in the rear to point out some of the sights that they passed on the way to Lalinde. Moore explained that O'Rourke and his wife were under arrest and being brought to Périgueux from Montauban, where they had been stopped and detained. Kelly, the man arrested in Bergerac, was refusing to talk and demanding a lawyer and access to the British consul in Bordeaux.

'I thought he was Irish,' said Hodge, looking confused.

'He was born in Belfast, so he's a British citizen,' Moore said. 'I suppose I should be touched by his faith in British diplomacy.'

They crossed the River Dordogne, drove past Lalinde church and then turned right up the hill. Bruno had already called his colleague Quatremer to warn that he was bringing visitors to the crime scene.

'Nice place,' said Hodge, unbending his great height from the back seat and surveying the house where Rentoul had lived as McBride and where he and Monika Felder had died. 'I wonder if Uncle Sam's money paid for it.'

Quatremer was waiting for them at the front door with the keys and a set of gloves and bootees for each of them, even though the forensics team had finished their work. He undid the crime scene tape as they approached and Bruno made the introductions.

'Better come inside,' said Quatremer. 'I don't want the guy from *Sud Ouest* coming out and taking your photographs.'

Moore and Hodge each had a copy of the crime scene report and they went first to the bathroom where Monika had been killed and then looked around the bedroom and kitchen.

'I didn't see anything about a safe in the report,' Hodge said. 'How hard did you guys look? Did you bring in ground-penetrating radar for the floors and walls? If not, that's something we need to do.'

'And what about metal detectors?' Moore asked. 'I already

suggested they use them at O'Rourke's place. It was standard practice in Northern Ireland, looking for buried weapons.'

'I'll check,' said Bruno, remembering that the forensics team had found the commando knife with a metal detector. 'Could be a good idea. You know a sniffer dog found cocaine at the market garden in Bergerac?'

'Yes, and I'd like a metal detector running over that site as well. Is there any progress on this sniper's rifle that might have gone missing?' Moore asked. 'The IRA is always in the market for them.'

'I've got a request in to our field office in Phoenix to see if the manufacturer can tell us anything,' Hodge said. 'But don't get your hopes up. Those things sell pretty well at gun shows and the second-hand market.'

Bruno led them into the barn and then up through the vineyard and orchard to the woodland and the clearing where he had found McBride–Rentoul. He described the scene, the big stepladder used for collecting apples, the way the rope had been secured over the limb and around the trunk, the placing of the knot.

'I read the pathologist's report and saw the photos,' said Moore. 'J-J seemed persuaded it was a suicide, that even if he'd been unconscious two men could never have got him up here and hanging without leaving a mark on his body. What do you think, Bruno?'

'It was dark, a lot of tricky undergrowth underfoot, but I think two men could have managed it.'

'How?' asked Hodge.

'Do you hunt?' Bruno asked his companions. They told him

they didn't. 'I know that O'Rourke, the man in Montignac, was in the local hunting club. He might have seen this done.' Bruno looked at Quatremer, who was grinning and nodding.

'Let's go back to the barn and we'll show you,' said Bruno.

Once there, Bruno found a stout pole, about two metres long, and a tarpaulin of reinforced plastic with metallic eyelets around its edges. It was the kind of covering placed over a car in the winter. He also found some of the blue plastic twine that was ubiquitous in the French countryside, used for everything from supporting tall plants and tying roses to temporary repairs of broken gates and fences.

'You look about McBride's size and weight,' he said to Moore. 'Would you lie down on that tarpaulin, please?'

Moore complied, surprised at first but then realizing what Bruno had in mind as he and Quatremer began to thread the twine through the eyelets. Once it was secure and Moore was lying in the centre of what was now a tube of tarpaulin, Bruno threaded more twine through the eyelets at each end of the tube to ensure that Moore could not slip out. He tossed a coil of rope, similar to that used in the hanging, to Hodge before pushing the pole through the tube to Quatremer at the other end. The two of them bent down, each putting his end of the pole onto a shoulder. As Bruno counted down from three, they rose as one to their full height and began walking out from the barn, through the garden and the vineyard, Moore swaying gently between them in his tarpaulin cocoon.

'This is how we bring deer back from deep in the woods,' Bruno said. 'And because his body is fully supported, there won't be a mark on him.'

It was much harder going over the undergrowth through the clearing, but Bruno and Quatremer were experienced hunters and they had done this often before. Every hundred metres they stopped and switched shoulders and they felt with their feet for a secure footing. Their progress was slow but it was sure. When they reached the hanging tree they put Moore down. Bruno took the rope from Hodge and asked him to bring the big stepladder.

'Okay to stay in there a bit longer?' Bruno called to Moore. 'I want to try something.' Moore grunted his assent.

Bruno secured one end of the rope to the tree trunk and then climbed the stepladder to pass it over the branch from which McBride-Rentoul had been hanging. He climbed back down, secured the dangling end of the rope to the tarpaulin pole with three running knots and asked Quatremer to haul on the rope while Bruno guided the tarpaulin cocoon as he climbed slowly, one step at a time.

Quatremer was grunting with the strain of lifting Moore's dead weight, but with a little support from Bruno on the stepladder, the blue tube rose slowly, steadily, until it was supported mostly by the large flat step at the top of the ladder. Bruno loosened the running knots and let the rope fall again to Quatremer's feet.

'Make me a noose, pull it up and then re-secure the other end of the rope around that trunk,' Bruno said.

Quatremer bent to his task and within minutes, a very convincing noose was slung over the branch, secured to the tree trunk and hanging at a convenient height for Bruno to slip it around the neck of the man in the tarpaulin. Instead, Bruno took the knife from his belt and cut the twine to free Moore, whose eyes widened when he saw the noose dangling before him.

'Bloody hell,' Moore said, swallowing and then looking down at the ground. 'Okay, you've convinced me. Two men could have done it.'

15

On their way back from Lalinde to St Denis, Bruno asked the driver to turn off from the main road to show Moore, a fellow rugby player, the town stadium. Built by volunteers, including Bruno, it was a handsome stand that could seat up to five hundred people, with changing rooms, showers, offices and storerooms in the space beneath. It was a source of great local pride. But as they cruised past, Bruno suddenly told the driver to brake, muttering, 'What the devil . . .'

Along the white wall at the back of the stand was scrawled some new graffiti that Bruno found shocking for the desecration of the town's cherished stand as much as the message itself.

Paulette – Papa Qui? it read, bad French but most people would recognize the refrain from a recent hit song. And at that moment Bruno knew the secret was not just out but that Paulette's devoutly religious parents must by now be aware of what they would see as their daughter's shame.

'Who is Paulette?' Moore asked in English. In the same language Bruno explained that she was St Denis's only hope of fielding a player for a national team and that he had been her coach for years. Something in his tone of voice made Moore look at him sharply.

'Does she have to have the baby?' Moore asked.

Bruno shrugged, directed the car round the corner to the Bricomarché store and bought a can of white spray paint. He drove back to the stadium and covered over the graffiti, wondering how long before the words would be replaced. He kept his eyes peeled as they drove to the car park in front of the Mairie but saw no more such daubs. But with a groan he spotted a gleaming new section of white paint on the wall of the flower shop that belonged to Paulette's parents. They must have found and erased it themselves.

'Another one?' Moore asked, following Bruno's gaze.

'It looks that way,' Bruno replied. 'That's her parents' shop.'

'You can't keep secrets in a small town,' Moore said. 'Who's the father? Another rugby man?'

'No, I'm pretty sure it's her drama teacher at the *lycée* in Périgueux but not many people know that yet. And it's Friday, the day she comes home from school for the weekend, to stay with her very religious parents.'

'So no abortion?' Moore asked.

'She's over eighteen so it's up to her but there'll be a family row if that's what she decides to do.'

They parked, and speaking quickly in English, Bruno asked the police driver if he would like to join them for lunch. The driver looked at him blankly, so at least Bruno did not have to worry of his spreading the tale around the entire police force of the *département*. He repeated the question in French and the driver eagerly agreed to join them.

Ivan's *menu du jour* began with vegetable soup, followed by a plate of *jambon du pays* with melon. Bruno and his guests had just been served with their main course of rabbit roasted in mustard when Hodge asked Moore, in English, whether Bruno's demonstration had persuaded him that Rentoul had been murdered.

'I accept that it could have been murder but for me the balance of probabilities still suggests suicide rather than murder,' Moore replied.

'But that would mean he murdered Monika, the woman he'd just been making love with,' Bruno replied. 'Is that likely?'

Moore shrugged. 'It's not unheard of. But for me it means we are going to have to find out more about Felder's marriage. He must have been in his forties when he met Monika and she was about twenty. I'd like to know where and how they met, where she was from and how a pretty young German girl meets a senior intelligence officer on a British military base. I've already asked London to find out what they can.'

Moore explained that his British colleagues in counterterrorism had picked up no word of any New IRA operation in France, nor of any renewal of contacts between the New IRA and their old connections in Libya. Moore was confident that the British intelligence networks were sufficiently comprehensive to have picked up hints of such a development. And both the human and electronic intelligence systems were on the alert for an IRA response to the events of the previous night.

'We're expecting to pick up some talk or phone calls about the arrest of Kelly and O'Rourke once the news gets out. Frankly, I expect their old friends will seem baffled by it all,' Moore added.

'How long can you hold these two before you have to charge them or release their names?' Hodge asked.

'Since the last terrorist attacks, the French government has declared a state of emergency,' Bruno said, not bothering to conceal his own doubts about the draconian new rules. 'We can arrest people, detain and question them for four days before bringing in a magistrate and starting the procedure of charging them. And we now have specialist magistrates for terrorism cases who can authorize preventive detention for as long as four years before trial.'

'Four years? Jesus,' said Moore, his eyes wide. 'How do you get away with that?'

'The same way we brought in the Patriot Act after 9/11,' said Hodge. 'Frightened people demand desperate measures. So you don't even have to announce their arrest? They just disappear?'

'In a way, but they can get a lawyer and there are various other procedures that can be applied, like house arrest,' Bruno replied. 'But now the sniffer dogs found cocaine we may announce their detention under the narcotics laws, saying nothing about any links to terrorism. The authorities might be embarrassed when the public learns that IRA men have been living and working here for years.'

'So they should be,' said Moore. 'We made sure you knew who and where they were. I thought there was supposed to be some monitoring system to keep an eye on them.'

Bruno shrugged. 'The IRA is old history. Our counterterrorism guys have more than enough work dealing with Islamists these days.'

Ivan brought four portions of apple pie and the bill. Bruno

put down a fifty-euro note and a ten and Ivan returned with some change.

'Four lunches, four excellent courses with wine, all for less than sixty euros?' Hodge said in disbelief. 'That's what I end up paying when I take the kids to McDo in Paris.'

'The nearest McDonald's is forty kilometres from here,' Bruno said. 'I don't think we miss it. We feed people better than that in the Périgord. I assume you'll both be here this weekend. Would you like to come to my place for dinner on Saturday for a relaxing evening and some home cooking?'

'Very much,' said Moore, and Hodge gave a slow nod and said, 'Mighty kind of you. I'd like that.'

At that point, Bruno's phone vibrated and he saw J-J's name come up on the screen.

'Bruno, can you get to Bergerac airport?' J-J asked. 'There's a flight from London City that gets in at three and a lawyer from Felder's company is coming in to make the formal identification of Monika. But make sure you take him from the morgue directly to the police *commissariat* and I'll meet you there.'

'Sure, but I have Moore and Hodge with me.'

'Send them back in the car that brought them and you head to Bergerac. Did you take them to Ivan's?'

'Yes, he was serving that *lapin à la moutarde* that you like.'

'And here's me with a sandwich. I'll see you in Bergerac, and whatever you do, don't let this man get on a flight out. We want to keep him here and talking so tell him he needs to sign something at the *commissariat*. Understood?'

'Understood. What's the lawyer's name?'

'Forbes, Alan Forbes. He's one of the directors of Felder's

company so he knows Monika well. I'll call the airport cops, make sure they treat him nicely, let him off the plane first. And take your police van.'

Bruno checked his watch. It had just gone two and Bergerac airport was less than forty minutes away if the traffic was reasonable. He went to say farewell to Hodge and Moore and found them huddled over Hodge's phone.

'Just got a message from Houston,' Hodge said, looking up at Bruno. 'It comes as no surprise but General Felder has died in his hospital bed.'

Bruno explained he had to leave them and strolled back to the car park by the Mairie, greeting acquaintances and enjoying the spring sunshine when he saw the black-garbed figure of Father Sentout bustling over the bridge from the direction of the flower shop, head down as though in thought. Bruno waited at the end of the bridge and touched the peak of his cap as the priest approached.

'*Bonjour*, Father,' said Bruno. 'I think I know where you've just been and what concerns you. It concerns me too, and the rugby club.'

Father Sentout's love of God was matched only by his passionate support for the St Denis rugby club. He rarely missed a home game and tried his best to attend away games even though they were played on Sunday afternoons and he offered an evening mass at six. Bruno recalled two occasions when the good father had changed into his vestments on the team bus and darted into his church as the clock began to strike six.

'Ah, Bruno, this should be such a joyous moment and yet it seems to be making everyone so sad.'

'How are her parents taking it?'

'It's not easy for them but they are strengthened by their faith in God. They are good people, Bruno, and it is heartbreaking to see them so downcast, so humiliated. Do you have any idea who has been scrawling these things on the walls?'

'No, but I saw one earlier on the stadium wall. I sprayed new paint over it but I imagine half the town will know about Paulette by now.'

'I'll be seeing her this evening when she gets in from the *lycée*. Her parents asked me to talk to her.'

'You know the law, Father. She's an adult in the eyes of the Republic and the choice is hers.'

'I also know the law of God and of the holy Church, Bruno. I have to counsel her as I think best. And I have known this child all her life. I baptized her, I gave Paulette her first communion, heard her first confession.'

'And I remember you blessing the team at their last home game.'

'We may differ on this, Bruno, but I think we can agree that Paulette must now be our main concern. She must be feeling very troubled. Tell me, if you can, is there a prospect that I might be celebrating a marriage?'

'None at all. If I'm right about the man in question, he's already married to someone else.'

'Heaven preserve us. Can we talk further on this?'

'Of course, Father, but right now I have to go, official business takes me to Bergerac. I'll try to be back in time for Paulette's return. I imagine she'll be on the train that gets in around six.'

'That's what her parents said. Go with God, Bruno.'

Bruno took the back road to the airport, avoiding the traffic on the main road through Mouleydier and Creysse and all the other villages that slowed the journey. As he turned onto the fast stretch of the Périgueux–Bergerac road he could see the aircraft turning onto its final approach. He was only a minute or two from the airport and by the time the plane's wheels touched down Bruno had parked and was shaking hands with the head of the Police aux Frontières who told him that J-J had already called and the pilot knew that one passenger was to be allowed off the plane first. They strolled together to the stretch of tarmac where the passenger jets parked to offload and board passengers.

'Monsieur Forbes?' Bruno enquired, saluting the middle-aged man in a dark grey suit coming down the steps, large briefcase in hand.

'I'm Forbes, here to identify a woman who may be Monika Felder,' he said in French.

'Welcome to Bergerac, *monsieur.* I'm sorry for the sad event that makes you come here,' said Bruno in his fluent but ungrammatical English. 'Your French is excellent, *monsieur*, but perhaps it may be easier if you pardon my bad English. Do you have any valise on the plane?'

'No, only this,' Forbes said, waving his briefcase. 'I'm flying back tonight, the six o'clock plane to Paris and then on to London. I hope this won't take too long.'

'I will take you directly to the morgue and then you will just have to call at the *commissariat de police* here in Bergerac to sign some papers. Allow me to introduce Directeur Baudouin, who arranged for you to come first from the plane.'

The *Frontières* chief led Bruno and Forbes to the small shed that housed two passport control booths, greeted the two officers and Forbes was waved through with a cursory glance at his passport. Ten minutes later, they were at the hospital and walking around the main building to the morgue where the attendant was expecting them. He held out a small pot of sharp-smelling menthol ointment – Bruno rubbed it around his nostrils and advised Forbes to do the same.

The room was very cold. The bodies were kept in what looked like a row of unusually deep filing cabinets and the attendant checked his register and pulled out one drawer on which a body lay beneath a white sheet. The only exposed flesh was a single shapely foot, and an identifying label was attached to the big toe. The attendant pulled back the cloth from the head, leaving the rest of the body covered. Monika's face was still lovely in death despite the grey tone to her skin.

'I confirm that this is Monika Felder, a director of our company and well known to me,' Forbes said in English, making an effort to show no emotion. Then repeated the same phrase in competent French.

He turned to Bruno. 'How did she die, exactly?'

'A stab wound to the heart. She was in the shower at the time but we believe she must have seen her killer.'

'May I see?'

Bruno gestured to the attendant who shrugged and then pulled the sheet back further, revealing the long gash of the autopsy down the length of her trunk, roughly sewn back together. Bruno pointed to the small wound beneath the left breast.

'She would have died very quickly,' he said.

The attendant replaced the sheet over Monika's face and slid the cabinet back into place. Forbes signed an identification sheet for the register and turned to Bruno.

'You said I have to sign something somewhere else. Was it at the police station here in Bergerac?'

'Indeed, *monsieur*, we now go to the *commissariat*. The detective in charge of the murder inquiry awaits us there and he will require a second signature. But first, I wonder if you might be able to help us with the identity of the second person who died at the scene.'

Bruno gestured to the attendant who pulled out a second drawer, this time a male figure draped in a sheet, again with the tag attached to the big toe. The contrast could not have been more grim between Monika's face and the gross, engorged visage of McBride-Rentoul. At least the bird-savaged eye sockets had been covered by small circular patches of white cotton.

'Good God Almighty!' Forbes put his hand to his mouth as if about to retch. 'I couldn't recognize my own brother looking like that. What's wrong with the eyes?'

'He was left hanging in the open air for nearly two days. The birds, you understand . . .'

Forbes swallowed and then, with a shudder, took control of himself and looked attentively at the body, as if trying to assess something from the shape of the head, the set of the jaw.

'I can't be sure of anything looking at that but I don't think I know that face at all. Sorry,' he said.

'My apologies, *monsieur*, I understand that it is not a pleasant sight.' The cabinet drawer slid shut again.

Another ten minutes took them to J-J, who was waiting in a well-appointed office, rather than the interview room Bruno had expected.

'Monsieur Forbes has been most helpful,' Bruno said. 'He identified Monika Felder but could not help us with the second body. He has a flight to Paris at six and he speaks some French.'

'Excellent, *monsieur*, and thank you for coming to France. We'll get a car to take you back to the airport, once the formalities are complete,' said J-J. 'If you could sign here that you have identified Madame Felder, and might I borrow your passport to take a photocopy to go along with your identification, just for the record.'

Forbes handed over his passport and signed as requested. J-J turned to a photocopier behind the desk, made two copies and then slipped the passport into a drawer.

'Just a couple of questions, *monsieur*, and I'll bring in our official interpreter. May I offer you some coffee or other refreshment while we wait?'

Forbes shook his head. J-J picked up a phone, spoke briefly and then beamed at Forbes, gesturing to him to take a seat. A young woman arrived, dressed very plainly, and then translated in almost perfect English J-J's next question.

'When did you last see Madame Felder?'

'At the last board meeting, about a month ago.'

'Where was that?'

'In London, Brook Street, our company offices.'

'She had returned from Houston for the meeting?'

'I believe so but I don't know her exact movements. She said she had just flown in from seeing her husband, our chairman and founder. He's in hospital there. She told us he was not doing well. She was clearly distressed.'

'What happens to the company now?'

'I don't understand. So long as General Felder remains with us, nothing changes. Then I presume it will go to his heirs but that's a matter for his personal lawyer. I work for the company. I'm not privy to his will.'

'Do you know this personal lawyer?'

'We met, once, in the chairman's office.'

'You've done no succession planning?'

Forbes remained silent for a moment, his eyes flicking towards Bruno, before speaking. 'It seemed premature. I'm afraid these questions are going beyond my competence. I was brought here to identify a body, which I have done and now I'd like to go, please. Could you return my passport?'

'Just a moment, *monsieur*. I'm grateful for your help but we are investigating a murder and I'm sure you would like to help us bring the killer to justice. Were you friendly with Madame Felder?'

'I only saw her at board meetings and at the Felders' annual party for senior staff at their home. Our relations were polite but businesslike.'

'Do you have any idea why she might have been killed?'

'No.' Felder was looking back and forth between J-J and the interpreter as if unsure which of them to answer.

'Since she can no longer inherit any of her husband's property, am I right to assume the children of his first marriage will inherit?'

'I have no idea but his will becomes public, if and when he

dies. Of course, in the circumstances you could with the help of the British police seek a court order asking for an immediate copy.'

'Do you know Monsieur Felder's two children?'

'I met them once, at one of those company parties I mentioned. I understand the son had worked for the company for some time but left before I joined. I've been there for three years. The daughter is a patent lawyer in private practice. That's all I know.'

Forbes looked at his watch, although there was a large clock on the wall behind him. Bruno noted that it was a few minutes before five. Would he be able to get back to St Denis in time to meet Paulette's train? He thought she might need an ally rather than come immediately under the influence of her parents. Maybe he could slip out and call Florence.

'May I go now please?' Forbes said, a quaver in his voice. 'I have nothing more to say, nothing more that I know and I have a flight to catch.'

'I have a murder to solve, *monsieur.* Did you ever hear anything about Madame Felder having enemies?'

'No.' Forbes was stone-faced but his hands were clenched.

'Do you know anything of her relations with her husband's children?'

'No, nothing at all.'

'You are aware that while the two children and their mother have rented an apartment in Houston to be near General Felder, Madame Felder was not invited to join them? She stayed in a hotel.'

'I did not know that. I know nothing of their personal lives.

I'm a corporate lawyer and I really don't want to miss my flight.'

J-J's expression, which had during these questions been coldly formal, broke into a smile. 'Flights can be delayed, *monsieur.* It just takes a phone call. So tell me, how is the company's health when its chairman is very ill? How will it continue after his death?'

'The company is trading profitably and it has good management at all the senior levels so it should continue to prosper should the chairman be unable to resume his duties. He has been ill for several months, nearly a year.'

'Ah, you see, I learn something from you,' J-J said, with another smile. 'I did not know that. Do you have a phone number for the Felders' personal lawyer?'

'I can probably get one once I'm back in London.'

'Perhaps you could try now, please.'

'There isn't time.'

'*Monsieur,* you may not be aware that there are terrorist aspects to this murder inquiry and I may detain you as long as I have questions for you to answer.' J-J was not smiling now. 'You will of course be allowed to see a lawyer and your consul, but this being Friday afternoon, you may have to wait until Monday.'

Forbes began to protest, thought better of it and pulled out a mobile phone. He dialled a long number, obviously international, and obviously someone he knew, judging by his friendly tone when he said, according to the interpreter's whispered but simultaneous translation, 'Sylvia, can you get me a number for Mervin Kahn at Cumberson and Hatch, the chairman's personal lawyer. You may have to ask his secretary. I need to talk to him urgently.'

He pulled out a pen and scribbled a number on the blotter of J-J's desk, ended that call and started another. 'Mervin, Alan Forbes here. I'm in France, with the police, identifying poor Monika's body but they want very badly to know who inherits if the general were to die. As you know, it's a murder inquiry and now they've just told me that they suspect a terrorist connection.'

Bruno heard what sounded like protests coming down the line.

'I'm sorry, Mervin, but I have to insist,' Forbes went on firmly. 'Under their anti-terrorism laws they have powers to hold me here indefinitely. Indeed, if I'm not allowed to call you back, I'd like you to start proceedings to get me out of here, the police station in Bergerac. Please tell me whatever you can about this bloody will.'

Forbes closed his eyes and listened for about twenty seconds, then said, 'That's it? Nothing else?'

Another pause. 'I owe you for this, Mervin, many thanks.' Forbes pressed a button on his phone, checked the screen and then slid it back into the breast pocket of his shirt.

'The will is very simple. The house and a private pension of fifty thousand pounds a year were left to Monika, but because of her death that no longer applies. So the house and cash and his life insurance goes to his two children. His shares in the company go into a family trust from which each child can draw fifty thousand pounds a year but the shares themselves are held in trust for any grandchildren. The house alone will be worth at least two million pounds and the company is private, not listed on the Stock Exchange, so it's not easy to assess its current market value. But annual profits range between three and five million pounds a year, depending on currency fluctuations and so on. Any outside buyer wanting to buy it as a going concern would have to pay at least fifty million. General Felder holds two-thirds of the shares and the rest are owned by his original partners in the business, most of whom are still there. Now may I go?'

'Indeed, *monsieur*, with my thanks,' J-J said when the interpreter had finished the translation. 'Bruno here will drive you to the airport and I'll call them to be sure you make your flight.'

16

The plane for Paris was waiting on the tarmac when Bruno arrived at Bergerac airport a few minutes after six. J-J had been as good as his word. Baudouin from the Police aux Frontières had held the plane for the English lawyer's arrival. Forbes shook Bruno's hand and scuttled aboard, perhaps wondering if he had said too much or too little. On the drive to the airport, Bruno had asked what happened to Felder's trust fund and shares if his two children had no heirs.

'I don't know,' Forbes had replied. 'I've wondered that myself. I've also wondered if General Felder ever let his children know the exact terms of his will.'

'It almost sounds as if he didn't trust them,' Bruno had observed.

'I wouldn't know about that.'

'You said Felder's son, Julian, had left the family company before you arrived. Have you heard anything about the circumstances of his departure? Was there perhaps some bitterness?'

'No, I heard nothing.'

'Not even gossip?

'I'm the company's legal officer,' Forbes replied. 'I don't mix much with the people in operations and when I met Julian and Portia at the General's parties the relations seemed amicable. Honestly, that's all I can tell you.'

It was enough to make Bruno pensive as he drove back from Bergerac towards St Denis, aware that he was already far too late for Paulette's scheduled arrival on the train from Périgueux. He pulled in to call her number but her phone was switched off. Then he checked his messages and found one from Florence saying that Paulette had left the train at Les Eyzies, before it reached St Denis where her parents would be waiting. Florence had picked her up and driven her back to her own home, where they awaited Bruno's arrival.

Bruno decided to drive home first, change out of his uniform and pick up Balzac before heading to Florence's apartment. He could understand why Paulette was delaying a reunion with her parents. She had probably heard from friends in the rugby team about the graffiti. He called Florence to say he'd be joining them in about an hour.

'Have you eaten yet?' he asked, and when she said she hadn't even thought about it he offered to bring dinner. He stopped to buy bread and potatoes and some cheese and drove on, wondering if Moore, the English cop, could find out more about Felder's relationship with his two children. If they knew about the will, and with their father suffering from terminal cancer, they might have a motive for getting Monika out of the way. And what of their mother, the first wife? There had been nothing about her in the will, although presumably there had been some sort of settlement when they divorced. Perhaps Hodge could get the FBI to make some detailed inquiries into the precise movements of Felder's family in and out of Houston. Bruno thought he'd better suggest that to J-J.

Bruno was startled as he turned into his driveway by the sight of a small van parked askew in front of his house. Sighing inwardly, he recognized it as belonging to the flower shop run by Paulette's parents. As he parked, Balzac came bounding towards him, abandoning the middle-aged man who was rising from the table on Bruno's terrace.

'*Bonjour*, Bernard,' Bruno said.

'Where is she?' Paulette's father demanded, striding angrily towards him, his face red, shoulders hunched and fists clenched. 'What have you done with her, you bastard?'

'Hey, watch your language,' Bruno said, wondering if Bernard was angry enough to take a swing at him. He shifted his feet a little, settling his balance against an attack, just in case.

'You're the father, aren't you? Don't bother to deny it, you piece of *merde*,' Bernard snapped, so furious that bits of spittle were spraying from his mouth. He waved his fist at Bruno. 'I'll have you run out of town for this, seducing a helpless girl. You're the one she's been spending all this time with. It's as clear as day.'

'Calm yourself, Bernard. I'm not the father.'

'And now you're lying!' Bernard roared. He leaped towards Bruno, both arms outstretched, holding his clenched fists together like a battering ram.

Bruno had never encountered an attack like it, the foolish assault of a man who'd never been trained and who had no idea how to fight. He simply swayed to one side, put out a foot to trip

Bernard and let the man's own momentum send him crashing to the ground. Bruno dropped onto him, his knees pinning him down and his hands wrenching Bernard's arms behind his back to immobilize the man while Bruno waited for the curses to cease.

'We'll stay like this until you calm down,' Bruno said, still finding it hard to believe that the overweight little shopkeeper would have dared to attack him, let alone make such an absurd accusation. He'd have been tempted to laugh but Bernard was a decent enough man who deserved to be allowed to keep his self-respect.

'I wouldn't struggle, if I were you,' Bruno added, his tone professional. 'You could dislocate your shoulders. Now, once again, I am not the father of Paulette's child and I'm sure she'll confirm that when she sees fit to talk to you. Right now, given your current state of mind, I'd advise her against it. You have to get a grip on yourself. Do you understand me?'

More curses met Bruno's question. He increased the pressure on Bernard's arms and noticed that Balzac was sitting near Bernard's head, staring quizzically at his master, perhaps wondering if this were some new game he had yet to fathom.

'I repeat, Bernard, we'll stay like this until you calm down. Then if you like we can go and see Father Sentout together.'

'Where is Paulette? Are you keeping her here?'

'No, I'm not, and you are free to search the place once you calm down,' Bruno replied, noting that at least Bernard had stopped cursing and the body beneath him seemed to relax.

'Get off me,' Bernard said. 'It's all right, I won't hit you again.' He paused and then added, 'Please.'

Bruno fought down the urge to laugh. 'You didn't hit me the first time. If you had, I'm in uniform so you'd be under arrest.'

He released the pressure on Bernard's arms and heard him groan with relief. Bruno rose to his feet and stepped back, still watchful although sure that Bernard's arms would be of little use for the next few moments. Bruno opened his front door and left it ajar.

'I'm going to see to my chickens,' he called back to Bernard. 'Feel free to look around but she's not here.'

'She was supposed to arrive on the six o'clock train,' Bernard said, shuffling towards him, his arms crossed in front of his body as though hugging himself. 'And she won't answer her phone.'

He followed Bruno who filled the water bowls for his ducks and chickens and his two stately geese, Napoléon and Joséphine. He scooped some crushed maize from the bin and scattered it over the ground of their run. As the birds darted off to eat, Bruno let himself into the coop and came out with his uniform cap full of fresh eggs.

'You want some eggs?' he asked Bernard. 'They're being prolific this week. I can let you have half a dozen.'

'If it's not you, do you have any idea who the father is?'

'If I knew, I wouldn't tell you. That's entirely up to Paulette.'

'She's just a child.'

'No, Bernard. She's your daughter but in the eyes of the law she's not a child. She's an adult, over eighteen, and wholly responsible for her own life and her own actions. And my job is to enforce the law. So if you try to deal with her as though Paulette were still a child, you'll have me to reckon with. As it is,

I could take you down to the Gendarmerie right now, put you in the cells and charge you with assault.'

As Bruno went into his kitchen to find an egg box, Bernard grunted something that might have been an apology. Then he added, 'She's going to have to get married.'

Bruno put six eggs into the plastic box and then put it on the passenger seat of Bernard's van before turning to face the man.

'No, she is not going to get married unless she does so of her own free choice. There's no shame in being a single mother, if that's what she wants to do. Whatever she decides, I'll support her choice and so should you.'

'The shame of it, those graffiti . . .' Bernard mumbled.

'The only shame involved here is the way you're behaving. And this isn't about you, Bernard, it's about your daughter. Now, do you want to come and see Father Sentout or can I get on with my day? If by any chance I happen to see Paulette or hear from her, I promise I'll advise her to get in touch with you. And if she asks me to come along, I will, just in case that temper of yours bursts out again.'

Bernard slumped against the side of his van, his arms still wrapped around his chest. 'Ah, *merde*, Bruno. This is such a shock. My wife's beside herself, she daren't show her face in the shop or outside the house.'

'These things pass,' said Bruno. 'Are you fit to drive home yourself?'

Bernard stood and swung his arms. 'I suppose so. Thanks for the eggs and I'm sorry about, er, you know.'

'I understand, and drive safely.'

Bruno saw him off and then went indoors to shower and change and to feed Balzac. He took a can of his home-made pâté from the pantry and from the freezer a plastic container filled with *boeuf Bourguignon*, then picked a head of winter salad from his garden. He put the food into a large bag with a bottle of Château de Tiregand red from his cellar and another of a dry white Bergerac from the fridge. Once Balzac had scrambled onto the front seat of the Land Rover Bruno headed, cautiously, into town. He kept stopping and looking down side lanes to be sure Bernard wasn't trying to follow him. He then checked that Bernard's van was parked outside the flower shop before driving on to Florence's place, where he parked his vehicle at the rear, out of sight.

'She's here,' said Florence as she answered the door. 'She helped me bathe the children before we put them to bed. But they wanted to wait up to see you. Paulette doesn't want to go home. She was very upset when I picked her up at the station. Her mother had called her and wept and ranted that she had to get married and claimed that her first grandchild was being sacrificed on the altar of rugby.'

'Bernard was waiting for me at my house in a rage, even took a swing at me. But I think I calmed him down,' Bruno said, glancing at the door to the kitchen and keeping his voice too low for Paulette to hear. 'Has she said anything?'

'She can tell you herself.'

Florence led the way into the kitchen where Paulette was sitting on the floor, Dora and Daniel on each side of her, reading to them. Bruno couldn't see the book's cover but with a flood of childhood memory he recognized it from the words Paulette was reading.

'Voici mon secret,' she read. *'Il est très simple: on ne voit bien qu'avec le coeur. L'essentiel est invisible pour les yeux.'*

'Here is my secret. It is very simple. One only sees well with the heart. The essential is invisible to the eye.'

Bruno saw on the table some paper and crayons. Rather than interrupt the rapt children, he put down his bag of food and wine and quickly sketched a long tube with a large bump in the middle. At one end of the tube he placed a small dot. Then he waited for the children's attention to flag. After a few minutes, Paulette closed the book firmly, looked up at Bruno with a familiar smile and said, *'Bonjour,* Bruno.'

As if released from a spell, Dora and Daniel jumped up and each clutched one of his legs until he bent down and picked them up, one in each arm, and held them where they could see his drawing.

'What's that?' he asked. 'Is it a hat?'

'No, it's the boa constrictor who swallowed the elephant!' Dora cried first and then Daniel demanded, 'Have you read *Le Petit Prince*? Is that where you got your drawing from?'

'I read it when I was a bit older than you are now and I never forgot that story. It made me want to be a pilot,' he replied.

'I'm going to be a pilot and have adventures,' Daniel said. 'So am I,' echoed Dora. Their childish delight was so catching that Bruno found himself laughing aloud and Paulette and Florence joined in. For a moment Bruno wondered whether the charm of the children might seduce Paulette and weigh upon the decision she was facing. At the same time, he knew there was another element that could influence her decision. He had expected to learn today whether or not she'd been picked for the national squad.

Bruno knew that the names of the thirty young women to be chosen would be placed on the website of the national rugby federation at midnight. But newspapers would be informed earlier, under embargo, so that they could arrange for photographs and brief biographies of those chosen in time for the following day's papers. Bruno had arranged with Philippe Delaron that Philippe would call him the moment the embargoed news release reached the sports desk of *Sud Ouest*.

So far, Bruno had heard nothing from the reporter and he was aware that time was running out. But his faith in Paulette's special talent for the sport remained strong. He was certain that if merit were the criterion, Paulette would certainly be picked. So he told himself that Philippe might have been sent on some other story, or that the sports desk had bridled at informing Philippe, or something had come up to delay the announcement.

Bruno had wrestled with the ethics of it all, whether learning that she'd been picked would affect Paulette's decision, or, if she weren't picked, would she give up the sport altogether and decide to have the baby? Bruno knew he was torn between his own doubts over abortion and his hopes for Paulette. This was new for him. Bruno seldom felt such conflict over ethical questions, and when he did, he could usually take refuge in the laws of France. This time the law was silent.

'Thanks for coming, Bruno,' said Paulette. 'I'm sorry to cause all this trouble for you and Florence.'

'I'm sorry that this has triggered such a breach between

you and your parents,' he said. 'Your dad came to see me. He's really upset, accused me of . . .' He broke off, thinking of the two children, and chose his words carefully. 'He thought I was responsible for your condition.'

Paulette grinned at him. 'And that I might finally have won for myself the most eligible bachelor in St Denis? That's what my mum calls you. I think she was quietly hoping it was you, despite our age difference.'

Bruno had to smile at her comment. Florence interrupted, saying it was time for the children to go to bed and as a special treat, Bruno could tuck them in and kiss them goodnight. Bruno put the *boeuf Bourguignon* into the microwave and said he'd better first peel the potatoes.

'I'll do that,' said Paulette. 'Let me set the table and make the salad. Where's the corkscrew for the wine?'

The children were already sleepy and once he and Florence had kissed them both goodnight they settled down quietly in the bed they shared. Bruno thought the time might be coming for him to build them a bunk bed. It shouldn't be difficult, just some wood and a ladder. He'd have to make a sketch, he thought, as he went back into the kitchen where Paulette handed him and Florence a glass of wine. The potatoes were already bubbling in hot water, the salad had been made, the baguette cut into thick slices and Bruno's pâté had been opened and turned onto a plate.

'I don't think there's room for me to stay here but I don't want to go to my parents' place tonight,' Paulette said, as the pâté disappeared.

'Normally you'd be very welcome to stay at my place but in

the circumstances, I don't think that's a good idea,' Bruno said. 'I'll call Fabiola. She and Gilles have a spare room and I can drop you off. But I really think you have to see your parents at some point. Maybe if Father Sentout were there . . .'

'Absolutely not,' said Paulette. 'I'm fond of him but I can't stand the idea of the priest and my father going on about the teachings of the Church and the law of God. I had quite enough of that in my childhood. Perhaps we could meet them somewhere public but I'd be grateful if you and Florence could be there. I feel that I ought to tell them what I intend to do. They have a right to know but not to stop me.'

'Perhaps you could let them know before you meet, a phone call, even a letter,' said Florence as Bruno called Fabiola, who said that Paulette was welcome to their spare room for the weekend.

'A phone call would be brutal,' Paulette said. 'I'd have to tell them and then refuse to discuss it and just end the call. Do you have some notepaper?'

'Let's eat first,' said Bruno, taking the *boeuf Bourguignon* from the microwave and stirring it to be sure it had warmed through. He poked a fork into the potatoes to check that they were done.

As he served the food Florence went into her own bedroom which she used as a study and came back with some writing paper and an envelope. She handed them to Paulette. 'Do you know what you're going to say?'

'I was hoping you two might help me draft something.' She bent her head to her plate. 'Mmm, this smells good.'

'The simpler you write it the better,' said Bruno. 'Just tell them that you love them but this is a decision you have to make for yourself and suggest that you meet somewhere. I wouldn't propose St Denis, you'd have too much of an audience. I'd suggest that place in St Cyprien, Le Chai. And don't put it in the post. I'll drop it off in their letter box.'

'Should I not add something about regretting the embarrassment this has caused them?'

'If you like,' said Florence, fanning her hand before her mouth as if the food were too hot. 'That's not a comment, Bruno. It's very good. I always have to let food cool down a little.' She turned to Paulette. 'You don't have to apologize for anything although it wouldn't hurt to add something like that. But I wouldn't say what it is you intend to do. That's your own affair.'

Paulette looked down at the table and bowed her head so that the hair fell forward and hid her face. 'They were badgering me about the father and why I couldn't just marry him and have the baby.'

'Again, that's your own business,' Florence said.

'What do you think?' Paulette asked Bruno, her voice muffled.

'I think that you and I know who the father was,' he replied, and then corrected himself. 'Who the father is.'

'Florence told me that you thought you knew who it was, and that his wife had another baby on the way.'

'About six weeks to go, she told me,' he replied, wiping his plate clean with a hunk of bread and avoiding her eye.

'I didn't know you'd met her.' Paulette sounded almost amused but then her voice hardened and she raised her head to look Bruno in the eye. 'And him?'

Bruno shook his head. 'I saw him by chance when you and he were arguing in the car park in Périgueux. I saw his car's registration number. As simple as that.'

'So you jumped to conclusions,' she said, half-smiling, but her eyes were glittering with some quite different emotion. 'Had you not considered that I might have turned to Gérard Bollinet for advice, as a friend, as a teacher I respected? Just because you saw us arguing in a car park doesn't necessarily mean he's the father.'

Bruno felt himself blushing as his surprise turned into a sensation of hollowness in his stomach. Could he have been so wrong, so arrogantly convinced of his own intuition that he had made such a foolish mistake? But already he was thinking who else the father might be.

'So it isn't him,' he said, thinking that Paulette hadn't directly denied that Bollinet was the father. She had only questioned his suspicion, but Bruno thought he'd better go along with her half-denial. 'I'm sorry for my misjudgement.'

Paulette nodded. 'I know you're trying to help but please don't put me on some kind of pedestal just because I'm good at rugby. Don't you think I'm capable of making a fool of myself, drinking too much at a party and taking a silly risk with someone I really don't want to see in the morning? You were young once, Bruno. Or did you never have a one-night stand?'

Ouch, thought Bruno, that's putting me in my place.

'I'm grateful for the support from you and Florence,' Paulette went on. 'And I think you have a right to know that I saw the gynaecologist, made a decision and that I have an appointment next week to terminate this pregnancy.'

'Would you like me to be there?' Florence asked her, as Bruno sat back in his chair, wondering why he felt no instant reaction of relief or even of sadness.

He took a sip of his wine, trying to absorb this rush of news. So he'd been wrong about the father and whoever it might have been it was no longer relevant – Paulette had made her choice. It did nothing to ease the turmoil in his mind even if it meant she could play for France. Then the thought struck him again that he'd heard nothing from Philippe Delaron about the announcement of the team. And with that came the sense of relief, that Paulette had made the decision without considering her future in rugby.

'No, thank you,' Paulette said, reaching out a hand to place it on Florence's arm. 'I have a friend at the *lycée* who's been close to me through this, another girl. But I'll stay in touch.'

At that point, Bruno's phone vibrated on the pouch at his waist. He looked at the screen and saw it came from the regional radio, France Bleu Périgord.

'I'd better take this,' he said, and headed out to the balcony as he answered.

'Bruno, it's David from the newsdesk. We've been trying to call Paulette but her phone's turned off. Do you know where we might reach her? We want to do an interview for the morning show.'

'She's on the list for the national team?'

'She sure is. Isn't that great news? And the only one of the thirty who comes from this *département*. Can you get her to call us?'

'Give me a couple of minutes to check where she is,' Bruno said. 'I'll call you right back.'

He closed his phone and punched a triumphant fist at the sky. He'd have given a whoop of joy except for the sleeping children. He felt the tension that had been building all evening fade away before heading back indoors with a beaming smile on his face and tears welling in his eyes.

'I should have brought champagne,' he said as he went back into the kitchen. 'Congratulations, Paulette. You've made the national squad. That was Radio Périgord. They were sent the list under embargo but they want to book you for an interview tomorrow morning.'

She leaped to her feet, raising both her hands in the air in joy and then coming round the table to hug him. 'We made it,' she declared. '*Mon Dieu*, I'm a *bleue*! I'm going to play for France.'

'I can't tell you how proud you've just made me,' Bruno said, returning her embrace. Florence joined them in a group hug and then everyone was kissing everyone else. 'It's wonderful and well deserved. They want you to call them back if I could track you down. Perhaps turn on your phone or you could just use mine.'

'Give me the number and I'll call them,' she said. 'Oh, what happy news in such a miserable week. It might even shut my parents up.' Then her face fell.

'*Merde*,' she said. 'I'd still better write that letter.' She let out a long sigh and then shrugged and her mouth grimaced into what might have been a wry smile. 'At least now there's something cheerful to add. Not, of course, that my mother will think so. She never thought I should play such an unladylike game.'

She bent over the sheet of paper and then looked up with a challenge in her eyes. 'But both of you should know that if

I wanted this baby, and if I wanted to spend my life with the man, I'd give up the sport tomorrow. But right now in my life, I don't want to be a mother, nor a wife.'

'I understand,' said Florence. 'And I think you're right.'

'And I certainly don't want its father. If you knew who it was, you'd probably agree.'

17

Bruno was home soon after ten, still thrilled by Paulette's news and feeling too alert to sleep after taking her to Fabiola's home and then dropping the letter into her parents' postbox. He logged on to his new laptop and went through the procedure with the USB stick to get onto the police VPN and check on the case file.

The report on the interrogation of Kelly and O'Rourke noted that they had so far refused to say a word, except to demand a lawyer and access to a consul. Bruno shrugged, not surprised that two such hard men of the IRA would give nothing away. He saw that J-J had filed a report on Bruno's reconstruction of the hanging to show that two men could have accounted for the murder of McBride–Rentoul. Then he scrolled back through the log to see what else was new to him. He paused at a section detailing the expenditures on McBride's business credit card, recalling that J-J had mentioned a great deal of international travel to countries outside the euro zone, but Bruno had seen no analysis of the man's travels in Europe.

He pulled up a pad and pen and began making notes of the trips over the past year, as indicated by restaurant and hotel bills. There were two trips to Dublin, one to Vienna, others to

Venice, Berlin and Barcelona the previous year. This year had one trip to Florence, another to a place in Switzerland called Sils Maria and one to Amsterdam. Bruno pulled out his diary to check the dates and found that every single trip except those to Dublin included a weekend. The Swiss trip, at a hotel called the Waldhaus, had lasted a week. Most of the hotel bills were for more than a thousand euros, which made Bruno whistle. The Waldhaus was even more. The man spent more on hotels than Bruno earned. He checked on Google and found that Sils Maria was next door to St Moritz, close to the Italian border, probably a winter sports resort.

The file also included information from the British police about his HSBC accounts, one current and the other savings, with eleven thousand pounds in the first and a hundred and twenty thousand in the second. Looking at the credits and withdrawals, Bruno saw that the accounts were mainly used to withdraw money from cash machines in the countries he visited. There was one extra payment in Sils Maria for ski hire. The payments into the savings account came from his company, McBride Creative Associates. There was a separate HSBC account in US currency, holding over two hundred thousand dollars. This showed more payments to McBride which were listed simply as 'travel expense refund'. They came from various companies that Bruno recalled J-J had mentioned, in Panama, the Caymans, the Channel Islands and other tax havens.

Bruno wondered how far Hodge's request to the US Treasury had got in investigating these sources of McBride's income. It would take a massive investment of specialist time to track everything down, and given the secrecy of most of the locations, even harder to identify McBride's clients. Certainly it was beyond Bruno's skills so he went back to the index and scrolled through, finding another listing of the expenditures on Monika Felder's credit card. She seemed to travel almost as much as McBride, again for three or four days at a time, and Bruno started to note down the dates and cities on his pad.

He began with the current year and a payment to a clothes shop in Sils Maria leaped out at him. It was for the same week that McBride had been there. He began cross-checking. Monika and McBride had been in Amsterdam and Florence at the same time. In the previous year, they'd been in Vienna, Venice and Barcelona as well as Istanbul. Their affair had evidently been running for a good while. Then he found another airfare to Bordeaux in Monika's credit card payments. He checked whether she had been travelling to the places outside Europe where McBride had been but found no matches.

Bruno checked the payments into her account. Her bills were paid automatically at the end of each month from the same British bank that issued the credit card, and each payment was listed 'Felder joint account'. That was interesting, Bruno thought. It meant that Monika's husband would presumably be able to monitor her expenditures and thus her travels. Did he know she was having this affair? Or with the difference in their ages, did he simply accept it? Between each of her trips that coincided with McBride's, Monika's credit card showed her to be in Houston, presumably at her sick husband's bedside.

He added a note to the case file, drawing attention to the parallels in the travels of McBride and Monika. What if her husband had not known of the affair, but for some reason had checked her credit card and her movements made him suspicious? And if he were too ill to check her card himself, could his children or his first wife have access to the statements on the joint account?

Under the heading 'Speculation', Bruno suggested that this might need to be checked. And it reinforced the case for asking the FBI to check on the movements of Felder's children. Could their presence in Houston be independently verified by eyewitnesses in the hospital?

Recalling the way a colleague had made use of social media in a previous case, he went into Facebook and looked for Monika Felder. She was there, but she would have to accept him as a friend to look into her account. There would doubtless be a way for the police to access it. He added a note to the case file that it would be worth checking, and that perhaps Felder's first wife and children would have a social media trail.

Bruno looked at his watch. It was midnight. He closed the VPN circuit and logged onto his own internet account and then onto the website of the national rugby federation to look with pride at Paulette's name on the list, followed by her accreditation, St Denis Rugby Club (Périgord). That was a battle Bruno had lost. Since St Denis was the most common name in France for a town, he'd suggested that their formal title should be amended to St Denis-en-Périgord. The Mayor would not hear of it and nor would the rugby club.

Ah well, Bruno said to himself, you can't win them all. He opened the door to let Balzac out, wondering if it was warm enough for his dog to start spending his nights in the kennel outside. It was the custom in the Périgord that hunting dogs slept outdoors the whole year round, but Bruno had raised Balzac from a puppy, when he hadn't the heart to put the little fellow outside. And now Balzac chose for himself. At some point each spring, he simply would not return from his nightly patrol of the grounds. In autumn, one cool evening he'd scratch at the door to come back in. It had become a twice-yearly ritual.

Bruno gazed up at the stars and felt at his waist the buzz of an incoming message. He took out his phone and tapped to open the text. No name was attached but he knew at once that it came from Isabelle. Only she ever contacted him this late.

'Sorry I snapped at you,' he read. 'It turned out well. Your usual luck. Or instinct. Tomorrow?'

Bruno sighed. It would take an army of psychologists to comprehend the layers of meaning that Isabelle could compress into a dozen words, some of them echoing from moments or incidents in the past that they had shared. Her comment on his luck, or his instinct – how many times had she spoken of them before? But she had said sorry. And what might she mean by that reference to tomorrow? He suspected these brief, tantalizing texts were her way of keeping him on edge, her way of maintaining the connection without commitment. It implied that she was still here, not back in Paris, and that was interesting. Isabelle was not a woman to waste her time in the provinces.

With the arrest of the two Irishmen, some of the urgency seemed to have leaked out of the investigation. Bruno knew that a police inquiry was a hungry but not very discriminating beast that needed to be fed and two suspects with motive, opportunity and means to kill would satisfy its appetite while the process of interrogation ground on. And *le bon Dieu* alone knew how long Hodge's financial sleuths would need to track the sources of McBride–Rentoul's income, or how thorough the FBI would be in checking the movements of the Felder family.

So Isabelle was staying in the Périgord. He would invite her to join Hodge and Moore for dinner the following evening. It should be something a little special. He had some of his truffles in the freezer and he could get some *magrets* of duck at the market in the morning and some of those slightly bitter Seville oranges that Marcel sometimes stocked. Or perhaps he could try Kathleen's advice about trying something more modern than the traditional *sauce à l'orange*.

His phone was still in his hand so he pondered for a moment what to say and then texted back: 'Dinner *chez moi* tomorrow. Help me give a Périgord welcome to Hodge and Moore. Grace our table.'

Almost as if summoned by some ghostly presence of Isabelle in the air, Balzac trotted back indoors and gazed up solemnly at Bruno before heading for the kitchen to lap some water from his bowl. He came and rubbed the side of his face against Bruno's leg before settling down on the floor at the foot of Bruno's bed, where a soft blanket awaited him. Shortly thereafter, Bruno joined his hound, and fell into a deep and contented sleep.

He was awoken, even before his cockerel greeted the dawn, by Balzac's soft growl, alerting Bruno to the coming of a car. He slipped on his tracksuit trousers and running shoes, kept ready by his bed for the morning jog, and reached his front door as his visitor knocked. It was Gilles, hair tousled, his smartphone held up in his hand so Bruno could see the image of a newspaper headline, **IRA Arrests in France.**

'It's today's *Daily Mail* in London,' Gilles said, and scrolled down to a sub-headline: **Police suspect IRA death squad behind murders.** 'What's going on, Bruno?' he demanded. 'And how come the Brits have it when we don't?'

'Come in, Gilles,' Bruno said, his heart sinking as he recalled what J-J had said about the relentless British press. He would have to be sure he said nothing that would make matters worse. 'I'll make some coffee for us. Can you call up today's *Sud Ouest* on that phone of yours? They might have something.'

'They don't, not in the paper,' said Gilles, following him into the kitchen as Blanco called out his morning *cocorico* from the chicken coop. 'But there's something on the website, written by Philippe Delaron and filed after midnight, saying some shock news had emerged from London about IRA terrorists living here and arrested. There was nothing on the radio as I drove here but that will soon change. How did he find out about it?'

'He probably monitors the British press. It's easy enough to set up an alert on Google News to cover any reference to the Dordogne or Périgord in the foreign media.' That was true, Bruno thought as he spoke, but he suspected that Kathleen might have been behind Philippe's news bulletin and that half the French media would be baying after the story today.

'What can you tell me, off the record?'

'Two men, one British from Northern Ireland and one Irish,

have been arrested, one in Bergerac for possession of two kilos of cocaine and the other in Montignac for a firearms offence,' said Bruno, turning to face his friend once he'd filled the kettle, set out two cups and put coffee grounds into the cafetière.

'Each man is a former IRA member who served time in that special British prison at Long Kesh for being involved in bomb attacks,' he went on. 'But they served their time. They were released and under European law they have paid their debt to society and as European citizens can now live and work anywhere in the European Union. Our authorities knew about them and kept a discreet eye on them, but being former IRA members was not the reason for their arrest.'

'The *Mail* says they're being questioned about the mystery deaths in Lalinde, that British woman and the Irish man.'

'Of course they're being asked about that,' Bruno said, pouring the almost boiling water into the coffee grounds and leaving them to steep. 'We'd be derelict in our duty if we didn't follow up on any possible connection.' He took care not to lie to Gilles while giving nothing away.

'The paper also says that British and American counterterrorist specialists are in Périgueux to help with the investigation. Is that true?'

'You'd expect that, given the close cooperation we've developed in counterterrorist matters. You ought to feel reassured.'

'Can I quote you on that?'

'No, you asked me to speak off the record. But I'd be surprised if the police spokesman didn't confirm that today, now it's already been reported.'

'The *Daily Mail* says the names are O'Rourke in Montignac and Kelly in Bergerac. Is that right?'

Bruno pushed down the plunger in the cafetière and nodded. 'Gilles, we're friends and I trust you but there's nothing more I can say about this. Do you want milk or sugar?'

'Just black is fine, thanks. Did you talk to Philippe?'

'No, nor did I say anything to the British woman, Kathleen, the journalist who's on the cooking course. Anyway, I have a bone to pick with Philippe. He was supposed to tip me off about the big news last night, that Paulette is on the French national team. All the sports desks get the news in advance under embargo but the young devil didn't call me so he'll be waiting a long time for any favours from me.'

'She's made the squad? That's wonderful!' Gilles's eyes lit up in genuine delight and he shook Bruno's hand warmly. 'And well done, I know what this means to you and I'm glad for both your sakes.'

'Drink your coffee and then I have to feed the chickens and take my morning run. Terrorists or no terrorists, I'm still the policeman of St Denis and that means being in the market this morning. Still, thanks for dropping in and make sure you tell Fabiola about Paulette's success. And by the way, we're reinstating the Monday evening dinners, only without Pamela and Miranda because of their cooking course. We'll have them here at my place, Florence and the kids, you and Fabiola, Felix and Jack Crimson when he gets back.'

'Where's he gone?'

'He had to go back to London for a few days,' Bruno replied. 'You know how he comes and goes.'

'Are you sure he's not involved in this Irish business?'

'I've no idea and that's enough questions, Gilles. Balzac and I need our morning exercise. Care to join us?'

Gilles laughed. 'That's too much activity for me.' He finished his coffee and put the cup in the sink. 'Thanks for the coffee and we'll see you Monday, if not before. Maybe in the market.'

The day had dawned clear, still chill from the night with the sun not yet above the horizon. But it promised to be warm and as Bruno reached the top of the ridge, the rays began to reach him slantwise through the trees, lighting up the first leaves, brilliant in the pure, fresh green of springtime and serenaded by the dawn chorus of the songbirds. The chirpy, descending notes of a chaffinch blended with the squeaky calls of the little wrens and the *me voici, me voici*, as French children called the 'here I am' of the song thrush, almost drowned out by the cheerful, assertive calls of a blackbird.

How could I live anywhere but here? Bruno asked himself. Here in these woods where I feel I know every tree and the birds that give each copse and clearing this gift of music that I know so well, where all the stars are familiar and where Balzac feels so at home. These woodlands give me truffles and mushrooms, wild garlic and sorrel and asparagus and the fresh young fiddle ferns. And in autumn come the acorns that Joe, Bruno's predecessor as town policeman, had shown him how to prepare to make the kind of makeshift coffee from toasted acorns that the French had drunk in the war years. Joe's wife had once baked for Bruno a loaf of the yellowish-brown, crunchy bread made from chestnuts that was another reminder of those hungry times of the Occupation.

Every shop and supermarket could close in St Denis and we wouldn't starve, Bruno thought, as he skirted the small outcrop of boulders that marked the last leg of his run towards home. National statistics suggested that this *département* was one of the poorest in France by average income, and yet the quality of life here didn't reflect this. Statistics could not show the reality of the local economy in a place like this, where people lived on their vegetable gardens for most of the summer, on the chickens they raised and the eggs they ate or swapped with neighbours for pots of jam and fresh-caught fish from the river.

Through his hunting club, Bruno was never short of a shoulder of venison or a haunch of wild boar. The *bécasse* Bruno most liked to hunt, the wiliest and most tasty of game birds, were always in demand among his neighbours. In exchange, Oudinot the farmer would always let Bruno have some of his milk-fed veal. His friend Stéphane, the cheesemaker, kept Bruno in butter, cheese, milk and yoghurt in return for the ducks, chickens and truffles that Bruno brought him, and the pots of blackberry jam that Bruno made at the end of summer from the abundant hedgerows at the bottom of his garden. The old ways of the barter economy remained vibrant here in the Périgord and the sense of community was all the better for it.

Bruno had reached home, showered and changed and was eating one of Stéphane's yoghurts with a spoonful of honey from another neighbour when the seven o'clock news came on the radio. Wars in Syria, an earthquake in Italy, a volcano erupting in Indonesia and a French minister caught with an illicit bank account in Switzerland gave way to the local bulletin, which led with the British press report of an IRA death squad at work in the Périgord. That wasn't quite what the newspaper had said, Bruno thought, but it would certainly get the attention of the public and set alarm bells ringing at police headquarters in Périgueux.

He assumed he was still in trouble with Prunier. Certainly he had not been invited back to the morning team meetings in Prunier's office but if they needed him, Bruno was always easy to find. The only message on his phone was from Isabelle, accepting with pleasure his invitation to dinner. He collected a dozen eggs from his chickens for Pamela and set off for the riding school and the pleasure of a reunion with Hector.

'It's wonderful news about Paulette being on the team,' said Pamela, hugging him when he handed her the carton of eggs. 'Give her our warmest congratulations and I'm also delighted for you. You worked so hard with her and I know what it means to you. Don't forget the farewell cocktails for the cookery class here tonight at six, before I take them all off to the Vieux Logis.'

'I'll have to miss it, I'm sorry,' he said. 'But I'll try to come to your oyster feast in St Cyprien tomorrow morning to say goodbye to them.'

Fabiola and Kathleen joined them as Bruno was leading Hector out into the yard. Kathleen didn't quite avoid Bruno's eye but gave him only the most cursory nod and there was none of that quiet air of triumph Bruno knew from Philippe Delaron after he had scored some scoop for his newspaper. Bruno guessed that Kathleen knew of the IRA story but could not claim personal credit for it. Besides, the Sunday paper she worked for was not attached to the *Daily Mail*. If anything, her own paper's news desk would be annoyed with her for failing to provide it. And today was Saturday. Her newspaper came out tomorrow. That meant she'd be under pressure to write something special for them today.

They rode out, the clatter of hooves in the yard giving way to the gentler thudding as the horses reached the softer ground. Pamela led them at a trot up the lane that climbed through some woods to the water tower, beyond which ran a long, level slope along the ridge to the village of Meyrals, home to a famous round loaf of dense bread and to a colony of local artists. Pamela paused at the water tower, announced that she planned a long ride that morning, but that Bruno and Fabiola might like to turn back early, since they had work that day.

There was time for a fine gallop, Hector taking Bruno into the lead ahead of Pamela mounted on her own horse, Primrose, and Fabiola on the Andalusian. Kathleen had trouble keeping up. She was riding the warmblood, a rather lazy horse who preferred show jumping to the kind of cross country rides that Pamela and her friends enjoyed. They paused at the turnoff to the shortcut back to the riding school and said their farewells, Kathleen asking if Bruno might be at the market later that morning.

'Maybe, but not for long,' he called back before turning away after Fabiola. 'But I'll see you for oysters tomorrow.'

Back in the yard, Félix was using a pitchfork to clear the stables of old straw which he piled into a trailer to take to the dung heap. The custom was that families whose children were taking riding lessons were allowed to help themselves for their gardens and each of them thanked Félix with five euros. Bruno chatted with the youth while rubbing down his horse and then heard a clatter of hooves as Kathleen came into the yard.

'I really need to talk to you,' she said, jumping down. 'Something important has come up.'

'You mean the IRA? I heard it on the radio this morning,' he said. 'I can't help you on that.'

'Is there a connection to the Lalinde murder?' she pressed. 'Please help, Bruno. I'm under a lot of pressure from London on this.'

Bruno sighed theatrically. 'I'm sorry but I don't know and even if I did, I couldn't tell you. I don't know who leaked that bit of information but if it was a French policeman, he'll be in real trouble.'

'It wasn't a French cop,' she said, almost interrupting him. 'The story came out of Dublin last night from the crime reporter for RTÉ, the Irish TV and radio network. Apparently one of the two men arrested is an Irish national so the Irish government had to be informed. My newsdesk got onto me to see if I could add anything. Can you at least confirm that two men have been arrested? You know the police spokesman won't talk to me because I'm not accredited.'

'If that's right about the news coming out of Dublin, then you're a lot better informed than I am,' Bruno replied. 'But you know Philippe Delaron so if I were you I'd try asking him. Philippe had some story about an IRA connection on his paper's website overnight. And now you'll have to excuse me, Kathleen. I have to get to work.'

18

The Saturday morning market occupied the whole of the square in front of the Mairie so Bruno parked his van outside the Gendarmerie and called in to say hello to Sergeant Jules and see if Yveline was in her office. Jules told him to go straight in and Bruno found her doing paperwork, preparing the schedule of drink-driving patrols for the following month. She put a manila file on top of the paper she was working on before coming round her desk to greet him.

'So after all this time you still don't trust me?' he said, grinning, with a gesture at the schedule she had hidden.

'I don't trust anybody with that file,' she said. 'But you've been around long enough to know how it works. The teams usually go out Friday and Saturday nights and Sunday afternoons after all those family lunches. That's when the pickings are rich and we have these arrest quotas to fill. But sometimes we mount a little surprise.' She shrugged. 'Count yourself lucky you don't get judged by the number of your arrests. What can I do for you?'

'I came to invite you to dinner at my place this evening, unless you're tired of the company of cops.' He explained that Hodge and Moore would be there, along with Isabelle, but it would be a social occasion rather than a working dinner.

'I never say no to your cooking,' Yveline replied. 'And it sounds like an interesting group.'

Bruno walked along the Rue de Paris, stopping every few yards to shake hands or kiss cheeks, and be slapped on the back by those who had heard Paulette's interview on the radio. When he reached the first stalls of the market that had overflowed from the town square he paused, looking for inspiration.

Other than the duck breasts, he'd hardly given a thought to the evening's menu. Since Hodge and Moore were foreigners, he'd have to introduce them to real foie gras but should he serve it cold as a pâté or sauté it with honey and vinegar? He'd need to get some cheese from Stéphane and for dessert he planned to make a chocolate mousse. He saw that the first young courgettes of the season were already on sale and also some of the early strawberries, the long-shaped *gariguettes* that were the first variety to ripen.

Bruno asked Marcel, whose produce Bruno always trusted, whether he thought the strawberries were worth buying. Marcel held out his hand palm down, waggled it and shrugged.

'They're on sale at other stalls but not mine, and congratulations on Paulette being selected for the *bleues*. Everybody's been talking about it,' he said. 'For the strawberries, I'd prefer to wait another week or so. But the young courgettes are good. What are you cooking?'

'Some foreign friends are coming to dinner so I thought I'd make a classic Périgord meal, foie gras and *magret de canard*, and I'm trying to decide between oranges or cherries for a sauce. And since you've warned me off the strawberries I'll make a chocolate mousse.'

'Wish I were coming. But if you're serving *magret* you'll be doing *pommes de terre Sarladaises* and I know you grow your own potatoes so how would you use the courgettes?'

'Slice them longways, deep fry them in batter and serve them hot with Stéphane's *aillou* to eat with our drinks before dinner.'

'Sounds good. I'll give you a kilo and pick out some of the bigger ones for you while you get your cream and *aillou* from Stéphane. How many are coming to dinner?'

'We'll be seven, maybe eight.'

'How are you preparing the foie gras? *Mi-cuit* or what?'

'I thought perhaps *poêlé*, with a sauce of honey and balsamic.'

Marcel shook his head. 'If you did oranges or cherries with the duck, that's two sweet sauces in a row. Why not offer them one of your *confits de canard* instead? That's what I'd do.'

Loaded down with the foie, cheese, cream and *aillou*, Bruno returned to Marcel's stall to pick up the fruit and courgettes. He was heading towards the Mairie with his purchases when he heard his name called from an outside table at Fauquet's.

'J-J told me I'd probably find you here,' said Hodge, standing up and towering over Bruno as he held out his hand. 'He also said you reckoned this place served the best croissants in the Périgord so I thought I'd give them a try. And I'll be sure to call in at your local wine store. J-J made St Denis sound like the culinary heart of France. I can see you've been shopping for dinner this evening. Let me buy you a coffee.'

'Give me a moment to put all this in the office fridge. Order the coffee and I'll be right back.' Bruno darted into the Mairie, stowed his food and then called Juliette in Les Eyzies to invite her to dinner.

'Is it formal?' she asked, nervously.

'Not at all, very relaxed, all cops, all French-speaking. One FBI man from the Paris Embassy and a very nice *rosbif* from Scotland Yard plus Yveline, the commandant from the Gendarmerie and a woman from French counterterrorism who used to be a detective in Périgueux. All colleagues.'

'I see, all top brass so no pressure,' she said cheerfully. 'I'd love to come. What can I bring?'

'Just yourself,' he replied. 'About seven.' He gave her directions and went down to join Hodge, who had that morning's *Sud Ouest* open before him. Fauquet, realizing the second coffee would be for Bruno, had automatically put a basket of croissants and *pains au chocolat* on the table.

'Nothing in here about the IRA,' Hodge said, pointing to the paper.

'It came in too late for the local edition but it's on their website and on the radio news,' Bruno said, picking up a croissant. 'There's a British journalist here who told me the story broke in Dublin on Irish radio. I suppose J-J had to inform their embassy.'

Hodge was already halfway through his croissant. Bruno was amused to see that with his mouth still full, he washed it down with a sip of coffee, just as Bruno did. They grinned companionably at one another.

'I thought the croissants were pretty damn good in Paris but this is in a different class altogether,' Hodge said.

'Where do you go in Paris?' Bruno asked.

'I'm working my way through the ones that won the prizes for the best in the city. My favourites are Poilâne on the Rue du

Cherche-Midi and Blé Sucré, just off the Rue du Faubourg Saint-Antoine. The coffee here is just as good too.'

'I'm glad you like them. Fauquet will be delighted, even more so when I tell him you're from the FBI.'

'I guess I'm not the first one from the Bureau to come here. My predecessor, Nancy, told me about this region, and about your cooking, in a long memo she sent me after she left Paris and heard I was her replacement. That was before she resigned from the Bureau. You know she's gone into politics, running for a seat in Congress?'

'Yes,' said Bruno, an image suddenly leaping into his mind of Nancy stripping off her sweater to stand amid a knot of soldiers in her black bra before putting on a bulletproof vest. 'She was a very impressive woman.'

'She says the same about you, except the bit about the woman. Her after-action report made for quite a read. She says you saved her life. The Bureau owes you a debt for that. So I brought you something.' Hodge pulled a large envelope from the briefcase at his feet and handed it to Bruno.

'I saw that note you filed on the case file about Felder's family and social media. That's something we do as a matter of course, so in there you'll find photos of the first wife and children plus some of their postings, along with the websites they've been using in Houston.'

'How do you get these?' Bruno asked, leafing through the photos.

He was sure the photo of Felder's son Julian had never come from Facebook. It had been taken in the street as he climbed out of a car and showed an athlete running to seed with a double chin and puffy eyes. The daughter, Portia, was blonde with a clear complexion, thin lips and hard eyes, very fashionably dressed as she climbed from the same car as her brother. In one photo that probably had come from social media she was wearing a strapless evening gown that showed off a gym-toned body. There was a photo of their mother smiling at what looked like a family gathering. She was plump and looked comfortable about it, happy in her skin, and her face still carried some hints of what must have been a striking beauty. He looked up at Hodge, waiting for an answer to his question.

'Don't ask.' Hodge gave a lopsided grin before adding, 'Our Houston field office is making checks on the movements of the family just to be sure they've all been where they say they have. J-J told us what the lawyer said about Felder's will, which could give them a motive to get rid of Monika.'

'I'm glad we agree but I thought your only concern was what had happened to the money stolen in the Baghdad ambush,' Bruno said, signalling Fauquet for more coffee.

'Well, you know how it is,' Hodge drawled, reminding Bruno once again of cowboy films. He could picture Hodge in a broad-rimmed stetson, squinting across some endless prairie. 'When it comes to crime one thing leads to another and you find yourself coming at the thing from a different direction. But you're right. My job is to find out what happened to Uncle Sam's cash, get it back if we can, and nail the bad guys even if we don't find a red cent.'

'Is there enough money at stake for your Treasury experts to make a real effort? They must have bigger targets.'

Hodge shrugged as Fauquet brought more coffee. 'We'll see.'

He reached for a *pain au chocolat*. 'If these are as good as the croissants I might just be tempted to move down here myself.'

'I'm grateful for this,' Bruno said, tapping the envelope. 'Is there anything I can do for you down here?'

Hodge grinned at him. 'Just point me to this famous wine store of yours.'

'Cross the bridge and go straight on for about four hundred metres. You can't miss it. There's a big pile of wine barrels outside. You can taste as much as you want and if you like it, you can order it here and he has a store in Paris where you can pick it up.'

'Right, I'll leave you to get on with your day. Since you're in uniform I guess you're still working.' He put a ten-euro note under his saucer and rose, waving away Bruno's attempt to pay. 'See you this evening, about seven. I may have some news by then. I asked J-J to organize a really thorough search of Rentoul's place, not just metal detectors but some ground-penetrating radar. I bet he has a safe buried somewhere, or a cache of some kind. A guy like that, he'd want to have a quick escape kit to hand, some other documents and cash.'

Bruno nodded, thinking that made sense. 'Any idea what Moore is working on?'

'Trying to backtrack Monika and find out just how she met Felder and how his first marriage broke down. There's no indication of her having any German family and that's unusual.'

Bruno made no secret of his surprise. 'A senior officer in military intelligence getting divorced to marry a foreign national? There must have been a security review at the time.'

'That's what Moore is trying to find but he's having trouble getting into the archives,' Hodge said. 'Felder was at Rheindahlen, the main British base in Germany just west of the Rhine. It was huge, over ten thousand people. The IRA hit the place with a car bomb in March 1987, injuring about thirty people, mainly Germans. You may recall some of our bases in Germany had been attacked by Libyan bombs so our army intel guys did their own report on the Rheindahlen attack. I'm hoping to dig it out, thanks to a buddy who's still in the military. It's interesting that the IRA keeps coming into the picture. Maybe we'll hear something from Moore tonight.'

Bruno did a brief patrol of the market, which was busy for this early season between Easter and summer holidays. He noticed several new faces who were clearly French. He knew from the Mayor that the population of St Denis was climbing as more and more people from northern and eastern France moved to spend their retirement here, which meant the average age in the *commune* was also rising. He wondered what that would mean for him, whether older people would be targets for burglary or confidence tricksters or the new phenomenon of cyber-crime. The *département* of the Dordogne had one of the lowest levels of violent crime and burglaries and Bruno wanted to keep it that way.

He crossed the bridge, glancing down at the anglers dotted along the quayside as he headed for Bernard's flower shop. It was always busy on market day as people bought flowers and plants when invited to a lunch or dinner, or took advantage of the spring weather to tend their gardens and fill them with colour. To Bruno's surprise, he found Paulette busy behind the cash register while her father offered advice to customers in the garden where he displayed his wares. He waited until she'd dealt with the various clients before asking if all was well.

'Dad and I are fine. Fabiola's working today so she dropped me off in time to join them for breakfast. Mum is still in a state but she's being kept busy with phone calls from people who heard the news on the radio about the rugby team.'

She broke off to attend to another customer who came in from the garden with Bernard, each of them loaded down with young geranium plants.

'I'm sorry about last night, Bruno,' said Bernard, once the customer had gone.

'Forget it, and I'm glad to see you two on good terms again.' That was one thing about running a shop, Bruno thought. The customers had to come first, leaving little time for moping. 'You both know where to reach me if there's anything I can do and the whole town is really proud of you, Paulette, me most of all.'

He left as more customers came in, one of them from the rugby club who shook Bruno's hand warmly before embracing Paulette and congratulating her father and then asking when the club would hold the obligatory celebration of Paulette's success. Bruno hadn't thought of that but knew there was a home match at the town stadium the following afternoon. Maybe they could organize something after the match. He called Lespinasse, the club president, while returning across the bridge and was told a *vin d'honneur* for Paulette was already in hand. Paulette would toss the coin before the match and the club would also take advantage of the occasion to celebrate the championship cup the young women's team had won. Bruno was glad to hear it, feeling guilty that with the murders and the other dramas of the week, he'd let that slip his mind.

Back in the Mairie, Bruno knocked on the door of the Mayor's office and found him at his desk, fountain pen poised over his manuscript, with some old documents beside him and his favourite pipe giving off an aromatic scent. The laws against smoking in offices could hardly apply to a Mayor in his own Mairie.

'I'm very glad to hear it and I shall certainly attend,' the Mayor said once he heard of the ceremony for Paulette. 'What do you know about her pregnancy?'

'She seems to be reconciled with her father and she is planning to have an abortion next week, something she'd decided before the news came through about the rugby. She'll be in her eleventh week so she's cutting it fine.'

The Mayor shook his head sadly. 'That poor child. I voted for the new law that extended the approved period from ten to twelve weeks when I was in the Senate. Now I wonder if we did the right thing. Perhaps it's for the best.'

Bruno recognized the manuscript the Mayor was working on, had watched his history of St Denis grow from a few sheets of paper to its current impressive dimensions, a stack of handwritten pages as thick as Bruno's clenched fist.

'How much further to go?' he asked.

'I'm just working on something that might excite your professional interest. I'm up to the chapter on the Revolution and I've come across some old letters of denunciation to one of your predecessors.'

'They were in the town archives?' Bruno asked, thinking

that perhaps it was time to add his own files of such letters to the archive.

'Yes, it's remarkable what you can find in the attic up there. And the same family names keep recurring. Here's a man called Marty denouncing a female Lespinasse for witchcraft. It's quite something to find in one letter two of the most common family names in St Denis to this day. And here they are again, Lespinasse and Marty, in muster rolls to be conscripted in 1793 when the Austrians and Prussians and the English declared war on the Revolution after we guillotined the King.'

'My predecessor who received the letters, who was he?'

'The letters were addressed to the Committee of Public Safety in Bergerac where some honest constable doubtless was told to do his duty, whatever that was at the time. The Revolution prided itself on a belief in reason so I doubt whether they'd have swallowed any tales of witchcraft. What we have here is a copy of the denunciation signed by a man named simply Taroupe.'

'Who was he? A clerk in the Mairie?'

The Mayor shrugged. 'It's an old name but it seemed familiar so I looked it up. It means hair growing between the eyebrows. He was conscripted, too. This *commune* sent a hundred and ten young men off to the Revolutionary armies, and then more each year for Napoleon's wars.'

'And two hundred names on the town memorial for the Great War,' Bruno said. 'It hardly bears thinking about.'

'Perhaps it will put your current concerns into some perspective. I saw Philippe's report about the IRA men. Any developments I should know about?'

'Jack Crimson was told to beat a hasty retreat back to London. Now the IRA men have been arrested he may think it safe enough to return.'

'How about your little difficulty with Prunier? Is that resolved?'

'I've heard no more about it,' said Bruno. 'But I'm no longer being called in to his morning case meetings at headquarters. That suits me since it means I don't lose half my mornings.'

'But you still know what's going on with the inquiry?'

'Yes, there's a special computer network which has all the case files, updated three or four times a day. And the British and American cops seem happy to keep me informed. In fact, they're coming to dinner tonight.'

'Good,' said the Mayor. 'I've always thought that a little judicious hospitality was an essential lubricant in most human affairs.'

19

Bruno took his sharpest knife from the bowl of hot water, dried the blade carefully and then sliced the raw foie into six generous portions, each about the thickness of his finger. The hot knife ensured a clean cut. Six big tranches of bread had already been toasted and he'd made the chocolate mousse which was now chilling in the fridge. The potatoes had been peeled, parboiled and dried, ready to go into the duck fat. The garlic had been peeled and sliced. One of the last of Bruno's black truffles from the winter had been taken in good time from his freezer and was now ready to be grated over the *pommes de terre Sarladaises*. The parsley and the salad had been picked from the garden and washed.

He had taken from the stores two big jars of *confit de canard* that he'd made in the winter, sealing them with the yellow duck fat that filled the top third of each jar. There were four generous thighs and legs in each one and they were all now roasting in the oven, almost filling his largest casserole. The Tomme d'Audrix and *cabécous* of goat's cheese were set on a plank of wood from a case that had once held six bottles of Château de Tiregand's Grand Millésime, a choice vintage from 2009 of which Bruno was especially fond.

The woodstove in the sitting room was warm and glowing, a fresh log of apple wood just added. A bottle of champagne and another of Monbazillac from Clos l'Envège were chilling in the fridge and his last two bottles of the 2009 Tiregand had been decanted. The table was laid for six and the champagne flutes were set out on the coffee table along with Stéphane's *aillou* and a pile of paper napkins for his guests to hold the hot courgettes which he had sliced, ready for the frying pan.

Hector had been ridden, Balzac had been exercised, brushed and fed and the chicken coop had been emptied of fresh eggs. Bruno had cleaned the bathroom and laid out fresh guest towels. He had vacuumed the carpets, changed the sheets on his bed, showered and changed into jeans and a plaid flannel shirt. Now he slipped a cherished CD of Jean Sablon songs from the 1930s and 1940s into his player and the haunting notes of the first song, '*J'attendrai*', began to fill the room. Bruno was ready for his guests.

He was not, however, prepared for the sudden phone call from Gilles, who began by saying he had just posted a story on the *Paris Match* website that might cause Bruno and his colleagues some embarrassment.

'It's about McBride's real identity as a former British intelligence officer called Rentoul who had been one of the planners of the SAS killing of three IRA men in Gibraltar,' Gilles said. 'So it looks to me like a revenge killing. And some official is on his way here from the Special Branch of the Guards, that's the Irish police.'

'You're doing your job as a journalist,' Bruno said. He remembered how good a reporter Gilles had been when they'd first met during the siege of Sarajevo. 'And I'm not going to confirm or deny your story so why should that embarrass me?'

'We're known to be friends so you're the one most likely to be accused of leaking it to me.'

'You and I both know that I'm not your source,' said Bruno, although he suspected that Gilles was right. 'But I imagine you aren't going to say who gave you the information. Just remember that people who leak stories to journalists usually have their own reasons for doing so, and their motives aren't always pure and leaks aren't always true.'

'I know. Anyway, I point out in the piece that the information came from a foreign intelligence source so I hope that leaves you in the clear.'

'We'll see, Gilles, thanks for the call.'

Bruno put his phone back in his pouch and thought that a foreign source was likely to mean Moore, Hodge or Jack Crimson, unless Gilles had been digging into diplomatic sources in Dublin. On the whole, and given that nugget about the Guards, Bruno thought Dublin the more likely and Prunier was smart enough to reach the same conclusion. He shrugged, knowing he'd rather live with a free press than the alternative. At his feet, Balzac twitched his long ears and gave his little bark to signal that a vehicle was coming up the lane, half an hour early.

Bruno looked out of the window to see Isabelle, alone in a rental car. She drove past him to park discreetly around the back of the house. What did that mean? he wondered. Was she planning to stay the night or did she simply want some time alone with Balzac? With Isabelle, he never knew what to expect. He opened the back door to let Balzac charge out to greet her and stood smiling as he waited for their reunion to take its course. The car door was hardly open before Balzac had scrambled into Isabelle's embrace with a sonorous bay of welcome that blended with her own delighted laughter.

Finally, she disentangled herself and came to embrace him with a bottle of Taittinger champagne, still chilled, in her hand. He hugged her in return, about to kiss her cheek but she turned her head to find his lips for a tantalizing moment that lasted just long enough for Bruno to overcome his surprise and appreciate it.

'I missed you as well as Balzac,' she said, drawing back her head a fraction before he could respond. And then, briefly, she kissed him again before tucking her head against his chest and squeezing.

Hand in hand, they went into the sitting room and Bruno opened the champagne as Isabelle gazed around the familiar space, spotting immediately on one wall a simple watercolour of St Denis, painted from the riverbank.

'That's new,' she said. 'I like it.'

'I bought it the other day at an exhibition of local artists.' He handed her a flute of champagne and bent to pour his own. He stood and raised his glass to her.

'You look wonderful,' he said. 'Lovelier than ever. Your hair suits you like that.'

She was wearing black jeans and ankle boots, an untucked shirt of heavy maroon silk with an open collar and hardly any make-up, just some lipstick that matched her shirt. She handed him the long black raincoat he remembered.

'There's news,' she said. 'The FBI in Washington has put out a press release about reopening the investigation into the loss of the money in Baghdad. I don't know why they've gone public but maybe Hodge can explain it to us.'

He told her about the call from Gilles and his story on the website of *Paris Match*. And the imminent arrival of someone from the Guards.

'I hadn't heard about that but I had to inform Dublin since they're represented on my counterterrorism committee, along with all the EU countries,' she said. 'The two Irishmen are still saying nothing and neither are their wives. We're keeping them all separate and I spent six hours getting nowhere with the women. But we got something from the GPS in their car. We think they were heading for an address in Ustaritz, near Bayonne. Their car had been there before, to the home of a known Basque militant, son of the old ETA veteran who first put the IRA in touch with the Libyans over forty years ago.'

'Has he been picked up?'

'Of course, and the Basque is not talking either. He was born in France so we can't threaten to deport him to Spain. Forensics have been going through his house and car but I haven't seen their report yet. We assume the Irishmen were hoping he'd get them another car or get them over the frontier into Spain. But there is some good news.'

'About time,' said Bruno. 'A link to Rentoul?'

'A perfect link, from the refuse bins nearest to Kelly's garden centre in Bergerac. Forensics got a yellow recycling bag that had envelopes addressed to him, English and Irish papers, the usual garbage. And mixed in were bits of two torn-up photographs from a computer printer. After we'd done the jigsaw puzzle of putting the photos back together, one was of a young Rentoul in British army uniform, the other was taken recently in Lalinde market. On each photo the words "Remember him?" were hand-printed in felt pen. Kelly's fingerprints were on it, but nobody else's so we don't know who sent it.'

'What about the envelope?' Bruno asked.

'We found it in the same bag. Brown paper envelope, addressed to Kelly in the same hand-printing and posted in Bergerac.'

'And then the person who sent it made contact?'

'Two days after the posting date on the envelope a woman speaking English called Kelly at the garden centre from a Bergerac call box. She used a ten-euro phone card that had been bought at the Leclerc supermarket in St Cyprien.'

'And we were monitoring his phone?' Bruno asked hopefully.

'Not live, but we were recording everything so we went back through the tapes for that week and found it. All she said was, "I just sent you something, Mr Kelly, and I think we should meet. I'll come to your business later today." That was all, but it's enough for voice recognition if we can find her.'

'So Kelly was the killer, or one of them,' Bruno said. 'Does he know he's now facing a murder charge?'

'No, we're working out how to play it.'

'You could try showing him these,' Bruno said, went to his study and brought back the photos of Felder's first wife and two children. 'Hodge gave them to me this morning,' he explained. 'The FBI took one of them from Felder's daughter's social media page, the others they took themselves. I'm sure he'll have copies for you. And I can take them to the Leclerc where the phone card was bought. I already sent them around my own little network, hotels and *gîtes*, car hire and campsites, you remember.'

She nodded. 'We'll share the voice tape with Moore. The British have a huge database of IRA voices but that doesn't stop us doing both.'

'This was meant to be a social evening without talking shop,' Bruno said, just as Balzac gave his warning bark again. 'You already know Yveline from the gendarmes and Juliette is also coming, my new counterpart from Les Eyzies.'

'I hope she's an improvement on Louis, but I suppose she couldn't be any worse,' Isabelle replied, drily.

Bruno turned up the heat on the vegetable oil for the courgettes before opening his front door. Hodge and Moore arrived together in an unmarked police car that Bruno recognized from the Périgueux motor pool. Each man had brought champagne, the bottles still very cold so they must have stopped at the *cave* in town to buy them. Almost immediately they were followed by Yveline who was dropped off by one of her gendarmes. She presented Bruno with a bottle of Tiregand. They had hardly been given their champagne when they heard the angry buzz of a trail bike engine revving hard as it came up the lane, skidding on the bend into Bruno's drive.

They all turned to watch as a helmeted figure in white leathers put the bike on its stand. The rider removed the helmet to reveal Juliette, running her hands through her short hair and taking a duffel bag from the bike's rack.

'Greetings, Bruno,' she said, handing him a large jar from the bag. 'Pickled mushrooms, made by me, and now, where's your bathroom so I can change?'

'Thank you and welcome,' he said, showing her the way. 'Or you could use my room to change, it's the door at the end. Would you like a glass of champagne?'

'Yes, please. I'll only be a moment.'

Bruno gave the batter a final whip and then dipped in a dozen sliced courgettes before dropping them into the sizzling fat. He went back to his guests in the sitting room, refilled their glasses and poured one for Juliette, who made her entrance in a plain white dress with a bright pink belt at her waist which matched the colour of her high heeled shoes. Bruno handed her champagne, made the introductions and went for the courgettes, replacing them in the hot oil with another dozen.

'I recommend using a napkin to hold these and then dip them into that *aillou*,' Bruno said, handing them round. 'There are more to come so don't hold back.'

Juliette's noisy arrival had inspired them all to talk of motorbikes, a topic which immediately created the amicable mood that Bruno always hoped for at his dinners. Hodge recalled a Harley-Davidson he'd ridden while in the military and Isabelle confessed that she'd only consented to go out with her first boyfriend so she could ride pillion on his ancient BMW before making him teach her how to ride it. Moore said his first purchase when he'd joined the police was to put down a deposit on a Triumph Bonneville and he'd spent the next two years paying it off. Yveline chimed in that as a student she'd been devoted to her Peugeot scooter. Bruno left them to it and went back for more courgettes and another bottle of champagne from the fridge.

'Can I help?' Juliette asked when Bruno returned. 'What are you making for us?'

Bruno described the menu and when Hodge asked if he could watch the foie being prepared they all piled into the kitchen, where Bruno gave them the last serving of courgettes and then brought out his two largest pans, turned on the gas beneath them and showed them the slices of foie. It felt a little like the class at Pamela's cooking school as they crowded round. Bruno asked each of them to bring their plate, and warned them this would not take long. He asked Moore to open the bottle of Monbazillac that was in the fridge and put his hand over the pans to check that they were hot enough before placing the slices of foie.

'We don't need fat because they already contain enough,' he explained as they began to sizzle. 'Right, I'd like you all to start singing the "Marseillaise" because that's how I time my cooking.'

Just before they reached *Aux armes, citoyens*, he turned over each of the slices with a spatula and told them to keep singing all the way to . . . *abreuve nos sillons*. Then he turned them again and took up the second chorus alone, but Isabelle's high clear voice soon joined him:

Que veut cette horde d'esclaves,
De traîtres, de rois conjurés?
Pour qui ces ignobles entraves,
Ces fers dès longtemps préparés?

With that, he turned out the gas beneath one pan, piled all the slices into it and then poured several splashes of balsamic vinegar to deglaze the pan that was still hot and added four generous spoonfuls of honey and stirred them into the vinegar and fat until it had become a runny sauce. Then he told them to bring their plates in turn, laid a slice of the cooked and slightly charred foie onto the toast he had made earlier and then shared out the sauce and invited them all to the table. He poured out a glass of the golden Monbazillac for each of them and raised his own glass in welcome.

'I've never had this before,' said Hodge, reaching for more bread to wipe up the last of the sauce. 'It's delicious.'

'I'm going to have to learn that second verse of the "Marseillaise",' said Moore. 'It's the first time I've heard it and I like that line about the long-prepared handcuffs. Very suitable for a policeman.'

'When we were kids, we sang a different version,' said Juliette. '*Mangeons bonbons de la patrie* – let's eat the sweets of our homeland.'

'We used to do that with Christmas carols,' said Moore, and launched into: 'While shepherds washed their socks by night . . .'

This was turning into a very promising evening, thought Bruno as he cleared the plates and went back to the kitchen to check on the roasting *confits* of duck and finishing the *pommes de terre Sarladaises* with duck fat from the top of the *confit* jars. He used the pan that still held some of the fat from the foie, added another generous spoonful and then poured in the sliced potatoes he had parboiled, and added the chopped parsley and the slivers of garlic. He took a jug of water into the dining room and told them to help themselves to the decanters of red wine. Back in the kitchen, enjoying the gales of laughter he heard from the dining room, he served the duck and then called Isabelle to help take the plates to the table.

'You haven't added the potatoes,' she said.

'I'll do that in there,' he replied. 'I have a treat that's best done when people can watch.'

Once they each had their duck before them, Bruno took the pan of potatoes into the dining room, a small grater in his other hand.

'There are two ways to make this dish of Sarlat,' he explained. 'The tourists are served it like this, cooked in duck fat and seasoned with garlic and parsley. But for the real thing, we add this.'

He took the truffle he had saved, about the size of a walnut, and began to grate it over the potatoes. As the flakes reached the heat the familiar aroma began to rise and swell and Bruno inhaled deeply. There was nothing like it. He continued grating until the truffle was entirely gone and then began to serve his guests in turn, advising them to lower their heads over their plates to enjoy the uniquely rich and earthy scent of his region's most treasured delicacy. Then he poured himself some of the Château de Tiregand, plunged his nose into his glass and sniffed deeply once more to savour a different but equally satisfying bouquet.

'A rare pleasure, Bruno, and let us raise our glasses to our host's generous hospitality,' announced Moore.

And then a silence fell, a compliment to the chef when a group of people who are relishing one another's company suddenly concentrate entirely on appreciating their food. For a few moments the only sounds were of knives and forks on plates and sighs and murmurs of pleasure, before the conversation picked up again.

When the salad and cheese appeared, Isabelle asked Hodge why the FBI had issued a press release on reopening the inquiry into the lost money from Baghdad.

'Politics,' Hodge replied, in his dry, drawling way. 'The Bureau is facing new hearings in Congress on our next budget so our leaders agreed that a judicious display of concern for recovering long-lost public funds would be helpful.'

With that, Moore chimed in with a story of his own about the way his political masters tended to see the police less as an essential system for keeping the peace than as a useful tool in their election campaigns. Isabelle followed this with a bitter description of how the politicians would greet each new terrorist outrage with promises of stern measures and more police on the streets, without finding the funds to pay for them. Under-resourced and exhausted, the French police no longer said they were going to work. Instead, they spoke of 'going into the trenches' like soldiers of the Great War.

'Politicians tell us not to be provocative by trying to police the Islamic quarters and then they complain when we can't recruit informers to warn us where trouble might be brewing,' she added. 'With these terrorist attacks making the President declare a state of emergency, there's hardly a cop in France who's had a weekend off in the last year.'

'Which is why I feel fortunate to be a simple country policeman in the Périgord,' declared Bruno, uncomfortable at the turn in the conversation and determined to change the mood.

'May you all return here often to remember that life can be sweet and that in the Périgord we never forget our friends.'

He turned to Moore. 'If you're interested, our village rugby team has a match here tomorrow. One of the young women players has just been selected for the French national team and we'll be honouring her with a small reception after the match. Since you're a rugby man do please come along as my guest.' He turned to Hodge. 'What about you? If you played American football would you like to come?'

'Basketball was my game, mainly because our high school coach took one look at my height and said no baseball or football for you. I'd be happy to come along except that we have the GPR team coming in tomorrow to search McBride's place.'

'What's that?' asked Juliette.

'Ground-penetrating radar so we can look underground,' Hodge replied. 'I need to be there for that.'

'And I have to prepare a briefing for the colleague coming in from the Guards before he joins in the interrogation,' Moore said. 'Otherwise, I'd love to come.'

Bruno brought in the chocolate mousse as Yveline asked Moore whether the interrogation was getting anywhere.

'No, for two reasons. One is that both these men have been arrested and questioned many times and they've both been in prison. They know the importance of saying nothing. The other reason is that all four of them, husbands and wives, come from Fianna families.'

'What's that?' Yveline asked.

'*Fianna* is a Gaelic term for a king's bodyguard, a chosen group of fighters who owe loyalty only to him,' Moore said.

'The Fianna families are the backbone of the IRA. It's a couple of hundred families, many of them inter-married, who have been the mainstay of the Irish independence movement or resistance for hundreds of years. The same families fought Oliver Cromwell in the seventeenth century and right through to the Easter Rising of 1916 and the Irish civil war. They've never gone away. The children are raised by their mothers and grandmothers and their family priests on the glorious legends and songs of the movement and hatred of us wicked Saxons. It's a whole tribal culture to itself, it's in their blood.'

'You sound as though it can never end,' said Isabelle.

'Sometimes I think you might be right,' Moore replied, shaking his head. 'And the Protestants on the other side are much the same. The reason I'm convinced that Kelly and O'Rourke are guilty of killing Rentoul is that there's a blood feud involved. They are both cousins of the two IRA men who were killed at Gibraltar.'

'That explains a lot,' said Isabelle, finishing the wine in her glass. 'And it makes a change from the jihadists we usually have to deal with.'

'Coffee?' Bruno asked, determined as host to break into the silence that suddenly fell after Isabelle's remark. On the way to the kitchen he placed two bottles on the table. 'And who would like a *digestif*? Perhaps a little Armagnac or some *Poire William*? Please help yourselves while I get the coffee.'

He was spooning coffee grounds into his cafetière when Isabelle joined him and began putting dessert dishes into the dishwasher.

'Your house is the only place on earth where I feel remotely domesticated,' she said, going unerringly to the correct cupboard for cups and sugar and the right drawer for coffee spoons. Without even looking, she then reached behind the door for his tray. 'It must be part of the strange effect St Denis has on me, and the way Balzac settled beneath the table with his head on my feet all through dinner.'

'He knows you're a soft touch to slip him the occasional morsel of duck,' Bruno replied, pouring boiling water over the coffee grounds. 'And he firmly believes that he's as much your dog as mine.'

'That's one of the sweetest things you've ever said to me,' she said, putting down the tray and reaching her hands up to his cheeks before kissing him.

He felt her tongue dart teasingly between his lips before she pulled away to take the loaded tray into the dining room. At the door she paused, looked back at him and when she spoke her voice was so quiet it was almost a whisper.

'I do hope the others don't stay too long. I'd like to have you to myself.'

20

Bruno was woken by his cockerel's usual greeting of the dawn. Isabelle, tucked into his arm with her head on his chest, did not stir. Bruno knew she'd be leaving later in the morning to drop off her rental car in Périgueux before catching a train to Paris and then Brussels for a meeting of her EU committee at nine on Monday morning. She might or might not return to Périgueux later in the week, depending on developments in the Rentoul case. So he'd probably not see her again until the French Open tennis championships in June, just as he had not seen her since their last meeting at the Château de Commarque, when she had so surprised him by inviting herself to lunch and staying for the weekend.

This was now becoming the pattern of their relationship; fleeting and passionate visits, followed by weeks of longing. It was the best that she could offer and Bruno hardly knew whether to accept these crumbs of an affair or to try again to end it once and for all. But he knew himself well enough to conclude that whenever Isabelle appeared in his life, he'd be unable to resist her. Would this hold over him last for ever? Surely not, if he fell in love and settled down with someone else. Strange, he thought, this mental turmoil in one's head while another sleeps peacefully just below, her breath faint upon his chest, one graceful arm across his body, the long warmth of her alongside. Her presence encompassed everything Bruno had dreamed of, except permanence.

Careful not to wake her, he slipped from the bed. Balzac was waiting patiently outside the door, as if aware that Isabelle was still sleeping. Bruno let him out and stretched mightily, standing naked on his terrace for a few moments enjoying the cool air on his skin before going back indoors to make coffee and set two cups on a tray with plates and orange juice, yogurt and a jar of honey. Isabelle was always hungry when she awoke and he loved this ritual of preparing breakfast when she stayed.

He put the remaining slices of last night's bread ready beside the toaster since they both liked their toast so hot it melted the butter. There was still no sound from his bedroom so he went to the bathroom to shower and shave, brush his teeth and don the silk dressing gown she had brought him on her last visit. Then quietly he unloaded the dishwasher they had filled after the last guests had gone and washed the cooking pots he had left to soak. He slipped on some sandals and went to feed and water his chickens and brought back ten fresh eggs. Thinking Isabelle wouldn't get eggs like this in Paris or Brussels, he put two of them on to boil and added salt and pepper, spoons and egg cups to the tray.

He was about to press down the plunger on his cafetière when he heard the bedroom door open, the bathroom door close and the shower being turned on. He put the bread into the toaster and heard his basset hound scratching at the door to be let back in. There was nothing left of the previous night's dinner so Balzac would have to make do with his usual dog biscuits this morning, along with whatever he and Isabelle chose to share. The sound of the shower stopped and the timer pinged that the eggs were ready just as the toast popped up. He put butter onto each slice and carried it to the bedroom as Isabelle emerged.

She was wearing his shirt from the previous evening, only cursorily buttoned. Her face was freshly washed and her eyes were shining. She tasted of toothpaste when she kissed him, then clambered back into bed while Balzac leaped up joyfully to greet her and nuzzle his nose into her neck. Bruno laughed to watch them and pushed the dog aside to make room for himself beside her, the tray still in his hands.

'Be good, Balzac,' she commanded and the dog lay still as she examined the tray. 'Oh my, fresh eggs and hot toast and coffee. I must have been spirited away in the night and woken up in the Ritz.'

They drank their orange juice and sipped at their coffee as she fed tiny bits of toast to Balzac. Bruno cut the tops from their boiled eggs and they ate in happy silence, Balzac watching each spoonful as it disappeared into Isabelle's mouth. When they had eaten enough, Bruno bribed Balzac out of the bedroom with the last morsel of his toast and half of his yogurt and turned back to see Isabelle putting the tray onto the floor and brushing stray crumbs from the sheets.

'I think I have rebuilt my strength,' she said, slipping off his shirt. 'You look delicious in that carefully chosen dressing gown, Bruno, but I think I prefer you without it.' She lifted the sheet to invite him to join her.

Two hours later, his mouth still remembering her kisses, Bruno stood at the top of the hill waving as she drove off to Périgueux. There had been time for them to enjoy a last walk through the woods with Balzac, and now his home was empty again. He sighed and went back indoors to open his laptop and check if anything new had been added to the case file. He logged on and had found nothing new when his phone rang. The screen said the caller's number was withheld but a familiar voice gave him a cheerful greeting.

'*Bonjour*, Jack,' Bruno said, smiling to hear Crimson's voice again. 'Are you still in England?'

'I was just calling to say I'll fly into Bergerac later today on the same flight as Miranda's next batch of cooking clients. I'm assured that all is now safe in the Périgord and the miscreants are in custody.'

'Were you told this by the French?' Bruno asked, not feeling quite as confident as Crimson that all potential dangers had now passed.

'No, by the same people who told me to come back in the first place, although I'm not sure they'll be so sanguine after they've read this morning's newspapers.'

'Why? What are they saying?'

'It's just one, a woman, Kathleen somebody, writing from St Denis,' Crimson said. 'She's reporting that a retired head of British intelligence was ordered back from his home in France to England to take refuge from an IRA death squad. But now I can go back again. I've never heard of her. Do you know who she is?'

'She's a travel writer, doing an article on your daughter's

cookery course,' Bruno replied, his surprise giving way to anger at Kathleen's report. 'She's staying at the riding school.'

'Bloody hell!' Crimson exclaimed. 'So she may have heard this from Miranda?'

'I'm sure Miranda had no idea it would end up in print,' Bruno said quickly, even as he wondered whether it had been Miranda or one of her children who had spoken of Grandpa's whereabouts. 'Maybe you'd better stay in England for the moment,' he added.

'No, I'm missing the grandkids and all my friends and I've no intention of spending my life in hiding. I'm coming back. And I return bearing gifts, copies of a couple of interesting files you might want to share with our usual friends.'

'They'll be happy to get them and I'll be glad to see you back, although I think you're putting yourself at risk.'

'It wouldn't be the first time and once we let our lives be governed by security, then the terrorists have won.'

'What time do you get in?'

'The usual time, just after three this afternoon.'

'I can't come to pick you up, I'm afraid. Paulette, our star rugby player, has just won a place on the national team so we're giving her a *vin d'honneur* at the club at five, after today's match.'

'Don't worry about that, I'll squeeze into the minivan with Miranda's paying customers,' Crimson said. 'And with any luck I'll be in time to get to the club and raise a glass to Paulette in person and to buy you a drink. I gather you made a splendid stand-in for me on the vineyard tour and Miranda told me Gilles and Fabiola and the Baron all back your plan to resume the Monday dinners. I'm delighted – I've been missing them, too.'

The call ended. Bruno added a note to the case file that Crimson would be returning later that day and asking whether any extra security might be advisable. Then he logged on to the online edition of Kathleen's newspaper to see a photo of a much younger Jack Crimson wearing some kind of medal after an investiture at Buckingham Palace.

Ex-Spy Chief Fled Death Squad, was the headline, Kathleen's byline beneath it and datelined St Denis. The second paragraph said that the arrest of the IRA team meant it was now thought safe for Crimson to return to his home in France. On an inside page was a photo of Crimson's home, with the caption **Spymaster's French chateau**. Beneath the photo were some words too small to read. He enlarged the image and read *Photocredit: P. Delaron.*

Bruno shook his head in disbelief. Did these newspaper people not understand that they had probably increased the danger to Crimson? The old diehards of the IRA were not the only terrorists who might see advantage in targeting someone like him. Or were the journalists too arrogant to care?

He sighed heavily before checking his watch, helping Balzac onto the passenger seat of his Land Rover and heading for Pamela's riding school. There would be time to ride Hector before joining the cookery class for a farewell lunch of oysters at the market in St Cyprien. The ride might calm him down, which was just what Bruno needed before seeing Kathleen again. In his current mood, he'd be tempted to stuff the oysters down her throat, shells and all, but that wouldn't help Pamela get the good publicity she wanted.

Pamela, Miranda and the guests had gone and their luggage was already piled up outside the barn where the lessons had been held, waiting for the trip to Bergerac airport. Bruno found only Félix and his parents, each making a useful twenty euros for cleaning the guest rooms and the barn, changing the sheets and loading the washing machines ready for the next contingent. They would be flying in on the same plane that took the departing guests back to England.

Bruno enjoyed his solitary ride, cantering along the ridge at a speed so that Balzac would not fall too far behind. In the back of his mind he was working out the economics of Pamela's cooking venture. He knew she charged eight hundred euros per person, reduced to fourteen hundred for a couple. This week she had only three paying couples since Kathleen was getting a free place so Pamela and Miranda would make four thousand two hundred. Their dinner at the Vieux Logis would certainly cost a hundred per head, and the lunch at La Tour des Vents fifty or sixty. The two professional chefs, Ivan and Raoul, were being paid five hundred each and Odette took a hundred for her guiding skills in finding and preparing the various local mushrooms. Pamela was also paying Lespinasse at the garage four hundred a week to rent the Ford Transit people carrier but that included the fuel.

In addition, the two women had to feed their guests, buy the wine, the Sunday oyster lunch, all the cooking ingredients and also pay the cleaners. Pamela's profit would barely reach a thousand euros, which meant five hundred each for her and Miranda after a long week's work. That wasn't all, Bruno reminded himself. They also had to run the riding school and stables and Miranda had her children to care for.

Not for the first time, Bruno mentally raised his cap to the small business people of the Périgord, on whose hard work the tourist trade depended. An extra couple, or some singles, would make a lot of difference to Pamela's business, but eight guests was the most they could squeeze into the minivan. Even though with all the *gîtes* filled she could accommodate seven or even eight couples, she would have to change to a small bus which would cost far more. And there would be less personal attention in the cooking lessons. So it was a good thing that he and Jack Crimson gave their services for free, Bruno thought, although Pamela had tried to offer him some money. In fact, Bruno rather enjoyed the lesson he gave, proud to show off the cuisine of his region. And it was good for his English.

Back at the riding school he rubbed down Hector, remembering that Pamela refused to accept any stable fee for his horse, and then sluiced himself off at the sink before heading off to St Cyprien with Balzac in tow. Bruno was fond of the medieval town up on the hill, founded by monks in the seventh century, who had begun building walls around their monastery after the first Viking raids. The old town clustered around the abbey and bell tower that dated back to the twelfth century, albeit much rebuilt after being sacked and burned in the sixteenth century wars of religion. Known as Montmartre, the locals liked to claim that their ancestors had called this district after the mount of martyrs long before the Parisians had stolen the name. Occupied by the English in the Hundred Years War, the upper town boasted a house that had been used by Talbot, the renowned English commander whose name lives on in the great wine of St Julien in the Médoc, Château Talbot.

The market was held every Sunday morning at the foot of the hill, more than filling the long, straight main street of Rue Gambetta. Bruno recalled that Pamela had planned to park at the top and give her guests a downhill walking tour so he strolled through the market to see if they had reached it yet. He knew some of the stallholders from St Denis, stopped to chat with his friend Stéphane at his cheese stall and heard that Pamela's group had already been buying from him and from old Gérard with his hand-woven baskets. He found the group stocking up on foie gras, duck sausages and dried mushrooms to take back on the plane. Since they had already been buying wine and cheese, he assumed their suitcases would be bulging.

'There you are, Bruno,' said Pamela as her guests shook his hand and smiled their welcomes. 'Ready for your oysters?'

The town was known for a fine fishmonger with his own restaurant, the Cro Marin, which on Sunday mornings offered plates of fresh oysters with white wine and bread. Pamela had originally planned to have a farewell brunch at the riding school but Miranda had persuaded her that their guests would appreciate a last opportunity to buy delicacies at the market. The sun was out and it was warm enough to sit outside. Bruno found himself between the two friendly older women, Alice and Vera, but was then not greatly surprised to find that Kathleen had manoeuvred herself into the place opposite him, and was now fixing him with a gimlet eye.

He bit back the angry comment he was sorely tempted to make. 'Sorry to be leaving?' he asked her.

'You don't get rid of me that easily,' she replied with a guarded smile. 'The paper asked me to stay on to keep up with developments so I'll be moving into a hotel in Lalinde to be near the action.'

'I don't think there's much action these days,' he said mildly.

'Not so, I was outside the Lalinde house early this morning and saw that tall one from the FBI and a big truck unloading a large machine which I learned was a ground-penetrating radar. So I presume you're looking for buried treasure, probably linked to that FBI press release about the eighteen million dollars that went missing in Iraq.'

'You have been busy,' he said. 'I'm just a village policeman so I imagine you know much more about all this than I do.'

'Come off it, Bruno. You've been awarded the Croix de Guerre and the police medal of honour, I'm told you're a bit of a legend in these parts.'

'Really, the Croix de Guerre?' said Alice. 'Goodness gracious, what war was that?'

'He was with the UN peacekeepers in Sarajevo and pulled men out of a burning armoured car during a mortar attack on the airport,' said Kathleen. 'Then he pulled two immigrant children out of a burning house.'

Merde, thought Bruno. She must also have been talking to Gilles, whom Bruno had first met in Sarajevo. Only he would have known about the airport attack. And no doubt Philippe Delaron would have been showing off his own local knowledge.

He looked at Kathleen, wondering if she might have become Philippe's latest conquest.

'Sarajevo, that was in the Balkans, wasn't it?' asked Alice. 'I remember seeing the pictures on the TV news and thinking how dreadful it must have been.'

Mercifully at that point the plates of oysters arrived, swiftly followed by the carafes of chilled white wine. Bruno busied himself pouring wine, handing round the bread and slices of lemon and helping Alice and Vera loosen the oysters from their shells.

'I hope you enjoyed your time with us,' he said to Vera in an attempt to keep Kathleen from the interrogation she doubtless had in mind. The women confided that they'd had a wonderful time, enjoyed every minute and learned a lot.

'We loved the visits too, all those castles and the caves. We could have done with more of that,' said Alice.

As Kathleen leaned forward to start again, Bruno forestalled her by turning to Vera. 'You've tried an oyster with a squeeze of lemon juice, so now try it with this.' He handed her the small bowl of chopped shallots in vinegar.

'And then with this,' he went on, still keeping Kathleen at bay by handing Vera a bowl of cocktail sauce that the fishmonger only made for tourists. Bruno had never tried it. 'These various sauces make the oysters taste different every time.'

'Thank you, dear, but I like them just as they come. Do you remember that trip we made to Whitstable, Alice? Those lovely fat oysters we had there.'

'Do you carry your gun when you're out of uniform?' Kathleen asked in French, interrupting Vera.

Bruno stared at her without answering, suddenly and with a touch of dismay seeing a parallel between this sharp and aggressive journalist and Isabelle. Like her, Kathleen's focus on her career and her ambition served to conceal, or perhaps to protect, something beneath that was softer and more vulnerable. But Kathleen looked both older and harder than Isabelle, with a tightness around her eyes and a brittleness in her manner that hinted at the price she paid for her work. Bruno wondered, was this how Isabelle would look after a few more years?

'Well, do you?' she pressed.

'Do you think before you write?' he retorted, speaking English so that the rest of the table would understand him. 'Or do you never worry about putting people's lives at risk as you did with your story in the paper this morning? You even published a photo of where Crimson lives, and another of what he looks like even though you know he's being targeted by the IRA.'

'The IRA team have been arrested,' she blustered. 'It's a legitimate news story.'

'And how did you find out Crimson was coming back?' Bruno went on, aware that the rest of the table had fallen silent and were staring at him. 'I can't believe Miranda would have told you if she thought you'd print it and put her father's life at risk. Or maybe her children told you their grandpa was coming home without knowing how you would use it. Do you have no sense of decency? No sense of honour?'

Kathleen had retreated as far as she could from Bruno's anger, her back pressed hard against her chair, her fists clenched, her mouth open. She glanced to left and right, at the fascinated faces of the rest of the table.

'You printed that in your paper today?' Miranda demanded. 'Is that why you were talking to my children yesterday?'

'Don't you believe in a free press?' Kathleen snapped in return but her eyes were on Bruno.

He was saved from answering by his phone. As soon as he heard Hodge's voice, he pushed back from the table and walked away from the group.

'I'm at Rentoul's place where we've found what we think is his safe,' the American said. 'If you want to be here when we open it, you'd better get moving.'

'On my way.' He offered his apologies to Pamela and made his farewells to the group. He was gratified to be given a kiss by both Alice and Vera, handshakes from the rest and a hug from Miranda. Kathleen, he saw, was left sitting alone. Alice, Vera and the others had shifted their chairs to turn their backs on her.

He called Balzac away from the chunks of bread and occasional oyster the English were slipping to the dog with such appealing eyes. Bruno drove back home, swiftly changed into uniform and took his new gun from the locked arms' cabinet and donned the holster. He left Balzac in the garden, refilling his water bowl by his kennel, and took his police van to Lalinde, half-expecting Kathleen to be there already.

But there was no sign of her at Rentoul's home. In the driveway was Hodge's car, a van he recognized from the Périgueux forensics unit and a large flatbed truck which presumably had brought the GPR system. Quatremer was standing in the doorway enjoying a smoke. They shook hands, and he told Bruno he'd find Hodge inside, in the wine cellar beneath the kitchen.

'Is the radar in the house?' he asked.

'No, they found something there behind the wine cellar. Now it's at work in the barn where we found the Range Rover.'

Bruno called Hodge's name as he entered the house, glancing once more at the hunting photos on the wall. Then something clicked in his memory and he stopped to study the coastline behind the beach scene. The two flat-topped buttes were the trigger. He'd seen them often enough when practising amphibious landings on the Ras Doumeira peninsula in Djibouti on the horn of Africa, where France had its largest overseas military base. Whatever had taken Rentoul there?

He heard an answering shout through the open door in the kitchen that gave way to a set of steps. Bruno went down, noting that this cellar was newly built, the walls to the staircase made of breeze blocks. Wine cellars were not common in the Périgord where the water table was usually quite high, but maybe up here on the slope it was easier to excavate one. At the bottom of the steps a door made of iron bars with a key in its formidable lock had been left open.

Hodge was squatting beside Yves, head of the forensics team, at the far end of the cellar. About three metres wide and five long, it seemed cool and dry. Cases of wine had been moved to expose the breeze blocks at the far end. Some of the lower blocks had been removed and stacked behind Hodge. The top box of wine would hold half a dozen bottles and the brand on its side said it contained Château Pétrus, 2005. Bruno swallowed; the contents would be worth as much as his annual salary. Another box beside it contained Romanée Saint-Vivant, 2007.

'Damn safe has been cemented in,' said Hodge by way of greeting. 'We may have to blow it.'

'You can't blow it, not without removing this wine to a safe place,' said Bruno. 'It would be sacrilege.'

'That's what I told him,' said Yves, turning from his task so Bruno could see he was wearing a stethoscope, the listening end held against a fat combination lock. On his lap sat a small computer with a wire leading from it to some attachment beside the lock. 'I've got the first two digits, three and four.'

'How many digits altogether?' Bruno asked, taking out his notebook and thumbing through it to the page where he had written Rentoul's details.

'Six.'

'Try his British army number, three-four-seven-four-eight-four.'

'You sure it's only six figures?'

'He was an officer, they only have six. Other ranks have eight.'

Yves turned back to his task and Hodge grinned at Bruno. 'Even if we don't get any cash back, I guess Uncle Sam will be happy to take all this wine as some modest compensation.'

Bruno laughed and glanced along the ranks of individual bottles in their racks above the cases. There was a row of four bottles of Château d'Yquem, with another four of La Tâche above it and Angélus above that.

'Does that mean they would end up in the White House cellars?'

'No, there would have to be an auction.'

'Shush,' said Yves, bending close to the lock and turning the dial slowly, his eyes closed in concentration. He grunted and then began turning it back in the opposite direction. Despite the lure of the wine, Bruno could not take his eyes off Yves at his work.

'*Youpi! Au poil*,' Yves announced with glee and swung open the door. 'No, wait,' he added, as Hodge leaned forward. 'We have to do this by the book.'

Bruno could see only two shelves inside, the top one filled with assorted papers, the middle one with bundles of what looked like cash and the lowest one with a bundle of something in a bag, a taut wire from it leading to the inside of the safe door.

Yves became still, craned his neck to listen, and then burst out, '*Putain!*' Bruno blinked to be sure of what he saw and shouted 'Grenade!' and tried to dive back through the door. Hodge flung himself to one side as Yves slammed the safe door shut and ducked away.

The muffled sound of an explosion came from behind the safe door.

'The bastard booby-trapped it,' Yves said calmly.

He opened the safe door gingerly, just a crack, and the stink of cordite filled the cellar.

Bruno picked himself up and felt his heartbeat racing. The palms of his hands were wet and his mouth had gone dry.

'*Merde*, but you're a cool customer,' he said to Yves, his voice unusually high. 'I thought we were done for.'

'I just hope it hasn't destroyed the contents but those looked to me like armoured shelves,' Yves said, his tone almost clinical. Bruno was amazed at his calm.

Yves opened the door more widely and looked inside with a sigh of satisfaction, seeing the contents of the upper two shelves untouched. The shelves themselves were at least four centimetres thick and extended into slots in the door. In the bottom space were some scattered lumps of metal. Yves put the back of his hand close to one and pulled it quickly away, saying, 'Still hot.'

He took a small digital camera from his bag and the room flared with light as he took photo after photo of the lock, the door and the contents of each shelf.

'Got your notebook ready, Bruno?' Yves called. 'Write it down as I call out. Middle shelf, one wrapped bundle of notes, pounds sterling in twenties, appear to be used. One bundle of US dollars, in hundreds, also used. Two bundles of euros, one of fifties, one of hundreds, also used. One bundle of Swiss francs, hundreds, used. One folder with assorted bearer bonds, another with plastic pockets containing postage stamps and stamped envelopes. Two smartphones, one Android and the other one Apple. You got that?'

'Yes, should we count each bundle now?' Bruno's hand was still trembling and his usually neat writing had become a scrawl.

'No, we'd better wait for someone from the *fisc* to come and do that. I'll call them when you've listed the documents on the top shelf. We usually reckon that a stack five centimetres high of one-hundred-euro notes would contain about fifty thousand euros, but that's clean bills. These are used so may be twenty per cent less.'

'Go ahead with the inventory,' said Bruno, trying to do the mental arithmetic before Yves resumed with his new list from the upper shelf. He reckoned that the total stash would be close to a hundred and fifty thousand euros.

'From the top shelf we have three passports bundled together, Canadian, Australian and Irish, in three different names, the photo in each one identical, and there's a national driving licence tucked into each one. There is a separate United States passport, same photograph, different name.'

'Let me see that,' Hodge interrupted, reaching out a hand safely covered with an evidence glove.

He leafed through it, held up some pages to the light, looked at the binding and the passport stamps inside before noting the number and date of issue. He handed it back saying, 'Go on.'

'There's a single account book, partly filled in, dating from the first entry in 2008 and the latest one in February this year,' Yves resumed. 'We have three cheque books, from HSBC, Allied Irish Bank and Julius Baer Bank, Zurich, along with bank statements. One Austrian post office bank book showing an account of forty thousand euros, no name, just a number. One German Postbank book, showing a credit of thirty-two thousand euros in the name of Patrick Flanegan, the same name as the Irish passport. There's another folder that contains sheets of paper with what appear to be computer passwords and PIN numbers. One small box with assorted SIM cards. Last item, a thick folder containing various share certificates in companies with registered addresses in Panama and Cayman Islands. And there's one in Dutch Antilles.'

'It looks like Uncle Sam's going to get something for his trouble, after all,' said Hodge, turning to beam at Bruno.

'I don't suppose Uncle Sam will feel grateful enough to let us crack a bottle or two,' said Yves, looking hopefully at the stacks of wine.

'I don't think he'd like that at all,' Hodge drawled with a smile. 'So it's just as well you've been photographing everything. Right now I'd like to take those four passports and check all the dates and stamps and draw up a coordinated list of his travels.'

21

Bruno arrived at the rugby stadium after half-time and saw that St Denis was leading by three points. He had left his uniform jacket in his van and taken off his tie and donned a plain black windcheater to look a little more like a civilian. He hadn't dared leave his gun in the van so it was tucked into the back of his trouser belt. He glanced up at the crowded stadium benches, where Paulette was sitting in the place of honour. The Mayor sat on one side of her, her father on the other with Father Sentout beside him. To Bruno's disappointment there was no sign of her mother. Paulette spotted him, smiled and raised a hand in greeting. He waved back and went to the kiosk for a grilled sausage in a bun and a plastic glass of beer and turned to watch the game.

'I'm glad you made it to the match, I was beginning to worry,' said Jack Crimson suddenly appearing at his side. Bruno had not heard his approach.

'Something came up at Rentoul's place in Lalinde. We found a safe, false identities, a lot of cash, bank books, share certificates and the most expensive wine collection I've ever seen.'

'Interesting. The FBI must be pleased.'

'The safe was also booby-trapped.'

'A careful fellow, we must have trained him well. What did he use?'

'An anti-personnel grenade. You remember Yves from forensics? He managed to slam the door closed just in time,' Bruno said between bites of his sausage. 'How's the game?'

'The two sides are pretty evenly matched but we may have the better forwards thanks to Karim. He's won a few lineouts but he gave away one penalty. The visitors have a good fly half. He made one lovely kick downfield to their very fast winger who managed to sprint downfield and reach it in time to score a try. Both our tries came from the forwards.'

The game seemed bogged down in the visitors' half, with St Denis trying charge after charge by the forwards and getting blocked every time. A pity Paulette wasn't playing, thought Bruno. She always varied the rhythm of her play and he was confident she would have found an unexpected way through.

And then it came. Instead of passing the ball, the St Denis scrum half gave a short kick over the heads of the maul that fell short of the opposing full back. The scrum half followed up fast, Karim and the two wing forwards peeling off from the maul to follow him. The bounce was lucky and the scrum half caught it on the run and as the full back came in to tackle he passed it to Karim. Their fast winger came in from the side and just as he committed himself Karim passed the ball to one of the wing forwards who raced over the line between the posts for a try.

Bruno thrust his arms into the air in delight, spilling the remains of his beer. The stadium erupted with cheers and applause. That was five more points and since the conversion kick was easy it was soon seven, giving St Denis a ten-point lead. The visitors would now have to score twice to win.

That was how it ended but the teams had been forewarned, instead of running off to the showers the players shook hands and then lined up as the Mayor led Paulette down from the stadium, signalling to Bruno to join them on the pitch. Alongside her father came Lespinasse as club chairman, brandishing the championship cup Paulette's team had won. Philippe Delaron was scampering around in front of them, snapping away with his camera, trying to find the best shot.

'I'd like to congratulate both teams on a very good game today, played hard and played well,' the Mayor began, speaking into a wireless microphone. 'But we're also here today to congratulate the captain of our women's team, Paulette, not only on winning the regional championship and this cup, but also on the wonderful news that she has been picked for the French national women's team.'

'Thank you, Monsieur le Maire,' said Paulette as the mike was passed to her. 'I'd like to thank you and my parents and teachers like wonderful Florence Pantowsky at the *collège*, here with her children, and Gérard Bollinet at my *lycée* who is here today with his wife and baby and all the town for their support. Above all I want to thank my teammates who really won this cup and our trainer, Bruno Courrèges, for his endless support and enthusiasm for the women's game. He first began teaching me rugby ten years ago and I think I'm finally getting the hang of it. And now I'd like to invite all my friends in the women's team to come out onto the pitch so you can all congratulate them properly. And I want every girl and mother and grandmother in this crowd to see that rugby is a sport for all of us.'

One by one, the town's young womanhood made their way onto the pitch to rousing cheers. In a move they must have rehearsed, Karim and Maurice, the next biggest of the St Denis forwards, advanced and picked up Paulette to place her onto their muddy shoulders. All the players on the pitch joined in the applause as Philippe darted around for the best picture and the Mayor rescued the microphone.

'And now the town of St Denis would like to welcome you all here to take a glass of our town wine in the clubhouse to drink to the health of Paulette and her teammates and to her future success when wearing the blue shirt of our beloved France.'

Paulette beckoned to him and took back the microphone, almost toppling from the shoulders on which she was perched.

'I'd just like to remind you that I'm not the first inhabitant of St Denis to be selected for a national sports squad,' she declared. 'The head of our gendarmes, Commandante Yveline, was in the field hockey squad for the Olympic Games, which means that we women are really doing well. So I'd like to tell all my male friends and colleagues here, it's time for you guys to catch us up. You can't expect the women to do all the work. Thank you.'

Bruno found himself laughing as Paulette's teammates whooped with joy and gathered round to embrace her. Paulette took Karim's brawny arm and slipped to the ground. Then the girls took up a shout of 'We want Bruno'. Little Amandine, the youngest of the team, darted out to grab Bruno's hand and pull him into the group. Delighted at being included, Bruno embraced every girl in reach, remembering how they had been when he first started to train them and the pleasure he had taken in watching them learn and grow into this terrific team. His chest was almost bursting with pride.

Finally, the group broke up as Paulette embraced first her father then Lespinasse, Father Sentout and finally the Mayor before they all headed to the clubhouse and the waiting wine. Bruno limited himself to a single glass, knowing he'd have to work, circulated quickly, shaking endless hands and kissing innumerable cheeks. He went to give Paulette a final hug. She kept a firm hold of his arm, turned, and said, 'I'd like you to meet my drama teacher, Gérard.'

Feeling himself blush as he shook hands with the young man who carried an infant in his arms, Bruno was at a loss for words. Gérard filled in the gap, saying how he'd heard from Paulette of the years of support Bruno had given her and the women's team.

'Training a team must be a bit like being a teacher,' Gérard went on with an engaging smile, even though his ear was being enthusiastically tugged by his child. 'This is one of those days when we realize how rewarding that job can be.'

Bruno liked him at once and managed to murmur, '*Enchanté, monsieur*, I heard Paulette's warm words about you so thank you for your own efforts.'

'Allow me to introduce my wife, Marie-Claire,' Bollinet said, and Bruno shook hands again. He saw the young woman's brows crease as she tried to recall whether she might have seen him before but then she smiled. Not for the first time, Bruno was grateful that a police uniform and *képi* were usually what caught the eye rather than the face of the wearer.

As Bruno tried to make his escape he saw Philippe Delaron approach Paulette. For once, Philippe's camera was not poised to shoot. He reached her side and bent to whisper something in her ear. Bruno watched Paulette's face grow cold and hard as she turned away, muttering something curt and dismissive. As so often, Bruno wished he could read lips. Philippe murmured something else but this time Paulette said not a word. She simply tipped the contents of her glass of red wine onto Philippe's shirt and turned away.

The glass was only half full and it was done so calmly and discreetly that no one in the crowd seemed to have noticed, even when a red-faced Philippe squeezed through the crowd to the door, holding his jacket to conceal the stain. Philippe was a few years older, an inveterate womanizer, and as a sports photographer he probably spent more time with the girls' teams than any other male except Bruno. Could he have been the father? Bruno found it hard to believe. Surely Paulette had better taste. But perhaps . . . he stopped himself. This was nobody's business but hers. He turned away and found Jack Crimson in the throng.

'You said you came bearing gifts,' Bruno said, leading Crimson outside, where he saw that Philippe was already disappearing through the stadium gates. 'But you didn't say who you wanted to receive them.'

'I thought you and I could discuss that. Perhaps I should pass them on to the Brigadier but I'm not sure it's worth his while. You know I saw him in Paris before I caught the Eurostar to London.'

'Yes, he told me. But he's not down here. I suppose Isabelle counts as his representative but she's just gone back to Paris.'

'I really don't want this to go through official police channels, and not to be shared with the FBI.'

'What about Moore, from your Special Branch?'

'Again, Bruno, I'm not sure. Maybe I should go to Paris, but could we talk it over first? I know you have your special ways of contacting the Brigadier.'

They took their separate vehicles back to Bruno's home and installed themselves on the terrace to enjoy the evening sun with a glass of kir, a Bergerac white wine with a splash of cassis. Balzac sat on the ground between them, gazing amiably from one to the other.

'You know, of course, that one of the key safeguards of our democratic freedoms is to keep our various intelligence agencies separate. If united, they could become far too powerful,' Crimson began.

'Like the CIA and FBI or your MI5 and MI6, or our gendarmes and our police,' Bruno replied.

'Yes, but in Britain we have five agencies. There's the Security Service, which you call MI5, and the Secret Intelligence Service which you call MI6. But there's also military intelligence and the old police Special Branch which is now part of the counterterrorist agency. And probably the most important and powerful of them all is GCHQ. It stands for Government Communications Headquarters, the listeners and the monitors and code-crackers of worldwide radio, phone and computer systems. We keep these five arms separate, although we coordinate them through the Joint Intelligence Committee.'

'Which you ran.'

'Not quite. I chaired the committee, which is not the same thing. But it means that I've been allowed to make handwritten notes taken from three separate files I was allowed to see in recent days. One is from military intelligence, dated 1988 and updated in 1989 and 1990 after the fall of the Berlin Wall, on Felder's divorce and marriage to Monika. I think that one is definitive. There's another, less complete file from SIS on the close relationship between them and Felder's company, and on that company's parallel close relationship with several different arms of American intelligence. The third one, also from SIS, is from a single-page report on the row between father and son that led to Julian's departure from the Felder company. It includes a separate note on Julian's less than brilliant career in the British army.'

Bruno nodded and topped up their glasses with kir. Balzac had wandered off, sniffing his way towards a long-abandoned rabbit warren he had searched in vain several times before.

'On the first and third files, I can be brief,' Crimson continued. 'Monika was the illegitimate daughter of an East German woman from Erfurt named Ursula Waskau who crossed to West Berlin in May 1961, at the age of seventeen, a few weeks before the Wall was built. Ursula was an orphan. In West Berlin she became a secretary but dreamed of being a pop star and actress. She had little success, no job and moved into a squat. She gave birth to Monika in 1968 and died the following year of a drug overdose. Monika was raised in a Lutheran orphanage and was a clever girl, did well in school and was gifted at sports, particularly tennis. When she met Felder, she was studying at the university in Düsseldorf. She played tennis at the nearby Blau-Weiss tennis club where Rafael Nadal started his career.

'Felder and Rentoul were at Rheindahlen at that time, HQ of the British army on the Rhine. Monika met the then-Lieutenant Rentoul at some local sporting event and became his doubles partner and girlfriend. Through him, she met Felder. Despite their initial suspicions, army security gave Monika a clean sheet. After several interviews they concluded that Monika and Felder were genuinely in love. He secured a divorce so he could marry her.'

'Did they interview Rentoul?' Bruno asked.

'Yes, more than once. Despite his own feelings for Monika, Rentoul accepted that she'd fallen for his boss and soon took up with another German girl, one of several, the report says.' Crimson sat up. 'Could we have some coffee, please? It's been a long day.'

They went into the kitchen together and Bruno put on the kettle, readied a tray with two cups and spooned coffee into his cafetière.

'There's not much to add about Felder's son, Julian,' Crimson said and explained that he'd gone to the Sandhurst military academy after his parents' divorce. He graduated in the middle of the rankings and joined the Parachute Regiment just too late for the Falklands campaign. He applied to join the SAS but failed to be accepted. He began drinking and was passed over for promotion. He resigned his commission, spent a year blowing his army gratuity on the hippy trail and then came back to London to work for various private security groups, including the UK-based Sandline. 'Have you ever heard of them?'

Bruno shook his head and carried the tray out to the terrace.

'They did a lot of lucrative work in Africa, mainly Angola and Sierra Leone, helping governments guard diamond and oil installations against rebel groups. Some called them mercenaries. That wasn't really true because although they operated paramilitary forces they wouldn't work for all comers, and Sandline liked to think they worked with the backing of Her Majesty's government, or at least bits of it.

'You should know that Britain in those years of Thatcher and her successors was a happy hunting ground for these private security and paramilitary outfits. This was Felder's world after he retired from the army and it became Rentoul's, just in time for the expansion of their business that came with the first and second Gulf wars.

'When Sandline went into decline,' Crimson went on, 'Julian tried working for some other private security groups with limited success before swallowing his pride and joining his father's company, by then very successful. He spent a few years running some of its security operations in Afghanistan and later Iraq, one of which ran into trouble when an American inquiry claimed serious mismanagement. His father withdrew Julian and settled the problem by paying a fine. Nonetheless, Julian demanded a seat on the company board, threatened once too often to resign and finally his father accepted the resignation.

'Nobody reputable in the security business would hire him,' Crimson added. 'So he spent some time in Dubai with a company providing anti-piracy guards for oil tankers. Then the official navies took over that job and Julian joined an old school friend selling prime London residences to rich foreigners, got married to an old girlfriend and was divorced within a year.'

'Would Julian have known Rentoul in Iraq?'

'No, he was in Kabul until a year after Rentoul's supposed death. I imagine he heard of the lost money. We don't know if he ever talked to his father about it but I'd be surprised if he didn't. And in the past few days the FBI attaché in the London embassy has started pressing us for information on Rentoul.'

'Did you have any?'

'Not much, but my old colleagues were rather surprised when the FBI started asking questions, in particular if we knew if Rentoul had ever had any dealings with the CIA.'

Bruno raised his eyebrows. 'And did he?'

'Nothing specific that we knew of, but it's a very big concern and a great deal of bizarre and questionable operations got under way, particularly in the years after nine-eleven. Lots of renditions – suspects spirited away to secret prisons in Poland, Egypt, Romania. And not a few of those suspects were deniable, that's to say they weren't picked up by the US military but by private operators, bounty-hunters, if you like.'

'You think Rentoul was involved in that?'

Crimson shrugged and finished his coffee. 'Nothing we could prove, but several people who were signed out by the British troops in and around Basra as being released after questioning were never heard of again. And Rentoul was often in and around Basra, where he had a lot of old army friends. We debriefed one of Rentoul's team, ex-British army, who told us that on three occasions he was present when Rentoul took a handcuffed prisoner from Basra to Abu Ghraib. Yet none of those prisoners from Basra was ever signed into Abu Ghraib. They were delivered to a special section that was known as CIFA. Rentoul evidently had some good friends there.'

Crimson explained that CIFA was a shadowy US military body called the Counterintelligence Field Activity, formed in 2002 by defence secretary Donald Rumsfeld before the Iraq war. It reported to him alone, much to the outrage of other agencies who saw it as a rogue outfit. CIFA was wound up in 2008 after a scandal when it was found spying on American peace groups which it was not authorized to do. Its activities, after supposedly being cleaned up, were later merged into the Defense Intelligence Agency.

'You think Rentoul was working for this CIFA group or with them?'

'We don't know. We do know that he had very close links to US military intelligence because that was his job at Rheindahlen. He was Felder's liaison officer with the US 66th Military Intelligence Brigade based at Wiesbaden, some of whose personnel later showed up in CIFA and at Abu Ghraib.'

'What a mess that war turned out to be,' Bruno said.

'Well, as China's Chou En-lai said when asked about the results of the French Revolution, it's too soon to tell.' Crimson gave Bruno a broad grin that lasted only a moment before his face turned serious again. 'I heard that Moore reported back to London that the FBI man here, Hodge, claimed that it was Felder who identified Rentoul's body after the ambush in Baghdad.'

'That's right,' said Bruno.

'Are you sure that Hodge didn't say there was a second identification made of the body by a US Army major? He'd have been a member of that same 66th Intelligence Brigade, who had known Rentoul in Germany.'

'Yes, I'm certain. A second identification was never mentioned nor was a US Army officer.'

'Well, it should have been in the file Hodge was sent. Or perhaps their military records are as jumbled as our own and that little detail was never included. Or perhaps our friend from the FBI is just playing his cards close to his chest. They have a reputation for doing that. What did you make of him?'

'He and Moore came to dinner at my place on Saturday,' Bruno replied. 'And he's been careful to keep me in the loop, even when I had a bit of a falling-out with Prunier over whether I worked for him or for the Mayor. Hodge strikes me as very professional and very much smarter than the slow-talking country boy he likes to play. He reminds me of those laconic, astute cowboys in Westerns.'

'You mean not so much John Wayne, more Gary Cooper?' Crimson gave one of his impish smiles.

'I suppose so, except that he has a French mother so his French is perfect,' Bruno replied with a laugh. 'But I can tell you that Hodge is taking a great deal of interest in Rentoul. He brought in a special radar that found Rentoul's secret safe, filled with cash, share certificates and four passports, one of them American. Hodge instantly began drawing up a chronology of Rentoul's travels by the various entry and exit stamps in all four passports.'

'That's interesting. What were the dates the passports were issued?'

'I don't know but I can find out from Yves, the forensics man who opened the combination of the safe. Oh yes, and the combination was based on Rentoul's British army number.'

'Where was the safe?'

'Cemented in behind a wall in his wine cellar, and there was at least a hundred thousand euros' worth of wine in there, Château Pétrus, Ausone, Latour, Lafite . . . You name it.'

'Nice to think that American money was spent in a good cause. What happened to the wine?'

'Hodge assumes it will all come to the Americans as compensation for the money they lost in Baghdad.'

'If he thinks that, he doesn't know the French,' Crimson said, with a laugh. 'The Americans would first have to prove Rentoul took the money and then that he spent it on wine. One suspects he had other sources of income after his supposed death. I should add that I looked very hard for any indication that he might have been working for us and found nothing. So perhaps he might have been doing odd jobs for some of his American friends.'

'The thought had begun to cross my mind as you spoke. I suppose you want me to pass all of this on to the Brigadier.'

'Just tell him I'd like to see him and you agree that I have some material that he might want to come down and see and hear for himself. How do they put it in those useful Michelin guides? *Vaut le détour*, something worth a special journey. It might be interesting for us all to think about what Rentoul might have been doing in those four years between his being reported dead and this CIFA organization being officially wound up. It might also be useful to find out what he was doing in the years since. I don't think he was the kind of man to spend his life in tourism and watching his vines grow.'

'I was thinking the same thing,' said Bruno. 'It's interesting that he didn't turn up in Lalinde until 2008, when you say CIFA was wound up.'

'Let's see if we can find out where Rentoul was in those lost years. You know his French was pretty good. His German and his Russian were even better. He reached NATO level four in both, just short of being taken for a native.'

'There's one thing I'm curious about,' Bruno said. 'You went through Rentoul's army file. Was there anything in there about his being wounded?'

'Not a thing.'

'He had a bullet scar high in his chest, near the shoulder, and what I think were grenade or shrapnel scars on one leg. So where did that happen and where was he treated?'

Crimson shrugged. 'I don't know but I suppose it might have happened in the Baghdad ambush that was supposed to have killed him.'

'In that case I doubt whether he'd have been in good enough shape to organize the robbery. Do you have any contacts in Felder's company to see if they have a record of his being injured?'

'Not really, but I could try,' Crimson said. 'Of course, his injury could have happened in those lost years. There were always lots of small wars under way in the Congo, South Sudan, Somalia, Colombia even before we get to the latest ones in Libya, Ukraine and Syria. Mercenaries never really go out of fashion.'

'Not that he needed the money,' Bruno replied, thinking of the hunting trophies and photos in Rentoul's home and the cost of his guns and safaris. He tried to recall the hunting trophies and photographs on the walls of his house, and suddenly something clicked.

'Bare-chested,' he said. 'He was bare-chested and there was no scar. One of the photos in his house, an African scene, on a beach I recognized in Djibouti. He was carrying a rifle.'

'Djibouti? I thought that was a Foreign Legion base.'

'It is, but I was on a training course there nearly fifteen years ago. Desert warfare and then amphibious landings.'

'Djibouti, next door to Somalia, that suggests the piracy trade. And Felder's son Julian was in the same business,' said Crimson, suddenly sitting forward in excitement. 'Could that be where Julian learned that Rentoul was still alive? The Somali piracy began about 2005, I recall, but it went on for years. A lot of former mercs ended up as security patrols on merchant ships.'

'And Rentoul was an excellent shot,' Bruno replied. 'It's cer tainly possible. But what interested me was that there was no scar, so Rentoul hadn't been wounded when the photo was taken.'

'Does it matter now?'

'It depends. Where were injured security guards taken from the oil tankers?'

'To one of the Western hospitals in Dubai. Why?'

'Can you find out if a man called McBride was treated there for a gunshot wound in the chest?' Bruno demanded.

'Probably. The security chief in the emirates is an old friend. But again, why?'

'That could be where Julian Felder found out that Rentoul was still alive and living under the McBride pseudonym.'

Crimson nodded slowly. 'His father could have told him,

presuming that he knew all along that Rentoul was still alive. But you could be right. I'll see what I can do. And there's another factor we should think about – how and when did Rentoul get back in touch with Monika? Was she aware that he never died? Or did he just turn up one day and surprise her?'

'I went through the McBride credit card that he seemed to use for travel,' Bruno replied. 'It showed a couple of years of him and Monika being in the same foreign cities. J-J ran the details through Interpol's list of unresolved cases looking for a match but without much result.'

'I don't think someone like Rentoul would have mixed business with pleasure.' Crimson shook his head firmly. 'You might get more from analysing the trips listed on his other passports.'

'The FBI man is working on that. Maybe they should look for unsolved killings by sniper.'

'Again, even if Rentoul was a contract killer, does it matter now? He's dead, so is Monika and the IRA did it. And I just heard that General Felder died in his Houston hospital and has been cremated. Isn't this when cops say the case is closed?'

'Not all of us,' replied Bruno. 'And not you, otherwise you wouldn't be thinking of telling all this to the Brigadier.'

'Let's see what my old friend in Dubai can find out,' Crimson said.

22

Summoned by a text message from J-J the previous evening, Bruno was in the Périgueux conference room just before eight the next morning. Once again he found himself the only man wearing uniform. Moore and Hodge greeted him warmly, Yves gave him a friendly nod and even poured him an excellent cup of coffee.

'Where's J-J?' Bruno asked. Yves replied that he was still in Bergerac where the Kelly couple were being held to keep them separate from the O'Rourkes during the interrogation.

'Ah, Bruno, good to have you back with us and I'm glad St Denis could spare you,' said Prunier, with the ghost of a wink as he entered the room and took his place at the head of the table. 'And thank you for taking such good care of our Anglo-Saxon friends. They told me you gave them an excellent Périgord dinner with some charming female company. I feel quite envious but we'd better get to business. I gather our new colleague from the Irish Guards arrives in Bergerac from Dublin later today, where he'll join J-J in the ongoing interrogation of Kelly and his wife before meeting us all at tomorrow morning's conference.

'One piece of good news has come from our colleagues in

Bayonne,' he went on. 'Based on our report of Kelly's connection to him they visited the Basque militant and found three kilos of Colombian cocaine on his premises. We have a significant narcotics ring here.'

'And Kelly was one of the IRA explosives experts who was in Colombia teaching the FARC guerrillas how to blow things up,' Moore interjected. 'That could be the trade, drugs for bombs.'

'Interesting,' said Prunier. 'We'll be following that up with our Spanish colleagues. But back to new developments in our own case. Based on the recommendation of our British colleague, we now have some crucial evidence linking O'Rourke to the deaths of Madame Felder and Rentoul.'

'Thanks to the metal detector, we found the sniper's rifle, the McMillan TAC-50,' said Moore, the matter-of-fact tone of his voice contrasting with the glint of triumph in his eye. 'It was buried in his garden. I suppose he couldn't bear to leave it in Rentoul's gun cabinet. A gun like that is worth more than gold to the IRA. It was all wrapped in plastic sheeting but the McMillan has Rentoul's prints on it.'

Prunier led a small round of applause and Moore nodded his thanks around the table.

'That's excellent news, hard evidence that links O'Rourke to the murder,' said Prunier. 'And the thought of such a gun being in circulation was very worrying. And now, Monsieur Hodge?'

'You all saw the report Yves and Bruno filed on Rentoul's safe and its contents,' Hodge said and handed Prunier a document. 'I'd like to give formal notice that the United States will claim ownership of the cash, securities and the wine that was found there.'

'Noted, but we'd better leave that to the diplomats and lawyers,' Prunier replied. 'And you said you had news from your colleagues in Houston.'

Hodge reported that the FBI field office had interviewed hospital staff, the rental agency and its cleaners, consulted travel records and established a clear chronology of when each of the different members of the Felder family was in the city over the three months of Felder's treatment. Felder's body had been cremated on Saturday and the family was booked on a flight back to London that very evening.

'We may have grounds to arrest at least one of them,' Hodge went on. 'We obtained voice prints of the first Mrs Felder and her children, and compared them with the voice print on Kelly's phone. We got a ninety-eight per cent match with Mrs Felder, and a ninety-one per cent match with the daughter. That's not unusual with close family members but it means we have reason to detain Mrs Felder and to cooperate in any extradition proceedings against her. We can also establish that Mrs Felder flew to London a week before the letter containing the photographs of Rentoul was posted to Kelly. If you guys could establish from flight or train or shipping records that she came to France, we have a case.'

'Excellent work by the FBI, thank you,' said Prunier. 'We'll follow up on that.'

Bruno raised a hand. 'I agree, great work, but there's one issue that perplexes me. I see that Madame Felder and her children had a strong financial motive to eliminate Monika but how could they be sure that setting the IRA onto Rentoul would kill her as well? They would have to have known of Rentoul's background and of Monika's affair with him and of her booking the cookery course.'

'Rentoul was working with Felder in Northern Ireland years before Monika met either of them, so the first Mrs Felder would have known Rentoul,' Moore replied. 'And if she didn't know about Rentoul surviving the supposed ambush in Baghdad, her son was part of the family company. He could have known.'

'They certainly knew of the cookery course,' Hodge said. 'Two of the hospital nurses told us that Monika mentioned it to them after the doctor recommended that Monika needed a break from Felder's bedside and she should take an activity vacation that would keep her busy.'

'Like a cookery course,' said Bruno.

'Exactly. He said the same thing to the Felders which is why Julian and Portia went skiing when Monika was in Houston. The travel records suggest that Mrs Felder was the only one who went to Europe. The children made one trip to Yucatán, in Mexico, and another to ski in Mont Tremblant in Canada. We have asked local police if they can confirm their continuous presence there. But all the family had to know where the others were so they could be told if the old man died. They'd all have to be at the funeral.

'One more thing,' Hodge added. 'I've been trying to fathom how Mrs Felder knew of Monika's affair with Rentoul. It turns out that while Felder was in hospital, the first wife and his children were added to his credit card to cover their expenses. That meant they had access to his and Monika's credit card records, so they could easily have tracked what she was spending and where. That's how they realized Monika was having these romantic trysts with Rentoul. They even knew about the cookery course Monika paid for, her air ticket to Bordeaux, even the train ticket she bought and paid for online.'

'So while the IRA wanted to kill Rentoul, Mrs Felder saw it as a way to kill Monika to be sure she wouldn't inherit from Felder's estate,' said Moore. 'That's very clever, she was killing two birds with one stone.'

Yes, thought Bruno, it all began to make sense. But he wondered if it was only her former husband's money that had inspired Mrs Felder. Might there not also have been some jealousy involved, a lingering hatred for the pretty young German girl who had stolen her husband all those years ago? Greed about money was one plausible motive but the passions and resentments of the human heart were often far more powerful. Even as he mused, Bruno was aware of Prunier's voice breaking into his reverie.

'Bruno, we need to arrange for that photograph of Madame Felder to be shown around hotels, restaurants, the usual places to establish that she was here,' Prunier said. 'I should add, gentlemen, that the reliability of voice prints is not yet established in French law, although our investigating magistrates do make use of them, so a visual identification would be important.'

Moore caught Prunier's eye. 'I have enough to apply for a warrant to look at Mrs Felder's own bank and credit card records in Britain.'

'Good, that'll be useful,' said Prunier. 'Anything else, gentlemen?'

'Yes,' chimed in Hodge. 'You should all have seen my report on the travel data from Rentoul's various passports, in addition to his travels as McBride. Colleagues back in the States are trying to analyse them but I'd be grateful for any further insights you can give.'

'Rentoul was a trained sniper, so it might be worth checking his travels against killings by rifle,' Bruno said. 'There's a photo of him on the wall of his house that was taken on a beach I recognized from my army days. It's in Djibouti and there's no scar on his chest. Guessing his age, the photo was probably taken around the time of the Somali pirate raids when shipping companies were hiring private security guards.'

Hodge scribbled a note and nodded his thanks.

Prunier closed the meeting and Bruno checked his phone as the others began to leave the conference room. There was one text message from Jack Crimson which he opened as he headed for the door, only to feel a hand on his arm as Prunier discreetly held him back until the rest had filed out. He closed the door.

'I gather your Mayor thinks I was guilty of a power play in asking you for an explanation of that business with Louis in Montignac,' Prunier said. 'Is that right?'

'Well, he's a politician and they tend to see many things in terms of politics and power plays,' Bruno said, choosing his words with care. 'And it's obvious that there's a lot of room for confusion about this new role of mine. But I think it's starting to work out.'

'Good. And I'm more than happy with the way you've been working with Moore and Hodge. I think we can agree that even though you don't come under my direct orders you'll help out where and when you can.'

'Of course. By the way, where was Ardouin this morning?' Bruno asked. 'I'd have thought the magistrate would have been present.'

'He had to go to Paris last night for a meeting on this loot that was found in Rentoul's safe. It's taking place at the Quai d'Orsay today but as well as the diplomats the finance and interior ministries are both involved. There's no sign of a will and Rentoul had no living relatives so Ardouin claims that under the law it all belongs to the French state. But now the Americans are getting involved, as you heard.'

'Maybe we should have seized that wine as evidence while we had the chance,' said Bruno, grinning. 'But I fear Yves took too many photos.'

'Interesting you should say that,' said Prunier, escorting Bruno to the door. 'I suspect that one or two cases might have escaped his camera. And by the way, congratulations to you and that girl of yours, Paulette. It's a great thing, playing for France. We'll have to raise a very special glass to her when all this is over.'

From Prunier's last comment, Bruno understood that some of the wine would never reach the French or American states, but it would certainly find an appreciative home. Smiling at the thought, he looked at Crimson's message: **'McBride treated for gunshot wound in Saudi-German hospital Dubai Sept '09 when young Felder based in Dubai. No further connection known.'**

Interesting but hardly conclusive, Bruno thought. He texted back: **'Were any of Felder's security guards treated at same hospital?'**

Thinking he'd better keep in touch with his team, he called Juliette on his mobile as he walked to the car park.

'Routine motorbike patrols today, I assume,' he said when she answered.

'*Bonjour*, Bruno, and thank you for that good dinner. It was interesting to meet those foreign cops, and those two women. I've just had a meeting with the Mayor about enlarging the parking area and this afternoon I plan to take those photos you sent around one or two places that aren't on your computer list.'

'Thank you. It's the older woman in those photos that we're most interested in. We're pretty sure she was here in the region but we need to prove it.'

'Understood. Are the three of us meeting this week?'

'Is Wednesday morning at nine possible for you? I'd like to meet on Louis's turf in Montignac. It would give me a chance to call in at the Mairie and the new Lascaux museum. I want to find out what surveillance cameras they've installed and how they store the images.'

'Wednesday at nine, that's a date. *A bientôt*.' She ended the call.

Standing by his van, Bruno phoned Louis. The call rang out unanswered so he left a message to call him back and began negotiating the one-way traffic system to return to St Denis. He remembered to put his phone on the passenger seat and insert an earphone into his right ear and just as he reached the roundabout with the trickiest crossroads, it rang.

'Bruno, it's Louis. Sorry, I was in the van and didn't get to the phone in time to answer. What is it?'

Louis's voice sounded nervous. That was to be expected after their last angry encounter. Bruno made an effort to sound cordial.

'Can you meet Juliette and me in your office, Wednesday at nine, just to review the week and see what we're all working on?'

'That's fine, Wednesday at nine,' Louis said, sounding relieved. 'Do you want to stay for lunch? And any word on that Irish guy, O'Rourke?'

'He's still in custody, not saying much but lunch on Wednesday sounds a good idea. I thought you might introduce us to some of the people in your Mairie. Then I thought I'd call in at the new Lascaux museum, check on their security cameras. That would take us through to lunchtime.'

'Ah, yes, cameras. That reminds me, those photos you sent. The younger one meant nothing to me but you know I never forget a face? The older woman, I saw her here in Montignac, two or three weeks ago in that café opposite the tourist office, with O'Rourke's wife. And a day or so later O'Rourke said he was planning to go to the new Lascaux place because his wife had just been with a friend and she was very impressed.'

Bruno pulled into the side of the road and put on his flashing hazard lights.

'You sure about that?'

'Oh yes, certain. I didn't say hello because I was with my wife, loaded down with shopping. It was my day off, Wednesday, the day after market day.'

'Can you remember the exact date? This is important.' Bruno pulled out his notebook and turned to the page with the date of the phone call to Kelly.

'Thursday, three weeks ago. I'm sure of it.' Bruno heard the sound of pages being flipped. 'Thursday, March fifth, it would have been about eleven in the morning. I can check because the wife bought a new food mixer and it will be on her credit card receipt.'

'Do me a favour, Louis, look it up, keep it safe and meet me at the new Lascaux museum in about an hour.'

Bruno called J-J and left a message to say they had a sighting of Felder's first wife and that he was heading for Lascaux to view the security tapes. Then he avoided the autoroute and took the back road through Fossemagne, knowing it would be faster, and he reached the new Lascaux in just over forty minutes. Louis was waiting at the entrance, credit card receipt in hand, saying the director would be happy to see them. Ten minutes later Bruno and Louis were scanning the digitalized film for the fifth of March and within thirty minutes Louis had spotted her. Madame Felder was not alone. She was accompanied by O'Rourke's wife.

'Told you, I never forget a face,' Louis said proudly as Bruno clapped him on the back in congratulation and they went to organize some printouts of the two women. The date and time were added automatically to the prints.

'I think this more than makes up for the other matter,' Bruno said. 'I'll take them over to J-J now and make sure Prunier knows you get the credit.'

'Whatever happened about that? You warned me of the wrath of God coming from Prunier and suddenly it went quiet.'

'There were two reasons for that. The most important is that it turned out well, in that your remark spooked your Irishman and made him and his wife run, and they got caught at a roadblock. Then O'Rourke called his friend, Kelly, in Bergerac, and he was caught as he was about to run, so it was a good result.'

'Ah yes, Sean Kelly from Bergerac, a very friendly fellow, I met him when he came up to visit O'Rourke for one of the Six Nations rugby games, Ireland versus England. We have this Irish-style pub in Montignac where they show the games on a big screen, and everybody was cheering for the Irish. I didn't have the heart to tell them we French weren't cheering for Ireland so much as against England.'

'I'm the same,' said Bruno. 'Unless France is playing I usually cheer for the Welsh or the Scots. England's so big, that makes the others the underdogs.'

'You said there was a second reason why Prunier didn't give me a hard time,' Louis said.

'Prunier went a bit too far. He demanded that I file a report on the incident and present myself in front of his desk the next day, as if I were under his orders. So I checked with my Mayor who said he was my boss, not Prunier, and as far as he is concerned there was no case to answer. Prunier is no fool. He doesn't want to pick a fight with a powerful Mayor.'

'I'll remember that,' said Louis, with a cheerful glint in his eye.

'I thought you might,' Bruno replied. 'But you haven't got long to go before you retire, Louis, so go easy on the booze. That Armagnac your cousin makes could get you into trouble. That would be a shame because you did really well today.'

When Bruno got to the police *commissariat* in Bergerac, he was told that J-J was still in the interrogation room. He went along to the observation chamber behind it and found Moore staring through the one-way glass, several empty plastic cups of coffee before him.

'You must be desperate, drinking that stuff,' said Bruno shaking hands and casting an eye into the room where J-J sat glaring at Kelly who was staring silently at his feet. He was wiry and looked fit and bronzed, probably from gardening in the open air. His grey hair was cut very short and he had the thick wrists and powerful arms of a man who worked with his hands.

'I'm getting desperate because that bastard won't say a word,' said Moore. 'He's been too well trained.'

'We might have a lever,' Bruno said, showing Moore the printed photo. 'That's Madame Felder, visiting our new Lascaux museum three weeks ago in the company of O'Rourke's wife. We also have an eyewitness of their meeting for coffee. The same eyewitness puts Kelly and O'Rourke together watching a Six Nations match.'

'That could do it,' said Moore, perking up. 'Does J-J know about this yet?'

'No, that's why I brought the prints in person. We just got them thanks to my colleague in Montignac. He's the eyewitness.'

'The photos are just what we need.' Moore glanced at his watch. 'It's almost noon so they'll break for lunch soon, thanks to your magistrate's rule. No more than three hours' questioning at a time, says Ardouin, and then they get lunch from the canteen. I have to admit it's a lot better than we get in ours.'

'You've been sitting in here this whole time?'

'I've been feeding J-J lines to try, based on what we know of Kelly. But the guy knows he's going down on the narcotics charge. I think he's waiting for the guard to arrive and then he'll start complaining of inhumane treatment. They usually try that.'

'So Kelly knows an Irish cop is coming?'

'He kept demanding an Irish diplomat so J-J mentioned that someone from the Guards was coming.'

'What about his wife?'

'Just the same, not a word. When she gets bored she starts singing old rebel songs.'

'This would drive me round the bend,' said Bruno. 'I'll just go to the toilet and be back in time to see J-J at noon.'

As Bruno was washing his hands J-J came in looking grumpy and frustrated.

'Hi, Bruno, have you come to share in our misery? This has to be the worst interrogation I ever suffered. I've never come across a more stubborn and tedious old bastard. At least his wife breaks into song from time to time.'

'I may have something that can help.' Bruno showed J-J the prints and explained the background. 'It was Louis, that cop from Montignac, who remembered seeing her in town and recalled the exact date. Make sure Prunier knows that. Then we went to the new Lascaux place and there they were on the surveillance camera.'

'So we can put them together with Madame Felder, the wife of an English general?' J-J raised his eyebrows. 'That won't be popular in the Dublin pubs. Do you think we can use this to get the FBI to arrest Madame Felder and start extradition proceedings?'

'I'm no lawyer but I'd have thought so. You weren't at the conference this morning but Hodge said the FBI already had enough to detain her and that he'd support extradition.'

'*Putain*, we're going to get this case all wrapped up,' said J-J, coming to the wash basins. 'I was supposed to meet the guard at the airport but Prunier wants me in Périgueux to tackle O'Rourke. Apparently Ardouin wants them all kept together, separate cells, but in one place. I must say I'm looking forward to seeing O'Rourke's face when we show him that sniper's gun we found in his garden.'

23

After picking up Balzac from home, Bruno was back in his office in the Mairie of St Denis ploughing through paperwork and thinking about dinner. Gilles and Fabiola, Crimson and the Baron and Florence were coming, along with her own and Miranda's children. Bruno would have to go home in time to put sheets on the guest beds and organize supper. He had lots of chicken stock and potatoes in the pantry and there were leeks in his garden so a leek and potato soup would be easy. He had some pigeons and a couple of rabbits he'd shot in the freezer which would thaw quickly. The idea attracted him but how would the children feel about eating bunnies?

Then he remembered one very successful evening when Miranda had let the children make their own pizzas, using whatever leftovers they chose as toppings. From tuna salad to pineapple slices, sliced beetroot to salami, meatballs to stewed apple, they had concocted some strange-looking dishes but had scoffed the lot. He grinned at the memory and thought he had enough assorted items in the fridge to keep them happy. He'd pick up some pizza dough and tomatoes from the supermarket when he went to buy bread. Crimson had said he'd bring wine and apple pie. He called the Baron to check that he was coming.

'I'll be bringing strawberries from my greenhouse,' his friend replied. 'I tried one this morning and they're perfect. Do you need anything else?'

'No, we're fine,' said Bruno. 'I'm making soup and I have a couple of rabbits and I'll let the kids make pizza for themselves. Crimson is back and he's bringing wine.'

'See you about seven, Bruno.'

Having reduced the pile in his inbox by a few centimetres, Bruno picked up his cap and headed with Balzac to the *collége* for the end of the school day, thinking he'd get the bread and other shopping on the way back. Then he might have time to exercise his horse before heading home to make the soup. He was greeting various mothers and teenagers when his phone rang. It was Philippe Delaron.

'What's this about a shooting on the *route nationale*?' Philippe demanded. 'It just came up on the police radio.'

'Which *route nationale*?'

'Périgueux to Bergerac. Haven't you heard? I'm heading there now.'

'I'll try to find out but it's not our district and I hadn't heard about it.'

Trotting back towards the Mairie, Bruno called the control centre in Périgueux but it was busy. He tried J-J's mobile and went straight to his message system. That was unusual. He called Prunier's office and reached Marie-Pierre, who said, 'I can't talk now, Bruno, there's an emergency and we've got chaos here. Please clear this line.'

Bruno called Yveline at the Gendarmerie, without success. But as Bruno reached the Mairie, Sergeant Jules answered his phone and at last gave him some answers. About thirty minutes earlier a truck driver had seen three men fighting beside a blue Renault Espace parked just off the road, one of them a cop in uniform. Then one of the others had pulled out a handgun and shot him. Police and gendarmes from all over the region were either heading there or setting up roadblocks. No word yet from the *urgences* on injuries.

'Was it a police vehicle?' Bruno asked, wondering where else the cop might have come from.

'I don't know, but we're trying to organize roadblocks throughout the region in case they come this way. Yveline has gone to the bridges at Limeuil and has another group at the bridge near Le Buisson. I'm surprised they haven't called you in.'

'Right,' said Bruno. 'Let your operations centre know that I'll block the bridge at St Denis. I'll get Juliette to block the one at Les Eyzies and Louis to do the same at Montignac. But make sure they know we only have handguns. After I call them I'll try to keep this line clear.'

His van was parked in front of the Mairie and he pulled it out into the road and then slewed it across the entrance to the bridge so only one car at a time could squeeze through. Leaving Balzac inside the van, he put on his flak vest, checked his weapon and then began to phone. He reached Juliette at once and there was a shocked silence on the end of the phone after he told her what he needed her to do.

'Whoever they are, these people shot a cop, one of ours, Juliette. There's no choice but you might try to get one or two hunters to bring weapons and join you, which is what I'm planning to do.'

'Do I stop every vehicle trying to cross?' she asked. 'The tailbacks . . .'

'No, they're armed and dangerous so don't try to stop them even if you have other weapons there. Your job is to deter them. If they see men with rifles they won't try to cross the bridge. And if they even see a roadblock they'll probably look for another route. Just park your police van so that only one vehicle can cross at a time. If you do see a blue Renault Espace let it through. I don't want you hurt. But please note the licence number and call me at once and the Police Nationale operations centre. You have their number.'

He called Louis without success, left a message and then called the Baron, to ask him to bring a rifle and shotgun to the bridge. Then he called Claire at the Mairie and asked her to inform the Mayor of the emergency.

'What's this about, Bruno?' called Lespinasse, pulling up his breakdown truck. It was too wide to squeeze through the gap.

'Somebody shot a cop on the Bergerac road so we're putting up roadblocks. I'll pull back a bit to let you through.'

By this time car horns and klaxons were sounding from a tailback that ran the length of the bridge and back the other way beyond the Mairie. There was no blue Renault Espace in sight but the Mayor arrived on foot, demanding to know what was happening. Bruno explained and the Mayor nodded.

'I'll get some big signs made and we'll put them up. People will understand,' he said and walked quickly back to the Mairie.

Minutes later, as Bruno waved cars through from alternate directions one by one, the Mayor returned with Xavier, his deputy, and Roberte from the social security desk, each carrying a big piece of cardboard on which someone had printed in huge letters: *SORRY FOR ROADBLOCK. POLICE INCIDENT.*

Roberte placed herself on the roundabout about fifty metres short of the roadblock and Xavier went to the far end of the bridge, where Bruno saw the Baron arriving on foot, a weapon over each shoulder. Xavier held up the sign as he passed each car and then walked on to the end of the tailback. The Baron handed Bruno the shotgun and then stood behind one of the big stone blocks that flanked the bridge, his body covered but keeping his rifle in full view. Bruno saw it was the Baron's favourite, a sturdy MAS-36 of the kind the Baron had been issued in the Algerian war.

'Who are we looking for?' the Baron asked.

'No idea,' said Bruno and explained how little he knew. 'We're here as deterrence so don't shoot unless they gun me down and keep your rifle like that, in full view.'

By now the drivers understood the routine and the traffic began to flow as Bruno kept waving them through. Louis called to say he'd got the message and was at the Montignac bridge. Bruno called his colleague Quatremer at Lalinde who was manning his own bridge. There were still some bridges unguarded so Bruno called his Mayor.

'Can you call the Mayors at Trémolat and Siorac and ask them to post someone to watch the bridges? I don't want a roadblock, just ask them to watch and to call me at once on my mobile if they see a blue Renault Espace.'

'I'll do so at once. I already had the Mayor from Siorac calling to ask if I knew what was going on.'

'And see if you can persuade the Mayor at Sainte Alvère to post someone to watch the crossroads.'

'Right, leave it to me.'

We should have rehearsed this and devised a proper plan, Bruno thought to himself. When this was over he'd draft a proposal and persuade Prunier to rehearse it and put it into effect. He kept waving through vehicles, ignoring people who slowed to ask questions and waving them on with his shotgun as he thought about what had happened.

He knew there were two prisoners at the *commissariat de police* in Bergerac, Kelly and his wife, and J-J had told him they were to be taken north that day to Périgueux. They would have been handcuffed with a police driver at the wheel and at least one armed guard. The obvious route would have taken them up the *route nationale* to Périgueux. Could they have broken free, somehow seized the guard's weapon, shot him and made their escape?

There would have been one other police vehicle taking that road, the one carrying the Irish policeman from the Guards who was flying in from Dublin that morning. Perhaps he'd already landed at Bergerac airport, where he'd have been met and driven to Périgueux. Bruno called Moore's mobile to ask if the guard had yet arrived.

'Not that I know of, Bruno, but it's chaos here. You know a cop has been shot?'

'Yes, I know, I'm manning one of the roadblocks looking for the blue Renault Espace the cop was driving. But do we know who was in the vehicle? Could it have been the Kelly couple?'

'Christ, I hope not but I don't know. Hodge and I are here in the conference room and Prunier and J-J are in the operations centre. All we heard was about the shooting when we were getting some coffee in the canteen.'

'They must know by now which cop was shot and whether he was on the Kelly escort. Could you get to the operations centre and ask? You and Hodge both have a right and a need to know.'

'All right, I'll call you back.' Moore hung up.

Let's assume it was the Kelly couple and they had somehow managed to escape, Bruno thought. Their priority would be to get out of France, perhaps to Spain or the much longer distance to Italy or Belgium, or to Ireland if they could. All the autoroutes and main roads would by now be blocked and the train stations watched. That left small aircraft and boats and Bruno presumed the IRA was sufficiently well organized to arrange such a voyage. There were yacht harbours all along the coast, airports at Périgueux, Bergerac, Limoges and Brive, private airfields at Belvès, Domme, Fumel, Agen, Cahors . . . *Putain*, if the IRA had access to a helicopter they could be picked up anywhere.

But what if they chose to stay? Given some support, they could hide out almost indefinitely in this region full of *gîtes* and rental properties. Any Irish, or British or American sympathizers could take a long vacation rental and hide them there for weeks or even months until new passports or escape routes were arranged.

What if they had a mission? A mission or a target more important than escape? Perhaps to free their friends the O'Rourkes in Périgueux? Or to take hostages to try and negotiate their freedom? They must know that France would never permit that, not after the murders and the cocaine and with the British and Americans already involved.

There was one obvious target, Bruno thought, and pulled out his phone to call Jack Crimson. It rang for some time before a woman's voice answered in English. It was Miranda.

'Do you know where your dad is?' he asked.

'He said he was going wine-tasting,' she replied cheerfully. 'He was here to arrange about picking up the children for tonight's dinner but he forgot his phone.'

'Any idea which one he was visiting?'

'He just said he was going to Montravel, I don't know which vineyard.'

'If you hear from him, could you tell him to call me very urgently? It's really important.'

'I will, and thanks for taking care of the children this evening.'

Montravel was on the far western side of the Bergerac wine area, on the border with the Bordeaux region. Bruno pulled from his van the map of the vineyards issued by Vins de Bergerac to look up some phone numbers but was interrupted by an incoming call.

'Bruno,' came Moore's urgent voice. 'Prunier has just confirmed that the shooting involved the police van that was bringing Kelly and his wife to Périgueux. Despite an armed guard and being handcuffed they somehow managed to escape in the van. The armed guard is in hospital, shot in the lung, and the driver is badly concussed. They were found at the side of the road. They were in a blue Renault Espace.'

'I'm looking for that van at my roadblock.'

'They might have switched it by now. They took the guard's weapon so they're armed and could easily have stolen another. They left the handcuffs at the scene, got the keys from the guard.'

'I'm worried they might be going after Jack Crimson,' Bruno said.

'Me too, he'd be a high value target for them. Can you call him?'

Bruno explained about the forgotten phone. 'Could you tell Prunier I'm going to abandon the roadblock and go to Crimson's place, just in case.'

'Where is it? I'll join you.'

'Just outside St Denis, on the way to St Avit, a small chateau called L'Aumônérie. It should be on the GPS in your car, which means Kelly can also find it, if he hasn't checked it out already.'

Bruno rang Sergeant Jules, alone at the Gendarmerie, to explain that he needed one of Yveline's gendarmes to replace him at the roadblock on the bridge while he went to protect Crimson.

'I'll come myself,' Jules replied. 'I'll get the wife to take over the phone here. You make sure Crimson is safe and I'll ask Yveline to send you reinforcements.'

As he waited, Bruno explained to the Baron the threat to Crimson.

'In that case, I'll come with you,' the Baron said. 'He's my friend, too. But leave your police van here at the block. If they see that at Crimson's place, they'll know it's a trap. My car's parked just across the bridge.'

'Good thinking,' said Bruno, and waited until Sergeant Jules, breathing heavily, trotted up the street towards the bridge. Bruno waved to him and let Balzac out of the van. He explained to Xavier that Jules was taking over the roadblock and then he, Balzac and the Baron climbed into the stately old Citröen DS and headed around the stalled traffic to Crimson's place.

24

As the Baron drove, Bruno began calling the Montravel vineyards. He drew a blank at the three best-known chateaux, Moulin-Caresse, Puy-Servain and le Raz. On an impulse, he called Château Marsau, which was mainly in the neighbouring *département* of the Gironde, and thus in the Bordeaux *appellation*. But one parcel of their land was on the Bergerac side of the border and they had a small vineyard in the Montravel called l'Enclos Pontys which Bruno recalled Crimson praising to his friends. And yes, they replied to his question. A charming Englishman with the credit card of a Monsieur Crimson who was driving an elderly Jaguar had been in their tasting room that day and had bought half a dozen of the Pontys and another half-dozen of their Château Marsau Merlot. He'd left less than an hour ago.

'If he's driving fast, Jack might just beat us back to his place,' Bruno said.

'How do you want to handle this?' the Baron asked. 'I'll park at the back out of sight but do we wait for them in the house or ambush them in the driveway?'

'One of us has to be at the head of the drive,' Bruno replied. 'That way we could see Crimson arrive and warn him to drive on and get the hell away. We both have our phones and we'd better put them on vibrate. We don't want them ringing at the wrong moment. I'll take the driveway and the rifle and you stay in the house with the shotgun. There's a landing on the staircase with a window that overlooks the driveway. That would be a good place to wait.'

'What's your plan? If you see them will you shoot?'

'That depends on them. If they drive in I'll probably try to shoot out a tyre and tell them to surrender. I can recognize Kelly and I think the only weapon he'll have will be the handgun he took from the guard in the van. His wife may have the driver's gun. She's long-term IRA so she should know how to use it.'

The Baron shook his head. 'Why do you think they'll just roll up in the car? I wouldn't. In their shoes, I'd leave the vehicle hidden and then creep up on foot using cover. One at the front, one at the back in case he makes a run for it. And first I'd try to check whether Jack is at home.'

Bruno considered this and then nodded. 'You're right, but I'll still need to stop Jack if I see him. And we might be getting reinforcements, maybe our gendarmes, maybe a British cop, although he must still be half an hour away. I'd better wait under cover at the top of the drive. And pull in here. I'll go ahead with Balzac and scout.'

They were still on a *commune* road, tarred and decently maintained, about a hundred metres short of the bumpy approach that led to Crimson's house. The Baron pulled off onto a hunters' track through the woods and checked that he was out of view of the road before he applied the brake.

'I'll leave the car here and come on foot with you,' he said.

'You know where Crimson keeps his spare key?' Bruno asked.

'Under the seat of his lawn mower.'

'How much ammo do you have?'

'Six each, buckshot and heavy birdshot for the shotgun, one already loaded in each barrel. Two spare deer slugs in my pocket. For the rifle, five rounds in the internal magazine, two more clips.' He handed Bruno the MAS-36 rifle and spare clips. 'If that isn't enough, they'll drum us out of the hunting club.'

Bruno went carefully through the woods, parallel to the approach to Crimson's driveway but keeping it a good ten metres on his left. Balzac was at his heels. The Baron was another ten metres to his right and slightly behind him, the distance they kept when hunting. They had trained Balzac together and hunted together frequently enough that Balzac would obey the Baron as if he were Bruno. When the approach road turned before reaching the stone pillars at the top of Crimson's private driveway Bruno stopped, crouched on one knee and waved to the Baron with one hand. Then he tapped Balzac on his left shoulder and the dog crept silently forward and slipped into the hedge by one of Crimson's pillars.

Bruno rose, signalled to the Baron to follow and moved quickly forward, knowing from his dog that the area around the pillars was clear. At the pillar, he sent Balzac forward again, watching his dog slinking quickly through the bushes that lined the driveway until he reached Crimson's garage. Then Balzac stopped and looked back at Bruno, his tail low and all four feet on the ground. That meant that zone was also clear. Again Bruno signalled to the Baron who went through the undergrowth to the garage, looked inside and shook his head. It was empty.

Crouching by the garage, the Baron sent Balzac to circle the house. When the dog returned, the Baron slipped inside the garage for a few moments and then went to the back door to let Balzac in before he followed. Bruno waited until his phone vibrated and answered it to hear the Baron murmur that the house was clear and he was sending Balzac back to join Bruno at the driveway.

'Right, I'm taking position, about ten metres back from the pillars and keeping them to my right,' Bruno said. 'I'm in cover with a clear view of the driveway and the approach road.'

The cover was patchy but adequate. He stood behind the trunk of a chestnut tree that would stop a bullet. A thick hedge of bramble sprawled to his left and to his right were fallen trees and undergrowth that could easily trip the unwary. Bruno told himself he would have to tread carefully. He bent down, spat onto his hand and rubbed it in the soil to make it muddy so that he could draw stripes onto his cheeks and nose and brow to camouflage his face. Then he waited for the sounds of the woods to resume, the birdsong and small animal rustlings that had ceased at his approach. He wondered if Kelly was a countryman. Running a garden centre suggested that he might be.

Minutes passed and then Balzac silently appeared at his side. Bruno bent down to caress him and heard a distant voice, a woman's voice, strangely rhythmic. As it came close he realized the woman was singing.

Bruno smiled. That was clever. Nothing could be more innocent than a woman singing on a country walk. Kelly would have sent her on ahead and he would follow, using cover but keeping close behind her. The fact that she was moving alone made the chances that the woman had a second gun much higher. Bruno put a finger on Balzac's head to keep him still and silent. Then he waited, rifle to his shoulder, for her to come into view. Suddenly, he began to pick out the words of her song.

In Mountjoy jail one Monday morning, high upon the gallows tree,
Kevin Barry gave his young life for the cause of liberty . . .

Bruno guessed that she was in her fifties, maybe a little older, a handsome dark-haired woman with an easy walk and good posture. Dappled sunlight shone through the trees, and he saw that she was wearing trainers, dark jeans and a leather jacket over a dark-coloured shirt.

Silently, Bruno pulled out his phone, hit the single autodial for the Baron and held it facing the woman, knowing that the Baron would hear her singing and understand that Bruno was indicating that their quarry was approaching.

The woman paused, still singing, when she saw the pillars and the house beyond. She turned her head to the right and slipped her right hand into the inner left side of her jacket. So that was where she kept her gun. She must be right-handed.

Bruno tried to follow her gaze, expecting that she'd be looking for her man. He used the hunter's trick, not staring directly but at a tree near where he expected Kelly to be, knowing that indirect vision caught movement more easily. He saw a branch shift down low in the trees beyond the woman, a shadow behind it.

Bruno waited, saw what might have been a hand gesture from Kelly and the woman walked on, in silence now. She was moving more slowly and with care, glancing briefly behind her and to each side until she paused at the pillar nearest Bruno. She stood silently for a long moment before peeking around it at the house. She moved back and gave a thumbs up to her right.

There was a long pause, some movement in the trees and then the man Bruno had seen in the Bergerac interview room slipped into view beside the other pillar. A handgun like the one Bruno now carried at his waist was in Kelly's hand. That meant he had at least fifteen rounds, less however many he had shot at the policeman who was the gun's rightful owner. He might also have a spare magazine.

Bruno had a clear shot at them both and he knew the rifle he was aiming. He had used the Baron's gun before. It was well-kept and it aimed true. Bruno knew he could work the bolt and load another round in little more than a second.

The 7.5 millimetre bullet left the barrel with a muzzle velocity of eight hundred and fifty metres per second. At this range Bruno knew it would hit the target with an energy of around three thousand joules, at least six times the energy of a round from the handgun that he and Kelly each carried. It would not just knock a big man off his feet, it would hurl him down onto his back. And the shock of impact would leave his central nervous system stunned for several seconds.

Should he shoot? He was facing two escaped prisoners who

had shot a cop and were armed and dangerous. They were known terrorists hunting a retired British official they saw as a legitimate target and were almost certainly intent on killing Crimson if they could. Since they had already shot their guard they would have no hesitation in shooting Bruno as well. And he knew already how efficiently they had killed Monika and how brutally they had hanged Rentoul.

He was tempted. *Mon Dieu*, Bruno was so tempted to fire that his trigger finger seemed to be twitching as if taking on a life of its own. Given who they were and what they had done there would be no recrimination, barely even an inquiry. They were legitimate targets.

At the back of Bruno's mind an insidious voice was suggesting he could nudge Balzac with his foot to send him surging forward, knowing the surprise of the dog's leap and sudden adrenalin peak would make the man and his wife lift their weapons and probably shoot. That would give Bruno every excuse to gun them down where they stood.

At this range he could not miss. Bruno held two lives in his hands but there was no need for a kill. He could settle for a disabling shot for each of them and the crisis would be over. But it would depend on how they moved, how they prepared to fire. Did they plan to kill Crimson or try to kidnap him? It would make a difference.

But Bruno knew that he couldn't shoot, not from an ambush like this, like a thief in the night. And he would not put Balzac at such risk. As that thought crossed his mind he heard the sound of a vehicle approaching.

The IRA couple cocked their heads as they heard it and

slipped behind their respective pillars, each one now with a gun drawn and ready.

From where they waited they might see the car and identify it before he could. They knew where Crimson lived so they probably knew his car. Bruno listened, recognizing the sound of a gasoline engine. The gendarmes used diesel.

So it was either Crimson or Moore. Crimson's Jaguar was white and he had no idea what car Moore would be using, nor if it would be a diesel. And Bruno did not know whether Moore would be coming alone or perhaps with Hodge or a police driver.

Putain, there could easily be three targets heading down that lane towards a possible ambush.

Would Kelly shoot or let them pass? Would his wife have the same fire discipline as her husband? Perhaps Kelly and his wife would assume that these new arrivals were innocent visitors, friends of Crimson dropping by and quite likely to turn around and leave when they realized he was not at home.

Bruno suddenly understood that Kelly and his wife would be making the same calculations as he was, wondering whether these visitors were dangerous or harmless, whether this was a time to kill.

Merde! A fierce new thought struck Bruno. Perhaps they already knew Moore's face. The IRA were professionals and they had been in this business for the last forty years. They had their own intelligence branch whose experts had doubtless collected photos from press clippings and police websites, even photos of police rugby teams, and distributed them among their militants to be studied. Know your enemy.

The sound of the engine was getting louder. Did it sound more powerful, like a Jaguar? Or did it sound like a modern saloon?

Even as the question framed itself in Bruno's mind his peripheral vision was aware of something white approaching. That would be Crimson.

Then Bruno heard a voice, a single phrase in English, a male voice saying quietly, 'It's him.'

Kelly stepped out from behind the pillar, already in the classic shooter's crouch, his arms stretched out before him, both hands on the weapon, his eyes focused and his finger whitening on the trigger.

Bruno shifted his aim a fraction, shouted 'Police', and instantly fired into Kelly's bunched hands at what seemed the very moment that Kelly pulled his trigger. Bruno worked the bolt to reload as he swivelled and saw the women adopting the same shooter's crouch.

In the millisecond before he squeezed the trigger Bruno recalled that she was right-handed and that therefore once hit in the right arm she would no longer be a danger and he could shift his aim back to Kelly. He put a bullet into the bone of her right shoulder, the one nearest to him.

Bruno saw her blown back into the pillar, stunned, her gun going off but firing wild as her arms flew up. Her gun rose into the air, spinning in what seemed almost like slow motion. Feeling he had all the time he needed Bruno swivelled back to see Kelly trying to get a leg beneath him to stand.

'Police, hands up,' he shouted in English.

There was no response, just another attempt by Kelly to lurch to his feet, his bloodied left hand on the ground helping him to rise on his right leg. Bruno couldn't see his gun. It could be in the hidden right hand. He aimed again and pumped another round high into Kelly's right leg to knock him down again and send him sprawling as he cried out in shock and pain.

Once Kelly crumpled to the ground, Bruno ran out and slammed his rifle butt into the back of his head. Then he turned to look at the woman.

Balzac, so accustomed to the sound of guns, had leaped forward with his master. He was now standing over the stricken woman, growling with bared teeth into her face. Bruno breathed out, the tension easing, muscles relaxing in the tiredness that came after an adrenalin rush. It was over.

'Think you're so fucking clever,' came a voice from the undergrowth behind Bruno where Kelly had made his approach.

Bruno turned his head, raising his rifle and tensing as he dived to one side. But even as he landed and rolled and worked the bolt again he knew it was hopelessly late.

A new figure had emerged onto the driveway with yet another gun aimed at him, the muzzle looking enormous.

And then this third figure disappeared in a red mist as the double sound of a shotgun's two barrels cracked from behind the pillar.

'There's always another one,' said the Baron, the shotgun still smoking in his hands. His voice was distant. Bruno's ears were still deafened by the sound of the shots.

'That's what they taught us in Algeria,' the Baron continued as he reloaded. 'Always another one.'

The door of the Jaguar opened and Crimson emerged, looking bemusedly from Bruno with his rifle to the Baron with his shotgun, and then from the still and silent Kelly to the man's wife, now keening as she lay on the ground. Her left hand was trying to staunch the bleeding from her shoulder as she stared at the snarling Balzac.

'*Putain, mon vieux*, I'd be dead without you,' Bruno said to the Baron. 'Can you call the *urgences*? And then the gendarmes?'

He walked across the driveway to look at the shredded figure, a stranger, in what had been a dark suit before the twin barrels of buckshot and birdshot had hit him. Bruno was startled to see that the man's shoes were black and highly polished.

He made sure he had turned on the safety catch of the rifle and that the chamber was empty before he handed it to Crimson. The Baron was already talking to the *urgences* on his phone. From his rear hip pocket Bruno withdrew a set of evidence gloves and pulled them on. He found Kelly's gun under the prone body and his wife's gun in the middle of the driveway. He left that one where it was, took Kelly's gun and put it beside the other one and then searched behind the bloody mess of death on the ground until he found the third shooter's weapon.

It was an automatic pistol but he did not recognize its make. Bits of the man's hands were still attached to the butt. Bruno pulled off a branch to mark the spot.

Another car appeared and braked behind the Jaguar. Still crouching, Bruno drew his handgun, only to replace it when he saw Moore emerge from one side and Hodge from the other, each with a gun in hand. Hodge glanced at the groaning woman and then advanced to stand over Kelly. He bent and put his left hand to Kelly's neck.

'He's still alive,' Hodge said. 'But he needs an ambulance.'

'We've called for one.'

'Bloody hell,' said Moore. 'What exactly happened here?'

'It's over, it's clear,' said Bruno. 'Kelly and his wife came to kill Crimson. But who was the third one?'

'The guard,' said Moore, looking down at the corpse. 'Or rather, the IRA guy who took the real guard's place. He was met by one of J-J's men at Bergerac airport and taken to be welcomed at the *commissariat* in Bergerac. He volunteered to help escort Kelly and his wife to Bergerac and then, we presume, freed them both when he overwhelmed the guard.'

'That's a very daring stroke,' said Bruno, a note almost of admiration in his voice.

'Daring or perhaps desperate,' said Moore. 'But it must have been one of their best men so I think I may know who it was.'

Moore walked across to the broken branch where Bruno had marked the third man's gun.

'It's a Walther P99, as issued to authorized officers of the Guards,' Moore said. 'It belonged to the real guard who has just been found gagged and tied to his bed in Dublin, still woozy from being given sodium thiopental. His passport, warrant card, air ticket and weapon were then used for the fake guard to fly to Bergerac this morning.'

Bruno was still trying to work out the complexity of it all and marvelling that he was still alive. 'How did you know he was not the real guard?'

'He left Bergerac in the van with the Kellys. Then he disappeared with them. We got the Guards in Dublin to fax a photo and fingerprints of the real man. The photo was ambiguous but the prints on the coffee cup he'd used at Bergerac didn't match.

That was when the Guards went to the home of the officer who should have flown here and found him tied up.'

Hodge joined them, glanced at the corpse and then at Bruno. 'Did you get him with a shotgun?'

'No, my friend got him, thank heavens,' Bruno replied, nodding to the Baron.

'Who are you, *monsieur*?' Hodge asked the Baron, eyeing the shotgun.

'Jean-Pierre Picot, *monsieur*, formerly a captain in the Chasseurs,' the Baron replied evenly. 'I'm long since retired from the army but I'm a friend and hunting partner of Bruno here.'

'He just saved my life,' said Bruno and he heard in the distance the first wail of the ambulance siren.

Hodge nodded and looked from the corpse of the false guard back to the Baron. 'So you're like what we'd call in the United States a deputy?'

'Really?' beamed the Baron, who was a devout fan of Western movies. 'I'm a deputy? How wonderful.'

25

Yveline and a second gendarme arrived as the ambulance men were loading Kelly and his wife into their vehicle. Yveline told her colleague to accompany the couple to the clinic at St Denis, and to call her as soon as they arrived.

'And stay watchful,' she called after him, before turning to Bruno. 'I need to take statements,' she said, pulling out a note-book. 'I'll start with you.'

Moore came to stand beside her, a small tape recorder in hand. 'Do you mind?' he asked Bruno, who shook his head and began to recount what had happened.

'You definitely shouted "Police" before you opened fire?' Yve-line asked.

'He did. I heard it just when I thought I was going to be killed,' said Crimson.

When she had finished, Bruno sat leaning against the pillar with Balzac's head on his lap as Yveline took statements from the Baron, from Crimson and then from Hodge and Moore. He knew the routine. A policeman who opened fire while on duty would be placed on administrative suspension pending an inquiry to determine whether his action was justified and that the standard rules of engagement had been followed.

Bruno's phone vibrated and he answered, to hear Florence's voice.

'I've just had a call from Paulette's friend,' she began. 'The procedure took place this afternoon, everything went as it should and Paulette is resting. She asked her friend to convey the message that she'd like to see us both in Périgueux later this week and I thought we could discuss when to visit her after we put the children to bed this evening. What time do you want us?'

'I'm sorry but we'll have to cancel tonight's dinner at my place,' Bruno said. 'We've just had an emergency. The Baron and Crimson and I will be tied up with the police for some time. None of us is hurt and I'll call you when I can.'

'I see. What's the emergency that includes you, Jack and the Baron?'

'I can't speak now, Florence, I'm sorry. Let me tell you later. But I'm glad it went well for Paulette.'

Sergeant Jules appeared and began stringing red and white crime scene tape across the approach road, just before Gilles arrived in one car and Philippe Delaron and Kathleen arrived in another. Bruno glared at them both as they converged on him.

'Do you realize that your news story about Crimson may have led to this?' he snapped at Kathleen.

'Stop this now,' barked Yveline, jumping in front of Bruno and pushing Philippe and Kathleen away. 'You cannot say a word to the press. You two get back behind that crime scene tape or I'll arrest you both.'

Philippe backed away, still taking photographs and Gilles shouted, 'You okay, Bruno?'

Bruno nodded as Yveline waved Gilles back.

'I can't say a word to the press,' Bruno called back to him. 'But the Baron and Crimson are civilians. They were here and they can talk. Ask them.'

'Shut up right now,' Yveline snapped at Bruno and then turned to Gilles. 'I'm sorry but you have to leave. Bruno and the Baron have been involved in a shooting incident and have to be detained.'

'You can't detain me, Yveline,' said Crimson and led Gilles away, talking as they went. Yveline looked after them and shrugged. Then she turned to Bruno. 'Don't worry, Bruno, but I have to take your handgun.'

'I know,' he said. He eased Balzac's head away, stood up, undid his holster and handed it to her.

'If I have anything to do with this, you'll have it back tonight,' she said. 'And I'm the one writing the incident report.'

'I know, thanks,' he said, looking at Crimson talking volubly to Gilles, Philippe and Kathleen. 'You might want to add that Sergeant Jules did well.'

'So did Jules's wife,' Yveline said. 'I'd better draft this report before Prunier and J-J get here.'

She went back to her van, climbed inside, pulled a small laptop from her case and began typing.

'Could we be in trouble?' the Baron asked him quietly. 'Not that I'm much bothered but do you think I should call a lawyer?'

'No,' said Bruno. 'It's just the rules we have to go through. But if you get any other official questions say nothing and refer them to the statement you just made to Yveline. You fired to save my life, that's what matters.'

Yves from the forensics squad and the scene of crime team from Périgueux were the next to arrive. They donned their snowman suits and began photographing the body of the false guard and the rest of the scene before collecting all the weapons and cartridge cases, labelling them and putting each one into a separate plastic bag. Yves examined the corpse and then Moore approached him to point out the dead man's gun.

Yves bent over, took more photos and then rose suddenly and went back to the forensics vehicle. He came back with what looked like a fingerprint kit and tubes for blood samples. He'd be trying to identify the dead man, Bruno thought as he watched Yves at work. Moore was on his phone, speaking English, Hodge at his side.

From the far side of the tape strung across the driveway, another phone rang and Bruno saw Philippe answer it with his usual cocky self-assurance. He listened for a moment and then his face seemed to slump.

'She what? Paulette's done what?' he cried in a voice more like a sob. 'When?' He paused. 'Are you there?' he shouted, then took the phone from his ear and stared at it. He punched a button to redial, his face a picture of frustration as he waited and waited for an answer that would not come. Kathleen put her hand on his arm but Philippe shook it off as if it were a bothersome fly and tried calling again.

So that was it, thought Bruno. Philippe must have got to know Paulette from covering all those rugby matches. He'd certainly published lots of photos of Paulette scoring tries in the newspaper. Bruno wondered how long it would take for Philippe to return to his usual jaunty self. It might even help him grow up.

Shortly afterwards, Prunier and J-J arrived in separate cars, brushed aside the three reporters and separated, Prunier going to speak to Moore and Hodge and J-J coming towards Bruno.

'The good news is that the cop who got shot on the Bergerac road is in intensive care but they say he'll live,' said J-J quietly. 'The bad news is that Prunier is under pressure. Have you given statements?'

Bruno nodded. 'Me, the Baron, Crimson, Hodge and Moore, all of us. Yveline is writing them up now.'

'What did you say exactly?'

'Acting on information received, I came to protect a civilian from what I believed was danger of assassination by an armed and known terrorist. I shouted a warning and then shot to save Crimson from a bullet. And I added that the Baron fired to save my life from another terrorist. That was it.'

'Right, say no more, not another word,' said J-J. 'I heard from Isabelle just before I got here. Moore called her and told her what happened and she told me to let you know that you are under the Brigadier's orders, so don't let Prunier tell you otherwise. The paperwork has been done and your Mayor is in the picture. Have you got that?'

'I think so,' Bruno replied. 'But why is Prunier under pressure?'

'Failure to provide an adequate escort for two dangerous prisoners. Failure to check the identity of the fake guard. He's responsible.'

'He shouldn't be,' said Bruno. 'The commander of the Bergerac *commissariat* ought to be responsible. He'd have assigned the escort and he should have checked the Irish credentials.'

'You're right but that's not how it works,' said J-J. 'The commander is on sick leave and the acting commander was called to a meeting with the Mayor. That leaves Prunier responsible. So it's a mess.'

'What's a mess?' Prunier asked, suddenly arriving at Bruno's side.

'The fact that the press got here before we did,' J-J said. 'We'd better get our version out fast.'

'Yes, but we'd better make sure it's right,' said Prunier. 'How are you feeling, Bruno?'

'I'm fine, thanks to the Baron here.'

'Good, I'd like to tell you that you did well but you know the procedure we have to follow in an incident like this. Now, tell me – under what authority did you bring in an armed civilian to accompany you to these premises?'

'It's all in my statement, sir, and I have nothing to add,' said Bruno. 'And I'm not under your command.'

'*Merde*, Bruno, I'm on your side so don't give me that.'

J-J put a hand on Prunier's sleeve. 'Sir, I've heard from the interior ministry that Bruno is currently under their orders on a counterterrorism operation, which means different rules of engagement. Maybe we'd better check with them.'

Prunier looked coldly at J-J, turned back to shake his head at Bruno and walked away, pulling out his phone. J-J rubbed a hand over his face, loosened his collar and sighed.

Bruno turned his gaze back to Yves, who was holding out

one of the cards used to take fingerprints so that Moore could take a photograph with his phone. Moore checked the image, pressed some buttons and then came across to Bruno.

'Yves has a good print,' he said. 'It matches the one they got from the coffee cup in Bergerac so the dead man is the fake guard, sure enough. I've just sent it to our records office and I already alerted them to carry out a rush check on known IRA prints. If that doesn't work, we have the DNA. We'll find out who the bastard was, don't worry.'

A car door slammed and Yveline was walking across, beckoning to J-J. Bruno heard her ask him if he would like to look at her draft report and the two of them returned to the gendarme van.

Bruno's phone vibrated again and the screen told him that Isabelle was calling.

'Moore just called to let me know you're okay and you did well and he and Hodge have already texted a note of appreciation to the Brigadier,' she said. 'You need to know that ever since we knew of the IRA involvement this has been an official counterterrorism operation and you were listed from the beginning as one of the team members. That means that the usual rules of engagement for use of firearms do not apply to you. There is no reason to worry. And we're in a state of emergency so whatever happened, Bruno, you're covered.'

'What about the Baron?' Bruno asked. 'I'm more concerned about him. He shot the IRA guy who was about to kill me.'

'You are empowered to call upon civilian assistance in an emergency so you and he are both covered. And it will get good media. Algerian war veteran uses hunting rifle to save cop's life. That's how we'll spin it and remember that I'm the one writing the official report.'

Bruno felt a wry smile coming to his lips. He knew about official reports, what their official authors chose to say and what they were determined to leave out.

'I've already drafted the first report saying this was a model of international counterterrorist cooperation,' she went on. 'What are you doing this weekend?'

'Gardening, visiting a friend who's been in hospital. Why?'

'To finish the full report I may have to come down to the Périgord to wrap up the loose ends and it would be lovely to see you.'

Bruno felt his heart skip a beat but made his voice sound normal. 'You know you're always more than welcome.'

'I'll need to interview you. I'm still not altogether sure of who planned what,' she said.

'I couldn't work it out at first but it seems clear enough now,' Bruno said. 'There were two separate murder plots that came together. The IRA wanted Rentoul but Felder's first wife and his kids wanted to kill Monika before the old man died to keep her from getting any of his money. So Madame Felder set the IRA onto Rentoul, told them where to find him and that he was going by the name of McBride. Rentoul had been on the IRA death list for years because of Gibraltar. And for the IRA, killing the wife of a former head of British military intelligence was just an extra bonus.'

'I already drafted an arrest warrant for Madame Felder,' Isabelle replied. 'I don't know that we have enough evidence yet to arrest her two children. But our FBI friend is already talking of prosecuting all three of them under the RICO procedure.'

'What's that?' Bruno asked.

'The Racketeer Influenced and Corrupt Organizations Act, or conspiring to commit organized crime. The Americans brought it in to deal with the mafia. It puts the burden of proof onto the accused to prove that they weren't conspiring. Hodge also thinks he can prove that the Felder company was built up with the American money from Baghdad. That way, the Felder family might not have much to inherit.'

'That's very clever,' said Bruno. 'I'm not sure it's a law I'd like to see in France but I know Hodge is determined to get Uncle Sam's money back.'

'J-J tells me Hodge is just as concerned about recovering Uncle Sam's wine from Rentoul's cellar.' She paused and when she continued her voice had softened and Bruno could imagine the smile in her eyes when she said, 'But J-J thinks he'll find that more difficult.'

'You might even find yourself sampling a glass or two if you come down this weekend,' Bruno replied. 'And you'll get a chance to congratulate Balzac for his own heroic role in the final shootout.'

'How do you mean?'

'He took care of one of the terrorists, the woman. He jumped onto her chest and gave a growl that scared even me. She must have thought he was about to rip her face off. You'd have been proud of him.'

'He did? That's even better. Maybe we can get him a commendation,' Isabelle replied, delight in her voice. 'The Minister will love that. Dog to the rescue – it's the sort of thing the media just laps up. If we can put Balzac into the story we'll get his picture in all the papers and on TV. And he's so photogenic. I'll need a really good photographer.'

'Better him than me,' said Bruno.

'I have other plans for you,' she said. 'But we'll save those for the weekend.'

Acknowledgements

Although set in the lovely valley of the River Vézère in the enchanting French region of the Périgord and including so many references to real places like Périgueux, Montignac and Les Eyzies, this is a work of fiction. All the characters are figments of my imagination. So the stalwart guardians of the peace in Montignac would never behave like Louis in this novel. The character of Paulette is not drawn from any of the magnificent young women who grace our rugby fields and make us just as proud of their skills as we are of their male colleagues. The growth of women's rugby has been a striking and welcome development during the twenty years I have now been devoted to the Périgord.

There are, however, real people who triggered ideas and inspiration for my fictional characters. My friend Pierre Simonet, our wise and genial municipal policeman with his passion for teaching rugby and tennis to the town's schoolchildren, gave me the initial idea for writing about a country copper in *la France profonde*. And I would like to thank him and his splendid wife Francine for two decades of friendship, for many wonderful dinners, and for Francine's tolerant and jocular comments on the energetic romantic life of my fictional hero. The first Bruno novel was rightly dedicated to Pierrot.

The second Bruno novel was dedicated to the Baron. My neighbour, Jean-Henri Picot, known to everyone as *le baron*, was the first to take me under his wing and introduce me around the neighbourhood. A major landowner (who donated land for the town rugby stadium), an entrepreneur and industrialist, and a passionate hunter and sportsman, the Baron was the proud son of Paul Picot, a Resistance leader in World War Two who was arrested by the Gestapo and came close to death in the Mauthausen concentration camp. The Baron was a young officer in the Algerian war, a passionate supporter of General de Gaulle and he invariably welcomed every British and American war veteran he encountered as 'my liberator'. When he learned that my father-in-law, Graham Watson, had landed in Normandy on the day after D-Day, the Baron gave him an unforgettable welcome. Along with Pierrot, the Baron and his wife, Claude, sustained and cared for me during the death of my mother. The Baron was a dear man, a larger than life figure, a regular tennis partner and we dined together weekly until his death. I was honoured to be asked to say a few words in his memory at his funeral and I miss him still.

As a young *Guardian* journalist in the 1970s, I reported briefly from Northern Ireland, interviewed IRA leaders and was guided around the republican stronghold of the Bogside in Londonderry by the journalist and civil rights activist Eamonn McCann, at a time when he and I each had rather more hair than we do today. But I am in no way any kind of expert on the Northern Ireland Troubles, so I must record my debt to Eamonn's books, particularly to *War and an Irish Town*; to Tony Geraghty's *The Irish War*; to Mark Urban's *Big Boys' Rules: The*

SAS and the Secret Struggle Against the IRA; and to Richard English's *Armed Struggle: The History of the IRA*. The account of the killing of the IRA squad in Gibraltar is based on fact and the New IRA is indeed active, just as the Northern Ireland peace settlement is looking politically fragile.

There are many people offering cookery courses and wine tours in the Périgord, but I am particularly grateful to Ian and Sara Fisk of Le Chèvrefeuille, just outside St Cyprien, for their insights on the hosting and teaching of clients in their well-regarded cookery school (see www.lechevrefeuille.com). I must also record my debt to my friends Caro Feely of Château Feely (www.frenchwineadventures.com), and to Emma Mayes and her husband Max of Duck & Truffle for their guidance on their own excellent vineyard tours (www.duck&truffle.com). I am thankful to Steve Martindale, editor of our local English-language newspaper, *The Bugle*, for encouraging me to write a monthly column on wine. The hospitality of the vineyards of the Bergerac, and the pleasure of visiting them and tasting their wines, can hardly be exaggerated. The Maison des Vins in Bergerac is an excellent place to start. Like Bruno and many other local inhabitants, I keep a copy of their free map of the vineyards in my car.

As always, I am deeply grateful for the hospitality and goodwill of my Périgord friends and neighbours. I deeply appreciate the honour, which came while this book was being written, of my election to the Académie des Lettres et des Arts du Périgord. As always, I owe a great deal to Jane and Caroline Wood in Britain, to Jonathan Segal in New York and Anna von Planta in Zurich, for their heroic work on my manuscripts. My wife Julia and our daughters, Kate and Fanny, are the first to read, correct and improve my raw drafts. Without Julia's guiding and restraining hand, Bruno's meals might turn into culinary disasters. And Benson, our basset hound, who died in his fourteenth year as this book was being edited, remains in my heart as a constant comfort and a faithful companion.

Martin Walker, Périgord